'Treachery!' he said through gritted teeth. 'It's an ambush! Get your heads dow-!'

The final word was obliterated by a discharge of cannon fire. A plume of eye-blinding fire stabbed toward them, and a split second later another and then a third. As the sound hit them, so did the shock of metal, smashing into the boat with hellish force. They were firing case-shot – bags of lead balls that dispersed on firing. It was like facing a giant's shot-gun. One thing was clear in his mind as he fell – that the Russians had rightly singled out the first boat as the vessel that carried the commanding officer.

The blast had knocked Smith down into the boat. He felt the burning embers of wadding where they stuck to his face and uniform. The acrid stench of powder smoke stopped him from drawing breath, gagged him. But no order would have been of any use because the roar had deafened those around him, and the flash and smoke had blinded them . . .

Robert Carter was born in Staffordshire and educated in England, Australia and Texas. Formerly with an American oil exploration company and then with the BBC, he has taught, worked in and travelled the wilder places of the earth. Now living in London, Robert Carter writes full time.

Also by Robert Carter

Talwar
Armada

COURAGE

ROBERT CARTER

ORION

An Orion paperback
First published in Great Britain by Orion in 1995
This paperback edition published in 1996 by Orion Books Ltd,
Orion House, 5 Upper St Martin's Lane, London WC2H 9EA

A CIP catalogue record for this book
is available from the British Library.

ISBN: 0 75280 347 6

Typeset at Deltatype Ltd, Ellesmere Port, Cheshire

Printed and bound in Great Britain by
Clays Ltd, St Ives plc

Courage is like love, it feeds on hope.

Napoleon Bonaparte

For Toby Eady

PART I

The Heart's Desire

17 JULY 1787
In an olive grove near Ajaccio, Corsica

You say, signore, *that you have gazed upon my tomb-stone, and know the day on which I am to die? Then tell me the date, for I would very much like to know it.*

You tell me I am to depart this life on the fifth day of May, in the year of Our Lord eighteen hundred and twenty-one? Excuse me for smiling, but how can you know such a thing, unless you plan to murder me? – If you are a fortune-teller, be off with you, signore. *I have little enough silver to spare on charlatans!*

What? You say you want no money, but that I must reveal myself fully to you if your prophecies are to come true? Is that all you are asking of me? In that case, why not? I have nothing to lose, and nothing to hide from a perfect stranger. I shall tell you all, for I am intrigued by you.

Ah, just to look again on those sun-washed hills, to smell olive trees and pine resin, to see my mother and brothers. After eight years in exile! Can you imagine how much I hate France? Almost half my life spent away from my beloved island. These are the hills of my birth. You cannot know, signore, *how much this handful of my native soil means to me.*

What else would you know of me? I am not yet quite eighteen. My family name is Italian – ah, but you must already know that if you have seen my tombstone. Above all things I am Corsican. That is why I hate the

French. They conquered my homeland in the year of my birth, and I have burned with the desire to make my island free again. Is that how I shall die, signore? Gloriously? At the head of my people?

I now hold the commission of junior lieutenant in the artillery regiment of La Fère. Some time ago we put down a riot in Lyons. That was the most instructive thing I have yet seen, I swear. My father sent me away to this land of conquerors, when I was eight years old – preparatory school at Autun, then a year at the Ecole Militaire in Paris. I hated that place. It was during that year that my mother was widowed. My one ally was Louis Bourrienne, and my principal enemy a gentleman cadet who goes by the name of Antoine Phelypeaux. I will always love the first and hate the latter.

Presently I am on leave of absence from Valence, where I have been studying the art of war. Valence is in France, a town situated on the river Rhône. That is where I have been finding out – for two years now – how to fight, and how to govern, after the French manner. They do not yet know what a viper they have nurtured, but one day they will. That much of the future I promise to you, signore.

So you see, I have stolen an education from the French. It was all paid for by King Louis's government: that's why I took so much of it away with me. Small good it has done me, so far, though. Military careers are open to talent, but they are rarely shaped by merit alone. My fellow juniors are mostly like Phelypeaux – sprigs of the nobility who have independent means. They laugh at my Italian speech. They scorn me because of my 'islander manners'. They mock me because I'm not well connected. We are paid hardly anything, signore, and they know I'm in debt. In my defence I tell them that luxury does not sit well with a soldier, but they continue to taunt me. Most of them are beneath my contempt, of course. They are high-born lordling bastards who drink and chase girls and know nothing of the heart of their profession. But I do. I made sure of that.

I don't know why I choose to talk with you, signore. Why I like the sound of the pact you have proposed.

The fifth of May, in the year of Our Lord eighteen hundred and twenty-one? Why have you told me that day?

Your answer intrigues me: I will die in exactly 12,345 days' time. Well, then, that allows me some thirty-four years. It means I will die aged fifty-one. It means that one-third of my life is already over . . .

You say you are offering me guidance along the road that leads to fame and greatness? And in return you want only to hear the unveiled truths of a human heart, and to use me as your instrument. That sounds a good enough bargain to me, signore.

Yes, on those terms I accept. I intend to abide by our pact. You may be sure I shall not be the one to break it.

Now, if you have heard enough, tell me: what are your other prophecies concerning me?

ONE

Is there really such a thing as love at first sight?

She asked herself the question, looking across the ballroom towards the Englishman. He was waiting to come into the duke's levee. She had never seen him before but she could not take her eyes off him. He is quite extraordinary, she thought, fanning herself. Quite the most magnetic person I have ever seen. The way he looks, the way he moves . . . I cannot stop myself from watching him. What can it be about him that so fascinates me?

Bewigged musicians played Herr Mozart's music under the light of a thousand candles. The floor of polished wood parquetry shone with a golden radiance. Four dozen guests danced, and twice as many watched, everyone in their best finery for the summer ball.

She was Berenice de Sainte Honorine du Fay, niece of the Duc d'Harcourt. She was eighteen years old. Her interest had been noted, she knew. Not by *him* – that would have been too embarrassing! – but by the older and more observant of her peers. All the principal families of the *Armorial Général* were represented tonight, many of them she had known at her convent school. There was her cousin, Marguerite de Tromelin, and Amanda de Tourville, and Louise de la Rochefoucault and Catherine de Phelypeaux, and several others who could place themselves on the highest social list,

7

then a number of girls whose families were of middling rank, right down to odious creatures like Marie Anne Corday d'Armans whose mother and father were little more than aspiring gentry. They had come all the way over from St Saturnin, fearing to leave her behind now she was nineteen.

Berenice could hardly bear to listen to them. They were already discussing the English captain in the way they discussed all new arrivals who were deemed worthy of their attention. But this time it was different. They had all become enthralled at the first sight of him.

The Englishmen's dress uniform coats were identical. Navy blue, with tails and standing collar, round white cuffs and white lapels fixed back with gilt buttons. Gold laced, but all in sober moderation. And this over short white waistcoat, white breeches and white silk hose. Their shoes were black with silver buckles, also neat and understated. And there was the inevitable slim dress sword, with gilded handguard and ivory hilt.

'I heard that the invitation was given by the duke himself.'

The fans fluttered. 'Indeed? Do tell.'

'They have lately been guests of the duke's regiment.'

'I have it that the duke repeated the invitation by two messages, one by his head servant, the other by a gentleman.'

'The Chevalier de la Grandière told me that the duke reviewed his regiment yesterday. As he passed the line he stopped some minutes to speak to them both – a mark of distinction he bestowed upon no one else.'

'This proves his attentions to be more than mere form, I think.'

'What about the other one? The blond one. Who's he?'

'Oh, who cares about *him*?'

Berenice looked from face to face, and saw the bright-eyed excitement the English captain had lit up in them.

It's sickening, she thought, feeling a burn of indignation. They're almost fawning. I wouldn't fawn over any man. I'm sure I wouldn't.

'It is easy for anyone who attends late at a ball to have themselves noticed,' she said. 'Disdainful latecomers are always the more remarkable. It is usually a mistake to show too much eagerness.'

Louise de la Rochefoucault caught an imagined barb in her words. 'Some think it an advantage to show a little eagerness. Whereas others think they are so beautiful they can afford to be aloof.'

Imbecile, she thought; she felt her cheeks colouring. 'I am not aloof, Louise. I simply give credit to men's intelligence. They find nothing so unappealing in woman as childish behaviour.'

Amanda de Tourville smiled blithely. She was a year older. 'I did not realize you were so great an expert on what men think about women.'

She smiled back tightly. 'My conclusion does not require me to be an expert.'

'He is a most handsome man,' Marguerite said in a faraway voice. They all looked again, and again the fans fluttered like a field of butterflies.

'But also dangerous . . .' Berenice took a deep breath. 'He looks to me like Pan – or a devil.'

He was slim. Well proportioned. His fine features and dark curly hair gave him a Hebraic air, she thought, or at least an origin somewhere on the shores of the Mediterranean.

She whispered to Marguerite. 'Are you *sure* he's English?'

'He's wearing an English naval uniform. So very plain, don't you think?'

'It's . . . marvellous.'

'What's his name?'

Amanda leaned across. 'Why don't you ask him?'

'Maybe I will.'

'I can't see what you're all fussing about,' Celestine, Berenice's younger sister, said.

'That's because you're too young to understand anything.'

Léontine d'Esparbes, a relation from Balleroy, joined them. She knew what was causing the stir. 'What's his connection to the duke?' she asked.

'Nobody knows,' Marguerite said.

'Catherine says he's a connection of the Bishop of Caen.'

'How does she know that?'

'She says he's lodging at the bishop's palace.'

Amanda's smile was poisonously sweet. 'Berenice – so you do know something about him after all.'

She could not help herself reacting. 'I told you before, if I really wanted to find out about him, I'd go and ask him.'

Amanda inclined her head. 'There's no need, Berenice. His name is Smith. I know because Adeline de Hergevault told me. And I'm quite sure your mother would disapprove of him.'

TWO

William Sidney Smith had so far escaped announcement. That pleased him, because his aim was to maintain a certain mysterious anonymity. He knew that was the best way to get what he wanted. Tonight the hunt was on. He could feel it in his bones.

He had arrived late, in the patrician company of Captain James Bonham RN. Within seconds, the modesty of their dress uniforms had drawn the unwelcome attention of the servants.

'How's your French?' Bonham asked, stiffening.

'Sufficient.'

'Those letters of invitation were genuine, were they not?'

Smith gave Bonham a sideways glance as answer. The man might be seven years older, and soon to inherit a title, but he was lacking in fineness of sensibility. He had been in France less than a week, and had been slow to make the necessary adjustments.

'Then, what do these people need with our ranks?'

Smith troubled to explain. 'The footmen are simply at a loss to know how we can be gentlemen without waistcoats got up like a pair of drawing-room curtains, and how we can be officers without wearing huge golden swabs on our shoulders.'

'Tell them to step aside.' Bonham had a cold haughtiness about him. His hand strayed automatically halfway towards the hilt of his dress sword. 'Or I shall.'

Smith saw the faces of the footmen harden. They undoubtedly carried cudgels in the tails of their coats, for an event of this social magnitude attracted all kinds of pretenders. Their spokesman, a big, watchful man, had detested Bonham on sight, but so far the delicate social membrane had not been pierced.

'A moment.' Smith seized the initiative, and moved forward. 'They need to be satisfied on this point.'

Bonham allowed the intercession. 'Tell them it's a question of style – simple elegance – something we have in England, along with a sense of proportion.'

Smith coughed into his handkerchief at Bonham's crudeness, continuing to explain courteously to the head footman that they were, in fact, English frigate captains, that they had attended at the invitation of the Duc d'Harcourt, and that, if there was still any doubt, any number of French officers present would vouch for them.

The footman seemed grudgingly satisfied. He motioned his trio of fellows away, and the two Englishmen were left alone.

'Ignorant peasants.'

'Lack of epaulettes is a frequent pitfall for English naval officers hereabouts,' Smith said smoothly. 'They did not know how to take us.'

'I've a good mind to make a complaint to the duke.'

Smith was irritated by Bonham's eagerness to make them so far known to the gathering. He had noticed a vinegary gentleman eyeing them. A large black dog, some muscular German hunting breed, looked to him and trotted after as he turned away. The comte, he thought, owner of this château, and younger brother of the Duc d'Harcourt. He forced a note of pleasantness into his voice. 'Bonham, why not let it lie? I'm no stranger to controversy. Wherever I go I'm obliged to explain how a fellow just turned twenty-three years of age could be a *capitaine de vaisseau*.'

Bonham grunted darkly, and Smith realized that an unintended dart had struck home. He had been the youngest man ever to become captain of a Royal Navy frigate. Now he had four years' seniority as a post captain, making him senior to James Bonham, a man of thirty. It undoubtedly rankled.

Damn his boorishness, he thought. And damn his jealousy. He's a cold snake. Can't think why I troubled to procure an invitation for him. Still, he'll not cramp my plans for tonight. And that's a certainty.

The early part of the evening passed uneventfully. Several parties introduced themselves, all seeking to draw him out. He refused to oblige, preferring to learn what he could while allowing no one to penetrate him. Always, at the back of his mind, was the real reason he had come to France, and he knew he must not compromise that.

A ship. That was what he wanted. A ship. For what was a captain without a ship?

He watched an elderly gentleman with a hooked nose fussing with his snuff box. There was a surprisingly feudal, almost mediaeval, quality to French society. The great hall was hung with family portraits, all larger than life – knights in armour and on horseback.

They still call the peasants *les vassaux* – vassals – he thought, looking around. Petitioners still turned up with their complaints, to be decided by *le seigneur* – like in England in Tudor times. While England has been forged in a civil war, tempered by troubles and edged by a revolution in the useful arts, complaisant France has become stagnant. Compared to industrious England, she has slumbered. And in consequence she has been caught and passed.

Bonham was disputing lightly with some French officers. The conversation was unwieldy in English. Inevitably it danced around politics. Smith felt the undertone sharpening. He heard gibes about the disaster of America, then Bonham replying that the jewel box of India made that loss insignificant. That the French had striven for forty years to get a grip on Hindustan, but had only succeeded in losing trade and influence to Britain.

With an old-style flourish the elderly man introduced himself as Charles de Hergevault. His Gallic pride was undiminished by his age, or his bearing by bandaged calves. 'I was at Pondichéry when you were but an itch in your daddy's loins, monsieur,' he said, taking centre stage to the delight of his young compatriots. 'I knew the great François Dupleix. I fought with Louis d'Auteuil.'

'And were obliged to surrender with him, no doubt?'

'As the English were obliged to surrender at York-town. To an army of colonists, no?'

There was laughter. Then a young officer with a heavy accent jutted his chin at Bonham. 'It was the French navy who lost you America. Our payment for Quebec.'

More laughter, and Smith saw how shallow the good humour was, and how fragile the truce. Of the last half century only eighteen years had been spent in peace between England and France.

Bonham disengaged himself and came alongside, speaking from the corner of his mouth. 'I thought this nation was supposed to be the first example of style and good taste in the world.'

Smith gave a short laugh. 'Great France, the populous and all-powerful – in the days of Louis XIV, perhaps.'

'I don't know what progress the arts have made at Paris, but in Normandy at least everything seems to be very fussy and old-fashioned.'

'Yes. They're living in the past. It happens to all nations that fall from greatness.'

'The making of chair seats is still ladies' work, it seems.' Bonham indicated an inelegant chair. It was decorated with a crudely embroidered hunting scene.

'And there is not yet such a thing as Wilton carpet in France. The bed chambers are all paved, or boarded with oak in squares, neatly enough, and dry rubbed, but terribly cold on the feet—'

'*Bed* chambers, did you say?'

Smith looked sharply to him. 'Ah . . . guilty, I confess. They play the age-old game just as we do.'

'Rather better, I sometimes think.'

'You must speak for yourself, Charles.'

They went their separate ways for a few minutes, to reconnoitre. The setting was perfect for an *affaire d'amour*. There were terraces and a wonderful garden with illuminations, and an old orangery. The château of Thury-Harcourt itself was magnificent. The ballroom was grand and well served. There was a long table loaded with cold morsels, a potent punchbowl, all manner of other drink, a small but vigorous orchestra providing musical entertainment. All the generations were present. So far as I can see, he thought, fascinated, there's already been plenty of manoeuvring among the *eligible* guests, and a good deal of speculation and intrigue among those content to spectate.

Bonham rejoined him.

'Ha, my God, look at them,' Bonham said, delighted by the excesses of taste he saw. 'Why, they're preening vanity itself.'

'Whereas . . .' Smith struck a pose he thought outrageous and worthy of a Spaniard. 'We are brothers-in-arms and ready for the fight. Who could resist us?'

He looked around now with veiled intent. His eye danced over the rose garden of fluttering beauties and picked out once more the young woman he had been watching. He had worked out the rules of engagement of this foreign world and saw that the prize lay at his feet.

'You're over-ambitious.'

'My dear Bonham, I am exactly ambitious enough.' He grinned, but there was sincerity in his tone. 'I am young and I am handsome and I am talented, and tonight . . .'

'Smith, you are selfish and wickedly ambitious and rather too dangerous to know.'

He laughed. 'I know what I want.'

The woman was by far the most beautiful. Fair and fine, tall, willowy. Very graceful. She was young, but something about her made him think of her as a woman, and the rest merely as girls. The small gold crucifix that hung at her breast flashed like a beacon as the light caught it.

'I like to make an *impression*.'

'You've already done that,' Bonham said. 'They've been sending after you all night.'

'It's a great game, and we've played it squarely till now. It's all in the eyes, d'you see?'

A fleeting frown darkened Bonham's face. He seemed in that moment to be deeply jealous. 'Smith, you will continue to bother them so exquisitely only until they have you pinned down. After that they will lose all interest in you.'

'Pinned down?'

'Once they discover your mongrel pedigree.'

He smiled, unashamed of what he was. 'Then I shall have to avoid getting myself pinned down, shan't I?'

Bonham laughed unpleasantly. 'You won't be able to. They'll want to know who their daughters are swooning over.'

'That's really not a problem. The duke's nephew is putting it about that I'm intimately related to the King of Naples.'

Bonham laughed aloud. 'I hope you disabused him of that!'

'On the contrary, I always encourage speculation.'

Bonham snorted. 'Smith, you're an adventurer of the worst kind.'

'Oh, yes. I'm certainly that.'

Bonham cocked a glance at the woman whose eye

Smith was pointedly avoiding. 'And a damned fox among the chickens.'

Smith looked past him. 'I think I have fallen in love with a demoiselle. Her name I do not know.'

He was playing dangerously with the truth, and felt the exhilaration of it.

Bonham followed his glance. 'Ah, I'm told she is a Tourville, a grand-daughter of the admiral's.'

'Oh, no. I've seen Mademoiselle Tourville, and that's not her.' He continued to watch her, even when she ventured him a candid glance back. 'I shall let my heart go as it will. According to the local proverb, Englishmen are famous for letting their hearts govern their actions. Or so said the lady to Sterne, at Calais.'

Bonham stiffened. 'I've never seen anything but impetuosity in you.'

'Only the brave deserve the fair, Bonham.'

'Plunder the virginity of one of these young prizes and there'll be trouble enough for you. Hook your heart to her, and you'd be utterly run ashore.'

'Why do you say that?' He knew perfectly.

Bonham shrugged at the obviousness of it. 'You could never court a Frenchwoman.'

'I could.'

'To what end? A liaison is impossible. Her connections and acres would be in the deal. None of them is allowed to have any truck with a *capitaine de vaisseau Anglais*.'

'It wasn't marriage I had in mind.' Smith folded his arms.

'Even so, you may forget those pretty flowers. For all their grace the French nobility are our implacable enemies. They've never forgiven us for almost making them extinct at Agincourt and Crécy. They will not let someone like you near their women. For myself, I shall be content to drink my fill of their excellent wine, then

17

go to see my village mistress tonight.' Bonham drained his wineglass, and turned away.

'Lucky lady.'

He mentally set Bonham's bleakness at a distance, and continued to watch the forbidden flowers. Ah, the frivolous French, he thought, filled with the heady exuberance of the night and the music and exactly the right amount of drink. What an obsolete crew their nobility are. They're completely obsessed with rank and status and appearances, and they seem to have no notion of what constitutes real worth at all – but, by God, they're magnificent when they set about enjoying them-selves.

He smiled back at the girl. 'Yes,' he said, his mind made up. 'She's the one I'm going to have.'

Bonham nudged his arm and handed over a bumper of champagne. He muttered above the rim of his glass. 'You'd better clear for action, I think.'

He turned to see the comtesse and her retinue approaching. She was the hostess, the lady of the house, a woman of forty-and-some, heavily made up and arranged, stately as a galleon in extravagant dress. She had been doing the rounds of her guests, but had decided to intercept them as a matter of urgency.

Bonham did not hide his glee. 'I'd like to see you charm that, Smith.'

He knew the kind of struggle it was going to be. So far tonight there had been a succession of sloops and gunboats sent against him. Each had pecked away at his mystery, tried to carry off essential information about him, something that would enable them to judge him. He had so far succeeded in keeping the enigma intact, but he knew Bonham was right: it could not last, even with a brother officer's connivance.

Smith realized the reason for the formidable lady's approach just as she came up. So heavy an armament is not required, unless— My God, it must be her daughter who's at stake!

He took the comtesse's fingers, bowed low, and held on a fraction too long, a little too firmly – an impudence that hinted at sexual interest.

She took it with utter sangfroid.

'I hear conflicting things about you, captain.'

'Indeed?'

'I am told you are of an ancient family.'

Smith smiled, and inclined his head, as if accepting a compliment. 'Everyone, madame, is of that.'

She tut-tutted. 'A noble family is what my informant meant, Captain . . . Smeet.'

He flashed a glanced at Bonham that acknowledged the onslaught. *Informant* – the strength of the word! And a pause, and a mispronunciation too.

In his crispest voice, he said, 'Madame la comtesse, you were *mis-informed*. Smith is the commonest name in the world. Mine is a family of captains, noble only in the loosest sense.' He turned to Bonham, unable to resist murmuring, 'Or perhaps loose in the noblest sense. It's always been hard to tell.'

The comtesse raised her eyebrows, witheringly. 'Did you say "captains"?'

He sighed with mock regret, enjoying the sparring and the theatre, but offering a hint of weariness. 'I'm afraid so. Humble toilers on sea and land, but honourable blood nevertheless.'

She looked him up and down pointedly. 'In France's navy, as in England's I have no doubt, a man becomes a ship's captain through the influence of his family.'

'It seems that considerations of blood are still paramount in France.'

The comtesse gathered herself up. 'They are. And they always will be.'

The sharpness of her answer surprised him. He judged the reactions of her retinue and ventured a thrust of his own. 'These days, in England, a blood-line counts for rather less – except among breeders of racehorses and hounds.'

'English ideas and English manners are of little consequence here.'

'Even so, madame, they may not be ignored. A modern world is in the making.'

'Let not the English imagine they will make it. They are an unfit people. Rude islanders. They struck off the head of their king and proclaimed a republic, did they not?'

She looked to her circle and they approved her point.

He smiled fixedly. 'I may say in our defence that we restored our monarchy.'

'Your monarchy?' The comtesse's eyebrows were raised theatrically. 'Please correct me if I am wrong, but did not the English have a dynasty of French kings to rule over them? Followed by Welsh Tudors and Scottish Stuarts? Then by a fool Dutchman, and latterly a succession of imbecile German princelings brought out of Hanover?'

Her retinue applauded, vastly amused.

His eyes glittered as he inspected his fingernails. 'However, madame, I think France may blame her late allies in America for today's talk of republics and democracies that seems so evidently the fashion wherever one goes in your country.'

Bonham guffawed and the comtesse's face hardened. 'Far better then that you tell me about yourself.'

He saw there was no escape, and decided to give in with good grace. 'Since you would have it out of me at all costs, madame, I am forced to tell you that my family may be traced no further back than my great-grandfather, a gentleman of piratical bent whose name was Captain Cornelius Smith. He was born at Hythe in the year of 1661. At least, a monumental inscription in New Shoreham church says as much.'

'Was he in some way – *notable*?'

'Alas, only within my family. And only then for being father to Captain Edward Smith.' He smiled, judging the moment to go on. 'He it was who commanded a frigate at the attack on Laguira, where he was severely wounded. He died on the island of Antigua.'

'This makes him what we in France call an *English* hero.'

Seeing his puzzlement at the remark an attendant cleric supplied, 'The kind who fall gloriously and against overwhelming odds – but who fall nevertheless.'

There was more amusement at that.

He put his hand to his breast. 'You're too kind to a lowly foreigner, madame. Hero or not, my grandfather did leave a cloud of daughters and at least two surviving sons, whereof the elder was Captain John Smith, late of the Guards, who is my father.'

Bonham had drunk too much. Smith had seen him awaiting his moment, and knew what was coming. He saw Bonham grin privately and heard him say: 'John Smith *was* a person of note, madame. He was once a gentleman-usher to Queen Charlotte – and aide-de-camp to Lord George Sackville Germain.'

Smith revealed nothing of his disquietude. He had anticipated Bonham's betrayal, but when it came it still burned like a brand.

The comtesse looked back blankly. Smith saw that she was unaware of the controversy that had surrounded Lord Germain's public disgrace and his dismissal from the army following the battle of Minden. He allowed a little amusement to show, then made the explanation that Bonham itched to make. 'What Captain Bonham is trying to say, madame, is that my father was so disgusted at the Prince of Brunswick's treatment of Lord Germain that he quit the service in sympathy, d'you see?'

'Then your father was *disgraced*?' The comtesse fired her broadside. 'He is a "black sheep"?'

Bonham brayed. 'Quaintly put, madame. But the whole flock of Smiths are as black as pitch, so none stands out particularly.'

Smith let the remark pass, so that his appearance remained genial. 'My father, I would rather say, is a man who knows what loyalty is and does not count the cost – as my mother, an excellent judge of character, doubtless recognized when she picked him out.'

The comtesse faced him stonily. 'To be so advanced at so young an age . . . one supposes you to have connections on your mother's side.'

Bonham snorted. 'Ah! There you have it, madame. Smith's father married the elder daughter of none other than Mr Pinkney Wilkinson – a most opulent London merchant. But a man with no son to be his heir.'

'A merchant?'

Smith saw the comtesse and her companions recoil from the idea of trade.

'Oh, yes,' Bonham went on, slurring his words a little now, but wickedly in command of himself. 'Unfortunately, the union of Captain Smith's parents was effected without the consent of Mr Wilkinson – indeed, he was in direct opposition to it – and that gentleman appears to have suffered his anger to have got the better of his feelings of affection. Isn't that so, Smith?'

The comtesse showed herself to be intrigued.

Smith chose deliberately to misinterpret her silence as sympathy. 'Alas, it is true that my maternal grandfather bestowed his great properties upon his younger daughter – that is to say, my aunt. I have therefore received no benefit from the Wilkinson fortune.' He inclined his head winningly. 'Perhaps my candidness has been of service to you, madame?'

The comtesse disengaged herself delicately, and looked towards Bonham. 'Your urbane young friend may think himself capable of toying with me, captain, but he is quite wrong. The Duc d'Harcourt is my brother-in-law, and at a word from me he will be required to leave. *Bon soir, Monsieur.*'

Bonham rolled his eyes upward as she sailed away. 'Savagery!' he said.

Smith smiled blithely. Even so he burned inside at Bonham's behaviour. Men like him must not be allowed to get away with it, he warned himself. His anger roasted a deeper dissatisfaction: the ending of the American war had seen the navy cut down to save money. More than half its ships had been put in ordinary, its seamen discharged, and its serving officers released on half pay. There was nothing worse for a talented man than enforced idleness. The leisure had almost killed him – until he had hit upon his secret plan.

'Didn't I say they'd have it out of you, eh, Smith?' Bonham's smugness blew the flames up inside him. 'Will you still have the daughter now, I wonder?'

'Yes, I think so.'

He showed nothing, just sipped at his champagne with a half-smile. He had seen the eyes of one of the footmen slide away from him. The man was in a pink silk suit and powdered wig. He had been listening to everything. He also smelled strongly of horses, and Smith knew he must be a groom who had been drafted in to attend the levee. So the French aristocracy have fallen to doubling up their servants, he thought. So much for the comtesse's pretensions of ancient and unassailable wealth.

Smith had seen the glint in her eye. He knew perfectly the understanding they had reached. He had touched her, and he knew the impression she had formed of him was far from unfavourable. Bonham had misread the outcome, because Bonham was a fool, and because it takes a social sophisticate to know another of the species.

He wondered at the aloof and ascetic man who was the comtesse's husband. There was a distant intelligence there. His favourite dog attended him like a magus's familiar. It would be interesting to ride to hounds with him . . .

Bonham's drawl broke in on his thoughts. 'Fifty pounds says you do not.'

'Hmm?'

'I have fifty pounds that says you do not bed that girl.'

The challenge was too crass, and he muttered back, 'Decorum, Bonham, is the mark of all civilization.'

'To hell with civilization.' Bonham's reptilian gaze fixed him. 'Will you have the bet, or not?'

'No, no . . .'

Bonham swaggered, and Smith knew that something about his own complete self-possession had got under the other man's skin.

'You know, I rather suspected you were just promises.'

He sighed. 'If you are so determined to defray my expenses, Bonham, who am I to gainsay you?'

'Fifty pounds, then?'

'Fifty pounds.' He offered his hand, and saw it instantly taken. 'And fifty more, if I take her before midnight.'

'Done!' Bonham snorted, pleased to have snared him. 'Now . . . what will you show me as proof?'

Smith laughed at the absurdity of the idea. 'Proof? Bonham, what proof could there possibly be?'

The other showed his teeth in a charmless way. 'I'm sure you'll think of something.'

Smith found himself repelled by the transparency of Bonham's mind. He thought, he's lacking in sublety, and now that he's drunk he's revealing his true nature. I do believe he's enjoying a peculiar kind of thrill from contemplating the idea of my bedding such a beauty. 'No proof,' he said. 'I am a man of honour. My word is sufficient.'

Bonham drank another draught. His manner wavered

on the verge of open hostility. 'Ah, but this is for fifty pounds. Men have broken their word for far less.'

'I care nothing about money. But honour is different. When I swear to something, you may rest assured I will carry it through.'

'Ah . . .' Bonham's eyes glowed as he broached a delicate matter. 'But there's still the possibility of a man not wanting to admit his failure with the fair sex . . .'

Smith raised an eyebrow in a way designed to disarm the other. 'My dear fellow, there's no question of that.'

'Oh, is that so?'

'Of course.' He smiled a smile of infuriating politeness. 'You see, I shan't fail.'

He saw Bonham's jealousy nakedly revealed now. 'You're remarkably sure of yourself, aren't you, Smith?'

'If there's one thing that women can detect at forty paces, Bonham,' he said, bowing his head pleasantly at a passing lady, 'it's self-doubt.'

THREE

'Oh, he's coming this way.'

The Englishman approached, heading straight for them, but at the last minute he veered away, seeming to ignore them all. He found the table, reached over to the elaborate floral centrepiece and selected a blood-red rose, not yet quite opened.

They all watched him do it, knowing there was to be a grand gesture. He had a knack of making everyone take notice of him. They all imagined his attentions must be aimed at them; but Berenice knew they were really for her alone.

She felt her mother's eyes on her. It was not yet half past nine, so she was safe. She knew it would be a wholly injudicious move for a hostess to bring her seventeen-year-old daughter to heel so early in the evening. Madame de Scepaux had recently attracted general disapprobation by gathering her four daughters into a game of cards whenever they showed interest in dancing.

The music was striking up for a quadrille. She saw Agnes, her maid, serving at the punchbowl and Gugnot looking strange in a footman's suit. Neither of them missed a thing, and certainly there would be talk among the servants.

She saw Smith pluck the flower and turn, leaning now nonchalantly against the edge of the table. He held the stalk of the rosebud elegantly between finger and thumb, and put the fingertips of his other hand to his lips as if considering. His eyes were intense.

She stood it as long as she could, then looked away,

feeling the heat flush through her. She felt herself trembling with anticipation, and damned herself for feeling that way. It amazed her that she could be made to experience such intense embarrassment by someone she had never met before. How his eyes hold me whenever they alight on me, she thought. And the antagonistic feelings towards my friends that he stirs up in me are nothing short of wickedness. I do believe I'm jealous of them when his gaze dwells on them. Is this what's meant by falling in love? And if not, then . . . what is it?

His charismatic pantomime continued. He discarded the rosebud, then made as if to stand up, and she turned away, terrified that he would ask her, and at the same time terrified that he would not.

She felt the heat of his approach as surely as if he had been incandescent.

'Mademoiselle, may I request the pleasure?' he said.

The quality of his voice was exactly as she had imagined it. It filled her with panic. She dared to look at him. '*Pardon, monsieur?*'

'The quadrille? You do dance, don't you?'

'Yes.'

'Then, shall we?'

He took her hand and led her across the dance floor, to join another couple, and thereby make ready for the quadrille. The dance, she knew, had originated as a peasant barn dance. It had become stylized into a series of fixed sets and evolutions. She walked through the complex formal moves, stepping close to him and away again in time to the music, curtsying to his bows and everyone rotated and precessed like the planets of her father's orrery, his clockwork model of the solar system.

When he came close she felt his breath on her neck. When their eyes met her skin tingled, though all correct form was observed. But still she felt herself stripped naked by him. She found herself blushing, amazed by the extent of her own excitement. This was like nothing she had felt before, or had even imagined possible. It couldn't be the same as the girlish flutterings and speculations that Amanda and Marguerite and Louise and the others were engaged in. They couldn't be feeling this way too. This was different. It had to be.

A little while ago she had asked her mother about love and what falling in love felt like.

'It will happen to you one day,' was all she had said.

'But – how will I know?'

'Oh, you'll know. Don't worry about that.'

And she did! The thought appalled her. The very impossibility of it appalled her. He's English. How could I fall in love with an Englishman? That was never my dream. I never wanted that. I never imagined it at all. He's not even a Catholic.

And it made no difference knowing that he's doing it on purpose, she thought. He knows exactly what he's doing. He knows quite well what effect he's having on me. Anyone else, and I wouldn't stand for it. He's making me feel this way quite deliberately.

She saw her father's best dog, Brutus, in the doorway. He was looking at her, until she saw her father snap his fingers and bring him away. Then the dance finished and the Englishman bowed to her and led her from the floor.

'Monsieur, you're perspiring.'

'It's a warm evening.'

He stared deeply into her eyes, and she stared back, like a fascinated animal. 'Yes.'

'Is it that you put drops of belladonna in your eyes? They are so very clear.'

It was as if he was looking into her soul. A strangling panic overwhelmed her. 'You must excuse me.'

'Please, don't go . . .'

'Monsieur, I must.'

'Meet me on the terrace. As soon as you can.'

'Monsieur . . .'

FOUR

He had made up his mind to take her, and he knew now absolutely that she would not be able to resist him. The pupils of her eyes had given her away. But there had been a terrible moment when she had panicked and excused herself.

She's completely besotted with me, he thought. He was elated, but instead of the discovery making him smile at the ease with which he had won over her emotions, the situation was making him strangely anxious. I can scarce believe it! he thought, trying to discipline himself. Who except idiots and dreamers can believe in the concept of romantic love?

Now that he had abandoned Bonham's unsophisticated company his thoughts were once more his own. He felt comfortable with the cool calculation that was his hallmark aboard a ship of war. He must straighten his thoughts immediately. The objective was clear and in sight. He consulted his watch; he would have Bonham's fifty pounds, and the other fifty too. Why, then, did his hand tremble?

The first rule of flirtation must be self-control, he reminded himself sternly. In bed and out of it. We sport for pleasure, do we not? We seek to receive the intimate pleasure of beautiful and convivial women, which is a joy worth all efforts. And without doubt the fair sex think much the same as we, or they would not flirt with us as eagerly as they do . . .

He put his knuckle to his lips, brooding now. He had been warned of the consequences of vulnerability by his brother. But what good is such a game when one party falls horribly in love? Then all is doomed to pain and heartsickness. I have seen the victims, so I know.

He had felt the loss of control in himself the first time she tried to get away from him, felt a little scared by it. He had met many women, had used his striking looks to hunt them down, then used his wit and his charm to hold them. He had managed to bring many of them to bed, but the play had always been conducted within the rules of the game of conquest. This time he had felt something far more earnest. It was as if something had torn loose inside him. And he had seen that the same thing had happened in his quarry. Whatever it was had escaped his discipline, and he was furious with himself.

'The biter bit, eh, Smith?' It was Bonham.

'What do you want?'

Bonham's tone was irritatingly triumphal. Now he saw his arrow had found its mark. 'Ah . . . I do believe the lady's got inside your defences.'

'Never.' He smirked back at the remark. Could it be that obvious? All he wanted to do now was call off the bet. To retire from the fray. This was too dangerous. Courting disaster. Throwing all his secret planning into chaos. But there was pride to consider, and he knew himself well enough to know that he was brimful of it.

'I think so.' Bonham's grin was toadlike. 'I think she's *smitten* you.'

He snapped. 'I'm right glad it seems that way to you!'

'Oh, it does. It does. And now she's fled away from you. Broke off, as you might say. I saw it all, Smith.'

'The wager stands.'

His own words sounded altogether too defensive in his ears. Bonham's laugh was gloating. 'That's understood. Midnight, then.'

'Yes. Midnight.'

Smith left him, angered by the way he felt the urge to look for the girl, angered more by the way he had reacted under Bonham's taunting fire. The man was grotesque; he had no compassion. And that fact, along with his own potent pride – he knew it very well – had gored him on the horns of a dilemma.

He clenched his fist. 'Damn me!'

He was a naval officer, and therefore accustomed to discomfort, used to disciplining his mind and being decisive. He was not a man given to worry; he had learned the trick of putting disagreeable but insoluble matters away from him. Why, then, could he not do so now?

He drew out a big silver *écu* piece.

'Heads I stay; tails I go,' he told himself under his breath.

The coin fell, showing King Louis's disembodied head in profile. He snatched it up, then went out on to the terrace to wait, sipping at his glass, before he splashed the remains into a flowerbed and set the glass down.

He noticed the footman again, the one in pink silk who smelled of horses. He was opening a pair of doors. Smith saw how he moved, where he chose to stand, saw how he studied the gathering, and recognized what it was he was doing. In the past, shipboard life had afforded Smith frequent opportunity to quietly observe his subordinates. It had been interesting to speculate what was going through their minds as his men went about their routine. It was helpful for a commander to work out what kind of man each was, how he fitted with the whole. This footman was not of the common run by any means.

As Smith watched him he was reminded of Skrimger, a foretopman aboard *Alcmene* back in '85. Skrimger had been a pressed man with less than a year's service, an individual swept from the gutter and into some stinking prison, and from there to the West Indies station. Skrimger had been trouble from the first day, because he had been full of something that made him awkward.

Some men were like that. In Skrimger's case it had been guilt, but it might just as well have been greed, or a belief that he was the equal of his officers, or sloth, or an undischarged passion.

So end all vanities, he thought. He took the silver coin from his pocket and idly tossed it onto the back of his hand.

. . . Heads.

Again . . .

. . . Heads.

And once more . . .

. . . Heads.

He looked up to heaven.

'It seems fate itself conspires . . .'

The ballroom was ablaze with light. He saw Berenice's immature friends regarding him. One or two of them tried to meet his eye. He recognized the storm of speculation his sulky behaviour had stirred up among the gossips. And then he caught a glimpse of her, and felt an intense pang, and knew he could do nothing other than follow his impulses.

FIVE

He had asked her to come to him, and she had done so, knowing she was violating her parents' instructions. He came to meet her at the doorway and they stood there, wordlessly, on the threshold, in a mutual bewilderment.

She put her hand to her breast, partly to calm her beating heart, partly to feel the comfort of the little gold cross with the silver figure upon it that hung there.

'Do you take comfort in your Christ?'

She wondered at the question. 'He is my little silver guardian angel.'

'I guess you must know that everyone has a guardian angel,' he said, and she thought his words somewhat eerie, because he added in a fainter way: 'Even I.'

'You?'

'Yes. Though mine is quite a pagan angel. One of whom your Christ would not necessarily approve.'

She felt herself flush as she regarded his elegance. His eyes were brown, his hair black and curly as a faun's, but his nose was aquiline and there was a challenging set to his mouth, so that he could easily be imagined the reincarnation of one of Caesar's more ruthless generals.

Changing the subject, she asked him something inconsequential about his travels.

He shrugged. 'The first town I visited was Bayeux.'

'A curious choice,' she said, thinking his looks were the very embodiment of the devil now. 'There is little there but the cathedral.'

'It is the see and residence of the bishop – to whom I had a letter of introduction.'

'You?'

'Why not?' He spread his arms, and she had the sense that there was a wordless communication between them at the same time as they were speaking. 'The bishop has his palace at Caen, but luckily for me he never resides there. Therefore I have the use of his pretty garden, into which all my windows look.'

She faced him, and a shiver passed through her. 'Monsieur, why did you really come to France?'

'Mademoiselle.' He hesitated. 'It is for the purpose of further qualifying myself for my country's service.'

'That makes your mission sound very serious.'

'Does it?' He smiled suddenly, making light of the matter. 'It is hardly a mission. The *Alcmene* – my ship – had little employment once the war was ended. Her services were not required in time of peace. Nor, apparently, were her captain's.'

For a moment his expression was that of a man rejected by his lover. 'But is it not in England as it is here in France?' she asked. 'Are you not retained on half pay?'

'I am. But this is not a condition of life at all suited to my constitution or feelings. My brother Charles urged me on to acquire knowledge of men and manners, and make myself better acquainted with foreign languages. *Et voilà*! Here I am.'

'Your French is already very good.'

'I have lately been so much under obligation to speak French that I am no longer distressed to express myself on any subject.' He gave her a significant look. 'The ladies have been polite and charitable enough to listen with attention to my Anglicisms.'

'Your accent is slight, and your voice is . . . quite . . . deep.'

'Mademoiselle is too kind.' Now his look quizzed her, and his mood darkened. 'Mademoiselle, I came to Normandy because I heard it was a place where many of the first families of France are in the habit of taking up their residence. I hoped that I would be, as it were, among people who would love me as one of their own.'

There was no doubt he had a remarkably well-stocked mind. There seemed to be hidden implications in all he said. 'Indeed?'

'I have visited all the polite families in the town – I know that is the custom for a stranger here.' He raised his eyebrows ironically. 'Alas, they went not an inch further than the custom – having returned my visit, I've heard no more of any of them.'

She fanned the warmth from her cheeks. 'You scared them, I suppose.'

He was taken aback, or feigned it. His eyes were dark and penetrating. '*Scared* them, mademoiselle?'

'Families who have impressionable daughters . . .' Her words petered out as she realized that her tongue was running away with her, revealing much too much. Such a thing was easy to do in his presence.

He laughed easily, and suddenly his intensity softened. He became affable, then confidential, then overly familiar in a space of seconds. 'Ah, well. The result of it is I have remained totally without evening society, except my landlady's circle – which is not quite *comme il faut* . . .'

The invitation to pity him was plain enough, but who could feel pity for one with such mastery over his own charm? Guardedly she said, 'Until tonight?'

'At last the Duc d'Harcourt had an invitation delivered to me. He asked me to come here – where he said he should have it more in his power to show me civility.'

'And has he?'

'Well . . . he is much taken up. But at least I have made your acquaintance.'

'You know the duke is my uncle . . .'

He looked directly at her. 'Yes.'

'He is very well liked. Very convivial.'

'I found his heart good. It was written in the country

people's faces how pleased they were to see him returned among them. Their hats were pulled off in a manner which indicated to me something more than mere respect.'

'You are very observant.'

'I see you are flushed. Shall we step outside – to cool ourselves?'

Her heart thundered. They're all watching, she thought. If I go now I shall be talked about above all else for the next month. But she was already walking on to the terrace. Anything was better than being watched so intently. She felt a tightness in her throat, so that she hardly knew what conversation she was making. 'As you see, the duke has abandoned the French rules of gardening in parterres and terraces for the English style.'

'Following nature,' he said knowledgeably. 'Destroying straight lines with individuality. Our landscapers give the reason that if every landowner follows the nature of his particular ground, then all shall have an original.'

She searched his face. 'Is it right, then, to follow nature?'

'Sometimes, perhaps, it is a sin not to do so.'

Something made her say, 'I meant in pursuit of art.'

He said, 'And I meant in pursuit of . . . anything.'

He steered her into the shadows, where they were no longer overlooked by the others, then walked her away from the house, saying it was his wish to view it in perspective, and she went, moving into the warm August night. The building blazed with the light of a myriad candles, and the merry sounds of the orchestra played through the open windows and doors. Conversation buzzed distantly as they stood alone in the darkness. She saw her maid, Agnes, hurry to the footman, Gugnot, with a message. Gugnot stooped and nodded.

I'm missed already, she thought, not wanting to have a chaperone imposed on her. Not wanting this to end.

The Englishman stood behind her and stretched out his arm to indicate the sky. She felt his other hand at her waist, and she wanted him to pull her close to him.

'I have been to many places and seen many things,' he said. 'See. Those are the stars of Gemini – my guardian sign.'

She looked at a pair of bright stars scattered among many, knowing that a navigator must be able to name them all.

'The stars of the Twins were my special companions when I was far from home. I looked for them ever in the winter season in those hot Caribbean skies.' He pointed suddenly. 'And there! Did you see that shooting star?'

She had caught the brief streak of light, and it seemed to be a celestial signal to her.

'The place crossed is betwixt the Virgin and the Herdsman,' he said, meeting her eye. 'Do you know the name of that region of the sky?'

'No . . .'

'In Latin it is *Coma Berenices* – the Hair of Berenice, Queen of Egypt.' He let down her tress of long, amber hair, facing her now in the half-light. She looked into his eyes, almost unable to breathe. And then he kissed her.

They remained fixed timelessly in an embrace, she tasting the sweetness of his mouth, feeling the smoothness of his clean-shaven jaw, he pulling her to him hungrily, touching the bare flesh of her neck. Their faces and bodies were pressed together.

'Where can we go?' he asked huskily when they broke away.

'The old orangery,' she said, amazed at her own daring. The warm night air enveloped them as they ran, hand-in-hand, into the darkness, and soon they were pushing through a confusion of rhododendron bushes and a grove of mythic statuary to a folly, a gallery built by a forgotten ancestor in Classical style, glazed long ago for the benefit of citrus bushes, but now disused and forgotten.

Berenice had played here as a child, among the empty terracotta pots, the lead gutters, dusty timber benches and tanks of green water. Greek figures posed, staring sightlessly from their wall niches: Artemis and Apollo, Aphrodite and Poseidon. She turned to him again and he pressed her against the wall, and her fingers twined in his faun's hair, like the grape vines twisted about the brow of the alabaster satyr that looked down on them now.

She felt the anticipation of discovery, the fear of mortal sin, but also the unbearable heat of desire mounting inside her. He grew urgent. Their mouths were locked, tongues moving. A plant pot fell from the table, smashed, unheeded. *Is this what it is like?* His hands exposed her breasts, lifted up her skirts and petticoats. He ran his hands over her flesh, delighting in her feel, and her hungry response. The encumbrance of their clothes made her want to rip his shirt from his back and his breeches from his hips. She longed for him to touch her, and when he did she could not stop herself from gasping, nor he from making a sound so bestial she thought him truly changed into a forest beast.

When he entered her there was a moment of pain, but that quickly passed, and as he thrust she found she could do no other than abandon her thinking mind to the waves of pleasure that led her up an inevitable ascent.

She reached the summit in an ecstasy that blotted everything from her mind, then she felt him withdraw from her, and it was over.

They clung to one another as a distant clock chimed midnight, as the real world reappeared around them. Then she put her clothing in order and tried not to consider the magnitude of what she had done.

PART 2

The Furnace Heat

How did you get into my house, signore? *If you have come here to taunt me, begone! For not everything goes well with me, and I cannot bear to hear your outrageous promises at this moment. Last time we met you told me I should leap from lieutenant to lieutenant-colonel in a single stride. You offered me greatness in exchange for the laying bare of my soul. What kind of greatness is this? Look at these four walls!*

You ask me to show patience? At a time like this, when everything is poised and ready for change? I admit that your small prophecies, such that they were, have all come to pass in the course of one month. Yes, that is true. You have not exactly lied to me.

Will you not step out of the shadows, signore? *It is a curious thing, but when I thought of you after our last meeting I could not recall the features of your face. Let me apologize for my brusqueness to you just now. I was rude because you startled me, and because I am worried. I'm a lieutenant of France's Royal Artillery who has outstayed his leave. Of course, I have written to ask my colonel for an extension, but that will not prevent him charging me with desertion if I do not return immediately. Still, the truth of it is: I cannot go back to France. Not yet.*

Do you know what my superiors have said of me? Look at my paper, signore – 'He is reserved and diligent.

41

Prefers study to any kind of conversation. Nourishes his mind upon good authors. Though he speaks little, his answers are decisive and to the point, and he excels in argument.' That's correct, is it not? But they are also mistaken. See, here – 'He is taciturn, with a love of solitude, moody, overbearing, and extremely egotistical. Much self-love, and overweening ambition.' They cannot bring themselves to say anything of my skill at mathematics. The French have little respect for true learning. They acknowledge form and love the superficial. When it comes to reality they think only of their stomachs – and their pricks.

So you see, signore, in France I am surrounded by others, but I am always alone. This has been my fate. It may surprise you to know that I have contemplated suicide – coldly, examining the arguments for and against – and before I came home I thought I would give myself up to melancholy, but this furlough in my homeland has now decided me another way. Oh, yes, I can see things differently now, and not everything I see pleases me. In the town I see how my leaderless countrymen cringe before their conquerors. The French tread all over them, while my compatriots kiss the hand that beats them. The land has been in bondage for as long as I have been alive. Its leaders imprisoned, its freedoms denied. Do you see the anger in me?

Where are our patriots? All jailed. Or in exile, like I was. Life under the French is vile. Demeaning. Who should know that better than I? They are foreigners, arrogant conquerors. Did I tell you that my father fought alongside the great Paoli? One day soon the Patriots and the sons of Patriots will drive out the French invaders. My instincts have always told me that my will shall one day prevail, that what pleases me must belong to me. One day my homeland will be free. I know that, for I will make it so.

I must tell you, signore – I've been reading Rousseau.

According to him, the root of all society is to be found in an unspoken agreement – a contract – between men. A nation may trust its ruler with power, but if the ruler abuses that trust then the contract between him and his people is shattered. The people must revert to the primitive state, which is founded on an agreement of equals with equals.

I approve of Rousseau, but I think he does not go far enough. I accuse Christianity of making men slaves to tyranny. Jesus Christ is the enemy of peace and justice – as are all men who advocate exchanging the rewards of this life for the vain glories of an invisible life hereafter.

Why did you ask, signore? What are my ideas about religion? That's simple. I have none, for I already feel the infinite inside me. There is good, and there is evil, but I can find no worth in religion. It works by trying to reform human character, and thereby the world. Whereas, if I ruled the world the State would compel men to be happy. Every obstacle to the State's beneficent despotism would be crushed. And my system would work, because most men are little better than sheep. And they would follow like sheep. All it would take would be one like Alexander, one who knew how to lead. But I see you understand that already, signore.

The priests say divine law forbids revolt, but what has divine law to do with politics? Hypocrites! A divine law that forbids the throwing off of a usurping tyranny would be absurd! And as for earthly laws, the French king has already violated them. We threw out the Genoese, we'll do the same with the French. One day. You'll see! You know how much I hate this world, signore. You must help me to change it.

ONE

'When will you be missed?'

She lay on her back, staring up at a sky so blue and faultless that the fancy came to her that she was an angel, falling endlessly into its depths. Summer birdsong warbled tantalizingly over the hayfields.

'Berenice?' He repeated his question in French.

She sighed. 'Not yet. We have one hour more.'

He whispered a single word, breathed it close to her ear. 'Good.'

He played with an inch-long golden crucifix that she wore about her neck. The gentle touch of Smith's hand on her pale stomach made her stretch and turn to look at him, hungry for more. A week ago, three days ago even, it would have been impossible to imagine lying naked beside an equally naked man. Yet here she was, in a nest atop a haystack, wanting only his touch.

Though he was naked, and the only thing she wore was her crucifix, nothing seemed strange, nothing shameful. She would not consider the judgement of God or man, either for her sins or her deceptions. If the only choice is to deceive my family or to defy them, it is surely better to deceive them, she thought. And anyway, something that brought such a feeling of completeness could not really be wrong. Could it?

She thought of her lies. Her mother thought she was out on the riverbank in the care of Monsieur Ponsardin.

He was an elderly painter who taught her how to interpret landscape scenes between four o'clock and six each afternoon. But it had been easy to bribe Agnes, her lady's maid, with free time because Agnes wanted opportunities to see the groom, Gugnot. And Monsieur Ponsardin had not always been elderly. He understood young love, and had accepted a bottle of her father's best brandy to share with a friend from Falaise this afternoon. To take her leave as normal and then to change into servant's clothes had been the way to meet her lover.

Smith made a noise of contentment. She let her eyes roam over him. The sweat of his exertions had barely dried on him. Her fingers played lightly over the soft brown hair of his chest, the scar on his ribs. His dark curls were flecked with fragments of grass. His chin was rough now; he had not been shaved since this morning, but everything about him was wonderful, even that, and nothing else in the world mattered but him.

She heard barking. Recognized the timbre and felt panic. Brutus. She sat up to see a hatless figure in a faded green coat cutting a diagonal path across the next field, no more than a hundred paces away.

She crouched down, and Smith was instantly attentive to her change of mood. 'What's the matter?'

'My father's groom.'

Smith raised himself to look. Gugnot had stopped, put one hand on his hip, the other up to shade his eyes. He was looking around like a landowner surveying the lie of his land. Then he bent to where the big black animal was moving expectantly. When he launched a stone out in a great arc over the reaped land the dog tore away after it, then Gugnot continued his journey in the same direction.

Berenice rolled her eyes with relief. It struck her that Agnes had not gone to see him after all, and she wondered what difference that made. Smith smiled at her, completely unconcerned. He lay back, basked in the last warmth of the day, feeling again the deeply relaxed sensations that could only be put into a man by a beautiful woman. To enjoy his bliss better he tried to identify its elements. Part of it was born of a sense of bodily gratitude, he decided. Part was the triumphant satisfactions of conquest and possession. And like the taking of fine wine, he thought, the rarity of a woman's grace and beauty makes the joy more special, more prideful. Berenice is certainly possessed of grace, and she is beautiful both in body and limb. She has the manner and face of an angel, but there is another aspect to what I feel.

And I cannot fathom what it is, he told himself, but the cleverest part of him knew that he was denying the nature of the emotion he had discovered in himself.

The figure of Christ glittered on her breast. The top part of the cross was most singular, formed into a loop through which the chain passed. He asked her about it.

'I've worn it ever since I can remember,' she said. 'It was given to me by my godparent, Monsieur de Hergevault.'

He recalled the fiery old man with bandaged legs. 'Yes. I think I know who you mean.'

'He respects the English, but will never admit it. He cannot forgive them for having stolen his dreams of a French Empire in India. He was an employee of the *Compagnie*, a protégé of Monsieur Dupleix.'

Smith smiled. 'Then it's well that I did not mention the name of Lord Clive. Or he may have taken an apoplexy.' He examined the strange cross again. 'This loop makes a curious kind of halo for the Christ. It looks quite ancient to me, like something extraordinary from the East. But perhaps not India . . .'

'Do you remember the night of the levee?' she asked him. 'You told me you had a pagan guardian angel? What did you mean by that?'

'I believe as the Greeks believed,' he said archly, 'that

47

everyone has their own attendant spirit. He is called the Tutelary Genius. I call him my Green Goblin, and touch wood to him three times when I call his name. He is quite invisible, but he sees all, and causes events to move towards good fortune and away from dangers.'

'Can you tell when he is with you?'

'Why, yes.'

Jokingly, she hid herself a little. 'Is he here now? Watching?'

'Yes. He must be present. For only when he is with me am I greatly fortunate.'

'And what happens when he goes away?'

'Then all manner of injuries and annoyances befall me.'

'I think, Smith, that whatever you say you really do believe in your Tutelary Genius.'

There came a moment, then, when their eyes met and there was nothing more to be said. They kissed. He marvelled at what her stroking fingers did to him, and that the peace that followed the sex act was so short-lived. Already the ache was stirring in him again, but there wasn't time to do such a feeling full justice.

'The sun has touched you,' he said. 'Your skin is not used to its rays.'

'It doesn't matter.'

'You'll start to feel it burn as soon as the sun goes down.' He grinned. 'And what will you tell your maid when she sees it?'

'I don't care what she thinks.'

'You should. Or you'll be found out.'

He propped himself up on one elbow, and looked ten feet down to the starlings pecking diligently among the stubble, then out across the rolling sea of well-farmed land: ripe cornfields, water meadows and hayfields. Straight hedges quilted the land, and dark wooded patches, and blue-misted hills on the edge of the world, and there in this shallow valley a bend of the River Orne, a ribbon of sun gold. The reapers who had been cutting here two days ago were specks in a far-off patch of the quilt, bonneted peasant women with sickles among the corn stooks, peasant men in smocks and wide-brim hats swaying in rhythm with their scythes. Their efforts had made this bed for him and he was glad.

Bonham had paid him forty of the fifty pounds yesterday, and that with considerable bad grace. The man had actually contested the issue, until Smith had asked him straight: 'Are you calling me a liar, Bonham?' Only then had Bonham seen the lee shore onto which his course was leading him. It had been ten seconds away from becoming a matter of edged steel, and that would have been the end of everything, for both of them.

'Forty pounds will have to do,' Bonham had muttered.

'The sum hardly matters. It is the principle.'

'Then take ten.'

'No.'

'Why not?'

'Because you agreed a wager.'

'If what you say is true, then you've had fifty pounds worth of pleasure in the winning of it.'

He had severed what tatters remained of their friendship then. 'Bonham, you have a great deal to learn, but I fear you will never learn it. I'll take all that you can pay now. You may owe me the rest. I will collect from you – or I will collect from your estate. But I *will* collect.'

He looked at Berenice now, and read the trust in her face. He had seen that look in a girl's face often enough, and he had betrayed it as many times with too little conscience. He felt a twinge of annoyance at what seemed like a whiff of guilt. What was happening to him?

What does a girl imagine a sailor can do for her, any more than any wedded man can? he argued back. A sailor is married to the sea, and beyond a few stolen moments of passion and pleasure what can he offer? There can be nothing lasting. To think otherwise would be madness.

The game of conquests was just that. A game. Dangerous, exhilarating and infinitely rewarding, but still a game. And there was other work to do. Work that would gain him the greatest prize. Work he must not neglect, despite the delights sent by fate to distract him . . .

He was reminded of something his mother had once told him. 'There are only two important things in this life, William: love and work.' Then she had smiled sweetly at him and turned away, adding, 'See you give due regard to at least one of them.'

Exhausted by the paradox, and overwhelmed by a sudden wave of desire, he bent to Berenice's perfect rose-tipped breasts and kissed them. She pulled him to her, feeling the strength in his muscles, wanting to dig her fingernails into them.

The first time is still ringing in me, she thought. She had been too nervous and too confused to concentrate on enjoyment the first time. It had been so impromptu, more like the coupling of two animals than lovemaking, and the shock had lasted longer than the pleasure. The music and dancing had continued until just after one o'clock. She had repaired her appearance and returned to the house as serenely as she could, fearing the sin she had committed must show in her face. He had arrived later – unobtrusively, she hoped, if such a man could do anything without attracting notice.

She had noticed. He tried to be so nonchalant, but was too pleased with himself, and so much so that she had burned with embarrassment, fearing that his self-satisfaction – and its cause therefore – must be apparent to everyone.

For the rest of the night she had glimpsed him, but he

had given her no more than the subtlest of acknowledgements. That had made her jealous, and she had wondered at the meaning of it. She wanted to be with him, to be reassured. Instead he had talked very nicely and deliberately at length with a group of naval officers – effortlessly, at urbane ease, she had thought – while the other Englishman had looked on icily.

Eventually he had passed pleasantries with the duke himself. Thinking about that now made her ask him, 'What did my uncle say to you at the levee?'

'Oh, I and the duke had something in common. He commanded the French at Havre de Grâce while I was cruising off the coast with Commodore Johnston.'

'Is it not strange meeting with your old enemies?' She looked into his eyes. 'Talking over your different hopes and fears?'

He laughed. 'D'you know, that is almost a pleasure worth all the pain. Scarce a meal has passed in France without my having dined in company with some officer against whom I've fought. I confess myself very fond of this country, and its people.'

Men, she thought. How their minds work is impossible to understand. One moment they would kill each other for the sake of honour, the next, they would drink a toast to their enemy's health. She said, 'Compliments should pass when equals meet, I suppose.'

He laughed again. 'How like you to say so. It is essential that men of war should honour one another in peace. We are all, as it were, brothers, made so by our profession. You know de Guichen?'

'The Comte de Guichen?'

'His son. He was in a ship that engaged with the *Sandwich*, when we were both midshipmen. He is still one, I fear, though older than I.' Hearing him boast of rank and career matters she thought he seemed guilelessly happy. She let him go on. 'De Guichen told me he supposes I must be related to King George, or at least the

Archbishop of Canterbury, to be so far advanced so young.'

She smiled. 'You must be.'

'Ah, mademoiselle, but ability counts for a great deal in our navy.'

'And modesty?'

'Modesty is a falsehood. I don't care for it.' His eyes sparkled, so she forgave him his vanities. 'I was in the action fought by Rear-Admiral Graves against Monsieur de Barras's fleet off the Chesapeake. It was inconclusive, but the following year we went against a French fleet commanded by the Comte de Grasse, in the Leeward Isles. That gentleman was captured in the *Ville de Paris*, along with four other ships-of-the-line. It was after a furious battle which lasted from seven in the morning until half past six in the evening. We gained a complete victory.'

'Victory matters much to you, I see.'

He met her eyes, and his smile gave his reply a second meaning. 'Oh, yes. Victory matters very much indeed.'

They kissed and lay back hand in hand, then after a moment she asked, 'What is that scar?'

He put his hand over the blemish on his ribs, an inch by two. 'That's nothing at all.'

'Tell me.'

He frowned. 'If you want me to, I will.'

He lay back, and the soft hay caressed his back and the warm sun played on his chest and belly and loins. The scar was an ancient memory, a memento of the hard past as he drowsed in the blissful perfection of the present.

He told her how he had entered His Majesty's naval service at the beginning of the war, and sailed to the coast of America, under the orders of Viscount Howe. 'I was appointed to the storeship *Tortoise* in June of the year 'seventy-seven. Then, in the January following, I was transferred to the *Unicorn*, a small frigate of twenty guns.'

She read his face, seeing the nature of his memories written there. 'How was that ship?'

'Like any ship of war,' he said shortly. Then he continued in a tone that told her he did not speak this way often. 'The *Unicorn* was commanded by a rather . . . austere man. Captain Ford was his name . . .'

Smith said he had learned much of value from a first lieutenant by the name of Hurd. Off Penobscot Bay they had chased the *Raleigh*, an American thirty-two gun frigate. She had run down a good many British privateers, and the *Unicorn* had engaged her single-handed in a hard action. It had been yard-arm to yard-arm for three hours, a terrifying blooding for a young boy. Thirteen of the *Unicorn*'s men had been killed and many more wounded, himself among them, struck severely by a splinter.

'The planks of the *Unicorn*'s side were four inches thick at the gundeck,' he told her. 'When roundshot hits oak it shatters like glass. The fragments fly about and can do terrible work to the men. I was very lucky.'

He lay quiet for a moment, but then the warmth returned to his face. 'After that battle the *Unicorn* had two hundred prisoners aboard. We couldn't lock them all up, so they were put on their parole – their word of honour.'

'How is it,' she asked, curious to know, 'when you must fight against your brothers? Englishman against English Americans?'

'It's not the same as fighting our cousins, the perfidious French. That's certain.' She saw he was joking and so hammered her fist on his chest. Then they wrestled for a moment. When he lay back he became pensive once more. 'It's strange. There came on one of those hurricanes they have off Nantucket, the kind we dreaded. I was mate of the watch. Lieutenant Hurd ordered me down with a gang of hands to get a trysail off the lower deck, but the squall laid the ship on her beam ends, and those Americans jumped up on deck as quick as you like to assist in heaving overboard our guns. We got safe back to harbour, when those men could have slit all our throats. Without honour . . .'

'You all would have died?'

'Yes. It made me think about the war, and what the fighting was really about. There was always something inexplicable about that war in my mind.'

'It is the same with all families,' she said slowly. 'They quarrel unless they face a threat from outside. So it was with England and America. Once the English had broken the French power at Quebec the threat was no more . . .'

He smiled at the irony. 'Yes . . .'

He went on with his story, and she listened with rapt attention, wanting to know every detail of his life, and how it could be that this man had come through so many dangers just to be with her. I cannot believe it, still, she thought. He has come through all these trials of life and death just to be here with me now. It is surely God's will, or else it is a mystery that true lovers can meet against such odds.

'. . . in the autumn of 'seventy-eight I left the *Unicorn* and joined the *Arrogant*, under a jollier captain, John Cleland – the ship was then fitting out at Portsmouth. I stayed aboard the *Arrogant* for some three months, after which I joined the *Sandwich*—'

She wrinkled her nose at the strange English word. 'Saundweesh?'

'As in *Lord* Sandwich, d'you see?'

She heard how the *Sandwich* had borne Admiral Rodney's flag through the victory over the Spaniards in 1780, and how, in the September of that year, the admiral had appointed Smith lieutenant aboard the *Alcide*. He had been sixteen years old.

'Can you get away for a whole day? Or a night?'

She nodded. She was unsure how such a gigantic deception could be accomplished, but still she nodded.

'Then let me take you to Cancale.'

She was puzzled. 'Cancale? Why?'

'I have a wish to see that place.'

'But it is only a small fishing village.'

'Ah, perhaps so, but it is more than that to me.'

'Why?'

He arched an eyebrow. 'For the moment that is for me to know.'

'Oh, tell me what—'

She stopped suddenly, turned to Smith with her finger to her lips. Someone was whistling, approaching the haystack. She dove down, hiding in the soft hay, her heart beating loudly. She could see him down below, could hear his voice prattling to the dog. He sat down and propped himself in the shade and took out a clay pipe, while Brutus hunted about the base of the stack, snuffling and snorting.

Berenice hardly dared breathe. She winced when Gugnot's gritty voice chastised the dog. '*Seulement les souris, alors Brute!*' Only mice. Then he growled, '*Les filles sont connes, Brute . . . Un de ces jours, je vais envoyer le seigneur chier.*'

The groom's crudeness of speech shocked her. She had never heard a servant express exasperation or use foul language in her presence before, but what Gugnot said shocked her even more. 'Girls are so stupid, Brutus . . . One day I'm going to tell the master to fuck off.'

He sat there, ten feet below and struck a light for his pipe, smoked for what seemed like an age in silence making her late for her rendezvous with Agnes. What about Agnes? The thought worried her. If she hadn't been with Gugnot that afternoon, where had she been? Maybe she had been with Gugnot, but they had argued. She was not patient enough or clever enough to wait for her mistress come what may. The chances were that

Agnes was as upset as Gugnot, or that she would decide something had gone amiss and go back to the house instead, plunging everything into jeopardy.

Finally Gugnot did as Berenice had been willing him to do. He stood up, knocked the dottle from his pipe against the heel of his shoe, and stretched.

For a few seconds Berenice worried that the sparks might set the stack ablaze, but the embers died quickly. Smith started to quake with laughter. She could not see any humour in the situation. All her careful plans had been ruined, and she turned to him with an angry look.

Down below the dog barked and barked, but Gugnot shouted angrily at it. '*Qu'est-ce que tu fous?*' What the hell are you doing? Then he started off up the hill, in the direction of the château.

They dressed quickly. She threw on her peasant clothes, frantic to get back to her rendezvous, but there was time for one last, lingering kiss.

He would not let go of her. 'You'll try to find a way to come to Cancale?'

'I'll try.'

'Until tomorrow, then.'

'Yes. Tomorrow.'

TWO

It was late, half an hour before sunset on this hot and windless afternoon. A figure moved against the violet sky, cresting the hill. A young woman, running. Then a second. This time a man.

At first Gugnot thought they had seen him. They were coming straight for him. But she dodged aside like a hare and he, like a lurcher after her, turned also.

He watched from the lip of the ditch as the pair cut through the poppy field. Tall grasses, speckled with tiny wildflowers, and dozens of butterflies flittering up as they passed.

You can't see me, Gugnot thought. Not in this coat of faded green. Nor shall you see me. My fieldcraft's too sharp for the likes of you, and Jupiter's tethered safe in the copse, and you're an aristocrat, Mademoiselle Berenice, even though you're dressed today like a country girl.

He pulled a stalk of grass and chewed the sweet end. And what if you did see me, anyway. I've as much right to be in this field as you, more than that damned foreigner. It's your father's land as far as the eye can see, and I'm his man. That's it, leap and laugh, while you may, my lovely. There's an end coming to your frolics that you little suspect . . .

Gugnot watched the Englishman gain on her and then down she went into the grass and out of sight for a moment or two. They're at it again, he thought. *Dieu*! They can't get enough of each other. And little wonder, for they make the handsomest pair.

57

Gugnot's eyes fastened on the sight of two bodies wrestling behind a curtain of waving grass. Then Mademoiselle Berenice rose up, naked to the waist except for the daisy chain plaited round her head. The sight of her breasts, suddenly unloosed and unhidden, gave him instant and intolerable pleasure. He gasped. Who could turn down an errand like this? he asked himself, reeling. And to think that yesterday I was half trying to convince my conscience that the task I'd been given was not at all loathsome!

Spying on people – especially lovers – may be called a sin under God, but it has incredible compensations. Ooooh, look at that! And there's a silver *écu* a day coming to me for this week too, and that means advancement, for it's money of my own, to increase or spend or dispose of as I like, which is something I never had before. *Dieu*! There's a kind of secret comfort in seeing this particular creature's true form. Ohhhh, yes!

He crouched down, sweating, his heart beating fast. It's as Father Fournet says in his sermons: we've ever to put ourselves in another man's position. 'Do unto others as you would have them do unto you' – that's what the good father stresses as most Christian. My God, I'd give more than a silver *écu* to put myself in that Englishman's place now . . .

Gugnot heard her warning plainly: she was worried they might be happened upon by chance. There were harvesters on the land, and going home. The Englishman pulled himself up, put his arm around her shoulders, and she her arm about his waist, and they hurried towards a wooded glade.

Gugnot crabbed around, stole from the ditch, and followed at a safe distance, peering through the hedge at last. He heard the piping of a fleeing blackbird, now he saw them kissing and embracing, now they sank down on to a mossy bed by the badger sets. The Englishman lifted off her underbodice and she slid down his breeches and he threw away his shirt in a hurry. They were both completely naked now. Then he kissed his lover's body and she lay back under his caresses in perfect view.

It's hard not to make comparisons, Gugnot thought, feeling the insistence growing intolerable in his own loins: milady's exceptional shape set against Agnes's ordinariness – hard to credit they're both of the same womankind, really. Agnes has enthusiasm, but she's nothing special to look at. Why should high-born gentlemen get the best of everything? he thought. You deserve something a bit special yourself, Gugnot. You do, my lad. And one day you'll get it . . .

For the moment Agnes will have to do, he thought. Her main charm is her availability. The way she dealt out her favours for straightforward considerations appealed to me from the start. A grope in exchange for my dead mother's silver pin. That's how I got going with her. She's a schemer, but so what? Fact is, there's not a lot of choice for a man in my position, but you can dream, Gugnot. You can still dream.

He heard the Englishman moaning. Mademoiselle Berenice was on her knees beside him, her long back and lovely pear-shaped rump well visible from the hiding place. He goggled at what she did next. It's a real education to see the way the aristos go about it, he thought, wonderingly. I didn't even know you could do that. My God, the pleasure must be incredible!

Her voice was soft, her laugh musical as she encouraged the Englishman. She leaned over him, back and forth, back and forth, her fair hair fanning out across her shoulders. Gugnot stared, enraptured. Sweat was spangling his face. He felt his own erection straining. Then the Englishman pulled her down and rolled over and they were doing it with great vigour and she was making the most exciting noises . . .

Watching from his concealment Gugnot felt himself swept up by their rhythm and the sounds they were making, and though he tried to stop himself the excitement was too much for him to bear. In that unstoppable moment he felt an intense pang of joy, a pleasure vastly heightened by the sinfulness of it. He felt his mind losing control, as it always did in that amazing moment. Then he was back, and everything was uncomfortable, and he was plunged into shame.

He turned on to his side and stared into the deep orange sun, still not quite back in his right mind. The sun sat like a golden *louis d'or* just above the horizon, beckoning. The buzz of intimate conversation a few yards away lulled him. Who would you have, he wondered, if any woman could be yours? Mademoiselle Berenice? Oh, think of that! Or maybe her dark-haired cousin, Marguerite de Tromelin. I love it when she visits. There's something incredible about her too, only in a different way ... but you'd be better served, Jean Gugnot, thinking about something else, something practical and possible, instead of fool's gold.

He waited in his hollow, huddled in silence while they dressed and took themselves off towards the lane. It was five miles to Thury-Harcourt, and it would be after dark when she arrived back. This time she might face questioning. What would she say to her father? What would he, Gugnot, say? The longer this affair went on the more silver *écus* would come tumbling his way, so maybe it would be possible to spin things out long enough to buy his own horse ...

He heard Jupiter whinny far away and got up, looking around warily. The far field was dotted with stooks of corn that looked like sentinels. There would be a good harvest this year, for a change. On a whim he walked in among the trees and stood for a moment, looking down at the place where the lovemaking had been. The pressure of their bodies had flattened the moss and grass and gave him a curious pleasure to see. He knelt down and put his hand there. It had a warmth to it like the warmth of a bed.

Then he saw it. A small book, four inches by three, bound in brown leather. The sight of it made him start. He grabbed it up, unable to believe his great luck. Then the thought struck him. What if the Englishman's missed it? What if he comes back for it? He looked quickly about, listening. But there was nothing.

THREE

Berenice moved the ring to her wedding finger as soon as she was alone.

She had managed to find a way to take two whole days away from Thury-Harcourt. She was to go with her sister Celestine, and they were to stay overnight at the summer residence of one of her godparents. In reality, she had sent her sister on to Adeline de Hergevault's care with a tale of last-minute changes in plan. She had chosen a plain habit, then she had taken a horse to ride to the Englishman. The deception had required the connivance of her sister and Gugnot the groom and Agnes, but she had not hesitated to arrange matters. All of them had been susceptible to either bribery or petty blackmail.

He had been waiting for her on the bounds of her father's estate lands. He had tried to dress like a member of the middle gentry, but his notions of Norman taste were somewhat eccentric, and he had too much élan about him and too foreign a cut to look much like the seigneurs of these parts. He brought with him a notebook and a little book of travels, that he consulted often as they rode together.

When he saw her looking at the smaller of the two books he asked her, 'I had with me two like this. I cannot find the other. You did not take it with you, by any chance?'

'No. I have not seen it.'

A flinty look came into his face, but was gone almost as quickly. 'Well, no matter. Since the whole morning stretches before us I cannot resist the temptation this fine, clear day offers to visit my element, the sea. Wraxall's guidebook says it is but two leagues away. Let's go as far as we can.'

She agreed and they galloped hard to the coast and followed the edge of the dunes to the westward. On the way he talked to her about everything he saw, and asked hundreds of questions. He noted the cliffs, measuring them with his eye.

'They're not so high, nor so white as Albion's,' he said after admiring the view that swept down to La Hogue and almost to Havre de Grâce in the east. Then they joined the great road again, and went on at his insistence until he jumped down, put one riding boot on a rock and opened his notebook on his knee. He began to sketch the view and nodded out into the bay, full of enthusiasm.

'The name of this region is Calvados,' she told him. 'Do you know why?'

He shrugged. 'I have no idea why. Should I have?'

'Yes. You are a man of the sea.' She watched him sketch for a moment, then she said, 'Calvados comes from the Spanish "Salvador", or "saviour". It was the name of a great galleon that was wrecked here during the invasion of England that failed.'

'Ah, the Invincible Armada!' He smiled. 'This coast is treacherous. It was almost a hundred years ago when our Admiral Russell discovered the French fleet, under the Comte de Tourville, lying just there. The fleets engaged, but a thick fog came down, so that for two or three days nothing could be done. When it cleared the French began to move off. Russell went in pursuit . . .'

She watched his eyes as he imagined the fight. Saw his ambitions burning bright then, as he sketched an aspect of the bay. He wanted to do as those before him had done. He enjoyed talking about his hopes and enthusiasms, but she sensed something guarded about him, and knew that he was unused to opening himself that much to a woman, or perhaps to anyone. To be a *capitaine de*

63

vaisseau is to have command, she thought. Ultimate responsibility for hundreds of men's lives. Personal isolation must come with such a powerful post. Perhaps that's one reason I find him so fascinating.

'. . . then Tourville ran ashore over there, and cut away his masts, and two others followed him. The admiral ordered Sir George Rooke to follow with fireships. The result was that France lost two great ships of a hundred and four guns and fourteen others of the line from ninety to sixty guns—'

'I think you forget that I am French,' she said sharply, suddenly conscious of how foolish the ring on her wedding finger must seem to him.

He sighed, somewhat deflated, then said: 'Yes, I believe I do forget that. I'm sorry.'

'I accept your apology,' she said, but his smile melted her and then he became serious, though in a different way this time.

He said, 'I don't care if you are French and I am English.'

She waited for him to say more. He seemed to want to, but he did not. Then she told herself that it was probably the imp of jealousy who had blighted the idyll. His love of the sea and all that happened upon it was so strong, she wished they could ride inland. There she would once more be his sole preoccupation. But if you loved him, truly loved him, she thought, you would not be so selfish.

What if it is in the nature of men that they can only love women who are prepared to share their obsessions? Then she would have to love the sea. She was not sure she could do that, for the sea had always frightened her. She stood beside him as he gazed at the play of light over the sea. A great glory shone in the sky, a cloud obscuring the sun with a hundred misty rays coming from it, like in the paintings of the Italian masters. Rays of hope, she always thought. The sight seemed to enthrall him.

Eventually he said quietly, 'The fury of that battle must have been quite hellish.'

She told him: 'The common people hereabouts remember the stories their fathers and grandfathers tell. They call that battle *le brûlement* – the burning. They see the wrecks at low tide between the island of Tatihou and La Hogue Point. Near St Vaas the local people still fish for iron from them.' She touched his sleeve. 'I think it's a pity that our countries must be so often at war.'

He embraced her, then, and they kissed. But he made no answer.

By six in the afternoon they had come right across the peninsula. Smith pronounced the tide in the estuary high enough, so they left their horses at the stables on this side of the river and took the ferry across to the small fishing village beyond.

On the way Smith engaged the ferryman in conversation, asking him about the peculiarities of wind and tide along the coast, and the local names for rocks and shoals. The Englishman seemed to know the geography hereabouts almost better than those he asked.

'Instead of going round eighteen leagues by land, we may as well take passage by water.'

'How?'

'Why, in a fishing boat. That way it's only five leagues to Cancale.'

'But why should we go to Cancale?'

He shrugged. 'Why not?'

He got among the stacks of lobster pots and negotiated with a fisherman to hire what seemed like a very small boat, and they climbed down into it. She, very conscious of herself; he, very adroitly. Then the fisherman's young son pushed them clear and Smith took the tiller as the man rowed them from the harbour and out to open water.

As the stained sail bellied in the breeze, the enormity

of what she was doing brought a powerful sensation into her stomach. She imagined the cold fury of her father when he found out. Her mind's eye pictured the crushing 'disappointment' her mother would demonstrate. But she had made her mind up, and here she was, despite their disapproval. The excitement of being completely away from her family for a night, of evading the care of all chaperones, seemed almost as great a sin as the sharing of that night with a man. What had he done to her in so few days to turn her from being an obedient young lady to being a make-believe eloper? How many times would it take to make her pregnant? She did not know. Nor could anyone tell her, for there was no one she could ask, except Smith himself. And that was unthinkable. Undoubtedly, tonight they would share a bed together. This time a real bed. She counted the times they had made love so far. Five times. Surely a woman could trust a man if he had made love to her five times.

She watched the fine, smooth water, and saw the pastel sunset give way to a disc of pale yellow moonlight. And the gigantic gulf in their experiences showed itself to her. Though she was quite assured at Thury-Harcourt, she knew little of the world beyond. And here was a man who had been everywhere and knew everything. No wonder he seemed so impressive. And to think he has fallen in love with me, she thought, feeling suddenly worthy and unworthy at the same time.

She said very little on the voyage. For the sake of their anonymity Smith spun a story for the fisherman's benefit of how he, an English merchant, and his wife, also English, had taken advantage of the peace to come across from Dover in order to follow in the footsteps of the intrepid Monsieur Wraxall. She was amazed at the fluency with which he lied. He was almost adept at it, and it occurred to her that such expertise must have required frequent practice in the past.

The boat tied up at eleven o'clock, and they had to

mount a slip of muddy cobbles. So firm a friend had Smith made of the fisherman, Marcouf, that he piloted them ashore, through the dark huddle of cottages to the *auberge*, stormed the people up, set their grate burning, and insisted that they all sit down to eat broiled mackerel, the only thing the house produced.

Berenice was amazed to find that the people seemed mightily pleased to see them. They were very anxious to know all about her, which was the only thing in which Smith did not choose to satisfy them. English, and a merchant's pretty young wife, was all they were told. Not even her name. She played the shy, anxious creature who kept downcast eyes, but her true state moved between excitement and hilarity. Smith paid the reckoning, and they were shown to a small room with a good bed, with linen bleached very white. They fell upon it, cackling like cats.

In the morning Cancale was quiet; most of the boats had gone out beyond the shoals. Old women in aprons smoked long clay pipes as they mended nets by the foreshore. The place smelled of salt and dried fish and she saw Smith draw a deep, appreciative breath of air as he sketched and narrowed his eyes to seaward.

'What are you expecting to see?' she asked.

He gave her a shrewd look and walked on. 'Old habits die hard. Aren't you hungry yet?'

The nearest approximation to an eating-house stood above the old quay. A tub of live crabs bubbled beside the doorway. It was a rude, tumbledown place of bare boards, rough wood and cracking plaster. They were its only customers.

While they awaited the tide and Marcouf's return, Smith ordered some cider from the owner, an overly deferential man, unused, she thought, to visits by people other than the local fisherfolk, much less to those by people of rank.

They sat down and ate and after a while Smith began to tell her about his strange childhood.

'I was sent at a young age to Tunbridge school. It was a most excellent establishment, under the guidance of one Doctor Knox.'

She watched his slim fingers peel the last of the fat boiled prawns and dunk it in melted butter. When he looked up his eyes were so dark they shocked her.

'Then I had to be . . . withdrawn.'

She wrinkled her nose at him. 'Because you were a very wicked boy, I think.'

He laughed. 'No. I was not a difficult child. I was obliged to leave school because of my grandfather. I was put instead into a frightful boarding school near Bath.'

'Your grandfather?'

'Yes. He plagued our family, you see. He could never forgive my mother for running away with my father.'

Berenice chewed her lip. 'Your parents *eloped*?'

'Oh, yes. Didn't your mother tell you?' He shook his head at his own foolishness. 'No, of course she wouldn't have. Despite telling everyone else in Normandy. Anyway, because of the elopement the old man confounded my parents at every turn. One of his ways of revenging himself on his daughter was through me, young as I was.'

She was horrified. 'That is a terrible way for a girl's father to behave.'

He shrugged. 'It often happens.'

A plate of mussel stew was laid before him by one of the young daughters of the inn, who approached the table with trepidation. She fled when Smith grinned at her.

'Your mother sounds very strong to have defied him.'

'Strong is not the word for it. My mother knows her own mind – and usually everyone else's too.'

'That must be where your wilfulness comes from.'

He regarded her with a sidelong glance. 'I dare say the

Wilkinson strand is in me too. But it's an unbending stuff, and better woven with a softer weft.' He blew the steam from a spoonful of mussel broth and consumed it with an expression of ultimate indulgence. 'Oh, braaaa-vo!'

The cook and innkeeper and three girls looked to one another with astonishment.

'They have never seen a foreigner,' she explained quietly. 'Much less an Englishman.'

'They know I'm English?' He seemed surprised.

'So half the town is speculating.'

'And how do they take their exotic visitor? Better than a crocodile in a waistcoat?'

'No.' She laughed. 'But they could not have hoped to see one who would show so civilized an appreciation of their speciality.'

He savoured another spoonful. 'Who could fail to appreciate the qualities of this divine ambrosia? In England we say that in all the world there are only three things the French can do better than we.'

'Only three?' She rolled her eyes. 'And what are they, pray tell me, sir?'

'The first is to cook food. No question.'

'And the second?'

'The second is their wine. A consequence of climate.'

'And what is the other?' She put her hand to her lips. Her eyes smiled, as she supposed what the third must be.

He said, 'The third is the building of ships.'

'. . . ships?'

'Oh, yes. French ships are superlative. And if the French could fight like us there would not be a power on earth who could stop them from ruling the entire globe. Fortunately, when it comes to fighting, they're a damned disgrace.'

'What about France's women?' She showed her indignation.

'Naturally I left French women out, for they are

goddesses.' He supped more mussel liquor. 'Good food and goddesses are both hard to come by in the Royal Navy. I know, because I have been in it for more than half my life.'

She reckoned his age. 'That means you must have been placed there before you were twelve.'

'Yes. I admit, my education could have been more extensive.' He smiled at her. 'A man-of-war was not exactly the best schoolroom for a young man. My education was confined mainly to the practical rules of seamanship, and to as much of navigation and arithmetic as were necessary to pass the examination for a lieutenant's commission.'

'Is that what you wanted most?'

He reacted to the question as if it was absurd. 'To me, as to all midshipmen, that is *the* leap. The one from boy to man.'

'And when you were made a captain?'

'Mortal to —' He stood up and struck a pose in imitation of a Greek hero. '— to *demi-god*!'

The children of the house watched him wide-eyed, so he cleared his throat and sat down again. 'It wasn't quite as simple as that. Though, I did win my goddess.'

'You did?'

'Oh yes.' His reverential tone gently mocked her disappointment. 'And she was *all* I ever wanted.'

'What was her name?'

'She was called *Alcmene*. Truly a goddess, and I worshipped her.'

Berenice folded her arms, pouting. 'I don't want to know.'

He leaned forward, his eyes on hers. 'She was the mother of Heracles by Zeus, and of Iphicles by Amphitryon, and wherever she went there were two hundred men dancing attendance on her.'

'Oh – she was your *ship*!'

'Of course, what else?'

She laughed with him, but the laugh caught in her throat as she saw an old woman standing in the doorway. The crone was ancient. She spat and then began to deliver a stream of insults. Finally she began to pelt them with oyster shells.

The innkeeper moved to intercept her. Then a fisherman appeared and the old lady was mollified and led across the alley to her cottage.

'Extraordinary,' Smith said, his eyebrows raised. 'Is she mad perhaps?'

'So sorry, monsieur. She is old. Perhaps she imagines some grievance upon you.'

Smith settled the bill generously, at the same time quelling the innkeeper's fawning apologies. 'Let's not have any embarrassment,' he said. 'Come, we'll all of us drink cider to the honour of Cancale.'

And so they toasted the village and then the port of Dover, and then France and then England, and after a couple of bottles had emptied everything was repaired.

As they walked with the fisherman, Berenice was interested to see him point out the marks of English bullets in the rocks and houses. She saw that there were many round holes in the window-shutters and doors of the houses, and Smith examined them attentively. He talked over the whole business very good-humouredly, and the fisherman took it equally well.

'So it was my English appearance that proved my having had some hand in the making of these holes six years ago?'

Marcouf nodded. 'The old women have not forgotten the injuries their houses were given by the English, but it is kings and lords who make wars, no? Not the common people.'

Smith nodded. 'Very true. But it's the common folk who always pay the price.'

The fisherman laughed. '*Bien sur*! Certainly. But not me this time.'

'No?'

'A fisherman can go where he likes and he can sell to whomsoever he likes.' Marcouf tapped his nose with a finger. 'All ships need provisions – water, fresh vegetables – even English ships, eh?'

Smith grinned back. 'I know what you mean.'

'I sold forty English cannonballs to our army. They fetched twelve sous apiece.'

Smith laughed. More than the anecdote warranted, she thought. Then he thrust out a hand and seized the fisherman's elbow. 'Excellent, Marcouf! An illustration of the English proverb, "It is an ill wind that blows nobody any good." '

A little later, as the little boat pulled from the harbour, Smith whispered quietly to her, 'Marcouf tells me he picked up forty of my round shot from the town and got twelve sous apiece for them. You see that windmill? I remember amusing myself with firing at it. If I'd known our good conductor was profiting from my actions to the tune of twelve sous per shot, I'd have given the place a much more thorough pounding.'

She was taken aback. '*You* were the one who bombarded this poor village six years ago?'

He nodded. 'Why else do you think I wanted to bring you here?'

FOUR

Berenice took her seat opposite Smith, and dared to meet his eye only briefly, so terrifying was the ordeal. This was her father's new table, and what seemed like the entire family was seated at it. There was her father at the head, her mother at the foot, her sister, Père Fournet from Caen, Adeline de Hergevault and her elderly uncle, the handsome artillery lieutenant Antoine le Picard de Phelypeaux, and six others of the family of René-Prosper Sapindaud, the Marquis St Hubert.

The invitation for Smith to dine at Thury-Harcourt had come without warning and had caused her great anxiety.

'Your uncle suggests I invite Captain Smith to help christen the English table,' her father had said neutrally and seemingly almost in passing. 'You remember him? He refused to wear epaulettes to our levee. He was almost thrown out by Faligan and Davout.'

Warning bells had sounded in her head. 'I don't . . .'

Her father had put down the quill and taken off his spectacles. 'Since he is lodging at the bishop's residence I thought he might stay here. Père Fournet can take him the invitation tomorrow.'

'Stay here?' She had felt herself colouring.

She had thought about the trip to Cancale many times in the week that had passed. So far the deception had remained intact. Gugnot and Agnes had been bribed with free time, her sister Celestine had been easily blackmailed. Her attachment to a certain music teacher had been a perfect lever. The spinster Adeline de

Hergevault had so far raised no query about the late change of plan regarding the visit, but now she was to come here in person. Something was bound to come out in conversation.

As Berenice took her seat, she crossed her fingers under the table. It was hard to know how Mademoiselle Adeline would take it if she had discovered the truth. She was herself forty, unmarried, and likely to remain so now that she had taken consolation in religion – or perhaps it was the religion that had been the cause of her chastity. Whatever the case, she seemed to be a good person, devoted to the care of her elderly uncle, and not otherwise bitter.

She might not approve of immorality and deception, Berenice thought hopefully, but that does not mean she will necessarily betray me. What she decides to do will depend on whether she follows Christ, or the Church.

The consideration was broken off as conversations began across the formally laid table. Smith found himself halfway down the table, seated significantly opposite Berenice. He was the only Englishman, in fact the only guest not intimately connected with the family du Fay. He played his part coolly; he had come prepared to fence off all enquiries, and would do so come what may.

He inspected the table. It was new, clearly English-made, of highly polished Malabar teak and quite superb. He decided it would be indelicate to compliment his irascible host on it, since it would bring up the question of the British smashing the French in India, and risk lighting old Monsieur Hergevault's fuse again.

Smith chose to hold his peace until the family turned their attentions on him. The comte did not seem to be a great conversationalist, nor a man with any taste for trivial talk. He had a long, narrow face, long nose, and pale features that his powdered wig did not flatter. He was stiff of bearing, but his choice of words was supple and his meaning precise.

He waited until what seemed a pre-arranged moment, then motioned gravely to the table servants, who bowed and took their leave discreetly. Smith felt an ominous discomfort as he noted the way Berenice glanced briefly and expectantly at her father, then down at her plate.

'You have seen much of our Normandy countryside, captain?'

Smith accepted Berenice's warning – her toe on his shinbone. The question was short, but placed with the accuracy of a dart. It alerted him. 'The duke favoured me with an official letter to the port commandant at St Maloes, which procured me a very gracious reception.'

'Indeed?'

'I saw with pleasure the inside of those batteries at St Maloes, which had so often tried to pelt us when we appeared off with Commodore Johnston. After that I spent three military days with the officers of the Régiment de Beauce at St Servan's, where our troops were in 1758, when—'

'We do not often speak of that episode, captain.' The comte's frigid humour balked him, but he doggedly tried to keep the conversation rolling.

'At St Servan's, sir, they talked of little else. I got into a scrape, not by abusing French arms, you may believe, but from defending Admiral de Grasse as a brave man. I discovered this is not the fashion.' He turned to bow his head knowingly towards the ladies' end of the table and dabbed at his mouth with his napkin before adding, 'But I hope it is the only unfashionable thing that I do.'

The comte seemed stung, on what account he could not tell. 'De Grasse is not a hero. He allowed himself to be defeated.'

'I don't really think he had much say in it, sir. And I should know, for I was there. At any rate I generally found one poor solitary soul at every dinner prepared to defend him until overpowered by numbers.' He grinned blithely. 'I must say I enjoyed the pleasure of seeing him recover and go into action again, reinforced with the ammunition of my facts. Of course, I left all the acrimony to him.'

A beat of silence passed. 'And where else have you been?'

He felt the unspoken word 'alone', implying that he had also visited places – sensitive places – when not under the eye of the French military. He fended the enquiry off easily. 'Well, sir, my reading of Wraxall's *Tour* raised in me a curiosity to see the famous Mont St Michel. We have a structure much the same in Cornwall, I believe.'

'You are fortunate to be allowed so much leisure,' the comtesse said.

'Most fortunate, madame.' He smiled. 'An advantage this glorious peace affords us.'

The comte held his glass before the light, examining the colour critically. 'But, I think you are a man upon whom empty leisure sits poorly. Hmmmm?'

'I am a naval man. And some would say that to see a man of war at his leisure can be no bad thing.'

The comte, still without looking to him, seemed to accept his words, but after another space he remarked: 'One is still forced to wonder why you choose to confine your Grand Tour to this locality.' His eyes moved briefly to his wife and back to his wineglass. 'When you have the whole expanse of Europe before you.'

Smith considered. 'But, then again, sir, why should a man bother with the lesser parts of a continent? This place has some rare beauties.' He resisted the temptation to look to Berenice.

'I know you ride very well. Did you ride to Mont St Michel?'

'Ah, only after the English fashion.' He coughed delicately. The comte had never seen him ride. He realized instantly that the remark was certainly designed to unsettle him, but why?

'Meaning?'

'The horses I took went under the name of *chevaux quittés*, because you go without a conductor. You leave one where you take the next. I was told I should find them an extremely hard ride. And so I should have done, had I not learned to ride in England, and so practise what nobody here has the least idea of, that is, rising in the stirrups. The French way is to bump it along like so many old women going to market.'

His attempt at humour missed its mark. Silver danced briefly on porcelain in the silence, then the comte said, 'So you rode everywhere without a conductor?'

He was determined to remain affable, despite the strained atmosphere. 'In the main. But on my excursion to that marvellous island mount I took a thing called a *cabriolet*, which is extremely like that in which Gil Blas and Scipio – or was it Dr Sangrado? I forget – performed their journey—'

The comte cut off his waffling with a briskness that bordered rudeness. 'And then you went to Cherbourg in it, did you not, sir?'

Smith divined the way the comte's questions were tending. He decided to direct his replies towards his own defence. 'Everyone is talking of the great works going on at Cherbourg. The building of a breakwater two miles and a half from the shore is a great and wonderful undertaking. I thought I must go there and see for myself.'

'That is not all you have "seen for youself".' The comte looked down the table, and it seemed to Smith that his gaze alighted briefly on Berenice, but then he stirred again, breaking the icy silence. 'It is not forgotten here that it was the English who destroyed the fortifications and harbour works of Cherbourg in 'fifty-eight.'

'I hope Monsieur le Comte will not hold that against

77

me personally.' He smiled charmingly, meaning to turn the man, and all of them, by a well-timed appeal to humour. Underneath, he knew with horrific certainty that all had been discovered.

'Monsieur?'

'That war was, after all, six years before my birth.'

The comte's voice remained stone cold. 'You were observing in Cherbourg on the eighth of this month, a day of great significance.'

That was the day the third of the giant cones was sunk, he recalled. They were circular, one hundred and sixty feet in diameter at the bottom, sixty feet high, and diminishing to sixty feet across at the top. They were built as strong as a ship, but of lower-grade wood. That morning at eight o'clock, at high water – a spring tide – one of them had been floated out. It had looked like a floating castle compared to the vessels that surrounded it. Empty casks had been lashed round its base. He had mounted another of the cones to watch the placement. After being towed into position the casks had been cut away in opposite pairs, and the task of filling the cone with fifty thousand tons of stones had begun.

'Yes, that was the day I saw one of the first cones put in place.' He was thinking the same thought he had at Cherbourg, that the techniques used to construct a floating castle could be used for other purposes too, not least the launching of invasion barges.

The comte looked at him directly, holding the exchange on its downward course. 'Pray tell me, what conclusions did you reach?'

'Conclusions? Only . . . that I remember thinking that each cone would take about five weeks to fill, and that if a gale should come on meanwhile then the woodwork above the stones would have no more chance of standing against the waves than the wreck of a ship does.' He shrugged. 'Nevertheless everyone must applaud the immensity of the work, which is nothing less than the making of a mountain piecemeal and carrying it a league out to sea. A deed worthy of the Romans.'

The comte continued to eye him freezingly. 'And what did you conclude was the purpose of all this work?'

Smith felt the rest of his sense of ease evaporate. The fortifications clearly face England, he thought. Of course it would pose a threat to Britain to have a great fleet stationed at Cherbourg, but that's elementary. What's he really trying to make me say? That I'm a spy? Could it be that he's found out about Berenice and me? Be careful!

He said, 'I was told that the Minister of Marine, Monsieur de Castries, began this work in 1783. That His Most Christian Majesty has found the want of a port in the Channel that is fit for the reception of his large ships. He seems determined to make one at any expense. From what I have seen, this will cost immensely, and – if I have any judgement as to the force of water – perhaps it will fail after all.'

The comte reacted as if Smith had admitted sabotage. 'Then you allow that you were, after all, assessing the strength of the harbour?'

'I am extremely glad I have seen it. The Duc d'Harcourt is the governor of Normandy, and commander-in-chief *pour sa majesté*, is he not?' He opened his hands in a gesture of frank incomprehension. 'I . . . the Duc d'Harcourt was there, sir. He expressed himself without objection to Britons viewing a French marvel. The day after I went thither, two other British captains of men-of-war arrived from Caen – on the same errand, I believe.'

The comte's tone was flat and cold. 'You appear to believe that you can hide behind my brother's hospitality. In that, I may say, you are mistaken, captain.'

He felt the remark cut like a whip on his cheek. He made his reply equally crisp and controlled. 'Monsieur le Duc received me most politely. He desired me to consider myself engaged to his party while I stayed. He himself conducted me to the place where the cones were constructed along the beach. And he showed them to me. We embarked with Monsieur le Duc, and attended the cone as it was towed to the place where it was to be sunk in a line with the two already placed—'

'Captain.' The comte cut him off. 'You are an officer, and a gentleman. But are you also a man of honour?'

Smith felt a faint nausea. His knife and fork appeared suddenly heavy in his hands. 'I have always tried to conduct myself according to that thesis, monsieur.'

'Good.' The comte turned to his elder daughter, then put his hand to his waistcoat and drew out a small leather-bound notebook. 'Berenice, do you recognize this?'

It took all of Smith's self-control to suppress a reaction, but he saw Berenice start as she recognized one of his two little notebooks.

'Father . . .'

'Do you recognize it?'

'I . . .' What's my father trying to say? she asked herself silently, but already knowing the answer in her heart. He knows about us. Oh, no . . .

The comte picked up the thread of the hanging moment with exquisite timing. 'I see that you do. Well and good. For it is time that I revealed to you, my dear daughter, the reasons behind Captain Smith's artistic interests – his sketching of the beaches and bays of this area, his academic attention to the new works at Cherbourg, his recordings of the depths of water in all of our harbours. And of course, my dear, his apparent attachment to yourself.'

Berenice felt her father's stern eye on her, saw the controlled but pale face of her lover. He knows, and he's known about us all along. Then her mind focused on what her father was saying, and her shock turned to panic. He's not disapproving, he's saying that Smith does not really love me.

'No!'

'I see you don't believe me.' Her father's pale blue eyes were unblinking. 'Why not ask him why he begged you to go with him to Cancale two days ago?'

There was a space of silence as Berenice's mind froze. How could he know that? What was in the little book? A diary? A diary of what? The embarrassment was too much to bear.

Just as Smith opened his mouth, her father went on in his coolly uninflected voice.

'He is an officer. A gentleman. As we have just heard he also thinks of himself as a man of honour. Surely then, he cannot lie to you. Ask him why he took you to Cancale. Why it was Cancale in particular?'

She turned her gaze to Smith, conscious that every other eye in the room was upon her. She searched his face. 'Why did you?'

Before the attentively silent table his eye avoided hers. 'It is my belief that England and France will soon be at war again—'

There was something different about his face now, something pale and waxen, as if the charm that usually animated it had departed. It seemed suddenly as if she was seeing him truly for the first time.

She shook her head slowly, her eyes pricking now.

'My dear,' her father said. He leaned back. 'He has been surveying our coastline. He knows that if his initiatives distinguish him at the British Admiralty he will get his true heart's desire – which is a ship of war!'

Smith made a gesture of denial, fervent now, his dark eyes flashing as he looked from face to face. 'I cannot deny making notes and sketches, nor that they were for the purpose you have identified, but my heart's desire is your daughter, sir.' He turned to her 'You *must* believe me, Berenice.'

She looked at him, saw the way his eyes implored, but then remembered all the other expressions she had seen there too. He was a charmer, a man who could compose his face to suit whatever occasion. How could she be sure that this was not a lie also?

'Must I believe you?'

He reached out to her across the table. 'Of course! My love for you is genuine! And since I *am* a man of honour you must believe what I say!'

The comte's voice seemed to come from far away. 'I am your father, Berenice. I am older and wiser than you, and I have your best interests at heart. Believe me when I say that this young man has played you false.'

Everything was poised in the balance. She looked from her father to Smith and back. Her heart was hammering. He is accused just because he is English, her own voice warned her. Father is bound to oppose us.

But what about the madness that had overcome her the night of the ball, the way they had ended up in the orangery together. Could it be that he had planned it as a deliberate seduction? A means to gain simple sexual gratification? Had it all been merely a *manoeuvre*? Her look questioned him. She felt tears begin to well.

'Men are men,' her father said. 'They have their needs and will go to any lengths to satisfy them.'

Smith was angry now. His voice sounded harsh and unfeeling. 'I admit, I started out simply to make you my conquest. But now I am as trapped by love as you are.'

She looked away from him. All the faces around were hardened, dutiful, censorious, betrayed – all except Père Fournet's, and her sister Celestine's. She felt the impulse to bolt from the room, but she knew there could be no escape.

Then her father closed the matter. He stood up, summoned them both to the head of the table, and they came, facing one another, a parody of bride and groom standing before the priest.

'The evening of the ball,' the comte said, filling the moment with his authority, 'Captain Smith, did you, or did you not, stake the sum of fifty pounds in a wager with Captain Bonham – that you would take my daughter's virginity before midnight?'

When the meaning of her father's words hit her she gasped. Tears began to well as she searched Smith's face for a denial, but what she saw was him clamp his lips together and turn his face away.

'Sir, I will have an answer. Do you deny such a transaction took place?'

'No. I cannot deny it.'

Berenice saw his spirit visibly dim. Shame? Was it shame that did that? She felt some kind of spell breaking.

Still trembling, she slapped his face.

He put his hand to his cheek, but did not look at her.

With a tremendous effort, she controlled her voice. 'Monsieur! You have disgraced me! I wish never to see you again.'

She saw him bow with rigid formality. 'Monsieur le Comte. Mesdames, messieurs . . . mademoiselle.'

He cast a dark glance around the table, then retired, humiliated and silenced, and was gone.

FIVE

Berenice sat at her dressing table, feeling a hollowness inside that she could only echo in sighs. Her chair's ornate back matched the table. The gilded looking glass matched the rococo decoration of the walls. Everything around her was of the best – finely wrought furniture, luxurious textiles, tasteful ornament, a delight to any cultured eye. But not to hers. Not today.

A Persian carpet had been brought in yesterday at her mother's order. Today a spray of tulips and irises had been placed in the empty fire-grate. They perfumed the room delicately, but despair made Berenice's senses dull and lifeless. Everything was as dry as dust. The spell was broken, the great pretence revealed. And there was only the flat reality of a mundane world to replace it.

The harpsichord sounds of Celestine's practising came to her from a far part of the house. Difficult sections repeated assiduously, time and time and time again, until she wanted to run to the head of the stair and scream at her sister to stop.

The room that pressed in around her was just so much fuss, a world without any power to interest her. Her eye took in the confining walls of her chamber. Everything from her perfumed bed pillows to the volumes of her bookcase had come from her father. His wealth and position had supplied them. Those things were the foundation of everything, he had said. It had been explained to her that she was nothing of herself. Nothing at all, and even less now that she had spent her virginity so shamefully. Her one function was to be the dutiful and obedient daughter of a great family, to marry at the appropriate time whomever was selected for her. To provide offspring who would continue the dynasty into the new century was what she had been put on earth to do. That was the great design. She was nothing outside that design.

'And I was so sure,' she murmured. 'So sure.'

Celestine had made her put into words something of what Smith had been to her. 'I believed he loved me, so at last I could begin to love myself. Do you understand?' But Celestine had not understood at all. That much had been obvious. She was too young. She had never been in love – except with her music. So how could she know?

And now? she thought, her feelings surging painfully from numbness once again. Now what? Fortunately it is not necessary for a person in my position to love anyone. Least of all herself.

The noise came again. Faint, but unmistakable. A brief small creeping sound, just like the one she had heard a minute before. She looked behind her. Nothing moved, but she knew now where the sound was coming from, and her imagination told her what had made it. The thought sent shivers through her . . . a rat in the wainscoting.

She tried to ignore it, but it came again.

Berenice knew that the château of Thury-Harcourt was old and held many secrets. The house had flourished in the age of Louis XIV, when the War of the Fronde had given an ancestor of the family du Fay reason to plan certain safeguards. There was a narrow space between two walls, a space a man's shoulder-width across, and perhaps four paces long. It could be entered by moving a wall panel in this room. She had played there as a child. It had been her secret place.

Hundreds of huge orange-toothed rats had run from the old piggeries when they had been demolished five years ago. The memory made her skin crawl. She had watched from horseback as the rat man's terriers shook dozens of them to death. The rats' anguished squeals and the bloodied muzzles of excited dogs were still vivid in her mind.

The idea of vermin making a nest in the sacred place of her childhood horrified her. Her first impulse was to call the servants. It was for them to deal with, but that would mean giving the secret away. She approached the panel, and forced herself to feel for the hidden catch. Recent paint had stiffened it in its recess, but she freed it and the wall section cracked open.

What if it jumps out at me? she thought, dreading the idea of looking in. It will run away from the light. Rats hate the light, don't they?

She looked in. Her eyes began to make sense of the darkness. The space was pierced by a beam of cold light coming in from a hole high up the end wall. The spy-hole overlooked the front of the château, disguised from the outside by an ornamental lion's head. She looked around the floor. The dusty boards were empty. What-ever it was had gone back the way it had come.

She looked again, just to make sure, but as she did the sound came again. It was louder this time. Something flew at her face and she fell back, dropping the panel. Something was whirling round and round her bedroom. She put her hand up in horror, trying to ward it off, but then she saw that it was trying to escape through the closed window. It collided with the glass pane and fell fluttering to the floor.

Her relief as she saw the part-stunned starling was tremendous. She went over and opened the window, then gathered up the starling in her hands. It tried to peck her, and the touch of it was wild and alien so she launched it out on an impulse of revulsion, watching as it flew away.

There was another noise – a different one this time – from outside her door, the creaking of a board. That meant Agnes would be lingering there, perhaps with one of the other maids, hoping no doubt to gather gossip with which to delight the rest of the servants. Agnes's taste for gossipmongering had budded in the past week. The scandal had driven it into full bloom.

Was it she who betrayed me? Berenice wondered.

She sighed again and composed herself. Her heart was racing. She replaced the panel and closed the catch. She was trembling, but she returned to the task of combing her hair. What did it matter? Nothing mattered any more. She looked in the glass and decided her eyes were red and puffy. She pulled a comb through her hair, knowing that life must go on as if nothing had happened. That much was expected of her.

How much clearer events are in hindsight, she thought. What a fool I was! What ridiculous castles I made in the air! I never thought about anything! Not with my mind. If I had only used my shrewdness instead of following the dictates of my heart the love of an Englishman would have been revealed as a ludicrous impossibility. It was quite laughable. Naturally my father did what was right. A man like him should never have been asked to tolerate such behaviour from a daughter. I denied him the one thing he has ever asked of me.

The furniture had been polished with beeswax, and the smell of it seemed suddenly cloying to her. She wanted to throw open the windows and scream. To run free across the lawn and fields. To plunge into the cold, brown waters of the Orne. Anything that would shock this terrible empty feeling out of her. But all she could do to dispel it was to sigh, echoing the void inside.

Three days ago she had run up to her room. Immediately Smith had departed the fatal dinner she had broken down, unable to do otherwise. She had rejected all attendance – the kindly Père Fournet, her mother, Celestine, Agnes, everyone – and flung herself onto her bed, distraught. Pride and anguish had warred inside her unbearably.

Then, hearing voices down below, she had gone to her window and looked down to see Smith waiting impatiently for his horse to be brought.

The sight had filled her eyes with tears. She had watched Gugnot bring the horse, and then help Smith mount up. It had been one of the Duc d'Harcourt's animals, a big bay hunter with a white flash. Smith had circled twice, looking around, as if expecting to see her. His face had been set in a grim expression, then he had dug his heels into the horse's flanks and ridden to where Faligan was already holding the tall iron gates open.

Did he really expect me to come to him? she asked herself. It was the sort of question that could never be answered. The sort of question that could drive a person out of their mind if they ever tried to answer it.

There was a knock at the door.

'Yes?'

Agnes entered, dropping her usual perfunctory curtsy.

'What is it, Agnes?' Agnes's hesitation made her turn. The maid was holding something in her hand. 'Well? Speak up.'

'Mademoiselle, I just found this. It was in what was supposed to be the Englishman's room.'

Berenice took the letter. The envelope was blank and unsealed. It contained a single sheet of paper. She drew it out. It was dated a week ago. The neat copperplate lines were in Smith's hand, but it was not addressed to her. She saw with disappointment that it was meant for Smith's elder brother.

Dear Charles,
I felt I had to write to you for, since parting from Captain Bonham, I have performed my intention of going over Wraxall's footsteps at Mont St Michel. The commandant of St Maloes, understanding my intention, furnished me with an official letter to the commander there, who is also

a Brother and the prior of the abbey of Benedictine monks. Another Brother gave me a letter to one of the monks, who was formerly an officer of dragoons in the same regiment with him.

The maid's curiosity was bothersome. 'Agnes, thank you, you may go.'

Agnes looked at her innocently. 'Who is "Charles"?'

The remark galled her. 'You've read it!'

'Mademoiselle Berenice, excuse me, but I didn't know what it was when I found it. Or who to take it to.' Agnes's expression of innocence was false, but her logic was unarguable. 'Besides, it's in the English and the mademoiselle knows I cannot read the English.'

Berenice pursed her lips patiently. 'Of course. I'm sorry. But please, leave me now.'

'Mademoiselle Berenice, I . . .'

'*Please*, Agnes!'

Agnes reluctantly did as she was told, and Berenice returned her attention to the letter. Her hopes had soared momentarily, then crashed to earth. It seemed to be a routine communication after all, just details of his stay in France, for the benefit of his family. She read on:

My letters procured me a most hospitable reception; they would not suffer me to sleep at the auberge, but gave me a most excellent old-fashioned room and a bed, which I will flatter myself was the bed of Henry I of England, when he was besieged there. I lived with *messieurs les moines* two days, dining and supplying *au refectoire*, and on the best cheer that I ever desire to meet with. From thence I rode to Caen, twenty-four leagues in one day. I have since been to Harcourt, and met Brother Dalrymple, who arrived here on the 15th.

Last week our Brother the Duke furnished me with a horse, and I enjoyed a most pleasant stag hunt for the first time in my life. He is gone to Cherbourg again, with *madame la duchesse*, and does not return till the middle of September, so I fear he will not be here when either you

or Brother Manners of the Apollo Lodge comes over. I
need not tell you how glad I shall be to see you. Bring
your apron, for you cannot wear better here, when
dressed. Brothers are Brothers regardless of nation, and

Berenice reached the bottom of the page. She knew she
was not concentrating properly, but the references to so
many 'Brothers' confused her. What does he mean by
'our Brother the Duke'? She recalled that Smith had been
invited to a stag hunt and otherwise honoured by her
uncle's attentions, but what did it signify that he had
referred to the Duc d'Harcourt as his brother?

The letter was broken off unfinished and unsigned. It
continued overleaf, this time in a more hurried hand, as
if this part had been added later. He must have penned it
in the afternoon just before the final dinner, she thought.

I must tell you urgently of an event that has destroyed all
my plans. I have last week met with a French lady who is
perfection to me. We are very much in love, and I do not
know how I can do other than propose a marriage to her.
Her family is high in the armorial of France, so if I am to
have her I must take her away to England. I cannot ask
our mother's advice in this for I know she will only tell me
to do as she did, and always to follow my heart. Dear
Charles, you know as well I that my heart was already set:
my life was to be the navy. But what can I do now?

She gasped, put her left hand to her breast, felt her
crucifix there, and squeezed it hard to comfort her. As a
child she had done the same thing to make special
wishes. Stupid! she thought. Stupid and childish! Men
hate nothing in women so much as childishness . . .

This changed everything!

He did love me, after all, she thought. He wanted to
take me to England! To England. To be his wife.

But now it was too late!

What could she wish for now that made any sense?
For Smith to come back? Impossible. For her to forget

him. Impossible. For time to peel back like the pages of a burning diary? That was impossible! She felt the anguish and pain overwhelm her, and sweep her away. She sat down and read the letter again, then she sobbed for relief, and sobbed again because nothing about the world made sense any more.

When she saw the bright crimson stain on her fingers a full second passed before she realized what it was. She opened her hand: the wound had been painless, but the cross had pierced the skin of her palm. The tiny golden spike that had held the figure of the passion upon the cross had broken, leaving a razor-sharp point.

The looped cross hung on its chain still, but the figure of Christ was gone from it.

PART 3

The Empty Hearth

Three years have passed

SUMMER, 1790
Ajaccio, Corsica

And so we meet once more, signore. *Welcome. The last time was three years ago in this same place, when I was so full of woes. Now you visit me again. That surprises me. As you must know, much has happened to me. And, yes, the prophecies you made of me have all come to pass.*

I have been at the training school at Auxonne. Such changes I found in France! And all come in so short a time. The aristocrats who once found my southern manners so very amusing have become a little less sure of themselves. My colonel could have locked me up for five months – by the letter of the law I could have been charged with desertion, having overstayed my leave by that period – but after following your advice, signore, *I faced him. Do you know, I could smell the fear in him? The regiment was close to mutiny. When I arrived I found most of the officers in a state of anxiety. I saw at once that the Colonel could do nothing, so I was brazen with him. I said I had been quite ill, and that that was the cause of my absence.*

Of course, I lied to him. It was simple expediency – I am learning always to do what is expedient, to use truth or lies to best advantage, as our ambitions demand. I am only ever completely confidential with you signore. *You alone are permitted to hear the real truth: in point of fact, I was not ill – I had made myself a freedom fighter.*

Last time we met I informed you that I wanted to rid my homeland of the French yoke. You told me that the changes overwhelming France would provide the very opportunities I was waiting for. It is my way to accord credit when it suits me, so listen: you were correct in every particular!

Since you encourage me, signore, I shall tell you all about what happened. When I came home it was with the red cockade. I brought to my island the three-fold promise: Liberty, Equality, and Fraternity! I told my countrymen: 'Henceforth we shall be free to rule ourselves. A new era has dawned in the world. We must proclaim our rights! Citizens, it is time to rise up! We shall form a National Guard, as they have in Paris! We shall rise up against the occupying soldiery! And since the French have imprisoned our leaders, I shall lead you!'

As you must know, signore, my family is well known on our island. Word soon spread through the capital. I gained followers, a crowd, some willing to fight, some eager to do so. I stood up for all their hopes. 'A leader among us again, at last!' they shouted. They cheered, and we marched, and I made them pledge themselves to our revolutionary ideals. We carried the streets, and there was glory for a while, but then armed troops arrived with muskets and bayonets fixed, and my brave revolutionaries scattered like mice. Spineless cowards, all of them. They ran away.

By nightfall they had all surrendered their weapons. The troopers did not even bother to arrest them, but sent them quietly to their homes. Can you imagine my disbelief, signore? The hole this made in my heart? That my own people could so betray me. I had placed my faith in them, but still they failed me. They made me look like a fool. They made me look small.

But I did not give up the struggle. Oh, no. I appealed to the National Assembly in Paris. I wrote a fraternal ode to the new freedoms. I made it plain to the revolutionary government that all my island wanted was equality – the same liberties they were prepared to award themselves – also that they must release our leaders – especially the great Paoli.

They deliberated, then their decision was made: our island was to become a French province. Only on that understanding were our leaders to be freed to return home.

I ask you signore: a province? My countrymen must remain Frenchmen! Do you call that liberty? For I do not.

ONE

It was the day of the flight – cloudless, with little breeze, and a lucid sunshine to bathe the stone façade of the château.

A grand marquee had been set up on the lawns, to provide refreshments. The philosopher, Professeur Oudot, and his assistants were still hard at work. All morning they had been laying out their alchemists' tools. Last night six wagons full of strange paraphernalia had arrived from Caen: a painted gondola, carboys and demijohns of acid, chests of iron dust – two or three thousand pounds' weight of it – netting, coils of rope, a small anchor, a flag, a multitude of lead pipes, and finally a great mass of proofed fabric, painted with celestial symbols.

The long windows of the château's great hall were open. Celestine's nimble fingers had danced over the keys of the harpsichord for the past hour, filling the gardens with the sounds of her virtuosity and the heart-tearing music of Jean-Philippe Rameau, François Couperin and Domenico Scarlatti.

Berenice wondered at the memories that these sonatas must be stirring in the minds of the more elderly visitors. Such music is the ghost of a vanished age, she thought, wishing Celestine would play instead something with heart and good humour, something by the marvellous Herr Mozart of Vienna perhaps. The cascading notes that came from the clavier were instead precisely patterned formal mosaics, almost mathematical sequences, the music of the rarefied court of the *Roi Soleil*. The sounds were stirring feelings in her own soul, but they were not feelings of pleasure, for they necessarily reminded her how far the might and civilization of France had fallen.

She surveyed Professeur Oudot's preparations with mixed feelings – excitement to see the great experiment take place, but also dread at the gathering, which would make her once again the centre of family speculation.

The nightmare had come to her again last night. The one where she was stalked through the snow by an ogre. The beast always caught her just as she awoke. Its meaning was clear enough. It was my birthday last month, she reminded herself. I am now twenty-one, a mature woman. I must make my choice soon – that's what everyone keeps telling me. They also tell me that it is my very great good fortune to have two suitors to choose between. I only wish I could share their joy at the prospect.

She had watched the gathering assemble. There were hundreds of people here to see the fantastic spectacle. Some were inside the gardens, but many more were outside the house's perimeter wall. The fields and hills were dotted with groups of country people; and yet more were coming up the public road from Caen, to crowd at the great iron gates in an effort to slake their curiosity.

All the family had arrived. The duke's sisters, the cadet branch, half the nobility of Normandy, or so it seemed. She looked at the scene, seeing its apparent normality as the thinnest of veneers. In recent months France had inched ever closer to a precipice. Everyone had seen it coming, had discussed it endlessly, but no one had known how to arrest the slide. A year ago the Paris mob, terrified by a surge in the price of bread, and haunted by the spectre of hunger, had found the strength to throw off tyranny. They had broken into the Bastille prison and hacked the governor to death – and all to liberate *seven* prisoners, one of them a nobleman, a notoriously insane sexual monster called the Marquis de Sade.

She had tried to make sense of all the news sheets and pamphlets, but little of the opinion coming out of Paris made sense to her. The Marquis de Lafayette – the hero of the American war – had broken from the extremist Jacobins and espoused a moderate line. Several other figures had joined with him in the *Société*, and had attempted to lead the country back to reason. But even Lafayette had been reduced to making grand political gestures. He had sent a golden key, meant to be that of the Bastille, to George Washington – the glorious token of triumphant liberty over oppression.

Berenice had little hope that the noble Marquis de Lafayette would succeed. She had sensed the morass, and feared that all the moderates and reasonable men in France would be gobbled up by it.

'Why trouble your mind with such matters, my dear?' her father had asked her yesterday, reclaiming his broadsheet from her. 'No wonder you have nightmares.'

'How can you ask me such a question?' she had demanded of him angrily. 'Am I not a human being too?'

Yes, here at Thury-Harcourt, she thought bitterly, a semblance of the old normality is still possible. She sighed, watching the flaccid envelope of the aerostatic machine as it was laid out sixty feet along the ground. It was a great doped bladder, an obscene tattooed skin stinking of glue and varnish, meshed in a tarry rope net, the whole lying on a wooden platform, symbol of a world turned upside down.

France is no longer a country at ease with itself, she thought. Gatherings, for whatever purpose, lack the innocence I remember from the past. These days there's always a tension in the air, an indefinable brooding – bad manners, inconsiderations, impatience. There was a kind of callousness abroad, an atmosphere that, at times, became quite ugly. A sense of violence barely leashed, of evil biding its time. Sometimes it frothed into riot. It was as if a devil moved among the people, a spirit, rapacious, threatening and malicious, one that wanted to consume all the foundations of life.

Two masts had been set up, the scarecrow figure of Professeur Oudot between them, hands outstretched, conducting her uncle's inspection. The ducal party was gathered in a semi-circle. The inventor was a thin man, with stick-like limbs. Just as well, considering his living, she thought as she examined his face. Look how his absurd, sandy moustache twitches and his bony hands move about as he speaks. He has that mad light in his eyes that only true enthusiasts have.

Oudot gestured at a structure in the middle of the stage. 'Here, Your Grace, is the lead-lined acid chamber . . .'

He still uses the honorific form of address, she thought, moving a pace or two closer to listen. Old habits die hard – especially when people want something. And my uncle remains commander-in-chief . . .

Many of the rising officials of the new so-called 'Departments' of Calvados and Orne enjoyed the patronage of the Duc d'Harcourt, despite their red, white and blue sashes. And many of them had considered the duke's scientific event of sufficient importance to attend. Three days ago aristocratic titles had been abolished, but most people, nobles and commoners alike, had taken no notice. What the advocates of instant change do not seem to understand, she thought, is that there are only so many skilled administrators in the country. If our class was to be annihilated, as the extremists seem to want, there would be chaos.

'. . . we use the sulphuric acid. It is made in England in

quantity these days by an entirely novel process, and so fortunately the price has fallen. As you can see, a great volume is required.'

The duke looked up from the globular chamber. 'England? I trust the iron filings at least are French?'

There was a ripple of amusement at the remark.

Professeur Oudot said, 'The action of acid on the iron gives rise to what its discoverer, Doctor Priestley, has named "the inflammable gas". Its most interesting property is its lightness compared to ordinary air. It is conducted along these pipes to this cock. *Et violà*! When the cock is turned the balloon begins to fill.'

Six men bore the ornate gondola forward. It was a kind of little boat, tastefully decorated with papier-mâché garlands and rosettes and swags of satin. There was seating for two occupants. A curious arrangement of levers was attached to it: four aerial oars made of hoops of willow and varnished brown paper – doubtless to propel and to steer it, she thought.

'We should have commissioned a poet to compose an ode to commemorate the qualities of the machine,' the duke said good-naturedly. 'That would have been appropriate, but where can a man find good poets these days?'

Professeur Oudot's shrug was dutifully hopeless, his face a mask of commiseration. She could tell he cared nothing for poets. He invited the duke a pace or two away from his entourage.

She heard the sound of metal meeting metal – now ringing, now dull – as one of the labourers hammered an iron stake into Davout's perfect lawn. Another man beside him coiled rope. Such an enormous amount of preparation is required, she thought. And at what cost? I'm sure Professeur Oudot wishes to demonstrate his machine to my uncle, and thereby sell his system to the government. Look at them talking together privately now. She saw the professor briefly grip the duke's hand.

The handshake struck her as meaningful. A gesture of a confidential kind that she had seen men exchange before. Their eyes would meet in recognition, and something would pass between them. Yet it seemed out of character for a duke to shake hands.

Doubtless their conversation concerns military secrets, she thought. That recalled Smith sharply to her mind. She felt a kind of panic seize her.

She sat down on one of the chairs, drew a deep breath and held it to combat the emotion in her chest. The sound of Celestine's syncopated figures came to her from the house, *Les Barricades Mystérieuses* – bare sequences of quills plucking wire in the key of B flat major, without any variation of touch. I wonder how my Englishman has fared through the peace? Did he get his ship, after all? Does he ever think of me?

But she knew: nothing lives in the cultivated mind quite so long as an injustice. I did him a great wrong, and now there is no chance of my ever righting it. My mother always said that for man and woman to part on unsettled terms is the greatest tragedy, because the good fades from the mind, but the evil is magnified.

She noticed the huge gardener, Davout. He swayed impotently from foot to foot, watching in dismay as the guests disported themselves on his lawns. Davout had been employed on the estate since he had appeared in the district fifteen winters ago – alone, unable to explain his origins, a giant idiot child of unknown parents, a mystery.

Faligan the gamekeeper had found him shivering in the forest, and taken him to Père Fournet, who pronounced him a miracle-gift sent from God. At first the village children had tormented him and called him 'cuckoo-chick' because of his great size, and his enormous appetite for food, and because they thought him a monster. They had broken his nose, and almost his heart, but the comte's one-time head gardener, Old

Davout, had taken pity on him. He had taken him in, and treated him like a son, and given him a real name. And in all that time the giant had never uttered a sound.

Poor Davout, she thought. Once there were five gardeners at Thury-Harcourt. He labours so heroically and so lovingly each day to keep the gardens in order, and now he must watch his lawn being trampled by strangers. He tends the beds, mows the grass, and keeps the fanciful hedges cut to the shape of birds and animals, even though he is alone now. He may not be able to speak, but he understands much.

'Ah, mademoiselle.'

She guarded her face. 'Captain.'

He was Antoine Louis-Edmond le Picard, Comte de Phelypeaux. Tall and lean and fair. By general agreement very handsome, but not in a way that seemed so to her. He is attentive, she told herself. Amusing. He has impeccable manners. He dresses well. Has taste. Is loved by his servants. He is – by far – the most eligible man in Normandy. And I admit that I do sometimes enjoy his company. It is obviously to my shame that, try as I might, I can feel no love for him.

Phelypeaux was two years her senior, of suitable family. He had studied at the Ecole Militaire in Paris, where he had been a gentleman cadet until his commissioning into the Royal Artillery. Now he was a captain in the National Guard, and her father's first choice for her. He had also been present at the dinner when her life had fallen apart, a fact he had had the delicacy never to mention.

'A marvellous day for such an aerial experiment. May I sit with you?'

'If you wish.' She sensed the tension in him, sensed the great unanswered question hanging in the air. He was too refined to approach it directly, too aware perhaps that to bring her to a crisis now would be to lose her to Jacques Tromelin, his rival. She noticed that for the occasion he had affected a lorgnon, a sort of monocle on a stick, the better to observe the balloon's flight, and the better, doubtless, to flourish his ruffled cuffs for the benefit of those who had come to watch him as much as they had the balloon.

'They say it takes two hours to inflate the machine.'

She fingered her cross. 'That long?'

He nodded his head. 'The very idea that a body can leave the earth and travel in space is so remarkable and so sublime. It seems so very far removed from the ordinary laws of Nature—'

'What about *birds*, monsieur?'

The comment stopped his fashionable rhapsodizing short.

'Birds?'

'Yes, monsieur. They are bound by natural laws, yet they manage to fly around quite easily, without the use of any inflammable gas, and without entailing a two-hour wait.'

'Forgive me.' He dabbed at his lips with his lace handkerchief. 'Delightful though birds may be, still they will not serve to carry two men into the sky.'

She sighed, feeling instantly guilty at her lack of good grace toward him. Antoine was a good man whose interest in her was genuine. He did not deserve rudeness. But then, for that very reason, he did not deserve to be falsely encouraged either. She stirred herself to be more civil. 'I suppose that soon mariners of the air will be spying on enemy fortresses and dropping arrows on enemy towns.'

He gave her a shrewd glance. 'I'm sure that idea has crossed the duke's mind. The English Channel has hitherto been an impenetrable barrier to us whenever the English have deserved a lesson.'

'I suppose such flights are commonplace in Paris.'

He grinned indulgently. 'No longer, alas. But I was at

the Champs-de-Mars when Monsieur Charles demonstrated the first of these new gas balloons. It was only a small one, just twelve or thirteen feet across. I was a student then, preparing for the Ecole Militaire. A pelting rain came down on us, I remember, but that did not prevent the machine from rising with extreme rapidity. The experiment was attended by the greatest success, and huge numbers of people caught their breath at it. It astonished everyone.'

She listened to him, liking him, liking the tone of his voice, but she was unable to think of him in the way her father wanted her to think of him.

'Ah, yes, Berenice! Picture it. So many ladies. All so elegantly dressed. All standing in that heavy, driving rain, and heeding it not at all! It was a most singular sight. After travelling a mile high for about fifteen miles, the pressure caused the envelope of the machine to split. Apparently it crashed back to earth near the village of Gonesse.' He smiled at her. 'Of course the peasants were terrified by the fall of this demon. Two of them dragged it back to their village where the inhabitants set about it and beat it with sticks.'

She put her hand to her mouth and laughed. 'Oh, Antoine.'

'It's quite true, though it was seven years ago now. Do you know that the king's government was obliged to put out a warning to the people after that? They were told not to be frightened of something that can do no harm to anyone and which one day will be put to a use for the benefit of society.'

Still she smiled, but mention of the king's government had made the smile die inside her. What sort of government is that now? she thought. A National Assembly that has abolished the ancient titles. The king and the royal family are, as we sit here, virtual prisoners in the Tuileries palace. The Champs-de-Mars is to be the scene of celebrations, the Marquis de Lafayette's

National Guardsmen parading there on the anniversary of the Bastille. It is no more than an obscene mockery of government.

She looked around, saw her parents. Her father was looking at the sky, his hands clasped behind his back, turning about on his heel. A characteristic pose. She had seen him adopt it many times as he studied the weather before going out on a stag hunt. Her mother acknowledged her coyly, clearly pleased she had settled to talk with Captain Phelypeaux. She gestured back obediently. Next her sister Celestine caught her eye – and Celestine's several young suitors.

Phelypeaux was watching them, too, with an amused expression on his face.

'They're gambolling about her like lambs,' he said pleasantly, squinting through his lorgnon.

She sighed. 'She seems so young.'

'Celestine is seventeen, is she not?'

'Yes. How strange to think that she's as old as I was when . . .'

His attentions deepened. 'When . . .?'

But she gave no direct answer, merely shook her head. 'My heart was lamenting the loss of innocence.'

'Your own?' he asked gently, but he saw a shadow pass across her face, and she turned away from him quickly.

'Monsieur, that question was impertinent.'

And before he could apologize, she had stood up and was walking away.

The balloon was half inflated now, the envelope lifted up by its tip and suspended by block-and-tackle from a rope slung between the two masts.

'Quite a sight, eh, Berenice?'

The voice was very familiar. It belonged to Jacques Jean de Tromelin. He was a distant cousin, a year her junior, who had served under the old regime as a lieutenant in the Limousan Regiment – the 42nd Infantry. She was attracted by his physical appearance, stockily well-proportioned and dark-haired, like a southerner. She liked his busy energy of mind, and he had an air of salaciousness about him that she found exciting, but there was something trivial about him that spoiled it all.

'Will you take a glass of champagne with me, in honour of this ridiculous bladder?' he said in a low voice, then sprang forward. 'Ho! Gugnot! I say!'

The groom was twenty yards away, on an errand. He stopped, and came back. 'Monsieur?'

'Fetch Mademoiselle Berenice and myself a glass of champagne each, there's a good fellow. In fact, bring us a bottle.'

She saw Gugnot's glance, his momentary hesitation, but then the groom bowed his head and went back the way he had come towards the refreshment marquee.

'Weaselly little man, isn't he?' de Tromelin said.

'He's a groom, Jacques. He's not here to wait on you.'

'He's not doing anything. You know, your father ought to keep an eye on him. He *trades*.' De Tromelin made it sound like Gugnot was a secret white slaver.

'Trades?'

'I've heard he does business of his own at horse fairs all over the district. And . . . did you know he's got two passions going – one with your maid?'

'Do you mean Agnes?' She feigned ignorance, though she had known for years, and knew that of late Gugnot and Agnes had been fighting like cat and dog. 'I don't believe you.'

'Oh, don't tell me you didn't know.' Then he laughed. 'Ah, you *did* know – you see, I can always tell when you're untrue to me.'

She eyed him tolerantly. 'Is that so?'

'What was Phelypeaux saying to you just then?'

'Not much of consequence. And if it had been it would still be none of your concern, Jacques.'

'Oh, you think so?'

'You're just jealous.'

He was thinking of a riposte when Gugnot came back with a tray and two glasses, and the bottle. She noticed him look to de Tromelin as if prompting a thank you, but de Tromelin ignored him and poured the champagne in a careless fashion.

Berenice said pointedly, 'Thank you, Gugnot,' and saw the look on the groom's face just before he bowed his head to her and went his way. I can well believe he's a secret horse trader, she thought. He's really nobody's fool. But I can't understand what he sees in Agnes. If he's waiting for her to grow up he'll wait a long time.

De Tromelin watched the bubbles subside, topped both glasses and sipped. 'Oh, that's magnificent! Lord God bless that divine monk. My sister sends her kind regards to you, by the way.'

'That's unexpected. Please give her mine.' She instantly regretted the cattiness of her tone because de Tromelin was on it immediately.

'Oh, what's happened?' he asked. 'What's put you against her?'

'Nothing.'

Nothing, she thought. Except that I've never liked cousin Marguerite. Ever since we were children, when I took against her. I can't explain it. She's just a bore.

De Tromelin became earnest. 'She really likes you, you know. She wishes you would visit us more often.' Then he came closer to her than she usually permitted and made a face. 'So, why don't you?'

She laughed. 'Oh, Jacques!'

He laughed too. 'I saw you send Phelypeaux off with a flea in his ear. Tell me you've done with him and I'll love you for ever. Marry me.'

She cooled her tone. 'I did not send him off.'

She saw her mother looking at her. There was another little wave. She turned away from it this time. It was obvious what was going on inside her mother's head: 'Berenice, you are twenty-one years old and still wilfully unmarried. You are at the crux of your life. You will be left on the shelf if you delay past this summer.'

Her father had issued a gentle but plain warning at breakfast: 'My dear, you must stop playing Lieutenant de Tromelin off against Captain Phelypeaux. I will not have it. Do you hear me?'

'If you do not consent to marry me at once I shall challenge Phelypeaux to a duel.'

'You shouldn't joke about such matters, Jacques. Antoine has a limited sense of humour. He is liable to interpret such remarks as aspersions upon his honour. And he is a rather accomplished swordsman.'

De Tromelin went into a fleeting sulk. 'I know his reputation. He also has an overblown sense of his own importance. He's only a captain of Engineers, you know.'

'And you are only a lieutenant.'

He assumed a pose of mock indignation. 'How can you say "only" of an officer of the Forty-second?'

The gas hissing into the balloon had caused the envelope to grow turgid. The attendants had anchored the gondola down to the iron stake, and there was some visible tension in the net of ropes that connected the two main parts together. De Tromelin cracked open his pocket watch like a silver oyster. She saw a strange device inscribed on it, a diamond shape formed of two instruments, a six-pointed star within, and the Greek letter 'gamma' in the middle.

'Everything's running late,' he said. 'It's the way of the world, these days.'

She imagined the scene if she were to go to her parents and say, 'Jacques has asked me to marry him.' She knew exactly how it would be. Both would show a fleeting regret that it was not Phelypeaux, then they would accept the alternative with hardly a pause. The relief would be palpable.

What choice is that? she thought. Antoine or Jacques? Jacques or Antoine? How to choose, when neither lights a fire in me?

'Consent! Or I shall challenge Phelypeaux to prove his courage by making an ascent in the aerostatic machine.'

She shook her head, smiling at his theatrical japery. 'Jacques, you will do nothing of the sort.'

'In that case, I shall make the ascent myself. And when we have soared high above the ground I shall throw myself out to prove my heart.'

'You are a strange boy.'

He pulled away. 'A boy? Is that what you think of me? You believe I won't do it?'

'Jacques . . .'

The balloon was fully inflated now. Valves were adjusted and the gas pipes disconnected from it. Professeur Oudot had climbed onto the stage, his arms raised in invitation. A crowd had gathered, pressed forward, and de Tromelin took her hand to sweep her along with it, but she hung back.

She had experienced a moment of strangeness. A shock. Had seen something that terrified her. And now she found herself suddenly breathless.

'Berenice, are you sick?' De Tromelin's face was full of concern. 'You're . . . pale.'

She felt herself drifting, and recognized the feeling as the light-headedness that comes before a faint. I've only ever fainted once before, she thought, annoyed with herself. And that was when I was sickening with a fever. The embarrassment of it made her fight the harder. She drew deep breaths, but discreetly, fearing that de Tromelin would make a fuss.

'I am quite well,' she said, and tried to reclaim her

arm, but he would not let go. He insisted she sit down before she fell down.

'What is it?' he asked, solicitous for her.

Phelypeaux was at her side instantly. 'Yes, what's the matter?'

'Nothing.' She felt foolish. The truth was too foolish to mention. She thought she had seen a man hooded in black, like a Black Friar. She had only glimpsed his face, but it had been enough to terrify her. Before she could look again, the crowd had closed around the stage and he was gone.

She wondered how she could have come to imagine something so terrible. The face had been fleshless.

She realized they were standing on the exact spot where she and Smith had come that fateful night to admire the house. Perhaps a ghost of that golden era had touched her, and she shivered, suddenly fearing for his life. I know he is somewhere in the world, but who can say where? Maybe aboard a ship on a far ocean, commanding his men. Maybe in London, lunching with admirals. Maybe in a port in the Americas, in his cot and dying of a fever . . .

She felt the warmth of the sun on her face and remembered her complexion. 'You must excuse me, gentlemen. I must go inside.'

The sun was bright. It was still only June. With luck, the summer would last for ever.

'We shall go with you.'

'Yes. You cannot walk to the house alone.'

'Gentlemen, for pity's sake, I'm perfectly well.' She forced a smile for them, then distracted them by pointing at the balloon. 'Look what you're missing. See! They're cutting the tethers now.'

The crowd fell silent, mesmerized by the spectacle of the balloon as it rose quickly and soundlessly into the sky above them. A single rope trailing with a small boy attached until he let go and fell ten feet into the arms of a man below.

She saw the professor and his assistant waving down from the gondola. The balloon soared quickly, drawing gasps of astonishment from the watchers. They shielded their eyes against the summer sun, and made sounds of praise and congratulations.

'It's quite marvellous,' she said softly, still feeling light-headed, but now caught up with the sense of wonder. 'And to think that one day perhaps, if what Professeur Oudot says is true, we shall all travel through the air.'

'Yes.'

Phelypeaux turned his attention languidly away from the balloon's flight. He dropped his lorgnon, allowing it to dangle on its cord. His eyes were following the shadow of the balloon as it passed across the lawns and briefly splashed the façade of the house with darkness. 'It's rising very fast. It must be cold in the higher regions of the air, a cold that we don't feel on the ground.'

The observation captured her interest. The idea of the air being cold high up in the sky was novel. That the temperature might affect the rate at which the balloon rose, she realized with humility, was something she had not considered. But Phelypeaux was a Captain of Engineers, and there were so many things a lady never seemed to have sufficient time to consider . . .

'Oh, look at that!' she said, her hand to her mouth. The sight made her laugh, and Phelypeaux laughed with her to see how the cows in the fields were bolting.

De Tromelin touched her arm proprietorially. 'Berenice, do you recognize the gentleman over there?'

When she followed his gaze she saw an avuncular man wearing eye-glasses on his forehead and a neatly cut brown coat. He was squinting up a telescope tube. 'The American ambassador?'

'Quite so.' There was a pleased look on Phelypeaux's face. 'Their ambassador is the duke's guest.'

De Tromelin folded his arms. 'He seems to be a sane and honourable man with an interest in science. Perhaps, after all, a republic can be a—'

But she did not hear his opinion. The sounds the crowd were making caused de Tromelin to break off and Phelypeaux to raise his lorgnon once more. The graceful rise of the balloon had arrested. Berenice saw the professor and his assistant throwing bags of ballast from the gondola in a frantic effort to lighten the machine. By now the inflated ball of gas had become noticeably pear-shaped.

Then someone by the telescope shouted, 'My God! It's tearing!'

A sickening moment passed. Fingers pointed as the balloon began to fall away. The gasps became cries of alarm. She saw a rag of fabric waving from the tangled balloon as the rush of air increased.

A shout went up all around. Berenice flinched. Halfway down the doomed fall the figure of a man parted from the gondola. His spreadeagled body cartwheeled, fell faster than the balloon, and she watched in horror as it slammed into a field perhaps half a mile away. Seconds later the remains of the balloon came to earth, the ground seeming to swallow it up. Then people, just white dots, were running towards it.

Phelypeaux watched aghast, then turned to her. De Tromelin looked to her also. And she was left with the powerful feeling that she was to blame. She knew it was irrational, but she was sure that if she had only gone to the house when she had said, then the accident would not have happened.

TWO

'It's a peculiar thing, guilt.'

Smith licked his lips, feeling the Baltic salt gritty on his face. 'Yes, damned peculiar. Affects some people more than it does others. I've met men – and women – who blame themselves for all kinds of misfortunes.'

Colonel Lilliehorn whispered back. 'Do *you*?'

'Me? Not at all. That's because I only do what's right.' He smiled, deliberately lightening the conversation and turning it away from the gloomy philosophy into which his companions had a tendency to sink before action. 'And to prove I do no wrong we're going to give the Prince of Nassau a bloody good hiding, what?'

They nodded at that, and he wished they were Englishmen, and therefore able to understand his peculiar English humour and be fully comfortable with his manner.

It was a calm, moonless midnight, but here the night was never quite dark. Smith looked out at the rugged land that continued to slide by the lead gunboat. In other circumstances nothing could be more sublime, he thought. In any event, it's still beautiful. And it had better be. You begged God to be here, and to have a chance to show your skill at war. This is what you wanted.

Two days ago the Swedish king had gone with Smith, by boat, to reconnoitre the position of the Russian flotilla. It was lying in Trongsund, the middle of the three channels formed by the islands of Uransari and Sommansari, at the entrance of Wyborg Sound. They had seen four large square-rigged vessels, about twelve large oared galleys and many smaller vessels.

Later, aboard the *Amadis*, there had been a conference. 'Your Majesty, I advise you to act as follows,' he had said. 'You should proceeed to the inner road of Wyborg, with the flotilla in three divisions. The left should proceed between Catilla and Sommansari by the westward of the three passages, while the right forces the passage of Actis Capel to the eastward.'

Count Rosen, a man he disliked on sight, had spoken up. 'There is no point in forcing Actis Capel.'

'Sir, there is every point. In fact, it is a necessity. The object is this: to land a body of troops on the island of Uransari. They will attack the rear of the batteries that presently command the middle passage of Trongsund, where the enemy's vessels lie.'

King Gustavus had been pleased. 'Splendid, Colonel Smith!'

Two dependable men, Colonel Lilliehorn and Captain Sillen, had been seconded to help him. They were at his side now in the sternsheets of the lead boat. Lilliehorn was without his large cocked hat; Sillen with a black silk kerchief tied round his neck. Both had volunteered for the intrepid attack on Actis Capel, knowing they might find death or glory in the enterprise. Let's hope it's the latter – for all of us, he thought, and felt the shiver of exhilaration.

His first meeting with the two Swedes had been auspicious. 'Your colleagues have a tendency to magnify every obstacle,' he had told them severely.

'And if they can find none they will invent them,' Lilliehorn had said mildly, giving him a significant look and offering his hand. It had been a handshake that Smith had returned with surprise. Then Lilliehorn whispered fiercely. 'God break the enemies of Gustavus, Colonel Smith, and give confusion to their bloody schemes.'

'We're the king's grenadiers,' Sillen said. 'And even if the enemy reduce us to the last mouthful of black bread we'll eat birch bark and fight on!'

'That's the spirit, gentlemen.' He smiled significantly, adding mentally, or I should say, 'Brothers'.

Both Lilliehorn and Sillen were initiates of the Aurora Lodge, Number Sixteen of Stockholm, the same whose Master was the Duke Carl, the king's brother. It was good to have the pledges of men like them, and once they had offered themselves to his service under the sign of the Brotherhood he knew he could rely on them absolutely.

He kept the crucial order with him in his pocket. It had been penned aboard the royal yacht, *Amadis*, and was in His Swedish Majesty's own hand.

Whereas, I have instructed Colonel William Sidney Smith, by word of mouth, concerning the operations which I have undertaken against the Russian coasting fleet in Wyborg harbour, my commanders and chiefs of division are hereby commanded to follow all such orders that the said Colonel Smith shall give in my name.

It was a perfect situation. Better than perfect, because it was carte blanche to do exactly as he saw fit, and it was in writing. What more could a commander want? Now his fate was in his own hands; it was up to him to show what he could do.

He sharpened his vigilance over the men as the gunboats penetrated deeper into the sound. General Wolfe must have felt much as I do now when he was upon the St Lawrence and approaching the Heights of Abraham, he thought, trying to suppress his mounting tension. The example of Wolfe's superb conduct inspired him, and he felt the attendant weight of responsibility gathering on his shoulders.

The prospect of a bloody conflict had awakened a sense of awe in the minds of the men. It was certain to come in the next hour, and likely to kill or maim many of them, and they knew it. A mass of tricorn hats rippled in the waist of the boat. Cross-belted uniforms were hidden under cowls of darkened sailcloth. He saw several soldiers cross themselves as they drew nearer to the enemy, their faces pale and grave. There were thirty-two rowers to each gunboat, eight placed on each quarter, a steersman, six gunners and fifty grenadiers. Muskets appeared with bayonets ready fixed, all held at the advance, their blades lamp-blacked. Cutlasses were stowed under the rowers' benches, boarding pikes lashed to the thwarts. A big twenty-four pounder cannon was mounted in each boat's bow, and there was another aft.

Smith had found a small metal figure in his pocket some time ago, and he rubbed it now between finger and thumb. It was something seemingly quite insignificant, less than an inch long, a small, indistinct silver figure, apparently a man, his arms spread wide, as if encompassing the world. He wondered how it could have come into his possession.

He had brought it with him wherever he went, at first treating it as a whimsical good-luck charm without believing in its powers at all, but then, as success had followed success, the superstitious part of his mind had begun to invest it with real properties. Lately it had become his amulet, the personification of his Tutelary Genius. Now he looked at it afresh, and was shocked to see it for what it really was.

'Christ almighty!'

The shock turned to irritation, as unwelcome memories were stirred in him. Damn it, he told his guiding spirit. I came here to put Berenice out of my mind. I even promised my mother I would do that. And *you* are not helping me.

He had worked hard to forget. After leaving France he had taken a passage to Galicia and then, during a stay in Gibraltar, had picked up rumours that the Emperor of Morocco was preparing to declare another war on shipping. So he had crossed to the Barbary Coast in disguise, surveying the main privateer ports, compiling several informative letters for the Admiralty, and begging them – as ever – for a command.

But the Admiralty had ignored him. 'Everyone must work their way up,' his brother Charles had told him. 'Their lordships will take no notice of you, for you have not sufficient seniority to be noticed.'

'Seniority! The system is designed to favour and protect incompetents. By God, if Lord Rodney were still at the Admiralty—'

'George has done enough for you. To those who remain you are a flea to be brushed off again and again. Unfortunately their lordships have something of a monopoly when it comes to appointments to ships of war.'

He had slammed the heel of his hand against the door frame. 'No, Charles, they do not! I'll be noticed – by my own country or by another. And I'll get my command, be it a British or a foreign vessel, one way or another. I will do that, if it kills me!'

'It might.' Charles had grunted at his brother's display of anger. 'I sometimes wonder if even that would stop you.'

The feeling of impotence had burned Smith up. He had raged inwardly as delay had followed delay. Then an increasingly cold exchange of letters with the Duke of Leeds had finally convinced him there was no possible route to a command in England, not while the peace with France held. Fortunately, there was a war to be had elsewhere.

In London he had explained his plan to both his brothers. 'I've written to Stockholm. A letter to Karl of Sudermania, Gustavus's brother. You remember him?'

'Yes. A long-faced, gloomy fellow.' Spencer was the youngest, but had by far the most brilliant intellect of the three. His manner was lofty and deceptively effete: he was being groomed as a diplomatist. 'If I recall correctly, Gustavus is a nephew of Frederick the Great of Prussia. You've decided to bring your peerless skills to his aid have you, Sidney?'

'Why not? Gustavus is struggling against the empress of all the Russias. He has good fighting men, but little in the way of naval strategy. I propose to teach him how best to proceed, that's all.'

Charles said, 'Except that I have heard the empress has procured her own Englishmen to advise her against the Swedes.'

'Then we shall see which of them has chosen the best Englishman, shan't we?'

Spencer had affected a yawn. 'There appears to me no finer way of clearing the Baltic of foreign warships.'

Charles raised his eyebrows. 'It's just as well that neither Gustavus nor Catherine decided on French officers as naval advisors.'

'Yes,' Smith had said, grinning. 'For then, none would ever be sunk.'

After a moment's reflection Spencer had asked, 'Are you entirely serious about Sweden?'

'Never more so, brother.'

'Then I'll ask Carmarthen if he'll help.'

Smith's hope had foundered again. Carmarthen was the Marquis of Carmarthen, Francis Osborne, the same who had become Duke of Leeds, and was presently Foreign Secretary. 'No good. He's adamantly against me.'

Spencer rolled his eyes. 'That was about getting you a ship. I happen to know he has a bee in his bonnet regarding the question of Russian armament. Therefore, I fancy he'll do you the honour of getting in touch with Liston.'

'Liston?'

'Yes, Robert Liston. Dependable. Highly regarded. Ex-minister plenipotentiary at Madrid. Presently envoy extraordinary at Stockholm. He was tutor to Sir Gilbert Eliot's sons. He'll be able to get you into the war, if anyone can.'

Smith felt a swell of bitter emotion at the memory of that very cordial meeting. Talk was easy, but the reality of war was blood and pain and horror and death. Many ships and many thousands of men had gone to the bottom of this frigid sea since Spencer had made his remark. Unfortunately, too many of them had been Swedish.

He cast a glance at Lilliehorn and Sillen, and the pensive faces of the king's grenadiers. When the boat passed through a huge ball of dancing midges that hovered over the water the men bore the irritation stoically. There was nothing wrong with Sweden's sailors and soldiers, but too many of their senior officers were taken up with political caballing, so that most did not have their hearts in the war. And not one of them knew how to go about winning a battle at sea.

The boats surged in unison at every stroke. The inexperience of the men had made him shudder. They had treated the rehearsal for the operation like a Sunday outing. Elementary understanding of what the mission required was absent from them. He had even had to command silence in the ranks, and to order the tholes muffled with rags, to deaden the sound of the sweeps. Once the men's minds had been properly focused on the nature of their undertaking it was essential to prevent them taking fright, and so he had shared a joke or two with his officers within their hearing.

He had lifted Lilliehorn's astonishing, outsize hat from his head and stowed it on the thwart beside him. 'We must create at least some small chance of surprising the enemy, eh, Lilliehorn?' he had said to his second-in-command, grinning, and Lilliehorn – and the men – had taken the pantomime very well.

Now the dead silence of the forests that covered the shore and islands was interrupted only by the splashing of the oars. The sound re-echoed through them eerily. He noted the exact order, the perfect intervals between the gunboats, the huge extent of the line, now perfectly straight, now in serpentine windings as it negotiated the shoals.

Iron-grey skies rolled over the sombre waters of the Gulf of Finland. A hundred miles to the east stood the Russian port of St Petersburg, with the naval base of Cronstadt on its strategic island guarding the approaches. He had almost, but not quite, convinced Duke Carl, and through the duke the king, that nothing succeeded in war so well as a fast and unexpected strike to the enemy's vitals.

Anchoring the main battle fleet during the short summer night, the Swedes had pitched tents on shore, and excursions had been made to seize such of the inhabitants as were likely to prove useful as pilots in the treacherous maze of islands and channels, and to obtain subsistence. Consequently, their progress up the Gulf had been incredibly slow.

Smith had learned from the Finnish islanders that the enemy had landed cannon and were erecting a battery on the point of Actis Capel. He had seen the root of the bigger problem as soon as he had arrived. The duke knew little of naval matters, and those like Count Rosen whom he trusted to keep him informed were not convinced of the necessity of the Russian war. At every turn they exaggerated the dangers of the navigation.

He had asked Duke Carl, politely, what he thought he was trying to achieve.

'I am advancing the fleet, Colonel Smith, though but slowly, towards Hogland, which is the station the king has indicated to me. I hope God will preserve the fleet from all the dangers we face.'

The duke's answer had mystified him. 'What dangers, Your Royal Highness?'

'I have been informed that it would be the loss of us all to proceed any faster among so many reefs and rocks. Heaven give us good luck, for we have need of much on this occasion. Notwithstanding, my heart tells me we shall extricate ourselves well, and I place my faith and my hope in Him who has conducted my steps to this day.'

Hearing that had made Smith's heart sink. Whatever anybody said, to depend supinely on the aid of the Almighty was not the way to encourage success in wordly matters such as these. As soon as he could Smith had drawn the duke a little way aside from his staff.

'If I may speak candidly, sir? On looking at the charts, I see the dangers your admirals so much insist upon do in fact appear fewer above Hogland than below it. And, whatever the difficulties and dangers might be, the enemy's fleet would be equally exposed to them – if there were any enemy here. Now let me tell you what's the remedy . . .'

The duke listened to him with suspicions against his own officers growing more and more evident in his face. 'It is the king's desire that we must have a battle with the Cronstadt squadron. Do you think that is wise?'

'I think perhaps it was I who put the idea in his mind.'

The duke had nodded thoughtfully. 'And you think that battle should be soon?'

'The sooner the better, sir. Before the Revel fleet can come out and place us between two fires. With twenty-one sail-of-the-line and so many heavy frigates we have reasonable grounds to hope for success against the seventeen of the Cronstadt squadron. It's better to attack them at their own doors, than to wait to be attacked by them.'

The duke nodded. 'And if we should be successful?'

'A victory gained at the gates of St Petersburg, won in sight and hearing of the Russian shore, could not fail to intimidate and humble the empress's court.' He looked to where the knot of senior Swedish officers regarded the conversation jealously. 'Thereby facilitating, Your Royal Highness, the peace that your admirals all so much wish for – and which the king has assured you is also the object of his wishes.'

The duke followed Smith's eyes to Count Rosen. 'And if we are not successful?'

Smith raised his voice so that Rosen could not fail to hear. 'Your action shall at least be honourable, in leaving nothing untried and thereby showing the court of St Petersburg that they have an enemy of spirit who will not lamely submit to receive the law at their own doors.'

'Gentlemen,' he heard the duke say moments later to his commanders, 'in Colonel Smith's opinion nothing is wanting to ensure success but to close with the enemy as soon as may be.'

Yes, Smith thought, looking at the troops making ready to go ashore. I certainly put the cat among the pigeons there. No men are braver than the Swedes when under fire, but they have not the necessary confidence in their leaders to make full use of their personal courage. And no wonder.

They arrived before the landing beach at exactly three o'clock. All was silent, and they proceeded stealthily. He gave orders to lose way and steer in to shore. Behind them, the five other craft started closing up, ready to follow his example. He was about to order 'Up oars', when the hairs began to rise on the nape of his neck.

He looked to shore and saw a movement a few dozen yards away. Boughs of evergreen were being pulled aside. Russians! The muzzle of a cannon appeared, then another. They were unmasking a battery of three guns.

'Treachery!' he said through gritted teeth, 'It's an ambush! Get your heads dow—!'

The final word was obliterated by a discharge of cannon fire. A plume of eye-blinding fire stabbed toward them, and a split second later another and then a third. As the sound hit them, so did the shock of metal, smashing into the boat with hellish force. They were firing case-shot – bags of lead balls that dispersed on firing. It was like facing a giant's shot-gun. One thing was clear in his mind as he fell – that the Russians had rightly singled out the first boat as the vessel that carried the commanding officer.

The blast had knocked Smith down into the boat. He felt the burning embers of wadding where they stuck to his face and uniform. The acrid stench of powder smoke stopped him from drawing breath, gagged him. But no order would have been of any use because the roar had deafened those around him, and the flash and smoke had blinded them.

As he struggled to get command of himself, he ran the fingers of his left hand over his lips. Something had smacked him in the mouth, leaving his lips and tongue completely numb. For a second he had the terrible suspicion that his front teeth might have been knocked in, or maybe cracked off, but he felt nothing solid when he spat, and there were more important things to worry about than a couple of teeth.

All around him there was a stunned silence. It lasted for a few seconds, then he heard oaths and curses, and the boat became a swaying hell. The smoke began to clear and someone started to scream. As his night sight returned he saw that both sides of the boat had been shattered just forward of where he had been sitting.

Luckily the damage was above the waterline, they were not shipping much water but it would not be so for long if the soldiers responded to their instinct to crowd to the side that was furthest from the shore. He was about to shout the order himself, then realized that only the Swedish officers knew French.

'Captain Sillen! Tell the men to keep their footings or they'll capsize her!'

When Sillen turned his face was a mask of horror. He had caught some metal and was staring at his shredded, empty sleeve. He gave only a single groan and mouthed the words, *'Dieu béni le roi.'*

Smith hardened his voice. 'Order the men to keep still, if you please, Captain Sillen. I shan't ask you again.'

There's not enough time, he thought, furious that they had been caught out. The Russians'll reload in under half a minute and we must do two things before then.

'Colonel Lilliehorn, I want us placed stern-on to that battery, and making sternway toward it.'

Lilliehorn was dazed, but he did as he was bid, shouting for the other boats to bring their twenty-four pounders to bear on the enemy.

To give the example, Smith snatched up an oar and poled it into the water, striking pebbles a fathom or so down. God damn it, he thought, it's still too deep to make a landing. He heaved with all his strength, turning the gunboat like a punt, so that it presented the smallest possible target to the shore, and so that his aft gunner could draw a mark on the battery.

The seamen were taking up their oars to propel the boat toward the shore. 'Fire as you bear, gunner!'

There was nothing more he could do, so he turned to Sillen whose ghastly face stared at him. He tore the man's sleeve back and saw that his arm was in a deplorable state. He would have to be brave. Without surgical assistance the amputation of the mangled stump could not be performed until he could be transported to the hospital ship. Smith took the black silk neckerchief from the man's throat and bound up the artery above the elbow, tightening it with a drumstick, to serve as a tourniquet. The blood flow was stopped, and he made Sillen hold the stick with his remaining hand.

By now the other gunboats were turning. The Russian cannoniers struggled to ram their muzzles, then the gunner touched off his big twenty-four pounder, and every sense was overwhelmed by the flash and roar. The boat was strongly built, but Smith feared the damaged gunwales would not stand the shock. The concussion was all-consuming – like Thor's hammer hitting them. Then he heard a plank spring somewhere in the boat's bottom, and water began to hiss in.

The devastation ashore was tremendous. At this short range their big naval guns had shattered the logs protecting the Russians and made an abattoir of the redoubt. When the second gunboat fired, three or four tree tops jumped momentarily above the smoke before falling down among the carnage.

A powder explosion in the battery marked the turning point. He felt the boat's keel ground on the beach, drew his sword, and ordered the attack. Lilliehorn had come to himself only a little, but enough to know his honour was at stake. Smith allowed him his chance to do his duty and lead his men. The Swede seized the opportunity with faultless courage. Wild-eyed, he soughed his sabre from its scabbard and shouted hoarsely, jumping down ahead of his troops, leading them over the side into two feet of oil-black water. The Swedish troopers threw themselves after him, and they dashed for the beach, Smith with them, admiring the high order of their bravery.

He saw movement behind the trees. From the silhouette of their headgear, they were a detachment of the empress's Life Guards, posted among the birches. When

their muskets flashed out, several of the king's grenadiers fell. Water squelched in his shoes, and it took all his
pride and shame to drive him up a loose rolling bank of
stones that fell away underfoot as he cleared the tide-
line. The treacherous footing sapped the momentum of
the attack, but did not stop it. His heart was thundering,
his breath coming in gasps. The sound of musketry
peppered the colourless night, and plucked several more
men down. Then they were among the trees and Swedish
bayonets were being driven home on the Russian line.
He hacked with his sword, its heavy blade and razor
edge notching a musket stock here, and cleaving into
what must have been a brass cap badge there.

Someone let out a bellow of triumph. The Russians
were giving way. Those who were able were running
back into the forest. Others were throwing down their
arms in terror. Prisoners were writhing hysterically on
the ground, screaming to save themselves. Men stood
over them with menacing bayonets, stabbing at them or
conceding the justice of the life pleas until their officers
got among them and made them stand back.

They had become masters of the battery. Above a
hundred men were ashore now, and Smith was first into
the exploded redoubt, where a litter of carcasses and
limbs was strewn around in the smoking ruin. Then he
saw a bloodied man, half of him gone, sitting propped
calmly amid a heap of shells, grinning at the fizzing fuses
in his hand.

A moment of paralysis overcame Smith's mind. The
utter horror of the sight froze him. It almost cost him his
life, but then he threw himself to the needle-strewn earth
and hugged it as the first of the shells burst.

The explosions went on for what seemed an age. He
lay down until the last of them shook the ground, then
he sat up and surveyed the scene, silently pledging to
hang from the yardarm of the king's flagship the man
who had engineered this piece of treachery.

The illumination had doubled since he had sighted the beach. Pale fingers crept across the north-eastern sky. The light was enough for him to make out the green coats of the enemy captives. He took post a little way up the beach, and ordered an encampment on the small island near the eastern point of Uransari. Then he ordered the prisoners and wounded to be sent back.

Among them he found the gallant Lilliehorn. A gaping wound in his thigh, sustained in the boat, had felled him. He had lost blood and was shivering. Strange how the human body reacts to war, Smith thought, offering his cloak. He was equal to the exertions of the attack while his blood was warm, but now the battle is won he's too faint and stiff even to stand up.

He took two men back to the beached gunboat and found Sillen sitting alone, still holding grimly on to his bloodied drumstick. He mumbled his thanks as Smith came to him.

Smith forced himself to be brisk. 'How do you find yourself, Captain Sillen?'

Sillen nodded to his hand, which was lying on the deck, and said, 'I see I am quite poorly.' Then he made a wan smile, and asked, 'How went the battle?'

'We did not find the sort of firmness the king of Prussia experienced from Russian troops. I'm pleased to say the Swedish king is completely victorious.'

Sillen showed himself to be relieved. 'Thank God, then, that I have lost my arm in a victory.'

To see Sillen's courage and loyalty uplifted him in a way that brought a tear to his eye. It was magnificent to see such a triumph of the higher functions of the mind and soul over the base weaknesses of the body. Without the capacity to overcome the limits of our own flesh and blood we would be little more than the animals, he thought. That's why honour and duty and glory and courage matter in the world.

Later Smith ran a finger over his teeth. They were all

there, though one felt somewhat loose. Apart from a few
scratches and a few bruises he found himself to be whole
and well, and no worse than a man pulled through a
briar by the heels. He searched in his waistcoat pocket
for the tiny silver figure, and was pleased to find it and
take it out. He could not help regarding it with a reverent
feeling of gratitude. As a fetish it's as good as any, he
thought, and better than most: a man, but also an aspect
of God, suffering and world-encompassing all at once.

He smiled. His Tutelary Genius had most certainly
been with him – guiding him, protecting him. At least, he
had fancied as much.

He went up the beach. The stony strand was his. The
Swedish flag of blue and gold was raised over it, hardly
stirring in the gentle morning air. His tent was being
erected and gear being brought up from the boats as he
watched. Now the passage of Actis Capel has been
forced, he thought, there's nothing to prevent our
proceeding according to our agreed plan.

The rest of the day passed without incident. He sent out
detachments to scout the island, mounted pickets, and
directed the rest of the tents to be pitched, and rudimentary defensive works to be thrown up around the
encampment in such a fashion that their approaches
could be covered by gunboats anchored to either side of
the landing ground.

After receiving reports he called his officers to him.
'Gentlemen, it seems the enemy have taken the road
toward Trongsund. Therefore . . .' He looked from face
to face among his officers, allowing his gaze to dwell last
of all on Count Dona, his new second-in-command. 'At
first light tomorrow we shall proceed with all haste in
pursuit of them.'

The next morning Smith led the column into the
woods, guided by the scouts whose reports had been
most useful. They arrived at a clearing where the wood

had been burnt, and came suddenly out upon the enemy. The Russians were at bay on the far side, drawn up in line, and waiting for them.

Smith halted. He saw their flank tailed into the thick part of the wood. How many of them are there? he wondered. It would be foolhardy to come out into the open without knowing more. He scanned the works on the other side of the wood, looking anxiously for cannon, and seeing places where they must be concealed, then he motioned the line back into the forest and considered.

As he waited an officer arrived in the uniform of a major of the hussars, and announced himself as one of the king's aides-de-camp.

'You must take the troops off immediately, colonel.'

'What? I intend to do no such thing.'

'You have been countermanded, sir.'

'Countermanded?' he asked sharply. 'How can I be countermanded? The king's order made me—'

The other thrust a letter into Smith's hand. 'This order is also from the king.'

Smith ripped open the letter. It was headed 'Wyborg Road'. As he read he was unable to contain his feelings. 'Damn them.'

'Sir?' Count Dona's eyes were fast on him. 'What does it say?'

'It represents the enemy's position on the islands of Uransari and Sommansari as almost impregnable. Count Rosen informs me that he fears the attack will be impossible, since his people have found the Russians have a battery close by the place where we plan to land.' He turned to the aide-de-camp, concealing his anger. 'As you see, it was not quite impossible. Would that this letter had arrived in our possession somewhat sooner, major.'

The other took it like an insult. 'I came after you with all speed. Alas, if the thing has been done. I shall inform the king that you will be pleased to follow his order and take the troops off.'

Smith turned square to him, his blood boiling. Captain Sillen's agonized face was immovably in his mind's eye. 'No, major, you will not. I see nothing in the line of Russian infantry now before us to lead me to believe the taking of Uransari is impossible – as your people have doubtless made the king believe. The attack will go ahead.'

The aide-de-camp protested. 'But there are thousands of them, and more are being landed from galleys on the far side of the island.'

Smith gave him a disdainful wave of dismissal, and drew the young Count Dona after him.

'The enemy are too near for any more debate. There's nothing for it but to retreat or close with them.'

The attack was immediate and grimly made. As the four hundred Swedes moved into view in the clearing the Russians gave fire. Their artillery volley was high, but the shot splintered the trees and sent lethal showers of splinters down, killing and maiming. The Swedes returned a musket volley, and then charged in under the cover of their own smoke, running in with the bayonet.

Smith willed the green uniforms opposing him to break, before the Swedish bayonets closed on them, but they stood firm. The last ten yards before the slaughter were terrifying; the faces of the Russians became those of individual men, and he saw the terror in those faces and knew that he must kill or they would kill him. He screamed, his sabre raised, and there was desperation and a brief flurry of stabbing steel and another moment of agony and death, before the nerve of the enemy suddenly broke, and he saw that all the way along the line the Russians were giving ground, fleeing.

He saw how the realization empowered every Swede, elating them, so that they charged after their enemy. No, he thought. You're throwing away your discipline, and without that you're dead.

'Drummer! Get them back! Beat the reform, damn you!'

But they did not listen. As the Russians ran the Swedes followed them, bringing down any man they could, but then, as Smith knew would happen, the Russians rallied. He stared around, breathless, unable to do more than judge the effect of the impetuosity of his troops. The stink of powder and death was in his nostrils, his muscles were shuddering with exertion and the excruciating tension of having faced death. Then he saw the appearance of a second Russian line; it had come up quickly to support the first, attracted by the sounds of battle.

'Lord God above,' he swore under his breath, 'the whole island must be swarming with them.'

He saw their officer out in front, his sword glittering, his black cocked hat turning this way and that. The way he moved gave the clue that he was about to set up a cross-fire, and Smith redoubled his attempts to make his Swedes withdraw and regroup. He ran among them, slapping them with the flat of his sword, pulling men to their senses until they started to obey.

This time the Russians advanced with bayonet, rending the air with their customary war cries. No more than a company remained of the Swedish force. Half had been separated by their eagerness to pursue the enemy. Smith found himself absolutely alone. His troops were uncohesive and facing greater numbers. He fell back toward the line of the enemy's abandoned cannon, a plan forming in his mind.

When he arrived at the guns he damned his ill-luck. The Swedes were turning them, but he saw that the effort was vain. The horses hitched to the ammunition waggons had been unused to gunfire and had bolted, taking the powder with them.

A few of the guards had rallied nearby when Count

Dona's company rejoined him. The count came up exhausted and out of breath, his bloodied sword clenched in his fist. He had collected a hundred more of the scattered ranks.

'We're surrounded. We must be taken!'

'No surrender!'

Smith felt the nausea of impending defeat sweep through his guts. It was vile and disgusting, and he fought it. But nothing could change the truth of the young count's words: wherever he turned he could see nothing but green coats advancing towards them.

'No surrender, do you hear me!'

He did not take his eyes off Dona's face until the man nodded his assent, then he gave the orders to try for a break-out.

'Tell the men to make for the beach and the gunboats. Your company'll fight the rearguard with me!'

They charged the Russians, feeling the desperate strength of men cornered and fighting for their last chance of life. It was enough to force a spearhead, then they ran like hares through the gap. The rush down to the shore was chaotic, with the Swedish rearguard and Russians mingled together in pell-mell flight. Musket shots crossed in all directions, but as they reached the camp's defences, the Russians drew off again.

Count Dona's boyish face was alight. 'They're not pressing the attack!'

'I presume – they won't care – to venture – within range of our – floating four-and-twenty pounders.'

They retired to the command post together. Smith was utterly exhausted, but absolutely satisfied that the ability of the men and officers he had commanded was proved beyond doubt. At the very least they had forced the Russians to land troops they could ill-afford on the island. Tomorrow, or the next day, with reinforcements brought over from Sommansari, they would be able to capture the lot.

He pulled back the flap of his tent and found Count Rosen waiting for him, immaculate in his uniform. He rose and held out a letter.

'From the king,' he said, and Smith felt the cut of his supercilious manner. 'I was on the point of opening it.'

'Thank you.' Smith threw him a deadly glance, and tore open the seal.

'You see, I thought you must be among the slain. Those of your scattered party who first came in could give me no better account of you than that they left you surrounded by the enemy.'

Smith addressed himself to the letter, but his face must have betrayed his surprise, because the count was emboldened by his reaction.

'Regarding your disobedience yesterday, one assumes. A pity you chose not to listen to my warning, my dear colonel. All that effort – and for nothing.'

Smith felt his irritation with the count come to a crescendo. He said, 'The king's sentiments are certainly . . . unexpected. Please excuse me.'

He cast the letter negligently onto the table for Rosen to read or not as he chose, and left the tent.

I cannot sufficiently testify to you how much I am sensible of your zeal, and the reiterated proofs you give of courage and ardour, and which you know how to communicate to those who accompany you. I beg of you to testify my satisfaction to them.
Gustavus

Outside the air was pure and clean. Smith drew a deep breath, feeling fully alive. The climactic battle would come in the next few days, he knew. It would come at sea. And now he was sure he had the power to make it a Swedish victory.

THREE

Berenice pulled on the postilion's boots, and prepared to leave the château. The question was hanging over her like a sword, still unresolved, still threatening. I am expected to consent to marry one or the other, she thought. Tomorrow I must give my answer. Either way that answer must be 'yes'.

'I have to decide tonight,' she had said an hour ago. The long room had been empty except for herself and Père Fournet. He had come to visit her father to discuss a particular matter, and to talk generally with the comte as he often did. The good father was the one person she had always felt able to confide in.

'It is your father's fondest wish.' He enfolded her hands; his were dry and warm, hers cold. He had been visiting the château two or three times a week since before she was born. Despite everything he was a rock of certainty in a sea of troubles. It was part of a priest's calling to make the loathsome seem palatable, but this was a duty she could not swallow.

'Berenice, he wants you to marry. He wants to see an heir.'

'I cannot do it. Even for my father.'

The priest was looking old of late. He had suffered intolerably during the past year. He had listened to Pope Pius, and refused the Oath of Loyalty demanded by the new French state. Because of that he had been sacked by the new government. They had taken his *curé*'s post and his official income away. He had joined the dispossessed, but he had continued to minister as if nothing had happened.

'Ask him to change his mind, Père Fournet.'

'He will not change his mind. Of that I am quite sure.'

'Then pray for me.'

'I shall, child.'

She thought regretfully how the lives of individual people were so easily caught up in greater matters, how easily mangled and smashed. The Church had been the special target of political attacks in the last year. According to *L'Ami du Roi*, the Revolution wanted to destroy the Church because the Church was rich: France is bankrupt, they said, but the Church holds 150 million livres.

So what is to be said of those poor women turned out of the nunnery of St Etienne? Turned out to starve in beggary or prostitution according to their age? What of *their* rights?

'You must do what your conscience tells you,' he said. 'That is God's voice within us. My task is to make clear exactly what your conscience is saying, to separate its purity from your other thoughts and motives.'

She disengaged her hands from his, heard her own voice, very definite now. 'Then, in conscience, I cannot choose.'

Père Fournet's eye was blear; its red rim watered. 'But think of the greater good. Think how your father suffers these days. Everything he stands for lies under threat. The extremists are growing stronger every day. That is why you must help him all you can.'

Père Fournet was right about her father. He seemed constantly careworn. Every decree the government made eroded him, added a new line to his face. He was not even allowed to hunt on his own land any more.

She felt the dilemma boxing her in. 'But how can I choose between two men I do not love?'

'What is the nature of love?' he asked. 'What does it mean? To love, or to be *in* love? Is not one a selfless state of grace, and the other the supreme selfishness? Satan is abroad today in our country. The more he works to undo us, the worse things will become. In such times as these a woman needs a husband.'

She squeezed her cross, shaking her head. Then Père Fournet surprised her by taking it from her and examining it.

'Why do you wear this?' he asked sharply. 'Where did it come from?'

'It is my . . . crucifix. Father, I have always worn it. You have seen it many times.'

'Child, this is no crucifix.'

'Yes, it is. You can see where the figure of Christ has fallen from—'

'No. This is the *crux ansata* – the looped cross. It is a pagan symbol.'

She was shocked at Père Fournet's anger. 'Symbol of what, father?'

'It is a sign devised by the ancient Egyptians to signify their idolatrous worship.'

'Surely they worshipped before the time of Christ, and so could know no better.' She searched his face for a clue to his fears.

'You must not wear it.'

'I have always worn it, father. It came from my godparents. It has never done me any harm.'

'You can't know that.'

She had stared at him wonderingly, seeing him in a sudden puzzling light. The episode had revealed an aspect of him to which she did not wish to admit. All her life Père Fournet had been her confessor and her spiritual father, yet at the greatest crisis in her life, instead of helping her he had grown angry over some silly detail.

You're not a child any more, she thought later, combing her hair and pinning it up on top of her head. An adult should begin to see through the unquestioned assumptions of childhood. When I was five years old I believed that God lived in the crypt of St Etienne's church. Perhaps a time comes in everyone's life when we outgrow those we thought wise. We all must shed our innocence, one way or another.

Last night she had dreamed the ogre dream again, but this time it had gone on longer. This time she had not woken up just as it caught her. There had been a splash of red thrown across the white snow, and the blue jacket of her lost love. Three colours. I shall go to St Etienne, and I shall pray for his safe delivery, then I shall beg God for the strength to put this romantic foolishness behind me, so that I may do my duty by my family.

She made her decision and rang for Agnes to attend her. The maid looked tired. She had put on weight recently. 'Mademoiselle?'

'Agnes, I want you to do me a favour.'

'Mademoiselle?' Agnes cocked her head with interest. 'What kind of favour?'

'I want you to speak to Gugnot on my behalf.'

She grimaced. 'Gugnot and I are not on terms at present.'

'I need him to take me into Caen tonight. I want to go without anyone knowing.'

Agnes's mouth dropped open.

'Caen? But why?'

She lowered her eyes. 'I want to go to St Etienne.'

'But that's dangerous. Your father would never allow it. There are gangs—'

'I know about the dangers. And I do not mean to inform my father. I shall wear a postilion's coat and hat for a disguise, and get aboard the phaeton when it is brought round to take Père Fournet back to Caen tonight.'

'But, mademoiselle . . .' Agnes seemed to realize it was useless to protest.

'If you will persuade Gugnot to do this for me you may have this for yourself.'

She held out a pearl pin.

A light came into Agnes's eyes. 'That? For me? To keep?'

'Yes.'

She took it, but then seemed about to hand it back as a thought troubled her. 'I would never tell anyone, mademoiselle, but . . . what are you going to do for Gugnot?'

'Won't he keep a secret?'

Agnes made another face. 'Not him. He's not worthy of anyone's trust.'

'My father would not agree with you. He has retained Gugnot while he has struck many others from the estate accounts.' She sensed a deceit. 'Why do you speak so ill of Gugnot's qualities? I thought you had an affection for him.'

'Pfhh! He had no qualities. When he spied on you—'

Agnes's hand went to her mouth, but she could not call back her words.

'Spied on me? What do you mean by that?'

'Mademoiselle Berenice, didn't you know?' The maid's eyes shifted. 'He's the one who spilled the story about you to your father.'

'Is he?' She felt anger, but controlled it, knowing that she could use Agnes's rift with Gugnot. 'You say he spied on me?'

'Yes, mademoiselle. He followed you all over Normandy, watching what you did. He's the one who stole that little book the Englishman had been writing in. And that's not all. It's why Père Fournet's here tonight. Over the matter of the theft of monsieur le comte's gold watch.'

Agnes was aware she had said too much, but the

pleasure of betraying Gugnot had been irresistible. Berenice's mind reeled; inside she felt as though she had been slapped across the mouth, but on the surface she remained calm. Well, well! So that was how it happened. Gugnot! And I imagined it was your stupidity all along, Agnes. What an injustice I have done you, even if you do listen at keyholes.

The thought of the groom observing in secret disgusted her. She cut off the thought and went to her purse, her plans unchanged by the revelation. 'Since it seems Gugnot has his price, you shall give him this.'

Agnes took the golden *louis d'or* reverently, but her eyes were full of bewilderment. 'Four-and-twenty livres? For *him*?'

'You may warn him that if this tale gets back to my father – *any* tale, by any means – I shall dedicate myself to ending his employment at Thury-Harcourt for ever.'

'I shouldn't worry about tales, mademoiselle,' Agnes said, her eyes green with triumph. 'He won't be here tomorrow.'

Berenice dismissed Agnes and left her room moments later, knowing that she must anticipate Père Fournet's departure to give her time to reach the gate. Both the comtesse and Celestine had retired to bed.

She froze on the stair when she saw the light spilling from the library. There were voices. The doors stood ajar; the two footmen Clissot and Dugommier had been dismissed over the affair of the stolen gold watch, and so the hallway was unattended. The actuality of it was that her father could not really afford to pay them any longer, and the theft had provoked him. Nothing is simple, she thought. Nothing is what it seems. So Clissot and Dugommier were right to curse my father. And it was Gugnot all along . . .

She felt pity for Gugnot, then caught herself. I belong to the aristocracy, she thought, feeling suddenly bitter, but my family is being dispossessed. My father must bear progressively crueller indignities. Insolence among some of the estate tenants has already given way to insults, and once or twice to unsheathed aggression. Our lives are falling apart bit by bit. What should I care for a servant who has broken faith by stealing? It was not pity for Gugnot I felt just now, only nostalgia for a time I can never recapture.

Yesterday, while combing out her hair, Agnes had said something with a strange look in her eye. 'It seems to me, mademoiselle, that your troubles began the day you slapped the Englishman's face.'

The cloying smell of recently snuffed tallow came to her. The house's greatest crystal chandelier hung motionless in the air twenty feet away, a structure, she had always thought, that seemed to be made from daggers of ice.

She strained to hear. The voices were warm with alcohol and a little slurred. Only two: her father and Père Fournet, discussing politics.

'. . . it seems the great battle was fought on the ninth of July last.'

'Will you have the rest of the decanter? Hmmm? You say the *Swedes* were victorious?'

'This is how it was stated in the English papers . . .'

Berenice moved another step lower on the stair to see Père Fournet adjust his spectacles and consult the cutting. At his elbow was a table on which stood her father's orrery. Ivory balls representing the seven planets stood on brass wires. An engraved sun beamed enigmatically up at her from the centre plate.

'. . . At that time the Swedes defeated the Russians with the loss of, let me see: "five frigates, fifteen galleys, two floating batteries, and twenty-one smaller vessels, along with a large quantity of naval and military stores. Also, there were captured some four thousand five hundred prisoners".'

'Hmmm. There it is.'

Berenice had heard her father say that a thousand times. It was a phrase he used to signal that his interest in a topic was at an end. He had been morose all week, oppressed by uncertainties, and worried about the financial management of the estate. His tolerance for old news regarding a foreign war would be predictably slight, but Père Fournet persisted, which meant he was making some kind of point. She listened closer.

'King Gustavus commanded in person, aboard the galley, *Seraphim*.' Père Fournet paused, then added: 'I mention it because two Englishmen of your acquaintance were at his side.'

She heard her father's surprise. 'Englishmen?'

Père Fournet took off his spectacles, then put them back on again. 'On this authority it is stated that an English officer, by the name of Bonham – you must remember him, *hein*? – commanded a Russian frigate named the *Venus*. It seemed it was he who captured the *Seraphim*.'

Her father's interest waned again. 'Indeed?'

On the darkened stair Berenice's heart began to beat faster.

'But only after Gustavus had left her. According to, ah, *Parker's General Advertiser*, "the King's advisor, observing the gallant and seaman-like style in which the *Venus* was bearing down, was sure she was under the command of a fellow-Englishman" — '

'Haw!'

Père Fournet produced a narrow smile. 'It is the kind of thing they will say in English papers. At any rate, this second Englishman advised Gustavus throughout the battle, and caused him to preserve his life by lowering a boat and having it rowed to the shore.'

'Courageous.'

'Apparently, King Gustavus's boat was surrounded. To penetrate through the enemy was a service of extreme danger.'

'There it is.'

'The record adds that the noble fellow Bonham was killed in the action.'

'Regrettable.'

'But . . .' She heard Père Fournet's voice quaver like an old man's, as it always did when he was obliged to deal with a tricky subject. '. . . Gustavus' protector was named also. He is also known to you.'

'Who was it? Hmmm?'

'One . . . Captain Smith.'

'Hmmm.'

Berenice felt the dampness on her face. Oh God, if he were only here now! Why can't he be here, to carry me away?

Faligan was not at the gates. Instead Davout opened them. Giant dumb Davout. He gawped at her as she sat up beside Gugnot in her postilion's gear.

The journey into Caen took about an hour. The river road was misty, the moon huge and yellow and low in the sky. All the way she could not get Smith out of her mind. Every time she had recalled Smith's leaving she had felt a pang of guilt. After so long the memory of him was still potent enough to stir up feelings of regret and of longing. Despite the passing of time, she was still in love with him. Sweden. A great victory. The saving of the king's life . . .

The twin towers of the church of St Etienne rose high above the surrounding houses. She entered through a small door set into one of the two great doors. Outside had been deserted, inside was almost so, yet still the church was a treasurehouse packed with wonderful works of mystery. Wooden pews and stone columns, carved chancel screens, battle honours. Great magic. Angels with gilded wings, saint's faces: pale cheeks and rosebud lips of plaster, unnatural and awesome. The language of Latin inscribed like spells. The images of saints and the smell of ages. Sounds echoed dead in here.

It was a place of symbols, a feast of ancient meaning for the eye, some glorious, some hideous, and the light was like something from another world.

She went straight to the heart of it, straight into prayer, implored God to speak to her: if I am a sinner, then tell me so. Why is my world being destroyed? Was what I did so very wrong? Was it? Tell me. Or if it is signs you speak through, then show me one.

She looked around, trembling, desperate to have an answer. Nothing. Or something so slight she did not know if it could count as a sign or not. The play of light on a brass plate, the stirring of an altar cloth in a draught, the impression of solidity created by the great grey incised slab in the aisle. Were these signs?

All was silence.

Has the passage of time soured me? she wondered. Can I ever help behaving as if the direction of my life has been thrown onto the wrong road? Look at Celestine. She's seventeen. She has her admirers, her music. She is not bedevilled by ridiculous obsessions. I fell in love with Smith, and I cannot forget him. And if I cannot forget him, how can I marry someone else?

Still there was silence.

She pressed her hands together until they ached. I know that every young woman in Normandy secretly wishes to have Antoine Phelypeaux as a lover. I find his attractions superficial and his attentions easy to resist. De Tromelin is amusing company, and he is ardent, but he seems to me a mere boy in comparison with Smith . . .

She waited and waited, and the feeling gathered in her that she was waiting in vain. Perhaps the silence is an answer in itself, she thought.

She rose, stood in the aisle, walked across the great grey slab. A seven-hundred-year-old tomb. William, Duke of Normandy, called the Conqueror. She went to where the votive candles blazed. Hundreds had been lit by the deacon on behalf of those who dared not come here in person any more. The flames that grew from curling, untrimmed wicks were huge, thin, a foot long. They reached up into still air, confounding themselves in ripples of thick smoke.

The translucent yellow columns mesmerized her. A long metal tray was crusted with dropped wax. It reflected a surprising heat, a radiance that in itself gave comfort. She saw impressed there in the softness the fingermarks of children, trapped in the amber the ash and stubs of spells used to transfer the good light of hope from one wish to another.

Suddenly she became aware of a presence some distance from her. The sight of the black-cowled monk terrified her, and she looked away from him. Still, like a statue in a niche, the figure hovered on the fringes of her vision. Then it knelt and crossed itself and fixed a single black candle in the array, and was gone.

When she moved to kneel on the polished flags, the disturbance sent the long flames into riot. Above her an accumulation of black grease on the ancient stone of the niche witnessed the prayers of thirty generations. The smell of newly snuffed stalactites. The vast grey pipes of the organ, ranged in their ranks. She lit a candle. Protect him. Protect Smith from falling in the Swedish war. Please, oh Lord God in Heaven. Protect him.

FOUR

Smith breathed deep and felt the warmth of late spring on his face. Sunlight drenched the palace of Tudor brick. He savoured the special qualities of the place. It was quiet, and the air smelled of daffodils. This was a palace from another century, a palace that continued here regardless of the hive of modern commerce that surrounded it. London may be the richest and most populous city of the civilized world, he thought, but her traditions will always be ancient and mystical.

He turned to the tall, elegantly uniformed figure beside him. 'It's good to be in England again, Charles.'

His elder brother's face became thoughtful. 'Yes. It's strange how we spend so much time parted from that which we love. You are right to savour this moment.'

Smith met his brother's eye. 'It's one I hope will come again and again to my mind.'

There was something gently mocking in his brother's manner. 'Ah, how sweet the maturing of ambition, how glorious the victory . . . Who would have thought it? You, made a knight before your thirtieth birthday.'

'I always said so.'

'But you never really believed yourself.'

'How do you know?' There had always been an element of competition between them, but he could forgive his brother almost anything. 'The victory is indeed glorious. And sweet.'

148

'. . . so long as there is someone to appreciate it.'

He realized that Charles had lost none of his capacity to read him accurately. *He knows I'm thinking about Berenice again. He knows how I've been unable to get her out of my mind since I arrived back in England. He knows that's the darker side of why I went to Sweden. To escape myself for a space of time, to lose myself in the smoke of war.*

The Baltic adventure had been one of high good fortune. In the greatest engagement of all, the battle of 11 July, he had saved the Swedish king's life, almost lost his own, then engineered a triumph against greater odds. In gratitude King Gustavus had conferred on him the Order of the Knight of the Sword.

He remembered how he had concealed his shock under a cool formality well suited to his Baltic surroundings. He had acquitted himself in a manner befitting a British naval officer, but to have a reward for that from a king's hands was incredible.

He felt a shiver pass through him as he recalled reading of King Gustavus's assassination. *I saved the man's life,* he thought, *but now he's dead, shot dead at a masked ball by an ex-bodyguard. Perhaps it's not possible to stand in the way of things that are meant to be. Maybe the pagan Greeks were right. Maybe the three Fates do spin and weave and then cut short the destinies of mortals, and sometimes not even Zeus can intervene.*

On his return from Sweden he had gone immediately to see his mother. She had received him in her boudoir. 'William, now your talents shall have proper recognition! You shall be "Sir William".'

He considered, then said, 'No, I think after all I shall have "Sir Sidney".'

She regarded him with satisfaction. 'What did your brother officers in the Swedish navy make of you?'

He returned an enigmatic smile. 'Ah, you may suppose I took care to have a most perfect good understanding with the Swedish officers – which was not very difficult, considering they knew the distribution of ranks and ribbons depended on my representation of their conduct.'

'How did they take your triumphs at the Admiralty?'

He laughed. 'I made the most of them, as you may imagine. After being so disgracefully treated by the Duke of Leeds over my permissions to serve in Sweden in the first place, I thought it only appropriate to play him up.'

He watched her satisfaction with him turn to disapproval, as if she thought it would be incumbent on her to repair his errors. It had happened often enough in the past. 'William, what did you say to their lordships?'

'Only that the King of Sweden had been pleased to think me worthy of the fourth rank, that is, the Great Cross of the Order of the Sword.' He paused. 'I then told them that, of course, I required my sovereign's permission to accept it, saying: "Will you be so good as to inform me of the mode of procuring this permission?" '

'One day, William, you will ride for a fall with such hubris. As a boy you were always showing off.'

'I may fall, mother, but not yet. And besides, at the Admiralty I was humble, as you shall hear. I wrung my hands for their lordships and said, "It seems I have been unavoidably included in the honours conferred on my companions on this particular service. The Swedish king was pleased to wave his sword over our shoulders on our return. This entitles me to a little cross at the buttonhole, which I suppose I must put in my pocket till I hear from you again." '

'William!'

He saw that his mother was unamused, and he became serious again. 'Actually, I was worried that King Gustavus's death might void the knighthood.'

'Nonsense. How could it?'

'Since formal protocol requires that my own sovereign approves the award before I may properly accept it, why, I supposed—'

His mother had briskly pooh-poohed the thought. 'Why should the king's death make any difference? You are already a knight by his hand, and all else is mere nicety.'

'His Majesty may not see it that way.'

'The House of Hanover are hardly absolute monarchs. His Majesty will do what he is told. I shall speak to my sister about it directly. What you must consider now is who is to attend you at the Palace.'

He had smiled at her, admiring her practicality and strength. She ran a network among the ladies of England every bit as influential as the foremost lodges of the Brotherhood. 'Mother, you are ever the architect of my ambitions.'

'Someone has to be.' She shook her head. 'You really must stop antagonizing powerful men if you wish to get on. Especially admirals.'

'Mother, I can't help it.' He smiled a cat-with-the-cream smile. 'It's in my nature, you see.'

Now he looked around, saw the little procession of bewigged knights gathering, and knew it was time. Their every ornament was crusted with ancient meaning: fur and feather, satin and velvet, cloak and chain, jewel and sword. It struck him suddenly, standing in the mild sunlight, how absurd their garments were, then he abandoned the thought, and chose to revel in the idea instead. Ceremonial's essential to the soul, he told himself, smiling at members of his entourage. Without oaths and symbols and uniforms and formality and pomp there would hardly be any civilization at all. Only fools attempt to strike ancient observances from the calendar, or underestimate their power.

As he walked he felt the presence of his Tutelary Genius strongly. His mind drifted back to that sombre sea in the north. The little silver figure he called the Green Goblin had been in his pocket throughout the

Baltic campaign, just as it was in his pocket now. It had seen him through then, and it would see him through for evermore – so long as he continued to believe. All that was required was to keep faith with his guardian spirit. If he did so, he knew, he would continue to make the right choices, and all his ambitions would be fulfilled. The smoke haze of battle had hung in the air. The tang of powder and salt had been on his lips. It had been in the aftermath of the climactic struggle of the war, a climax whose outcome he had done so much to influence. At the close of the final battle between the Swedish and Russian flotillas, they had landed on a forbidding coast, and he had approached King Gustavus.

'Your Majesty, if I may make report of a successful operation . . .' That afternoon he had been in the centre of the line directing battle against the largest ships of the Russian force, those commanded by the Prince of Nassau. '. . . I should like also to mention efforts I have made to organize certain Turkish prisoners. I've had them released from captivity following the surrender of the Russian galleys. These men were employed at the oars, and deserve their freedom . . .'

Gustavus had heard him out while standing on a rocky island, without shrub or shelter, and seeing Smith's exhaustion and the way he had felt the cold after the hot work of the day, had called to a trusted soldier of his guard. 'Why not give the English captain your cloak?' The guard had answered, wrapping it tighter round himself, 'Because I want it myself, sir.'

Smith chuckled inwardly as he remembered his own surprise at the guard's lack of grace and obedience. But Gustavus had not lost his good humour. Instead he had told his page to bring one of his royal cloaks. It had been brought and put over Smith's shoulders, then the king had gestured at the star of the Order of the Seraphim embroidered on it, and had said, 'Only because it is cold,' adding, 'You know, Smith, if I did not use those words, you would have been regularly invested with the Order of the Seraphim, just as a nobleman of the court of Spain would be made a grandee of the first class if the king ordered him to put on his hat without the badge of the Order being covered.'

'You don't say so, Majesty.'

'I *do* say so! Have you not heard it?' Then the king had punched him playfully on the shoulder. 'Ah, you English. So hard to understand. It is not the Order of the Seraphim, but that of the Sword I destine for you, Smith.'

He smiled inwardly at the memory now and, dressed in the surcoat and mantle, wearing the sword and spurs of the Order, and in his hand his cap and feathers, he fell in with the procession.

'What is it?' Charles asked.

'I was just thinking about Gustavus. The injustice of it.'

'I read they caught Ankarstrom, the fellow who pointed the pistol. He was flogged in public for three days before they executed him.' Charles leaned close and lowered his voice. 'Spencer told me Gustavus was shot because he had decided to send troops to France to help Louis crush the Revolution.'

'I'm not the least surprised by it.'

Charles looked long at him, smiling finally. 'What *happened* to you out there?'

'I'm sorry?' He gave his brother nothing.

'What did you learn? Look at you: still the youthful vanity, still the outward conceits, always your roaring ambition, but . . . you've changed inside.'

'I thought it was Spencer's place to open our eyes to our faults.' He tossed the remark away jocularly, but he felt it hit to his heart.

'You've changed, Sidney. I think you've started to believe in yourself – or something – at last.'

He wanted to tell his brother about the certainties he

now felt, but the time had come to move off, and they were obliged to start from the Presence Chamber and go at a sedate pace towards His Majesty's Closet. Smith's three esquires carried ahead the coronet, helmet, shield and banner as far as the Levee Chamber. There they would remain until the procession returned.

Around him the palace's motifs caught his eye, like words speaking to his soul in a secret language: carved wooden lions, roses, dragons, thistles, harps, fleurs-de-lys . . .

This is a long way from the fashionable Robert Adam drawing rooms that are to be found in the great houses of England, he thought. No, this place has the spirit of an earlier age. The cool halls were flagged, the stone steps footworn, the walls panelled in dark wood, above white ceilings of Tudor plaster, ornamented with crude cherubs and heraldic devices. Sun shafted the dusty air through leaded, narrow lancet windows, shadows lurked in corners. The sounds here were muted echoes. He fancied the ghosts of former ages, invisible as the pure stream of history, a flow running down the centuries, resonating in the relics, and he knew what it was to be heir to an ancient heritage.

A chamberlain announced the dignitaries in a loud, formal voice as they moved slowly toward the doors. First Smith's personal friends, young men, like himself:

'George Cook, Esquire, Ensign in his Majesty's First Regiment of Foot Guards . . . Hugh Pigot, Esquire, Lieutenant in His Majesty's Navy . . . William Lindsay, Esquire, late his Majesty's Secretary of Legation at the Court of Saint Petersburg, here represented by William Cosby, Esquire, captain of an independent company of foot, Charles Douglas Smith, Esquire, Captain . . .'

Then the witnesses, an incredibly distinguished company, Knights of the Bath, following in the dress of their order. Smith felt a flush of pride, but also gratitude for his mother's efforts. She had moved heaven and earth to surround him with representatives of the most powerful families in the Union. But this is astonishing, he thought, feeling humbled by the privilege. It's almost like a meeting of the Privy Council.

I knew she'd been pulling strings, he thought, but something's not quite right. As he walked he wondered what had really been happening behind the scenes. It seemed that someone had chosen to make the occasion into something other than a simple investiture.

'His Majesty's Secretary at War, The Right Honourable Sir George Yonge . . . General Sir Henry Clinton . . . Sir William Gordon . . . General Sir George Howard, Viscount Morpeth . . . Lord Macartney . . . Sir Ralph Payne . . . Lord Amherst . . .'

He was introduced into the royal presence by the Right Honourable Lord Grenville, His Majesty's Principal Secretary of State for Foreign Affairs. Smith instantly noticed the distracted impatience of the man, as if the ceremony and its main players were incidental to his own agenda.

The sight of him recalled his brother Spencer's acerbic remark about Grenville. That had been designed to keep him from getting carried away with his reward. 'Grenville's only six years your senior,' Spencer had said, 'yet he's been Foreign Secretary a year, and Home Secretary for two years before that. And that's nothing compared to Pitt. By the time *he* was your age he'd been Prime Minister for three and a half years!'

That had certainly put things in perspective, he thought with a measure of chagrin. Strange how Spencer has adopted so many of our mother's mannerisms. He's the youngest, yet he takes most upon himself when it comes to keeping our feet on the ground. A shame he can't be here, but I could not expect him to turn down his first foreign posting, it being one of such notable importance.

Grenville's smiling eyes sized and dismissed Smith

with a haste that was almost slighting. That's it, he thought, calculating from Grenville's glances. I know why he's here. There have been some savage rumours about the king's 'health' lately – and we all know what that means. Also there's a war on the Continent. I think Grenville's chosen to make a demonstration for the benefit of Europe's ambassadors. He's taken my investiture as a pretext to convene an impromptu meeting with them.

Grenville turned away to talk to a man who wore the collar of a Knight Commander of the Swedish Order of the Polar Star. That's Nolcken, he thought, knowing him to be Envoy Extraordinary and Minister Plenipotentiary from the Court of Stockholm. Liston spoke well of him, and there are others present too that he mentioned – ambassadors from half a dozen European states. Good God, Grenville looks preoccupied, doesn't he? Almost anxious.

Smith felt suddenly engaged himself, more engaged than he had ever felt in action. This was not simply a group of oddly dressed men in an over-ornamented room, but a ritual of tremendous symbolic potency, a rite of great and ancient significance. And, whatever his state of health, the monarch who was about to conduct it was the most powerful man in the world. Smith felt an almost tangible sense of knocking and being granted entry, and going through in innocence into a different, higher world.

Charles touched his arm, and it focused his mind. He entered the room known as the Royal Closet. The heavy curtains were almost drawn, so that thin slits of sunshine were all that penetrated the gloom. As his eyes adjusted he saw that the monarch's seat was a gilded, Gothic chair, mounted on a dais of two steps, and the king himself was arrayed in white silk hose and a suit of dark blue velvet with fur-trimmed cape and soft black velvet hat. Despite himself, Smith found the experience of coming suddenly into the presence of the sovereign awe-inspiring.

He approached with the approved reverences, advancing and kneeling on a velvet cushion before the seated king. Then he felt the tension in the air, and he knew that something was badly amiss.

Only when Smith looked up at the red mottled face of his sovereign did he realize how right the rumours had been. The king staggered as he got to his feet, and there was a wild look in his eyes. His hand shook as he presented the Collar. There was a dank smell about him too. From the corner of his eye Smith could see a shrivelled, bespectacled man hovering anxiously in the corner, His Majesty's physician.

The king really is out of his mind, he thought, appalled. It's common knowledge that he's periodically 'unwell', but this is worse than anything I ever imagined. No wonder Grenville seems so nervous; he's surely over-reached himself. By trying to show the king off, Grenville's only managed to reveal the extent of his frailty.

The king wavered unsteadily. There were white flecks of spittle at the corners of his mouth. He hardly seemed to know where he was.

Smith rose, kissed the royal hand as it was proffered. His Majesty grinned emptily, and was helped to sit down by two pages. His teeth were brown, his hands beetroot red, and the backs of them scarred as if by blisters. Good God, Smith thought with horror but showing no sign on his face. He's our head of state. Our king. The most powerful man in the world. Everything the British nation does is done in his name, but look at him . . . he's little better than a vacant idiot.

He cleared his throat, ready to begin the speech of thanks that was required of him.

'Your Majesty, in order to express my gratitude to . . .' Suddenly he saw the king's face tremble. His eyes rolled. Then a dark patch began to spread along the leg of his velvet breeches, and a sickening smell came from him.

It was a moment of excruciating embarrassment, then Smith realized the truth. Good God, he thought. I'm closer to him than the ambassadors by twenty paces, and none of them have yet noticed. But what happens when they do? I must do something. I *must*. But what?

He struck a pose that carried him a step to his left, and continued his speech, knowing he must not pause, or rush it, or he would draw attention to the incontinence, whereas – perhaps a hint of flamboyance in his own delivery might just succeed in creating a distraction.

'. . . since the late Swedish king, Gustavus, the third of that name, has seen fit to confer upon your humble servant and subject . . .'

With horror, he saw that the king's seat had begun to drip.

He raised his voice, vapouring now, talking nonsense and wrecking formal protocol in an effort to divert attention. When he felt he could bring his blethering speech to an end he did so by stepping forward onto the dais and seizing the seated king's hand. In the guise of kissing it for a second time, he took the corner of the king's cloak and pulled it hard across his knees.

His move drew audible gasps from the nearest courtiers. Smith felt his palms bedewed with sweat. To touch the monarch, even in informal circumstances, without invitation, would have been utterly against the code; to rearrange His Majesty's clothing in the middle of an investiture was tantamount to treason. He retired over-hastily, repeating the ceremonies he had made at his entrance. He was burning, aware that he had been taken for a man ignorant of how to behave properly. He looked to left and right, hoping he gave no hint on the surface of the turmoil he felt inside, and saw that his modifications to the accepted ritual had outraged several of those watching.

He felt tremendous unease, and knew that the experience of seeing the king's state had affected him far more deeply than he had at first thought.

His entourage filed out with him. As he left the august halls, his brother murmured fiercely, 'What on earth were you thinking of?'

He said only, 'I'll tell you later.'

My assumptions are shaken, he thought, because now I have seen with my own eyes that the governance of Great Britain – my country, and the biggest commercial and maritime power ever seen – is being carried on as an empty charade, and what could be more shocking to a man than that? He halted, still feeling the burn of embarrassment as a nebulous fear overtook him.

When they reached the hall where the formal procession dissolved, the congratulations he received were less than wholehearted. Sir George Yonge shook his hand faintly. His disappointment showed. A moment later Smith overheard him saying, 'Unlike a son of Mary Smith to lose his nerve, what?' Others were able to show their disapproval of his conduct in more subtle ways.

He endured the shame and reflected on the disaster. He would certainly be the laughing stock of London society for a few days, and then the ghost of it would haunt his career. The word would reach his mother soon enough. He would tell her the truth, of course. He could tell no one else, except perhaps Charles. There's always a damned fly in my ointment, he told himself. Always something to blight my life's special moments. I wonder why?

Charles came to him solicitously.

'Have you any idea—'

He turned, lips pursed. 'Of what? How badly I behaved? Oh, yes, *I'm* quite aware of that.'

'Then, what happened to you?' His brother's expression showed sudden irritation. 'Sidney, how can you smile at a time like this?'

'I'm simply amused at the irony of it.' He heard the smoothness of his own voice, and knew he must look inexplicably pleased with himself. 'You really didn't see?'

'See what?'

Excellent, he thought. If Charles saw nothing then it's a sure bet that no one else saw what happened. They all think I forgot my words and gabbled nonsense and forced myself upon the king's person through ignorance of the correct form.

Charles said, 'What I saw was you making a deliberate fool of yourself.'

'That's a pity,' he said. 'It wasn't meant to appear deliberate.'

PART 4

The Tempering Fire

SUMMER, 1792
Ajaccio, Corsica

How I have longed for your return signore; *I have so much to tell you! Great things have happened since our last meeting. Your predictions – pardon, I should say* prophecies *– continue to fall true, despite my doubts. It's very curious, but I can never see how the results you foretell are to come about until they have done so. Then, suddenly, my world is made different. For a long time* signore, *I thought that yours were self-fulfilling prophecies, that your suggestions were acting on my mind, causing me to do as you say. But it is not like that. Yours is a strange kind of magic,* signore, *and I am ashamed ever to have doubted your powers.*

Just as you prophesied, Paoli did return home. A month before my twenty-first birthday he came back to us. He had been exactly twenty-one years in exile. I asked my brothers: 'Can this really be the Great Man?' This was the same who had been my father's commander before my birth, the great hero of my youth, now returned to his homeland, yet to me he seemed very ordinary, very – insignificant.

He rejected me, signore. *Just as you said he would. Me, the most fervent supporter of his cause. I burned to die for him, and yet he rejected me! . . . But I cannot bring myself to talk about that 'great general' any more.*

I went back to my regiment in Valence, a place I knew well enough. But it was not easy for me in France. I ate stale bread to make ends meet! We shared a room in a peasant's hovel, but at least we had enough to read. Perhaps it was my diet that gave me such a sallow complexion. You see how the skin flakes from my face, and neck and wrists? Physicians call it 'the tetter'. It itches. But have you not told me that a soldier must disregard personal discomfort? That much is surely fundamental.

I almost fell in love. With a girl who used to walk with me in a cherry orchard. But of course you know that, because you know everything. Well, then, you'll know that I chose to leave her rather than suffer more disappointment. I learned enough of love then to regard it as something injurious to society and destructive to the happiness of the individual. What use is a man who cannot eat, cannot sleep, cannot think of anything but the face of a girl? Pains in the belly like fear. Is that love? Men should think themselves saved when they are quit of it.

The people have faith in me. I was elected lieutenant-colonel of Ajaccio's new National Guard, just as you said I would be. So it was that I went from lieutenant to lieutenant-colonel in one stride – who would have thought it, except yourself?

You know what I think, signore? I think that damned liar, Paoli, will not throw the French out of Corsica. I think he's come to accept their terms. You know I even dedicated some of my writing to him? I sent him a manuscript, but his reply to me – me, to whom he owes his liberty – has been lofty. He said: 'History should not be written in youth.'

Bastard! What a farce! It is clear he considers me a person of no importance, that's all! I told my brother Joseph to ask for my manuscript back, but the great patriot says he has not the time to go through his papers.

Do you know the word 'vendetta', signore?

It means a blood-feud. Among the quarrelsome

families of my island a man soon learns to study the human heart. What I have learned is that every man has his price. It follows that the differences between men can be measured by a few pieces of silver more or less.

If my nature is anything, signore, it is persevering. And time, as you have told me, is very much on my side.

Now, signore, shall we talk business?

ONE

Smith felt the heavy door close behind him. Despite the pain in his head he peered into a hellish scene. Human flesh cooked like dough amid rising clouds. Six tortured bodies, old and young, lay draped across the stone slabs, some with their loins wrapped in towels, some with their heads made up in turbans, others pinkly naked, sweltering as they endured the moist heat.

He rubbed the salt sweat from his eyes, then opened them again on the steaming room of Almack's Romanesque baths. The basement labyrinth had been built on the profits of the gambling club that stood above it.

London society, it sometimes seemed, was a maze of interlocking clubs, all dedicated to one pursuit or another. The steaming room was the latest vogue. Far longer than it was wide, low-ceilinged and lined with classical Italian marble, all of it hot to the touch, it was fed with steam from an underground boiler, steam that passed along pipes and issued from the nostrils of a leaden dolphin's head, proving, Smith surmised, that the artist had never seen a dolphin in his life.

His bare feet felt their way along the misty outlines of wooden duck-boards. They reminded him of the *Alcmene*'s gratings. Charles's fashionable club had hosted him a drinking party last night, and he had overindulged. On waking he had found that to move his head too suddenly set up a bass aching that rang in it for half a minute. Breakfast had been out of the question. Jeklin, his housekeeper, had told him that the only recourse was to cook out the poison, with repeated scaldings and plungings. After three such cycles of torment he had begun to feel the benefit of the method.

Last night the drink had flowed freely, and Smith had partaken of it after playing three indifferent hands at brag. He and Charles and an elderly Whig peer with a taste for moral conundrums had been discussing the politics of France, and the ways of the world at large.

'Don't you think we should at least give asylum to France's men of genius?' the peer had asked.

Smith raised his eyebrows. 'If you mean their politicians, I've found that "men of genius" are rarely either prompt in action or consistent in general conduct.'

'Is that so?'

'The daydreams with which self-styled intellectual persons amuse their solitude have usually adapted them splendidly for esoteric speculation, but it's a habit of mind that renders them unfit for the helm of state. You see, contemplative indolence spoils a person. And I think it would be a perfect hell to be ruled by philosophers of that kind.'

'Are you saying that *you* are a man of genius?'

He laughed. 'If they're saying that, then it's with considerable irony, my lord. If you'd have brilliant thinkers as opposed to sophists, then I'd say let French politicians well alone. You would do better to rescue that celebrated chemical fellow, Monsieur Lavoisier. He's a tax-farmer by profession, and he's made an enemy of Marat, so he's as good as dead, which would be a great crime.'

The peer had then evinced more enthusiasm for the sciences. 'Scholars have recently determined the age at which a human brain becomes truly the brain of an adult.'

'And what age is that, my lord?'

'What would be your best guess, Smith? – I beg pardon, I should say Sir Sidney.'

He had taken the enquiry at face value, not knowing how else to take it, replying, 'In my experience, my lord, most young men, midshipmen at least, are ready for a semblance of responsibility by the time they are fifteen or sixteen years old. Much, however, depends upon the individual.'

'The scholars say the crucial age of maturity is four-and-twenty.'

There had been something appraising in the other's expression, so that Smith had begun to suspect some oblique reference was being made to his record, which was the swiftest promotion to post rank to date. He said mildly, 'So late in life?'

'Oh, yes. Until four-and-twenty, so they say, our main faculties are adolescent, and therefore untrustworthy.'

'My lord . . .' He paused just long enough to give a shade of emphasis to his words. 'In that case it is perhaps a sobering thought that when the Right Honourable William Pitt was my age he had been Prime Minister of Great Britain for three and a half years.'

Before moving away the other had cracked a yellow smile and tapped the side of his nose. '*Quod erat demonstrandum*, Captain Smith. Ha. Ha.'

The steam pipe gurgled and belched, throwing up an obscuring cloud. Smith considered the way events had turned. Something about the ancient peer had called his mind to action stations, but then Charles had reappeared and distracted him from pursuing the suspicion that some intercourse of the highest importance had just taken place.

In the next moment Charles had got him alone and thrown him off the scent entirely, first insinuating about the changes that he had seen in him, then trying to prise him open as if he were an oyster.

'You often think of France, don't you?'

'I'm sure I don't know what you mean.'

'Sidney, admit it. Once you were extraordinarily single-minded. There was a sort of ruthlessness about you that had people in awe. You were very predatory. But now . . .'

He smiled as if at a compliment. 'Am I not still?'

'Well . . . no.' Charles wrestled to put the observation into words. 'You appear to me to have turned somewhat introspective.'

'If you want a receipt for my ennui,' Smith said, rousing himself to his old outrageousness, 'it's that I recognize that the most penetrating insights of the most brilliant minds of government are in fact on a par with my own hum-drum thoughts and utterances on a day when I feel slow and reluctant. That's how I know I'm made of more visionary stuff than them – and why it irks me to have to deal with their blunderings so respectfully. They should promote me to a command and save themselves a lot of trouble.'

'Bravo!' Charles clapped his hands languidly, 'But . . . I detect that your heart's not wholly in it.'

He snorted. 'Creeping maturity.'

'Nonsense. I knew a man who was wounded once—'

'Wounded?' He echoed it, falsely bright, but the drink had been in him and the echo had died maudlin in his mouth. 'Well . . . I was in love then.'

When Charles had broached the subject last time, he had, with revealing understatement, admitted he had once or twice wondered what might have become of the girl.

Now Charles nodded and gave him a look of such compassion that it triggered him to say something he would never have thought to hear himself say.

'For the first time in my life I cared for someone else more than I cared for myself. It was quite a shock to one who thought as I did. And for it to end as it did – I was not ready for that. I was really very . . . disappointed.'

'You're still disappointed now?' Charles was tentative, knowing he was probing an exposed nerve. 'After all this time?'

He sighed. 'I shall be disappointed, my dear Carolus, till the day I die.'

He felt his brother's consoling hand on his shoulder, and he brightened himself. 'But, don't trouble over me. I've decided that France was, all in all, a good thing. For that's when I began to see there was something more to this life than the satisfaction of narrow and selfish ends. And the French war is now certainly overdue.'

At that moment the old Whig had reappeared and taken up the threads of his dormant conversation with another hypothetical question. 'Then, Smith – I beg pardon, *Sir* Sidney – what of the French?'

He had smiled indulgently at the spritely octogenarian. 'What of them, my lord?'

'I read that the Republicans are voting on questions in their fleet.'

'Questions?' A passing Tory member was hooked by the word 'Republican' and attached himself to the discussion.

The peer revolved his hand, irritated by the interloper, who was of the opposite political persuasion. 'Why, *sea* questions. What to say? Shall the ship set a course north-by-east? Shall the crew reef the maincourse or whatever is the proper term to turn a corner at sea? And so on?'

'Shall we close with the enemy?' The member suggested wickedly. 'Or shall we run away?'

The peer fluttered his eyelids. 'Ah, but you pre-empt me, sir. Let us suppose there is to be a battle. The life of Sir Sidney's youngest midshipman and his lowliest landsman are to be staked on the outcome just as much as his own, are they not?'

They turned to Smith in appeal, and he favoured them. 'In general, my lord, that is quite true.'

'Then . . . are they not first entitled to an explanation of what the battle is to be about?'

'Pooh!' The Honourable Member for Desborough trod him down. 'That, sir, is like saying that the sheep of the fields should be taken on a tour of the kitchen pantry and otherwise indulged with descriptions of their fate. It avails most men nothing to understand their fate, and often impairs their happiness and efficiency through nervous reflection on what is to become of them.'

'So, men of lower station are but *sheep*?' Smith asked with mock innocence.

The member seemed surprised. 'From your own experiences in captaining a man-of-war, you must surely think so.'

'I do not think so, sir, and never have. The Royal Navy generally respects its personnel. Even the lowliest.'

'You *flog* them, don't you?'

'Only for proven crimes, sir. And then in comparative moderation. I venture to say that the men of His Majesty's ships are better fed and housed than most ashore. And one could never control the world's most efficient fighting force unless one was seen to be fair.'

'But you must be able to imagine what would be the result of taking every man jack aboard a frigate into your confidence before a battle, as the French are now said to do.'

He realized that to avoid the tedium of these two buffoons and remain within the bounds of good manners would be impossible. Devil's advocate and drunk judge, he thought, and allowed himself a delicate yawn. 'I do not think the newspaper reports can be correct. For one thing, it would not be possible to run a ship that way, sir. For another, it would serve no purpose.'

The member sprang a triumphant witticism. 'Then what of the Ship of State? Tell me that.'

'Ha! The royal barge is the only ship he has ever seen.' The peer's interjection came with a peevish humour that made Smith roll his eyes. 'And that only from Whitehall Steps. Ha! Ha!'

The member's self-conscious dignity trembled, and he resorted to exaggerated patience. 'I am merely saying that, for whatever regrettable reason, most men are uneducated, and therefore – for that reason alone – they are unable to make the same sense of the world as you or I.'

'They should be lied to, eh?' the peer said. 'Is that what you would propose too, Smith? – your pardon, I mean to say *Sir* Sidney.'

'No, my lord, I would not. When I commanded *Alcmene* I regarded all my officers and crew very highly. They were, for the most part, worthy men. However, they were specialists, and trained to their own main work, which disqualified them from the taking of such decisions as I was obliged to make.'

'But may it not also be said that the captain is a specialist?'

'Again, no, my lord. In my opinion the captain is the one man aboard a man-of-war who absolutely requires a wide diversity of understanding. I say it is the job of a commander to know his ship and the jobs of all his people. Many of our captains leave too much to their first lieutenants.'

The member was flummoxed by Smith's forthrightness. 'Well, sir! Is that so?'

'Yes, sir. It is.'

The peer grunted. 'Not afraid to speak his mind! Ha! Ha! Above all a commander must know human nature, isn't that the case, Smith – beg pardon, *Sir* Sidney. Why when I was a young man—'

The member said, 'La, sir! Then why not hear our expert?'

Smith hurdled the two-edged compliment, sticking to the point. 'It was my duty – and my desire – to see to my people's welfare, which I did as best I could. I took advice from them whenever it was appropriate, but this did not extend to holding a plebiscite on whether or not we should join battle, or what were the virtues of the war. Captaincy is a privilege, an exalted distinction, but it does carry with it the loneliness of responsibility, and necessarily so. A ship cannot be run by a committee.'

'The Swedes seemed to think so, and they were victorious, were they not, hmmm? Your opinion was often made reference to, so you've said. Is that not ruling an entire fleet by committee?'

The member's probe irritated him, and there seemed nothing to lose, so he said what he thought. 'My dear sir, I've seen navies beaten before a shot was fired, beaten merely by the presence of the enemy. Such is the effect of numbers and size of ships on the minds of men not used to the business. Under those circumstances it is in vain that kings and commanders are firm in their resolve, calm in danger, or clear in their orders, if those who are to obey them employ themselves in weighing the probability of success, and making most humble representations, which are neither more nor less than refusals to obey. It is in vain that subalterns are brave, if they are not obedient, which they cannot be with a bad example in their immediate chiefs. In Sweden I was exasperated beyond measure to see so many men in military uniforms without the requisite qualities to be soldiers.'

'Bravo, Smith!' the peer said. 'Bravo indeed!'

The member, disputatious and in his cups, seemed to see the way to bring the argument back round to its origin. 'Then what of our English democracy? Magna Carta? Our parliament, whose rights were so hard fought for a hundred and fifty years since? Shall the people not decide who shall rule them?'

'Tell me which country has a true democracy?' he said. 'Even the United States is a long way from that. Though one may applaud their intentions at least.'

The member was on him again instantly. 'So you applaud General Washington, your late enemy?'

'I believe history will come to regard him as a great man.'

'And great men make the world, do they not? Who can really believe that history proceeds by random leaps and bounds? If it did there would be no progress.' The elderly peer had fixed a watery blue eye on him. The iris carried the arc of old age, but there had also been the glint of a dangerous intelligence. It shocked him that he had missed it. 'You do believe in progress, don't you, Smith?'

'Yes. I do.'

'And you believe that good government necessarily entails the keeping of secrets?'

'Who really knows the truth about anything, my lord?'

His recollection of what had followed was hazy, because he had got drunk soon afterwards, but the last impression was that he had been expertly cross-questioned, and had allowed himself to be drawn on a hundred issues.

What can my beliefs matter? he wondered, nonplussed by the unaccustomed attention being paid to his views. Then he looked up through the long windows to street level and saw one of Almack's occasional but most celebrated members arriving. His suspicions deepened.

Ordinarily Smith would have welcomed a chance meeting with Lord Grenville, but presently he felt less than enthusiastic. Grenville was dangerous because Grenville was a power, and Grenville was also fickle. He was Spencer's chief into the bargain, which gave him a direct lever. I had to endure my brother's political theories regarding the coming importance of the East, he thought dismally. Spencer wanted to rehearse himself before putting his ideas to Grenville, but it's more than I could take this morning to have it all again from the other side. What's going on?

After a few moments Grenville came in, stark naked. He was always artificially brisk and did not suffer fools at all. His conversation was energetic and all fencing. He made a point of cutting subordinates, so they jumped whenever he appeared. It was a character role Smith had rarely seen played so well, but it was a role all the same. Half of those present left the steam room the moment he appeared.

Smith regarded Grenville discreetly, sure that the man's no-nonsense manner was an adopted style, a piece of theatre that bore little relation to the inner man. What's his true nature? he wondered. It was useless to attempt an answer. Who could know what Grenville was like at the core? Neither his wife, Smith suspected, nor even his closest friends, would know much about that.

Grenville opened in characteristic style with a swipe to the head. 'Your conduct at St James's did not pass me by, Smith.'

In front of three strangers it was a hair's breadth from being an insult. 'And good morning to you, Lord Grenville.'

'Your conduct, I say. Hmmm?'

'Conduct, my lord?'

Grenville leaned forward and made his tone confidential. 'The way you covered His Majesty's – aberration. You thought no one had noticed when the imbecile pissed himself, didn't you?'

Smith found himself wrong-footed. 'It was . . . simply a question of good manners.'

'Yes, and manners maketh the man. Isn't that what they say?' Grenville narrowed his eyes at him. 'You intrigue me, Smith. I think you have all the qualities we need. Everyone says you are able. You appear to have a natural understanding of the hard realities of the world –

the *actual* realities as distinct from the myths that most people are content to accept. You are also clever. Though that is in a practical way, a way that many clever people are not. That's the difference between you and your younger brother.'

'My lord, I . . .'

'Yes. I realize I'm embarrassing you, but my time is valuable, and I don't care a twopenny damn about your feelings. Those who dislike you tell me you're notably unafraid to express yourself straightly whether or not it is politic to do so. You'll find me no different.'

A sweltering figure got up and left. There was a space of silence that invited Smith irresistibly. 'You may tell them – whoever they are that *dislike* me so – that I have always held discussion with fools to be a fruitless endeavour.'

'Don't be dry with me, damn you, Smith.'

'My apologies, if I was that.'

'Pitch yourself according to what company you're among. That's my advice to you. You abuse your wit and ingenuity otherwise. And damage your cause.'

'I believe I had to expend more wit and ingenuity commanding the *Alcmene* than has been expended in the last decade in the governing of England.'

Another bather got up and slid out. The steam pipe gurgled and dripped. Grenville ignored the barb. 'Is it perhaps that you feel out of your depth with me, Smith?'

'No, my lord.'

'Then, is it that you think I'm one of your fools?'

He refused the invitation to stab. 'Not that either, my lord.'

'Then be prepared to talk with me on terms of equality.' Grenville's eyes looked him up and down. 'Much as I may regret it, there is a specific need for me to be candid with you.'

'I understand.'

Grenville waited for the other two men to leave the

room. Eventually the heat overcame their curiosity. Grenville made the sign, and Smith returned it, knowing that now their formal ranks could be laid aside.

Smith raised his eyebrow questioningly. 'A little while ago you said "we" – you used the phrase, "all the qualities we need". What did you—'

'And last night you said that good government must often require the keeping of secrets.'

He had suspected that something was going on, but was still amazed that his conversation had been reported to Grenville. 'I believe it does.'

'Recently you've had proof, if you had none before, that this nation is no more governed by a king than are the United States of America.'

'Every country must have its conceits,' he said carefully.

'You know damned well that the king is to England little more than a figurehead is to a man-of-war.'

'Exactly as I would put it.'

Grenville seemed to find the thought appealing, and smiled at it. He got up and walked up and down through the vapours. 'Norman, Frenchman, Welshman, Scot. A Dutchman, a German . . . What does it matter, eh? So far as I can see the last English king was Harold, what?'

Smith stepped with extreme care over Grenville's jocularity. 'There is the question of advice, and that of influence and form, but if we are discussing executive *power . . .*'

'Well? Go on.'

He wondered if he should limit himself to telling Grenville only what the man wanted to hear, but abandoned the idea as too risky. 'I now believe,' he said, feeling his way, 'that since mediaeval times our royalty has become a kind of show, a necessary focal point, first maintained for the sake of keeping the superstitions of the Romish church off the minds of our people, then maintained to allow our trade to prosper in the face of

Spaniards and Dutchmen and the French, and latterly to keep the Union. Since the integrity of Great Britain is now assured, it follows that the illustrious House of Hanover is reduced to something else.'

'So much for your loyal oath, Smith.' Grenville threw back his head and studied the dripping ceiling. 'You're aware that to say our royal house is partly an historical relic and partly a device to awe the lower orders is tantamount to treason in a naval officer?'

'But I am not speaking as a naval officer. And you did say you wanted candour.'

'Well, then, if the kingdom is not governed by King George . . . by whom do you imagine it is governed?'

'Why, by the cabinet, of course,' he said, thinking of the eleven men who managed the realm. 'The First Lord of the Treasury and Chancellor of the Exchequer presently combined in the person of the Prime Minister, William Pitt. By you and your colleagues, the three Secretaries of State for the Home, Foreign and War departments. By the Lord President and the Lord Chancellor and the Lord Privy Seal. The First Lord of the Admiralty and the Master-General of Ordnance. The Lord-Lieutenant of Ireland and the Secretary at War. They decide our national policy.'

'But let us cut the cake another way.' Grenville loomed out of the steam, tapped a marble cherub with his fingernail. 'When you think of political power you must also think of families.'

'Yes. There's the Pitt dynasty, the Dundases, and Yonges, and your own family . . .'

Grenville chuckled. 'A very few families have controlled Great Britain since the Civil War. A very few institutions too – Eton School, certain colleges in Oxford, the Navy, and . . . the Craft.'

Every time Grenville's body passed him, the moisture hanging in the air wafted him with a blast of heat. He reclined sweating, on the grey marble slab, where it was cooler. His apparent lassitude belied his state of inner excitement at what he was hearing. The Brotherhood – the Craft – could count among its membership just about every man of power, influence or talent in the entire civilized world. Of course it made sense that it had a say in the government of nations, but to hear the fact stated so matter-of-factly, and by Lord Grenville himself, was extraordinary.

'Smith, you have been raised through the three degrees, and therefore a certain knowledge will have been revealed to you. It was the duty of your Master of Lodge to have acquainted you with the basic tenets.'

Grenville reappeared from the scalding fog, sat down, laced his fingers together. 'The Church of Rome undertook the raising of our souls from the pit. In the same way the Craft's task has been to set the minds of Mankind on the path to a higher moral and intellectual realization. We have tried to build that which the Perfect Architect would have us build.'

Smith felt a surge of interest and sat up, his entire body streaming with sweat. The clouds of steam had thinned momentarily and Grenville's sweating nakedness was revealed once again.

The Brotherhood's philosophy is one of personal development, Smith reminded himself. It's all about the fostering of good fellowship, and the realizing of the potential that lies within us as human beings. He said: 'I believe I know the ultimate aims—'

'I daresay you do. What you don't know are the means we have settled for achieving them.' Grenville rose and wandered away. He paused halfway down the room. Smith saw Grenville's misty silhouette draw a deep breath and brace itself before continuing. 'Some have called our project "Albion", others "the New Jerusalem". Alas, nothing more can be revealed to you at present.'

He recognized the approach. It had always been the

same among the initiates of the Brotherhood: a veiled invitation laid before him to move on to the next circle of knowledge. An intimation that if he would only ask, it would be given.

Smith wiped the sweat from his eyes, and longed to draw a breath of cool, dry air. He tried to disregard his bodily distress and focus his attention on Grenville but the silhouette had almost entirely disappeared. He glanced down at his fingertips; they had puckered. The humid heat was suffocating, and he realized he would soon find it unbearable to remain any longer among these stifling vapours, no matter how exalted the company or how illuminating the conversation.

He spoke into the boiling fog. 'I've heard there are higher degrees in the Craft, my lord, and I . . .'

But then he heard the door bang and he knew he was talking to himself, and that Grenville had gone.

TWO

LATE 1792
Thury-Harcourt

Berenice had come upstairs to find a little gift, something to distract her young cousin, Catherine, something to make her forget the horrors that had overtaken her. A sudden sensation made Berenice pause at the door of her chamber. Then she heard a noise, the rustling of stiffened fabric and the sound of light footsteps inside the room. She pressed herself against the wall to see through the half-closed door.

Her own heart was beating loudly; she saw the triple rope of pearls at her breast reflecting a nacreous glare as they shivered against her pale skin. The light in this passage where she had played as a child, where she had kissed the only man she had ever loved, was now grey with the gloom of late afternoon and the coming of winter.

Beyond the window panes the garden was deserted, except for the lone, scarecrow figure of Faligan. The two long pheasant feathers in his hat trembled in the cold wind. Davout had been driving fence posts for a month now, rudimentary defensive works thrown up against the outside world at the suggestion of Bonchamps and Rochejaquelein. Weeds had appeared in the lawns, the parterres had gone unclipped, withered flower-heads brown and stark stood now like starving beggars in the rose garden, raked by a wind that rattled the sashes. There was no defence against the poor.

Downstairs the hum of conversation remained ominous. The servants' nerves had been put on edge by the arrival three days ago of the Marquis de Pont-Courlay's household. Berenice remembered how the cook, Madame Cozette, had wrung her hands at the sight of their pale faces, and brought them a hot meal. Since then horrifying gossip had spread from the drivers and footmen to the groom and from them to the cooks and maids.

'Terrible massacres in Paris, monsieur le comte.'

'Those monsters Marat and Robespierre have murdered everyone detained in the overcrowded prisons of Paris!'

'A ruthless purge of all the Jacobins' political rivals.'

'Hysteria!'

'Blood frenzy!'

'It's come upon us at last!'

Two carriages had drawn up at the gates three mornings ago. They had come from Lisieux, mud-spattered and heavy laden, their occupants muffled against the autumnal chill. The horses had been lathered, taxed by difficult roads, routes made next to impassable by the rain. Cousins from a nearby branch of the great dying tree of nobility, she had thought, staring at them as if they had been ghosts stepping out of their coaches. These relatives had arrived to a sympathetic reception. They had warmed themselves by the fire, drank coffee and told harrowing stories.

Fear had begun to seep into her bones when the Marquis de Pont-Courlay had begun to speak. He had paced the withdrawing room as he spoke. Always a rational thinker, he could not understand the reason for any of the horrors that were happening around him.

'Alarm is being spread on all sides,' he said. The skin of his face was taut and sallow. He had lost much of his hair. 'The population imagine bands of murderers where none exist. Malicious, ill-designing persons are going

183

about reporting that this village has been burnt or that family have been cut to pieces. That's how so many have been persuaded to quit their towns and villages, to hide themselves in the woods and wheatfields. They're all terrified of having their throats cut in their own houses. Everyone is arming himself for defence.'

His wife's back was very straight. Her hand clasped the silver knob of her stick like a claw. 'And some are using defence as an excuse to arm themselves for another purpose entirely – to plunder.'

Bonchamps shook his head. 'They're forming themselves into large groups, taking the law into their own hands, cousin. In parts of Orléanais they've started going to the houses of the nobility. They're calling upon us to give an account of our "tyranny".'

The marquise's eyes flashed away from her husband. 'That's what they called it. Uncle Joubert was never a tyrant!'

The Comtesse de Bernay looked up, her eyes red, her hands wringing in her lap. 'The justice they gave us was to burn our house, and assassinate poor Joubert.'

The Chevalier de Martel's face had been bloodless, watching his niece begin to cry. He had later admitted what he had seen done to Joubert's dismembered body. The memory of what he said had terrified Berenice so completely that she was certain she would not be able to sleep tonight. The chevalier had been delicate in earshot of the ladies, but his words had been specific enough. Berenice had dreamed in hellish detail how they had raised Uncle Joubert's head and empty ribcage aloft on a pike, a ghastly, dripping bust, the arms dangling limply from the shoulders this way and that. The bloody trophy had stared with wide-open eyes, and a wide-open mouth that seemed to howl with the swelling crowd.

'We always treated our tenants well, yet this was how they repaid us.'

'The better you treat them, the more ferociously they

turn on you. One of our most trusted men stole my pocket watch from me. Then he wished the Republic down on us before I saw the back of him.'

Catherine, just twelve years old, had continued to stare at the wall wordlessly. Her mother said that she had not spoken since she had been raped.

'There's no reasoning with them. Nothing stops them. There's no restraint any more. No government.'

The Marquis de Pont-Courlay's face was more lined than she had ever remembered it. 'It's always strangers who act as their leaders. They call themselves Jacobins. They're the spawn of the devil!'

The chevalier turned to Berenice's father then. He said, 'There are only two alternatives left to us, Charles. To seek safety in a foreign country as so many have already done—' He looked away, allowing his gaze to extend through the long window and rest like a promise on the distant hills to the south. His back straightened in a way reminiscent of the Marquise de Pont-Courlay. 'Some prefer the defence of their country to the abandonment of it. I count myself among this number.'

Berenice had seen the grim look on her father's face then, the way he had nodded. It reminded her of the day when Smith left.

Throughout the summer she had kept up with the increasingly unbelievable news coming out of Paris. War had come, as she had known it must. Emigrés – refugees, flooding into the imperial fief of Trier on the Moselle had been the immediate cause. There had been an exchange of diplomatic insults, then France had declared war on the Austrian emperor, who had instantly allied himself with Prussia in a coalition against the political cancer that had destroyed the heart's flesh of Europe's greatest nation.

The news the refugees had brought was so shocking that the world seemed suddenly unreal, like a dream. France was plunged into chaos of a kind that would have

185

been unimaginable a few years ago. Last month the royal family had been besieged at the Tuileries by a mob. Twelve hundred had died, two thirds of them the king's Swiss Guards. After that the National Assembly had deposed King Louis. Then it had fallen itself, to be replaced by the Convention, the body that had declared France a republic. Their ideals sounded magnificent, but the reality was the precise opposite. Now the nation was being run by the Paris Commune – a venomous lawyer called Robespierre, and his Jacobin radicals.

Alone in the silent corridor, Berenice crossed herself. She asked herself how long this bad dream would go on. How long would it be before the world returned to normal? Where will it end? she wondered, but just as soon the answer came to her. It won't ever end, because it's not a dream, and because that's the nature of jealousy and self-seeking, and the lust for power. The devil himself is in Paris, hardening the hearts of men and twisting their minds. A great evil has been unleashed on France, and it will not end until we're all dead . . .

She fingered the pagan cross, and it made her think about the Englishman's love for her, and the love she had had for him. It was possible to look back on the inexplicable affair now and see it fondly, though not quite painlessly. It had receded into the past, and it felt like something from that remote world that dwelt down the wrong end of the telescope. That summer she had felt an emotion so strong that it had changed her. She had felt incomplete whenever she had been out of his presence, so much so that the separation imposed by her family duties had amounted to cruelty. How could it be that something meant to be had not happened? It was a mistake. God's mistake.

She recalled her confidences last summer. Admissions made to Madame Cozette. She had talked while the cook had cored apples and nodded in sympathy.

'I feel there is a hole in my heart. A nothing where once something was.'

And what had prompted her to reveal herself? The apples! Apples – from that wonderful orchard where Smith had waited for her. Apples, it might have been, from the very tree where he had carved her name and his, enclosed in a heart, saying that it was one of the most solemn customs of England so to do . . .

Berenice forced a breath, and put away the aching memory. She looked out of the window and thought of the orangery where she had lost her virginity. Last time she had gone there she had found the roof fallen in. Miles away over the wooded horizon, she thought, as far to the east of Paris as this garden is west of it, war is burning. At least it's a timely war. At least it has saved me from marriage.

She tore her gaze away from the view and passed on along the corridor. When she reached her own bed chamber and opened the door she saw a figure posing in front of the mirror. Whoever it was wore her finest ball gown, and was laughing.

'Agnes? Is that you?'

The maid turned instantly, shocked. The laugh of private and conspiratorial delight ceased. Agnes was stunned to be discovered so brazenly made up and flaunting herself in her mistress's gown.

'Agnes . . . what are you doing?' There was disappointment in her question, rather than anger. She saw from the sly expression on Agnes's face that she could not find a suitable explanation, but suddenly the maid's expression changed and she turned back to the mirror, examining herself again, this time in a thoughtful, preening way.

'This dress suits me quite well, don't you think so, milady?'

Berenice felt her anger rise. 'Take it off.'

The insolent face regarded her in reflection, head and

shoulders adorned by the gilt frame of the mirror. 'That's not what you said when you borrowed my bonnet to go to Cancale with your Englishman.'

'Take it off! At once!'

Agnes danced away from her. 'Ah-ah! You should be more respectful, citizeness,' she said emboldened by her mistress's words. 'Yes, more respectful. You should do a bit more asking, and a bit less giving out orders.'

'Agnes, have you gone mad?'

'Mad? Not me, citizeness. I've just come to my senses. Like a lot of people just lately. We've let ourselves be pushed around by the likes of you all our lives. We ate bread while you ate the meat. We drank water while you drank champagne. We worked in cotton rags while you walked around in silks. We've taken it all, and said nothing – for fear of losing our livings.'

'Agnes, whatever references—'

Agnes's eyes narrowed. 'Yes, that was always the threat, wasn't it? Because without *references* we'd never get employment in any other great house. You're bloody bastards and foreigners' whores, the lot of you.'

Berenice opened the window and shouted, 'Davout!'

'That's right, call bloody Davout. You can depend on that dumb animal, all right. He'll never answer back. He'd follow you all the way to hell, so call him while you still can.'

When the massive gardener appeared at her door, his dull eyes gave no hint that he had taken in the situation.

'Davout, Agnes is very upset. Please guard the door, until she has changed her clothes. When she has done so – but not before – you may escort her below stairs. Do you understand?'

The gardener nodded his massive head once.

'Agnes, I will talk to you when you are calmer. This is a difficult time for everyone. It makes no sense for any of us to lose our good temper.'

It had been a stupid incident. Nothing to get upset

about. But on the way down the stair, Berenice had found herself trembling so violently that she had almost missed a step.

THREE

Smith examined the enamelled cross of the Order, and turned it over in his fingers thoughtfully. He felt an echo of the slap that once reddened his cheek, and the embarrassment of it burned him until his mother appeared.

'So William. Now you have your knighthood.'

He grinned at her loftiness. She was only put out because he had had a perfect explanation for his behaviour at Court. 'You must call me Sir Sidney now, mother.'

'You shall always be Baby William to me, sweet lamb.' She looked askance at his medal. 'Insignificant little thing, isn't it?'

'A small cross of white metal hanging on a blue ribbon, but it's the key that will open a good many doors for me.'

She looked over her shoulder at him, unable to resist the enquiry. 'And did Sweden solve your other problem?'

'What?'

'I mean your heart's sickness. I'm sorry to have to mention it, but you were in pain, were you not?'

'I was. But all that's over now. Mother, I very much did as you told me – or rather my heart did. I found myself another. Oh, mother, you cannot imagine how it was. She was quite exquisite . . .'

'Your heart, William, was by fate designed never to be free from passion.' She rang for tea, and he knew she would not be put off. 'Who was this young beauty from the north who was capable of perplexing and inflaming you so vehemently?'

He detected the scepticism in her voice, and tried to counter it. 'Her name was Aurora, Countess of, ah, . . . Köningsmark.'

'And what was she like?'

'To an eminent birth, mother, she joined the most astonishing bodily graces imaginable.' He fell silent.

'Go on, then, describe her to me!'

He sat down, shrugging. 'I'll try. Her size was moderate. Her shape rather free and easy. An unparalleled delicacy and regularity was to be seen in the features of her face. Her teeth were so nicely placed and of so beautiful a colour that they could scarce be distinguished from a row of pearls.'

His mother shook her head. 'A row of pearls?'

'Yes. And that's not all. Her eyes were black, but also bright and full of fire and tenderness. Her hair, that was of the same colour, set off most exquisitely her beautiful complexion, like a very fine carnation. Her neck, breast, arms and hands were very white.'

'Nature seems to have exhausted all her charms in this lady's favour.'

'Ah, but . . . to all these uncommon bodily perfections she joined equally uncommon faculties of the mind. She had an engaging address, her jests were diverting, her banters most pleasant, she had a bright and lively knack when describing the character of, or ridiculing, a person.'

'Uncommon ideas expressed in an uncommon manner, I suppose?'

'Just so.' He began to suspect his mother of irony, but pushed on regardless. 'Mother, I tell you she was incomparably gallant. No opportunity for generosity passed her by. Also, she never thought herself too much troubled to do me favours. There was no animosity, no spleen in her. What more can I say? She forgave and forgot all offences, was humble, modest, and . . .'

'Did she speak English?'

'Er, no. But she spoke French, Italian and German languages just as well as her own Swedish. She even knew some Latin. She loved music and grandeur and diversions, was well acquainted with history, no less with geography, and understood all the fables and fictions of ancient writers. I thought her the very mistress of polite literature.'

'Is that so?'

'Absolutely.'

'Then London society will be unsurprised, William, to find that she captivated your heart.'

'Oh, but you mustn't tell a soul.'

'And why not?'

'I conceived an instant passion for the countess, but alas . . .'

'Alas?'

He smiled and shrugged. 'Married.'

She scowled and returned to her list of names. 'William, you're as transparent as window-glass to me, and the most appalling bad liar to boot. You swore to me that you wanted to go to Sweden to get the Frenchwoman out of your soul. And, as I suspected, you've done nothing whatsoever about it.'

'Mother . . .'

She rose, picked up the Order of the Sword and looked at it. 'It is a pity the demoiselle Berenice de Sainte Honorine du Fay cannot be here with us today. As it is, she can know nothing of your great successes – nor how accurately you remember her.'

'John, thank you for coming.'

William Wyndham Grenville, latterly Home Secretary to His Majesty's Government, presently Foreign Secretary, welcomed his visitor with the relaxed warmth that he reserved for members of his family.

Sir John Pitt, Second Lord Chatham, presently First Lord of the Admiralty, entered the study, sat down and waited for one of Grenville's servants to pull off his boots. Like Grenville he was in his mid-thirties, with the same penetrating grey-blue eyes as his younger brother, the Prime Minister. He had only walked a few yards along Whitehall from Admiralty House, but his boots were new, and the leather stiff.

He's worried, Grenville thought watching him. His mother's a Grenville, and I know what a look like that means.

They passed a few forced pleasantries, then glasses of port arrived. After the first sip, Grenville asked his visitor's opinions about the Continental war.

'It's a bloody mess, and growing bloodier by the day,' Pitt said. 'Since France declared war on the king of Austria the situation's got completely out of control. And we can blame the Girondists for that . . .'

Grenville agreed with Pitt's sentiments. In the spring news had come from his Paris embassy that the Girondin party had obliged the French king to dismiss his ministers and appoint their men instead. King Louis had been forced to appoint Demouriez at Foreign Affairs and de Grave as Minister of War.

'They've made Lacoste Minister of Marine, and put Roland in at the Interior Ministry,' Pitt said gloomily.

Grenville sipped at his port, remembering that dispirited meeting. He had said, 'It's the Jacobin Club that causes me to lose sleep, what?'

Pitt had snorted. 'Mad dogs, the pack of them!'

The Jacobins were the most virulent section of the popular party in Paris, the cabal most responsible for smashing the Great Design to renew the state of France.

'Yes, the Jacobins're our greatest worry – violent idealists and as infectious as any disease – and they're also making clever moves. By forcing a declaration of war on Leopold they've locked France irrecoverably into war with us.'

Pitt had flashed him a glance, then looked dismayed. 'Irrecoverably? So, you think as I do now?'

'Yes. Leopold may be the Holy Roman Emperor, but more important than that he's Marie Antoinette's brother.' Grenville had compressed his lips, feeling the bitterness inside him stirring. 'The Revolutionaries've thrown down the gauntlet deliberately.'

Now Pitt regarded him with the same baleful look that had been in his eyes six months ago. 'You know my brother would keep us out of a war at all costs?'

'God willing, he may succeed – for a few months. But eventually he'll have no choice.'

'You think they'll send Louis for trial?'

Grenville grunted. He stood up and dismissed his attendants, then slipped the bolt on the door and made the sign of the Brotherhood. He leaned forward and whispered. 'My dear fellow, I think Louis is about to be tried in the worst possible way. I think they'll feel obliged to *execute* him.'

Pitt's eyes searched his face in alarm. 'Well, Brother Grenville, you'll recall what I said a year ago. Even then the Design had been pushed so far into instability that Brother Lafayette had no hope of recovering it. All efforts since then appear to have been in vain.'

Last summer Brother Lafayette had marched his National Guard to the Champs de Mars, the Hyde Park of Paris, to disperse a lynching mob. They had flown the red flag of martial law, but hysteria had overwhelmed the people. Radical elements had taunted the Guard until they had opened fire on the crowd. Fifty unarmed people had died in the fusillade.

Since then, Grenville reflected, the situation had gone

from bad to worse. Impoverished émigré armies had mustered on all the borders that surrounded France. At Coblenz on the Rhein, at Baden and elsewhere, tens of thousands of Frenchmen were assembled. Badly led, badly equipped, more of a burden to their hosts than a threat to the Revolution.

They're an army of haughty and frivolous nobles, Grenville thought, creatures of the *ancien régime* – aristocrats who, if the latest reports are to be believed, have a greater inclination to fight among themselves than to turn back the Revolution . . .

But a Revolutionary decree in July had pronounced the French homeland in danger. Queen Marie Antoinette had been accused of passing secret messages to her countrymen, the Austrian enemy. By August they had deposed her husband, after a bloody fight at the Tuileries, and proclaimed a new rule, 'the Convention'.

Grenville looked sourly into the empty fire grate. A display of dried grasses and oak leaves rustled in the draught that came down the chimney. Pine cones and wooden balls carved in the likeness of pineapples stared back at him. 'The whole experiment has become a stinking morass, what? An outcome worse than any of us imagined.'

Pitt gestured hopelessly, his dismay seeming to turn to despair as he faced the truth. 'Yes. And now it's slipping into disaster.'

Grenville studied Pitt's countenance and reflected that now was not the time to bring up the question of the state of unreadiness of the navy. It would be wise to spare Pitt's feelings and in any case there was a more important matter to discuss.

He looked up after a suitable lapse of time. 'So, what did you find out about our Swedish knight?'

A fleeting smile lit Pitt's face, but Grenville could not decode its meaning. The First Lord drew out a file of papers. 'Ah, *Sir* Sidney . . . a fast riser under Admiral

Rodney. Quite the apple of the old man's eye. Yes, certainly that – if I recall correctly, the youngest post captain we've yet known.'

Grenville's next question was incisive. 'Was it through interest, then? Or merit?'

'Largely through merit, it seems.' There was a grudging tone to Pitt's voice. He looked up. 'I daresay you know my cousin's wife is his aunt?'

Grenville raised an eyebrow. 'Lady Camelford?'

'The same.' Now Pitt gazed back with what seemed false innocence. 'Tell me, why are you really asking after him?'

'His name has been put to me in a *particular* connection.'

'By whom?'

Grenville paused for deliberate effect, then said, 'By the Grand Master.'

Pitt took the port from his lips and set the glass down. His demeanour changed. 'Oh.'

'Brother, what's Smith's record?'

'Apparently he's that rare thing a *blemishless* naval officer, who is, I've heard it said, very good with the lower deck. Had command of the frigate *Alcmene* until she was paid off in 'eighty-five.'

'Has he seen any action?'

Pitt consulted his papers. 'A few times – as a middie, in the action off Cape St Vincent, then in two or three actions against de Guichen. And twice as a lieutenant, under Charles Thompson in the *Alcide* off the Chesapeake and in the operation at St Kitts.'

'Any as commander?'

'None. He was just too late for the American war. He was posted down to Antigua in the *Alcmene*. He was put on half pay in the spring of 'eighty-five after he brought her home.' Pitt gazed back in his unsettling way again, but this time Grenville caught a glint of amusement in his eye. 'And then there are these . . .'

Grenville took the papers, looked at them. They were unofficial reports, closely written in a neat hand, with diagrams and sketches. They seemed to be detailed reports on a variety of coastal works: Normandy, Gibraltar, Morocco . . .

'Fancied himself as some sort of freelance Admiralty intelligencer for a while, before going off to Stockholm in search of laurels for his brow.'

Grenville felt the stirrings of irritation. 'He was in France . . .'

'Yes, for a while. The Secretary says that he was always pestering us with his views on the likelihood of another war, and giving his considered advice on how we might prepare for it.'

Grenville smiled narrowly. 'You don't like him very much, do you.'

'I don't know him,' Pitt said carefully, but Grenville continued to regard the First Lord in silence until he made his admission. 'Well, since you ask, Brother, it's the *type* I don't like. He's impertinent. And an attention seeker. I have the impression he's annoyed quite a few by panting so desperately after glory.'

Grenville breathed in the rich, sweet odour of the port. Smith's obviously brilliant, he thought, and what's more, he knows it. His great fault, and it is a great one, is that he has hardly any modesty. That's the part you can't stand, John Pitt. You never could, even when we were at Eton. I know your record – when you were serving in the 86th Foot in America – and it's hum-drum. You're a reasonable First Lord, but Smith is of another calibre entirely. The way he reacted to cover the king's embarrassment was absolutely astonishing. It's time I went to see the Supreme Master.

Grenville put the port glass down. 'Did you know that his younger brother, John Spencer Smith, is one of my chosen men?'

Pitt seemed to feel himself caught out. 'No, I didn't.'

'Spencer's a very clever fellow. I have it in mind to accredit him ambassador sooner rather than later.'

Pitt's interest stirred. 'Where?'

'The Sublime Porte.'

'Constantinople?'

Grenville smiled, correcting the delicate balance of what he could say to Pitt as a friend, what as a family member, what as First Lord of the Admiralty, and what as a Brother of the Craft. 'Seems Spencer Smith has an affinity for the Turks – if you take my meaning. And, now that the Russians are no longer occupied by the Swedes, I have a mind to let him indulge it.'

Grenville entered the study that always smelled to him of lavender and polished leather. He made and received the sign, and was no longer in the company of a peer, or a soldier, or even a subject of the king, but of a Brother, and the most perfected Brother of them all.

The news from France was terrifying. Marat, Danton and Robespierre were the tribunes who had taken control. They were doing all they could to stir the people up and turn them against the National Assembly. They had set up a star chamber and maintained an army of thugs whom they bribed to do their bidding with what they had stolen from the Tuileries.

An intercepted letter had reached him from the salon of Madame Roland, wife of the man who had been designated Minister of Marine only half a year before. It had been meant for the deputy, Bancal des Issarts, and described the massacres of two months ago.

> If only you knew the dreadful details of the killing
> expeditions. Women brutally raped before being torn to
> pieces by these tigers, guts cut out and worn as ribbons,
> human flesh eaten dripping with blood. You knew my
> enthusiasm for the Revolution. Now, I am ashamed of it.
> It has become hideous. It is forbidden to leave Paris. We
> are being shut in so that we can have our throats cut at

their convenience. Adieu! If it is too late for us, save the rest of France from the crimes of these madmen.

Bryce, the Supreme Master's servant, and a Brother himself of Secret Degree, came in. He lit the lamps, bowed and went out again almost unnoticed. Grenville strolled to the wide-open garden window, took a deep breath. The early evening air was soft, the sky pastel washed. The dark lawns were freshly scythed; the Green Park chestnut trees were in bloom like towering, unlit candelabra. He heard the sound of iron-shod wheels – hand carts negotiating the cobbled lane of Catherine Wheel Yard in the dying light.

The Supreme Master said, 'Ah, what a glorious piece of work is London.'

'Mmmm.' Grenville was silent for a long while, appreciating the moment, then he turned. 'This scene has some quality that reminds me of a picture I bought at a print shop in Broad Street some time ago. A sketch drawn by one of the owners. An artist ... William somebody-or-another ...' He tried to remember the man's surname, and failed. 'At any rate, I found out he was apprentice at a Lodge near Poland Street. His is a most mystical talent. He has lately taken to poetic flights concerning the French Revolution and the nature of America.'

'Flights too close to the truth for your comfort?' the Supreme Master asked. 'You want to know what's to be done with him?'

'Oh, no. He's no threat to us, after all he is a Brother. I merely think his talents could serve us better were he made more *aware*.'

The Supreme Master tapped the rim of his brandy glass. 'Then I shall enquire if his Lodge judges him ready to be initiated to a higher degree.'

'Brother, I think you know that Mr ...' He sought the name and this time found it. 'William Blake's artistic and poetic endeavours are really not why I'm here.'

'No? The defection of Brother Lafayette to the Austrians, Perhaps?'

Grenville scratched his chin. 'Our diplomacy has already guaranteed his safety in Liège. No, it's about the Turkish mission. I think I may have come across exactly the right man.'

'Where did you find him?'

Grenville started, then smiled at the coincidence. 'Why, I never thought of it, but I suppose it was in a Turkish baths.'

FOUR

Thury-Harcourt

The mob came to the château with beating drums in the middle of the afternoon. Berenice watched them from her bedroom window. There was already a name for what they were doing – they called it 'the Terror'.

Late January mists clung to the banks of the River Orne. The mob carried fire-brands to light their way through the gloom, fire-brands and pikes and other weapons were raised, some with bundles impaled. They came steadily up the Caen road, close by the river. There were hundreds, some of them local men singing raucously, some were obviously drunk. They arrived at the house, assembling as if for some fête before the tall, iron gates.

The dogs were barking at maddened pitch, driven there by the sense of danger. Berenice watched the Revolutionaries gather. She wanted to tell them that they had chosen the worst possible time to come to Thury-Harcourt. The Comte du Fay and most of his loyal establishment were four leagues away at Conde, organizing the defence there with Bonchamps and La Rochejaquelein. Part of her was filled with a cold fury that wanted to throw open the windows and harangue them defiantly, but another part of her knew that there were seven women in the house and that incitement would make things worse.

She moved behind the curtain, and watched the crowd swell. The wall surrounding the house was no more than fifty paces away. It was head high, but they could scale it if they chose to. Instead they just milled about. Half a dozen zealots shouted out to the servants, calling on them to open the gates and join their comrades. Berenice wondered if any of them – Agnes perhaps, or one of Madame Cozette's kitchen helpers – would be sufficiently intimidated to come forward. She prayed it would not happen, for they would shower any defector with congratulations and that would raise jubilation and excite the mood of the hotheads still further. Perhaps they'll be content just to hurl insults at the house and rattle the gates. She clung to the hope as a hideous carnival atmosphere began to develop. The ringleaders chanted and danced the carmagnole.

'Ça ira! Ça ira! Ça ira!'

'Tremblez, tyrans! Et vous perfides!'

The words were unmistakable – encouragement to the Revolution and exhortations for tyrants to tremble. She could hear them despite the frenzied barking of Brutus and the other dogs. She began to dare to hope that the mob would content itself with a demonstration. Don't unleash the dogs in the grounds, she prayed. Please God, don't let anyone do that. They'll go wild. Then she recognized the bundles on top of the pikes, and knew what it was that had put the dogs into so uncontrollable a state. They could smell human blood. The bundles were people's heads.

Her mind was so repelled that she could not make herself believe they were real, but what else could they be? She gasped, her mind racing now. My God, she told herself, it's all true! The worst is not rumour – they're glorying in their murders. They're really going to kill us. Oh, God save us all!

She started from her panic as a hail of stones came against the façade of the house. She heard the sound of windows breaking, saw her father's gamekeeper, Faligan, break from cover and run for the house, a long musket in his hand. Somewhere in the house her sister began to scream hysterically. Suddenly shards of glass exploded from the window pane. Berenice stood, paralysed with fear, as she watched the stone that had come through the window roll onto her hearth rug.

The sounds outside were louder and clearer now. There was a musket shot, and it seemed to act as a signal, because when she dared to look she saw agile figures climbing the iron railings, and the mob heaving in rhythm against the gates. Then the gates burst open, and dozens of people were spilling onto the carriage drive.

Berenice felt pure horror as the crowd closed on the house. Her eyes stayed on a man who was dancing madly in the vanguard. Both his hands were aloft, one holding a loaf, the other a long knife. An expression of insane rapture was on his face. She remembered what the Chevalier de Martel had said about Uncle Joubert's body being spitted on a pike.

How can they hate us so? she wondered, aghast. What have we done to them that we deserve it? We are rich and they are poor, but none of us have maltreated any of them – far from it – father is known famously for his charitable giving, and our tenants have never been left in want when prices were high and others were starving. Does this count for nought? If so, the whole world has been seized by the Devil.

She watched the lusting crowd invading her home in a turmoil of noise and destruction. She saw women and children among the rioters, red-capped and ragged. Sansculottes – literally 'those without breeches', because knee breeches had been declared the symbol of feudal subservience and universally replaced by trousers among the Revolutionaries. They streamed forward, a monster of demonic destruction.

Berenice did not move. She could not; she had lost the use of her limbs. She had heard of the ferocious acts of the Marseilles Battalion, those terrible shock troops of the Revolution whose wild provocation had caused so much bloodshed at the Tuileries in the summer.

Rumours spoke of columns of men streaming out of Paris, men mobilized by the Commune to resist the Prussian army in the north, but in reality to thrust the Revolution into France's own reluctant provinces. The vilest scrapings of Paris, the filth of the whole city and of all the gaols – idlers, thieves, maniacs, murderers – all had been deliberately armed by an insane government. These were the demons they had unleashed on the quiet towns of the west. They carried a mandate to murder and raze, to torture, to empty the gaols and dispossess all those of property or standing.

She recognized some of the local people caught up in the frenzy. They were ordinary people: peasants, fishermen, millers, blacksmiths, innkeepers, house servants . . . Individually they were civilized, but their coming together had created a howling monster. They were rushing across her father's lawn, a tide of evil, brandishing knives and bearing on high the standards of the Devil's own army. They kicked down terracotta urns and smashed the lovely statue of Aphrodite, stamping it to pieces with such venom that she cried out.

She was shaking uncontrollably, but then revulsion rose in her. Revulsion at the stupidity of it. She saw, as they could not, how in a week, or a month, or even a year from now, these same mindless braggarts would be cringing and begging for mercy from an even more hellish gang of leaders. But you will receive none, she thought. Don't you see that? Because that's the nature of the madness that makes devils of men.

She felt the violence of the mob breaking against the house itself – the terrific sound of the ground-floor windows being shattered and their frames pushed in. Wild yelps and heavy thuds came, this time from inside the house. War cries. She turned to see her mother and Celestine clutching one another at the top of the stair.

'*Mother*!'

The hoarseness of her own scream amazed her. Her mother did not see her, nor come towards her. Berenice shouted again, frantic that no one should catch sight of them. She realized that the advance guard were intent on looting the treasures of the house, and were not yet climbing the stairs.

'In here! Quickly!'

Her mother and sister were both white-faced and shaking. Both had been made stupid with fear. They stumbled against each other in the gallery, not knowing where to go or what to do. Then Berenice heard lumbering steps coming up the stairwell, and knew there was no time. She dashed forward.

'*Mother*!'

She pulled them both into her dressing room, but her mother stumbled and fell on the threshold as the door was slammed and it caught her hem. Berenice fumbled with the fabric, but it would not come free. Nor would it tear away. The noise in the gallery swelled. The light spilling from beyond the door dulled, and she felt a physical presence on the other side, the fine hairs on her neck erected like needles, and she braced herself against the door, frantically motioning Celestine to do the same. But the force that came against the door was irresistible.

A huge strength drove them back like children, so they sprawled back, cowering in terror on the carpet. But no red-capped Revolutionary appeared.

'Davout!'

The giant gardener bent down and tore the hem from Berenice's mother's dress as if it were tissue paper, then, picking her up, he deposited her on the bed. Berenice was at the door instantly, slamming and locking it. She looked around for something with which to prop the door, but could only see a chair. She jammed its ornate back under the handle, then began to feel around the rococo decoration of the gilded panel beneath the bookcase.

Château Thury-Harcourt had been built during the endless reign of the Sun King, when religious and political factions had fought one another for favour. The prudent architect had provided for every eventuality. The concealed entrance led into the secret chamber that Berenice had played in as a child. Inside, it was dark, a musty, narrow space sandwiched between two walls of rough-mortared brick, all dust and cobwebs. There was just enough space for three.

Appalling yells came up the stairs as the servants fought for their lives. They were being slaughtered. Then an axe-head slammed through the door and was levered out.

Berenice pushed her mother inside the hole, then her sister. The secret panel was in Davout's hands. He waited for her to climb inside, but she hesitated to leave him to certain death. The axe struck the door again, this time shattering the panel and sending wood splinters flying across the room. Two violent kicks and the lock gave way.

As the door flung open Davout turned and stepped forward. Berenice saw him thrust his hand at something or someone and struggle briefly. The axe rang to the floor, then Davout had his opponent in a stranglehold. The victim was big and muscular, but he was dwarfed by Davout, who shook him then threw him to the floor so that he landed at Berenice's feet. She tried to grab the dazed man by the hair, but Davout took him by the shirtfront and crutch and lifted him bodily, this time throwing him full at the window. He crashed through it in a shower of shattered glass and disappeared.

Berenice stared at the gaping hole where her window had been, then, as she recovered from her astonishment, she saw the red woollen bonnet that now lay on the carpet. She picked it up.

'Davout! Wear this! Save yourself!'

The gardener, slow to be roused and equally slow to calm, refused the hated symbol, but she screamed at him. 'Davout! For my sake, you *must*! If you still love the family du Fay, wear it! It is your duty to make good your escape! Go to Faligan's cottage, if you can.' She squeezed his great hand as hard as she could. 'Promise me you will do that. Davout, promise me!'

This time he allowed it. The Phrygian cap sat on his great head like a child's. For the first time she heard him make a sound, a deep rumble but enough to seal the promise.

She climbed inside the secret chamber. Then Davout bent to replace the panel, she saw his troubled face, then all became blackness.

FIVE

NOVEMBER, 1792
Dover

He had come here to make a final decision.

It was five o'clock in the afternoon, but the November sky was dark and the grey sea wild beneath it. The figure that stood on the strand was gazing at the horizon, despite the biting wind. Boats were drawn up on the shingle like a line of giant beetles, and just above the high-tide mark an ingenious house made from the upturned bow section of a wrecked ship stood defiant against the weather. A rag of smoke issued from the tin chimney and the glow of an oil lamp escaped the opaque glazing.

The sight of the place sent a poignant memory into Smith's mind. His early youth had been spent in the boat-house in Dover, the one everyone called Smith's Folly. It had been all his disgraced father was able to afford at the time, but they had been memorably happy times.

Despite the cold he felt very warm inside. He had spent half an hour throwing pennies for ragged local children to scramble for. Partly for amusement, partly to test the hypothesis that it was better to give than to receive. That had been impossible to answer, but it was certainly an activity that fed some region of the human spirit. Exactly what region it was hard to tell, but it had been more warming than spending the money on a bottle of liquor.

Beyond a certain point, he concluded, recalling the Brotherhood's wise teaching, there's really no direct relationship between wealth and happiness. So long as a person has enough of a material nature to sustain life and to maintain a few comforts he has every chance of happiness. Thereafter the pursuit of wealth becomes nothing more than the indulgence of greed.

Other factors . . .

He felt the ice tighten round his heart again, driving out the temporary warmth. Its grip had been there for years, something faint and forgettable, at other times squeezing until his whole inside ached.

They tell me time is supposed to be the great healer, he thought wryly, then laughed. Mother knows me too well. Too well.

War's coming. It's certain now. Only a matter of time. Six months at most before Pitt stands up in the House. Doubtless I shall have my ship. A fine frigate. The *Ceres* or the *Winchelsea* or the *Hebe* – he had submitted plans to the Admiralty for a new design of floating batteries to carry two long twenty-four pounders and two sixty-eight-pound cannonades. So what else is there for me? Only the sea. And duty. Hopefully honour. Hopefully rank. Or at least recognition. Perhaps prizes. Perhaps glory. I must ask what best can I do for my family? What for my country? What for the Brotherhood? What for mankind?

But he heard a tiny voice nag at him, 'What best for you, William? And what for her?'

It had come to the point where he dared not think of her. Throughout the autumn the news from France had been bad. His stomach had been churned and his sensibilities revolted time and again by the reports he had read in *The Times* and the *Public Advertiser* during September. The Prussian army had entered France. Longwy had fallen to them, and they had threatened the fortress of Verdun, the last defensive line before Paris.

The panic-stricken Commune had ordered a hasty general mobilization of troops that had almost emptied Paris of Jacobins. Those who remained had seen the prisons bursting with their political enemies, awaiting trial. The Commune's Committee of Surveillance circulated false reports that the inmates were plotting a mass escape, and when the panic was at its height the vile Marat had called for their slaughter.

The beach was deserted. His boots crunched down over the ridges of pebbles and wreaths of sea-wrack. Wind-whipped spume flew off the rollers and freshened his face. She must be dead, he thought for the first time, staring in the direction of the invisible French coastline. I could discover no news of her family among the community of émigrés in London. They say that excellent fellow Phelypeaux is serving in Condé's army with the Austrians, but the Comte du Fay has not come to England. The word is that Normandy has been the special target of the Revolution. Ergo . . .

The wind tore tears from his eyes. He felt his breast seized by pain, and he held the little silver figure in his hand ready to throw into the grey breakers as a kind of remembrance to someone he had never been able to forget.

The probability was that the monsters had murdered her.

PART 5

The Iron Forge

WINTER, 1792
Paris

*Ah, monsieur, how you have neglected your chosen one.
I had begun to doubt that we would meet again. But
now we are here again, together. Paris has been a
maelstrom of blood! You will excuse my great buoyancy
of mood, but I suppose this is an effect of the extraordinary new energy of which you spoke. It is a marvellous
gift, and one for which I thank you, for so much more
can now be achieved.*

*Why do I call you 'monsieur', instead of 'signore'? It is
simply because while I am in Paris I choose to adopt the
French mode, nothing more. I have also been considering a modification of my name. The 'di' sounds too
Italian here, too much tainted by aspirations to the old
nobility. Things being what they are, I shall have to drop
it.*

*In settled times I certainly would have been executed
for treason. But these are not settled times, are they,
monsieur? I knew there was war in the air in France. I
could smell it. All sorts of rotten political matters
simmering in the capital. I knew the most daring plan
would be to come here, direct to the heart, to explain
myself in person. A little finessing. I claimed the right to
do so before Paoli. And Paoli – the old fool – just
shrugged and approved my going. He thought they'd
shoot me as soon as spit, you see.*

*When I arrived in Marseilles the first thing I heard was
that we had declared war on the Austrians. At last, I*

thought, we're carrying the Revolution beyond the borders of France, making all the crowned heads of Europe quake with fear. I knew very well that nobody in the Paris ministries would have so much as an hour for my insignificant case, let alone the time to expend trying me for high treason.

That was the time I began to doubt you, monsieur. In Paris melancholy crowded in on me. I had neither money nor position. Everything you promised me had vanished in an instant. In France I was a petitioning Italian nobody, a suspected traitor, a deserter to boot. Quite a comedown for a man who two months earlier had been a lieutenant-colonel.

I've found Paris too expensive. I pawned my watch, and for the first time in my life I'm in debt. That's why I began drinking. That's why the last embers of my idealism have been stamped out. I listened to you when you told me that youthful ideals such as I used to have were an impediment, that I must root them out. But I needed to see at first hand what the shining principles of the Revolution had become. I needed to see the degradation for myself, before I could crush it out of me. You see that, don't you?

It did not take long for Paris to do that, monsieur. This city, even then, was all insanity. Law and order had broken down. Criminals and the filthiest of the lowest classes were roaming the streets, sporting the red bonnet of the Jacobins, but really only out to grab what they could by way of plunder. I learned the lesson very well then: that you can always rely on self-interest.

Oh, you put the city in a fine state. Let me tell you, Paris, even when I first went there, was chaos. Now it is complete insanity. You remember that once upon a time I was as ardent as anyone for the Revolution? Well, no wonder. I was depending on the fall of the King to save me from the firing squad. But I hated to see what was happening out there. Louis Bourrienne and I watched *that huge mob overrunning the Tuileries, hurling insults at the royal family. We saw the Montmorency dragoons and the Swiss Guard threatened by a rabble of civilians. Utterly astonishing! It demonstrated to me that without leadership the finest of troops are just a line of uncertain children.*

I thought: if the king would only show himself on horseback, he'd send the canaille *running. I felt the mood that morning. What fools! Why didn't the king order his guns loaded with grapeshot? What folly to treat scum like that with forbearance. If a few hundred of them had been shot down, the others would have cleared off soon enough, I'll tell you.*

It wasn't long after we last met that I received the marvellous personal news that you forecast. You said that my twenty-third birthday would fall five days after Louis Capet, King of the French, was dethroned. You were absolutely right! There was to be a new, republican assembly, called 'the Convention', but you know the Commune are really running things now. Monsieur, I cannot tell you how I despise the common people of Paris. Anyone who sees what is going on here must admit that the filth need to be controlled by the army. They're creating chaos, ruining everything. They are base and malicious, none of them seeks anything but his own advantage, and everyone tries to push his way into the first rank.

But to tell you of my marvellous news: there has been one very shining outcome for me, this summer. The king – for that's what people continued to call him even though he was locked in the Temple prison – was obliged to appoint Servan as Minister of War. And he wiped my record clean, saying he would offer me a captain's commission.

Don't you see? I can be French now. And I've come back here just as I said I would. I'm a French Revolutionary captain, and in charge of six thousand French volunteers. Vive the Republic, one and indivisible! I'm going to claim my homeland and smash Paoli. He would rather sell out to the English than submit to France. But I intend to grind his face into the dirt for the way he treated me.

You see this bottle? It came from Louis Capet's own cellars. What do you think of that? I saw thousands emptied then smashed outside the Tuileries, so that the place seemed to be paved in emeralds. I have been saving this one for a certain occasion. Please, monsieur, you will drink a little with me? We shall down half each, then you may treat me to some more of your wonderful oracular presentiments. Excellent! Ah, you know what they say in England, don't you? In their navy they have this grim toast: 'Here's to bloody war, and fast promotion!'

Salut!

ONE

'The King is to be tried,' Berenice whispered. 'The National Convention have appointed three commissioners to gather evidence against him.'

She saw the whites of Celestine's eyes in the gloom. She was shivering.

'The king? It can't be true. For what crime?'

'Treason. That's what they're saying.'

'Oh, no!'

'Why not?' She heard the flatness in her own whispered voice. 'The people have thrown off the yoke of political servitude, and with it the law and all morality. The truth is now whatever they say it is. They will put the king through the humiliation of a trial, they will find him guilty, and then they will kill him. What else do you expect?'

She saw how the emotionless cut of her voice had brought Celestine to tears; her mother sobbed, aghast at the idea. For a perverse moment Berenice enjoyed the cruelty of it, feeling superior. She recognized the feeling of emptiness that they were suffering. They're not used to it, she thought, her mind cool and crystal sharp. They don't know about loss. But I do. I've lived with emptiness for years.

The whole royal family had been jailed at the Temple prison in Paris. The king, his sister, young Louis his heir, the queen, the princess royal, Mademoiselle Elisabeth

217

. . . Then, in the same month, at Valmy, the Prussian advance into France had been turned back by General Kellerman, and all hope of the nightmare being ended by the forces of the outside world had been stamped out.

A shaft of flickering firelight came from the loophole that overlooked the front of the house. When she pressed her face to it she saw people below. They were walking back and forth in front of the house, past a bonfire that cast hideous shadows and sent sparks up towards her. She saw the chill breath rising from them, felt the cold draught against her face.

Warm your hands, good people, she thought, hearing her mother offering an almost silent prayer for the fate of Louis of the House of Bourbon. Yes, warm your hands by our funeral pyre. It is apparent to me, if it is not to you, that others will warm themselves by your pyre soon enough.

The worst of the violence had passed in a chaos of looting. Her mother had become hysterical. To save them from discovery Berenice had lain with her hand clamped tightly over her mother's mouth until she had passed out. She had come round, moaning softly, but since then she had not uttered, except in prayer.

Looters had come into the bedroom, their voices loud and wild. They had ripped out everything, destroying whatever they could not remove. Through a crevice that acted as a spy-hole into the room she watched her drawers and cupboards being flung open, women rummaging through her clothes and jewelry, grabbing combs and perfume, trinkets and undergarments. Fighting one another to stuff their pockets in an orgy of thieving. She heard someone shout urgently, 'Get the carpet! Get the carpet!' Then others had come, smashing wine bottles on the bare floor, one of them even urinating against the walls. Then they had moved on, all but a young boy, no more than seven years of age, who pulled a thick rope of pearls from his shirt, polished them for a moment, then put them away and left too, disdaining a room where nothing remained to be stolen.

What had happened to Davout? What had happened to Faligan and Agnes and the other servants? Were they dead? Suddenly she remembered hearing Gugnot's threats the morning of his dismissal.

His face had contorted, and his voice had sounded supernaturally calm. 'I say I did not steal your watch, monsieur le comte. You sent Dugommier away for that crime. Now you have accused me and found me guilty without cause. If you now send me away I shall have no means to live. Please . . .'

'I repeat, Gugnot. You are dismissed.'

'Please, monsieur le comte!'

'Get off my property!'

She remembered the servant's eyes the moment Faligan had been called. His face had been white with a mixture of frustration and rage and desperation, then his anger had broken out, signalled by a stabbing finger. 'A new world is coming! I shall tell that world how you have mistreated me! I shall make sure you are called upon! I shall have my redress. One day, monsieur le comte, I shall have my redress!'

How fully those predictions had come to pass. Perhaps it was Gugnot, she thought, who had showed the mob the way here. She felt the pearls she had neglected to remove. When she took them off they gleamed dully, and she bit gently on one of them as she thought, feeling the peculiar graininess against her teeth, before putting them down her dress, where they could not be seen.

Celestine moved closer to her, whispering. Her face signalled she was anxious that their mother should not hear. 'Berenice . . . what if they – what if they should try to burn down the house?'

Berenice stared back at her. 'Don't even think of that, Bébé.'

'But what if they *do*? We will be burned to death.'

'Shhhhh.' This time Berenice looked into her eyes to give her courage, and was reminded of the night some months ago that she had told Celestine how she had read of the sudden death of Herr Mozart. He had been thirty-five years of age. Celestine had cried.

'How?' was all she had said.

'It says here – a fever.'

'But he was surpassing himself every year.' There had been tears in Celestine's eyes, and an injured sense of justice. She had risen and left the room, accusing Père Fournet in the doorway, 'How can God have robbed us of so much beauty?'

Perhaps you have known loss, after all, Berenice thought, relenting. Suddenly she felt her own self-indulgence, and recalled what the religiously inclined Adeline de Hergevault had once told her: 'Help others if you would help yourself.'

She hugged Celestine. 'I know you are scared, but the worst is over. We will get away from here. In the early hours. When they have gone to sleep. We will escape. I promise you.'

In the failing afternoon light she had watched them carrying off carpets and chairs and paintings of her ancestors, some slashed, others intact, all still valuable because of their huge gilt frames. Ornaments, kitchen utensils, crockery. There had been a frenzy of greed. No one had wanted to be left out. The wardrobes had been ransacked, the beds stripped of their covers and mattresses. She had seen two men fighting over the tall case clock that had stood near the foot of the stairs. They had fought until it was broken, then they had abandoned it on the lawn for some other prize.

Throughout the grey afternoon she had sat in the darkness, cradling her mother's head, and going at intervals to the loophole until, eventually, the monster had begun to dissolve, its parts melting slowly back towards Caen, carrying away the booty.

Enjoy your Rights of Man while you may, good people, she thought ironically, staring down now at the blazing pile of broken furniture and the wine bottles scattered all around. You know your Rights well enough, but which of you has considered what will be your Duties? Now that your priests are gone, and your landowners dispossessed, now that you have murdered your king. What will you do with your freedom? Who will lead you? Which of you has even thought about that?

She shivered at the thought. *Who will lead. . . ? Who will be your new lords, for lords there must be? The chief Revolutionaries? The Jacobin theorists of the Paris commune? Marat? Danton? The brothers Robespierre? Maybe. But they will eat one another alive, for that is in the nature of such men. And what will happen when the Revolution, like Saturn, has devoured all its children? Inevitably there will come one strong man. That's what happened in England a hundred and fifty years ago, when they cut off their king's head. After Charles there came a Cromwell, and after him another Charles . . .*

Her eyes followed a severe figure in black, his tricolour rosette and sash marking him out, as he approached the fire. He took off his kid gloves and gave orders to ragged men who carried muskets with bayonets. His manner was authoritative.

You see, she told herself silently. It's happening already.

The night air was cold, and a feathering of snow began to fall, haloing the fire like fairy dust. It was the kind of snow that fell in fine flakes which seemed to disappear instantly into the ground leaving no moisture behind. Strangely it did not console her at all to think that these naive children of the Revolution who warmed their hands below would disappear into the ground in exactly the same way. It was foreseeable only because it was inevitable. Once it had been avoidable, now everything was inescapably heading for tragedy. It was all such an unnecessary waste, but no force in the world was strong enough to stop it now.

Firelight flickered on to the ceiling of their narrow cell. She listened to the sounds, straining to hear. Her bedroom seemed to have been abandoned. It was impossible to see even half the room from the spy-hole, but she had heard nothing moving there for a long time.

My darling, strength of mind is simply a matter of choosing what to think ... That was something she remembered her English captain saying long ago. A valuable lesson, she thought. And it was now time to lend her mind to more immediate matters. First, there was the matter of appearance.

She spat into her hand and patted her palm in the dust, to begin smearing down her sister's hair.

'Ugh, what are you doing?'

'We must look the part, Bébé. Come, mother, you must undergo the transformation too.' She took the pins from her mother's hair and removed all trace of the colour from her lips.

'God help me,' her mother said, and began to languish in pity.

'That's it,' she told her kindly. 'Cry your best tears. They will help wash the rouge and powder from your face. You'll see.'

'We must comb down our hair and dirty our faces, mother,' Celestine whispered. Then she turned to Berenice. 'But what about our attire? These are finely made gowns. They will know us straight away.'

'I don't think so. Half of those down below are wearing *la mode du Fay* tonight. We shall wear one another's – filthy them, rip them, undo them. We shall be a little mussed, a little *déshabillé*. Do you see?

Come, take off your shoes and let me dirty your feet, Cinderella.'

Her mother was aghast. 'We cannot go barefoot in the depth of winter, Berenice. We shall *die*!'

She tossed her head toward the loophole. 'Mother, *they* do not die. Nor shall we.'

'But where shall we go? I refuse to move from here!'

'I see you are returned to your old self, somewhat.'

The comtesse clung to her misery as her sleeves were torn from her dress. 'Surely you cannot make a joke of our situation,' she said.

Berenice shook her head. There is only one way to combat pathetic words, she thought, and that is with briskness. My God, I am as terrified as they, but they are depending on me. She said, 'What better way to raise our spirits than with good humour?'

They tried to smother as best they could the sounds of ripping fabric. After a while her sister sighed. 'I'm so cold and hungry.'

'That's why we must go soon. We stand a better chance in the middle of the night.'

'Go *where*?' the comtesse pleaded.

'I take it you have no absolute preferences?' she said, a hard edge in her voice. Her mother looked back at her hopelessly, on the point of tears again. 'Then, I suppose I shall have to make the plans. Are you ready?'

She bolstered their hopes as well as she could, told them how best to go about things – not to carry themselves as if they still owned the house, but not to creep too fearfully either. To be casual, but not to talk to anyone. 'Our mode of speech would be enough to betray us instantly. Try to copy their manners, but try not to catch anyone's eye. And remember, they are not looking for us, and do not expect to see us.'

'Are we to go singly?' Celestine asked.

'It would be best.'

'I dare not.'

Berenice sighed. 'Then we shall go together.'

'But, what if we're recognized?'

'Celestine! We *have* to do it!'

She pushed past to the entrance, took hold of the wooden block attached to the back of the panel, paused to listen for a brief moment, then lifted.

The panel came free and they crawled out into the room. Bonfire light played across the ceiling and cast dancing shadows on the once elegantly painted walls.

'Be careful of the broken glass.'

Their soft, bare feet were already numb with cold. They stepped carefully towards the corridor and were soon at the head of the main stair. The sight that met them there was shocking. The great chandelier had been pulled down and lay like a wrecked galleon on the lobby below. Hundreds of books from the Comte du Fay's library had been scattered across the marble floor, many fine volumes were torn and trampled where they had escaped being heaped onto the bonfire. All the landscapes had gone, and even the walls had been hacked and defaced. The carcass of Brutus, the German guard dog, lay stiff among the bloodied rubbish.

The comtesse gasped, but her daughters took her arms to steady her, and led her down the staircase. A skinny old man in a dark greatcoat and a bicorne hat snored on the bottom step, dead drunk. They filed past him and made for the door to the kitchens. Every entrance to every room they passed showed a scene of total devastation. The library, the sitting rooms and the great hall – all had been ransacked and gutted.

Celestine bent to pick up the case of her beautiful new five-key clarinet that had come all the way from Vienna. The sections of the instrument had been discarded nearby, their keys smashed up. Nearby the brass orrery lay disembowelled. Most of the little ivory balls were missing, and the clockwork innards that had once driven the planets in their orbits were broken and the cog wheels scattered about.

Berenice tried to shield her eyes from the awesome sight of the desecrated ballroom. The hanging tapestries from Arras, the ones depicting the campaigns of Louis XIV, had been torn down, and the plaster behind daubed with slogans written in excrement. The painted panels with cherubim and seraphim had been grotesquely defaced, their eyes and mouths and privates cut out.

In Madame Cozette's kitchen the floor was ankle deep in icy water. The great coppers had been overturned and the tables and counters ripped out. Every useful item had gone. Not a saucepan or tea caddy or pastrycook's whisk remained. Dozens of huge glass jars of preserves had been smashed and all the fittings ripped away in the mad scramble to get into the wine cellars. The portly lady herself was not here.

Berenice saw her mother's agony and helped her wade to the door that opened on to the yard. From there, cutting through the herb garden, the orchard was only a short distance, and as soon as they reached the shadow of the trees she felt her anxieties subside a little. The bare black branches laced the night sky. She could not stop herself breaking a knuckled twig from the apple tree where Smith had carved their names. It was brittle and dry.

The trees seemed so dormant to Berenice in that moment that it seemed they would never come to life again. They waited among them, teeth chattering and breath steaming, until she had got her bearings.

Faligan's cottage was almost half a mile away. She decided it would be safer to cross the five-acre field than to go by the lane. The hedgerows and ditches would protect them, and the field was ploughed, so no one but a fugitive would think to cross it.

They came to the end of the orchard, and climbed the

gate, eventually finding some way to help their mother over it. The rutted earth on the far side was frozen hard under their feet. There were no stars and no moon, and the wind had dropped. As they walked up the hill it seemed to Berenice as if a thick, sound-absorbing blanket had been cast over the sky, an overcast pregnant with snow. It reflected the bonfire dully. Orange light flared like a corona round the Château of Thury-Harcourt, throwing the house itself into silhouette. The towers and spires and chimneys of the familiar roofscape seemed to be on fire too, but she knew that was just an illusion.

Everything else was dark, grey on grey, so they hardly knew where their feet were falling. They struggled on breathlessly uphill, until the comtesse stumbled for the fifth time. Then she sat down, stupefied by fear and conquered by exhaustion. She felt snow begin to sift down again. A fox cried somewhere in the night. The sound was like a tortured child.

'I cannot go on.'

Berenice knelt. 'Then we shall wait until you get your wind.'

Her mother looked at her through the large falling flakes. They were black against the orange glow of the sky. The night was too dark to make out any feature of her mother's face. 'I keep thinking of your papa. What will he say when he hears about his books.'

It was absurd, but Berenice felt the poignancy of the remark knot her up inside. After a while she said, 'Let's go on now, it's not far. There will be food and clothes and the worst of our troubles will soon be at an end.'

But even as she said it she knew that it was the sort of lie people told one another because they could not face a terrible truth.

Then she heard a noise and an unbearable sensation passed up the back of her neck. She turned, and for a moment she could hardly see. She had become aware that there was a figure nearby. A living, moving thing, large and clumsy.

Hope screamed that it was a cow, only a hungry cow, escaped into this frozen turnip field. Let it be a cow, she prayed. Please let it be a cow. But she knew as it loomed above her that it was certainly human.

TWO

Smith sat in the yawl's sternsheets beside Mr Varnham, the owner and helmsman. Two others were aboard, no doubt wondering at a man who travelled with no luggage but a small chest. He lowered his head as the bow slammed into a wave. Spray flew aft, spattered the sail, dripped from his hat.

Ahead, the *Deal Castle*, the ship that was to take him to Jersey, stood hove-to. She had been delayed by the weather. From Jersey it was just twenty miles across the Passage de la Deroute to any landing place he desired. And then he would be in France.

The decision to give up his best chance of a command had been made on the very beach from which he had stepped aboard this little sail-boat, the day before he had read of King Louis's impeachment. Devil take the Admiralty, he had thought. It's their loss, for I'm sure I was not about to spend another year begging to be allowed a damned ship!

He felt the water swilling under his boots, the bits of wave-smoothed gravel there. The notion crossed his mind that it might very well turn out to be the last time his feet touched English ground. The self-monitoring part of his mind detected the outburst of pride, and reprimanded him. It was becoming customary for his Tutelary Genius to speak to him in this way. To react against infractions like these by driving him to think balancing thoughts of humility, or at least to a superstitious respect for the manifold ways the future could unfold to his detriment. Fate had to be propitiated.

Yes, you're quite right, Goblin, he thought, tapping the wooden transom three times, pride goeth before a fall. And he could hear above the noise of wind and wave the words pronounced in his mother's voice. *Pride goeth before a fall* . . .

France and Britain remained at peace, and doubtless would remain thus until the year's end, but thereafter one thing was certain. And even in a nominal peace France itself was in the throes of unparalleled violence. It would not be a safe place for an English gentleman, let alone one asking pertinent questions, offering gold, and perhaps even occasionally attempting to pass himself off as French.

They were fast closing now. As the *Deal Castle* grew beyond the spindrift, her details caught his eye, the Frenchified rake to her masts, the sharp prow, the white wales along her side interrupted in a way that mimicked gunports. She wallowed, so she must be fully laden. Stores and provisions of war for St Helier, he thought.

The news of King Louis's impeachment has sealed the course of events, he thought. Now the Revolutionaries have chosen to try him, they'll have to find him guilty. And once he's found guilty they'll have to punish him. And the punishment for treason is death. So they'll have to execute him. And once that happens His Britannic Majesty's government will not take long to manufacture a *casus belli* – a reason to go to war. It therefore follows that the French have already taken the irrevocable step.

The wind was on the boat's quarter now, and whipping the tops off the whitecaps. Time to turn, he thought as Varnham bore away. He felt the old anticipation, and wished she was the *Alcmene*, and the *Alcmene*'s old crew waiting to pipe the side for him. But that ship was in the Medway with her masts unshipped, and her marvellous crew dispersed and gone, never to be again, and her erstwhile captain was resolved on another mission.

You're coming alongside handsomely, making it easy for your bow man, Smith thought. That means he's a landsman, and no wonder, for the press is active in the ports now, and taking experienced hands off merchantmen in all the approaches.

'Luff up now,' Varnham said.

Ten to one the landsman's never been out of sight of land, he thought. The other man in the boat was another matter. A prize. He knew his trade, his competence was something ten years in the learning, smooth and well-timed as he secured the vibrating halyard. Under his jacket his arms would bear tattoos that could be read by any knowledgeable eye. They would show the man's ships, his history. Six months and he'd be back aboard one of His Majesty's frigates or a ship-of-the-line, an able seaman, and old Mr Varnham would have to bring on another landsman to keep his yawl in business.

They were half a cable from the *Deal Castle*'s lee side now, but still he smelled fresh tar and lampblack, the melted turpentine of her new-daubed yards. It was a smell that tore at his heart. Was it possible for a man to know when he was going against fate? How did it feel to fight against what was meant for him?

The weather was too choppy for a gangway. As the yawl came up into the wind she began to plunge and heel. The *Deal Castle* towered above them. Waves slapped and buffeted against the strakes. Smith's boat-cloak parted to show a civilian coat of sage green. On Jersey he would trust himself to his mother's maiden name and be Mr Wilkinson, or maybe use his old first lieutenant's name of Mr Underhill, while in France he would be . . . well, it was perhaps just as well he had not thought that far yet.

'Bows!'

The end of the flung rope-ladder clattered down, just clearing the water. The landsman balanced uneasily in the bow, stiffly holding out his boat-hook.

'Down sail!'

The lugsail flapped twice then crumpled to be gathered in. Then the yawl was wallowing close by the ladder. Two ropes trailed down and were brought in. The yawl's clinch-work side grazed barnacles off the *Deal Castle*'s green timbers as the chest was lifted up and swayed inboard. Then Smith paid his dues and readied himself at the gunwale. One hand grasped a stay. He leapt for the ladder and got a footing on it.

The mate looped a hand under his arm to help the passenger inboard.

'Now then, zur. You take care.'

Smith's feet found the deck. He felt wrong without his uniform. The ceremony accorded a Royal Naval captain when going aboard a ship was one of considerable respect, and it appalled him not even to be recognized as wholly capable of climbing across a gunwale. He disengaged himself as soon as he could without giving offence, thinking, damn me, if only you knew what you are manhandling, my well-meaning fellow!

'Stand off!'

Someone shouted down to the yawl, 'Belay that, Mr Varnham! Remain alongside, if you please.'

The officer of the watch came up. He spoke to a junior: 'Take the deck.' Then he turned to Smith with a lowered voice. 'If you'll follow me below, Sir Sidney. A gentleman requires to speak with you urgently.'

The remark was impossible. For a split second he was tempted to protest that some mistake had been made and that his name was Wilkinson, but that was so patently absurd that he merely followed the officer down the companionway and into the captain's cabin.

There he was welcomed by a man in his forties, a man with high cheekbones, a beak-like nose, and an air of

231

command about him. He rose partly from his seat, and took Smith's hand in a faint grip.

'A very good day to you, Sir Sidney.'

His voice was acid and nasal. He nodded to the captain, pleasantly enough, but in a way that dismissed him too easily from his own cabin. Short of the *Deal Castle*'s owner, Smith could not imagine what sort of man could accomplish such a manoeuvre.

'I may say, you're the very devil of a person to track down.'

Smith felt both anger and suspicion rising inside him at the man's presumption. He said crisply, 'And who are you, sir?'

'Who I am is really a matter of no importance. Now I think—'

'It's of importance to me, sir! It's a habit I have to know at all times the identity of those who address me so familiarly.'

The other met his eye bleakly. 'Please don't take that tack with me, Sir Sidney. I've been aboard this wretched mudlark's clog thirty-six hours in wait for you, and my temper is not presently at its best. As I was in the midst of explaining, I'm here at Lord Grenville's behest, to ask you if you would be so kind as to accompany me back to London.'

A vision of the *Alcmene* came to him. A ship, he thought, excitement rising inside him. That's it! Grenville's found me a ship! But still he returned the other's graceless stare, and then he said with severity, 'You have a most singular way of making *requests*, sir.'

There was a brief flash of bad teeth. 'You'll pardon me for that, I'm sure.'

'Since you ask it, yes. But if you think I am to come back with you, then you have another think coming.'

'I have this letter for you, Smith.' The deck moved again as the ship was buffeted. A pair of dividers shifted across the chart and fell. The other rolled his eyes and put the letter in his lap while he held a handkerchief to his mouth. He was desperately unwell. 'Oh, this wretched heaving! Is it always like this upon the sea? How do sailors ever *live*?'

'The motion affects some people rather more adversely than others. Most sufferers get over it quickly enough.' Smith continued to direct an unyielding gaze at the other, pointedly ignoring the letter. He had made his decision, and even the offer of a ship would not be sufficient to change his mind. 'Now, sir, you have heard my answer. I therefore hope you will excuse me.'

The other raised his voice with difficulty as Smith reached the cabin door. 'And what would you say if I told you that I am a Stranger who Travels to the West, to seek for That which was Lost?'

Smith took the envelope as if it was a sentence of death. As his fingers tore into the paper he felt an intolerable lump forming in his throat.

Foremost in his mind now was the searching of his soul, the turmoil that had kept him from restful sleep on too many nights. He had finally understood the only way he could be made whole again. The crisis had come as he had stood on that desolate beach at Dover, and once passed it had taken only a moment's thought to decide what he must do. He had set his course irreversibly.

He looked back at the stranger, feeling the intolerable tension of the moment, knowing he must appear to the other as a man looking down into the Crack of Doom. He held out the mutilated envelope. It was torn in two, the letter inside destroyed, unread.

The affront was graceless, tantamount to an insult to the sender, and the messenger interpreted it as such. 'Will you not at least *consider* it?'

'No.'

The other reacted angrily. His voice rasped, ' "For the Sake of the Widow's Son" – did you not hear me say it?'

There was a rap at the cabin door. It opened and a seaman's head poked in. 'Begging your pardon, Sir, but the capt'n says the sea's getting up. Those as might be going ashore—'

'Yes. All right, man!' The messenger watched the door close, then turned to Smith. 'Well, sir?'

Smith softened his tone a fraction. 'Brother, I mean no disrespect, but I *will* go to France. Widow's Son, or no.'

The other's anger dropped away as quickly as it had arisen. His face was hollow, shadowed, almost cadaverous, but those hooded eyes suddenly showed an unexpected measure of compassion. He reached out to touch Smith's arm. 'Brother, please, for your own good – obey and have faith in our higher wisdom, as you promised you would do. Pay me good heed when I say that a different destiny awaits you. You *should* return to England with me. This is your duty.'

Smith faced the man, moved by the appeal, but knowing his own heart very well, and the only way to proceed with honour. He said quietly, 'My mind is quite made up.'

And it was done. The spell was broken. Both knew that it would have been poor form for one gentleman to try to press another beyond so final a statement of intent.

'Then, I am sorry.'

'Yes. But there it is.'

The messenger let out a lingering breath, then nodded sharply. 'You know what this means?'

Smith was touched by the other's disappointment and his regret, but he also detected the faintly implied threat, and that made it easier for him to keep his sang-froid.

'Yes, I know what it means. But I also believe that, at this particular moment, no one is better qualified to shape my destiny. No one.'

'Sadly, sir,' the other said, turning away, bleak with a fresh upwelling of nausea, 'that belief is specious. For you are in no position to judge.'

THREE

November, 1792
Normandy

The ground was iron hard. All day freezing mists had clung to the earth, making the world silent and wraith-like and unreal. Now the watery sun had sunk, and darkness had closed in again.

Berenice cocked the flintlock and crawled forward from her hiding place, the pistol heavy in her hand. The powder in the priming pad seemed to be dry, and the flint was properly knapped and set, but there was no way to check the charge and ball without disturbing them, and there was neither worm to reach down the barrel of the pistol, nor another charge to renew it.

It was last night that Davout had surprised them in the snow-swept turnip field. He had brought with him half a roast chicken and a pair of pistols. Where he had found them, he could not say, but the violent mime had shown her more than enough.

She was cold and desperately fearful of the consequence of running across anyone. Those who lived within five leagues of Thury-Harcourt would almost certainly recognize them. Davout could be distinguished at a hundred paces, and there was no way of disguising his great size.

For the remainder of the previous night and most of today they had lain low in the woods of Bois d'Harcourt while Berenice had formulated her plan. She had explained herself to her mother, who was huddled in a ditch, groggy with cold and fear. 'We are faced with two problems. The first is our own survival: we need to find food and shelter. The second is that father is at Condé.' It was a place some leagues to the south and east of Thury-Harcourt, where the comte was organizing a contingent with other noblemen. 'It is possible that the Revolutionary mobs have not yet penetrated so far up the valley. It is also possible that papa has not yet heard about the sacking of the house. He might try to return there.'

'Oh, no!'

She had seized her mother by the upper arms. 'Listen to me! That is why I must try to warn him. Do you understand me, mother? You must wait here with Celestine tonight. Be very quiet, and do not stray from this place. I will come back for you. I promise you that.'

She had turned to Celestine, offering her sister what advice and encouragement she could. Then she had left at six o'clock in the evening. They had reached the mill a quarter of a league from Donnay half an hour later. It belonged to two unmarried brothers.

'They must not see you. They must not recognize you, Davout.'

Davout kicked the door in and withdrew, and Berenice entered the house, her face tied up in a kerchief, and pistols waving like a highway robber.

She attempted to disguise her mode of speech as she spoke to the astonished man who stared back at her.

'Who else lives here?'

'Only my brother.'

'Where is he?'

'In Caen.'

She stared back, not knowing what to say next, but sure that she must say something, or he would see the fear in her. At last she said, 'We must get safely to the house of the Marquis de St Hubert, which is five leagues from this place. We will have a better chance if you will give us what clothing you possess, monsieur. Your pardon, but we shall also require a sack of your flour and your horse.'

'Not my horse.'

She did not know whether it was the prospect of losing his cart-horse or the fear of what the waving pistols might do to him that caused the miller the greatest pain. His anguish animated him. He waved his hands, and tore at himself, and the fear rose in her like vomit as she followed his demonstration with her pistols.

She could not stop herself from shouting at him. 'Keep still, or I shall kill you!'

'I'm sorry, monsieur,' was all he said, though what kind of monsieur wore the remnants of ladies' hose under a giant's worsted jacket she did not know. Perhaps he was too scared to notice.

She made the miller undress and lie face down. Then she covered his head with a jacket, and Davout came in and trussed him and blindfolded him properly. She changed her clothes as Davout got the horse bridled. She could feel the warmth of the miller's body, his personal smell was in the garments and the fabric was stiff with flour dust. Davout threw a sack of flour across his back and took it outside. Then she went to look in the other rooms of the house for things to fill her stomach and shirts and breeches and whatever else she could find.

'Burn everything by which we may be known,' she told Davout, handing him the torn rags she had taken off. The rope of pearls she had kept hidden in her dress was now safe inside her new shirt.

The miller's struggles to free himself stopped when she reappeared. She approached him.

'You must remain here, monsieur. Whether or not that is agreeable to you.'

He turned his head, blinded and bound, and swallowed hard, but he said nothing.

They set off back to where her mother and sister

waited. On the way Berenice recalled the miller, thinking, was his silence a matter of fear? Either fear of the pistols, or the fear of freezing undiscovered? Did he guess my rank? What would he have done if the power to kill me had been suddenly put into his hands? Would he have killed me? And what would I have done if I had had to fire on him. Could I have done it?

They reached the rendezvous on the fringes of the Bois d'Harcourt just after midnight. She tethered the horse and plunged after Davout, who carried the flour sack on his back. Once in the clearing Davout gave the signal, the hoot of an owl, cleverly made by cupping his hands together and blowing between his thumbs.

They waited for half a minute, but heard nothing. She urged Davout to try again. Again nothing.

Davout mimed sleeping, and she understood.

'They might have. Try again.'

Still there was nothing, and she felt the panic growing in her. What if they had wandered off? What if they had taken fright and—

'Are you sure this is the place?' she demanded.

Davout took a broken twig he had placed in the crutch of a tree and showed it to her. He was right.

'So . . . where *are* they?' She brushed strands of hair from her face. 'Give the signal again.'

Davout made the eerie noise once more.

Berenice strained to listen, but the hideous fear began to seep into her mind that her mother and sister had been taken. She wrapped her oversized jacket closer about her. There was a breeze in the tops of the trees. The sounds were faint. They came and went like the sea. That's what becomes of thieves, they told her. That's what happens to people who threaten others at gunpoint and steal their property and leave them to freeze: they forfeit their good fortune. You're no better than those who dispossessed you.

No! We're different! her mind screamed back. We're not sinners, we're the sinned against. We're the victims!

She strained again, desperate to hear a twig snapping, a footfall, or the rustle of leaves, but all she heard was the faintest accusing laughter and the words 'Victims . . . That's what everyone says . . .'

Davout sat down, slouched inside himself. An hour passed, then another, and he made no move to rouse her. But the night was wearing older. The futility of remaining here was obvious. She knew that once they went from here there would be no way to make contact with her mother and sister again. They were meant to be here, but they were not here. If they were lost there was no way she could find them; if they had been arrested by the Guard there was nothing she could do. Her father, on the other hand, might still be able to escape, given warning.

A simple matter of logic, she thought. But what in life is ever a simple matter of logic. The affairs of humankind are seldom straightforward. I am tired, and hungry and over-wrought by emotion. I don't know what sense of duty drives me to save the life of the man who caused me to be in this world, the man who sometimes made me wish myself out of it, but I must do what I know is right. I must.

Finally, she took herself from the clearing. 'I'm going to ride to Condé, Davout. I must warn my father. Will you wait here for me?'

He stood up, looking forlorn, looking mistrustful of her decision, and she felt suddenly unwilling to go against his instinct. But she did anyway.

The fringes of the forest were dark. The underfoot was treacherous and slick with frost and full of animal holes. She stumbled and slipped on the way to the place where she had tethered the miller's cart-horse, landed awkwardly and skinned the palm of her hand on the flinty ground. She lay there in the moment between accident and pain, blowing warm breath onto her wet, cold hand and waiting for the pain to crescendo and the blood to seep.

Then she heard the voices.

They were dull. A monotone. The horse snorted. Ragged shapes, dark and moon-silvered figures, moved beyond the mesh of coppice striplings. Whoever they were, they were less than a stone's throw away, and they had found the horse.

She waited for them to take their leave, but watched after them. They moved out of sight at a bend in the road two hundred paces away, and it was only by crossing to a new vantage point that she saw a knot of half-a-dozen men gathered on the roadside. They were admiring the prize like so many horse-dealers. She saw a covered wagon, and someone pulling a heavy iron brazier from the back of it. The Guard, she thought. They're putting up a checkpoint. I would have ridden right into it.

She made her way back to where Davout waited, and told him what she had seen. He nodded, and in that moment as she stood almost dizzy with fatigue she felt herself suddenly aware of Davout's great size, and his great power to protect her, and the limitless goodness of his spirit. Instinct – perhaps his, or maybe hers – had saved her.

From then on they made the moonlit River Orne their only guide. They followed no path, but went over hedges and ditches and water meadows like two creatures of the night. By cock-crow they reached a church she recognized. Within a league was an estate of middle size, and a house that she knew to be the parish manor of St Siffren. A distant relative, the Seigneur du Plessis, lived there.

During the last hour before sunrise she recalled the seigneur's visits to Thury-Harcourt in the days before the darkness descended. She had seen him many times, asking favours and advice about his horses. She told

Davout to stand back where he could not be seen, and threw a pebble at the window of the main bedroom.

The window opened, and a head appeared. The title Seigneur made du Plessis, squire, lord of the manor, the major landowner in the parish of St Siffren, and as such gentry, rather than nobility.

'Who's there?'

She tried to make her whisper loud. 'It is I, Berenice.'

No sound of recognition came.

'Berenice de Sainte Honorine du Fay. You remember me?'

There was another space of silence, and Berenice recalled the opinion her mother had entertained of the man as having a calculating and self-centred nature. 'It seems he asks himself a question of every situation,' she had said. 'And that question is: "What is there in it for me?" '

He came down, and opened the door a fraction. 'What do you want from me, citoyenne?'

'Sanctuary – until nightfall.' Though she pleaded, her hopes had already foundered at the guardedness of his voice and on being addressed as 'citizeness'. 'Please, Seigneur du Plessis, I beg of you.'

Again there was the calculating pause, then the rumbling voice, gruff with reluctance. 'Ah, this is not a good place to hide. The whole area round here's thick with Revolutionaries. You've picked a bad time, citoyenne, you surely have.'

'I did not pick the time at all, seigneur—'

'I am to be addressed as "citoyen" now. Listen, I cannot help you. I'd like to, naturally, but you have no idea of the risk we should both run if I did. Believe me, I'm only thinking of you, citoyenne – the risk you would run in remaining here would be insupportable.'

'Will you not take me in? Into your barn at least. I am freezing!'

'I can't help the weather.'

She had come to the telling moment, and she faced him with a single hard question. 'Why?'

'The reasons I've already given lay me under the hard necessity of refusing you. I'd go towards Condé if I were you.'

He stepped back, and she suddenly felt her weariness, her wet stockings, the ache in her limbs, her hunger. 'In that case – citoyen – I'm sorry I called at such an inconvenient moment. I am surprised you are so little inclined to help me, after all my father did to advise you in the matter of bloodstock.'

The seigneur muttered another refusal, before he closed the door fully.

'A little food, perhaps—?'

She knew she had timed her appeal wrongly. She had let her desperation show, then she had accused him. She had failed to secure any advantage at all. Du Plessis's cold ingratitude had infuriated her, and the pleading she heard in her own voice. Well? she demanded of herself. What do you expect? You know nothing of begging or persuasion.

She banged on the door with the heel of her hand. Amazingly it opened again, but this time du Plessis's pale face was taut with anger. 'The world has changed, citoyenne! I told you to leave! Go now! If you do not I will call the *gens d'armes* down on you.'

The door slammed. She heard the barking of dogs somewhere at the back of the house and knew it would be useless to persist. She felt like weeping, but the anger was too hot in her breast. Instead she threw up her hands, and returned to Davout.

'Come on. At half a league from here I know there's another gentleman, Monsieur Hergevault. He's over seventy years old, and is laid up with the gout, but with him lives a spinster, his niece, Mademoiselle Adeline. She is known to all my family.' She sighed, refusing to lose hope. 'She is a person to whom I have in the past rendered some essential services.'

Davout looked at her as if to ask: what does that count for, since gratitude has been abolished?

She touched his sleeve. 'I know, Davout. The light of the world is going out.'

He shook his head and pointed to the golden disc of the sun that had lifted itself above the marsh mists, and seemed to say: then shall we bend our steps that way, my lady?

'In daylight the getting there will be all the easier. The difficulty will be in finding Mademoiselle Adeline. The chances of her being at the house may not be so good.'

It seemed strange travelling in the light of day. The danger of being seen by anyone with authority to stop them had given way to the need to find a refuge. Her imagination plagued her the whole of the way, but Davout's looming presence a half pace behind her right shoulder gave her confidence.

'Thank you, Davout,' she said softly. 'You are a great comfort to me.'

She heard him grunt, and realized how much of his thoughts she could interpret from his wordless utterances. She smiled, her eyes filling close to tears, and found the strength to laugh at her predicament. 'Not many of those we might meet on this road would dare to annoy you gratuitously.'

They arrived at the house within the hour, seeing no one on the way. She again told Davout to hide himself, then she began to throw pebbles at the window of the room in which she thought Mademoiselle de Hergevault slept. The window opened and a voice demanded to know who was there.

'A friend.'

'Friends are rare in these times. I do not know you.'

'You do not recognize me, Adeline?'

On Berenice's speaking her name the spinster withdrew her head. Without another word the window closed. Berenice stared up at the sky-reflecting panes, the ache in her limbs making her sway on her feet. She was so tired that she wondered if she had just imagined Adeline looking out, but moments later she heard two bolts being shot back and the door opened.

'Quickly. Come inside.'

The lobby was hung with rugs from India and decorated with strange oriental weaponry. Berenice explained what had happened and asked for shelter until night.

Adeline de Hergevault put her hand to her mouth, shocked, then hugged her. The woman's pinched features were unbeautiful. She was not yet forty years of age, but her face was careworn. 'Of course you shall stay here.'

'What about Davout?'

'Who?'

Berenice called him, and he came.

The spinster glanced up at the massive frame of Davout. 'Do not make the least noise. Go up into my chamber. Not a soul must know you're here.'

They climbed the stairs and Berenice was revived by the sight of the fire that burned in the grate. As she sat down beside it she began to feel the blood flowing once more in her legs. Her stockings were clotted with mud and stuck to her legs, her feet swollen from having travelled continually in wet shoes for so many hours in freezing weather.

Adeline said something to her, but she found she could not make sense of it. She realized that she was for the moment beyond speech; she and Davout had gone two days and two nights without sleep. Adeline began to undress her by pulling off her coat and then her shoes and stockings. 'Poor kitten, you're quite frozen! And half starved.'

She went downstairs and returned with bread and butter and a bottle of wine. They ate gratefully, Berenice's own manners ludicrously genteel next to the ravenous wolfing of the giant gardener. She saw the spinster glancing at Davout with a certain amazement.

'Excuse me, Mademoiselle Adeline,' she said, remembering her manners. 'May I present Monsieur Davout? He is a man who does not make unnecessary conversation. His special genius is the care of formal gardens, but, as you may know, there has been little call for his skills of late. He has been my loyal protector.'

'I'm sure of that,' Adeline replied faintly, still watching him. '*Bon appétit*, Monsieur Davout.'

Davout grunted, his mouth stuffed. He lifted the bottle in a toast.

Berenice said, 'He bids you "Salut!" mademoiselle.'

After a few moments looking anxiously out of the window the spinster took the empty glass from Berenice and her expression hardened. 'My dear, I think you have no idea of the dangers you have negotiated in coming here.'

'I'm sorry to have put you—'

The spinster tutted. 'It would be against my faith, which I still hold dear, if I were not to help a friend in distress.' She gave a little shrug. 'It's quite simple.'

'Mademoiselle Adeline . . .' She began to shake. 'You are so kind. But we must go. I cannot put your life at risk. I think we would all be killed if I was to be found here.'

'No, no, my dear. Too often have I prayed to God that I might have someone to care for. In this way He has given His answer, therefore nothing shall intimidate me.'

Berenice felt a vast tide of relief overcome her. The love in the woman's heart was real and unconditional.

'Fortunately, my *femme de chambre* is no longer in my employ. No one else comes here. I shall lock you in this room and you may sleep.' Turning back to Davout,

Adeline said, 'Monsieur, please avail yourself of the adjoining room. It is my dressing room, and has a small bed. It may be somewhat inadequate for you, but there is nothing else.'

'Adeline, you are a true saint.'

She smiled at that. 'No, I'm not that. I just try to do unto others as I would have them do unto me. Whatever happens just stay in your beds. Don't make the least noise. The National Guard comes daily to investigate every house, but I have treated the men well, and so in consideration of that their searches here are quite cursory. If God wills it you shall remain unmolested.'

'One day I shall repay you, Adeline. You may count on that.'

The spinster made small of the suggestion. 'I already have my reward.'

Berenice tried to remember when she had last been in bed with her clothes off, but the thought drifted away from her and she slept dreamlessly.

FOUR

Cancale

The grey-green waters were marbled white with foam as Smith made his landing in France in the early morning. November seas were churning, surging against the sill at Cancale as they reluctantly ebbed. It was so different to the high summer of '87 that he could easily tell himself this was another place.

An accident of stars, a damned conspiracy of fate, had brought him here from Jersey. Gone was that strangely comforting sense of inevitability that a man felt when he was in tune with events and treading the path that his destiny decreed. Yes, he thought bad-temperedly, it's the Goblin, chastising me, telling me – as if I need any telling – that I've broken a sacred trust and wilfully thrown my due fate up to the skies like a boy or an imbecile. My guide's deserted me and, by God, I feel his absence.

It was no good pleading that his conviction had been so very strong back on Dover beach, or that he could not possibly have been mistaken. The power of self-deception was very strong. In truth he had closed his mind, lost his sixth sense, and therefore his way. In consequence the mission that had seemed so essential had turned into blind stumblings.

I've begun it, so I'll see it through, he told himself stubbornly for the tenth time. Fortitude! This is no time to let doubts plague you. Away with them!

247

But inside he knew it was all going wrong. How, he could not say. But he *knew* it was so.

He had first felt the pangs watching that cadaverous figure departing down the side of the *Deal Castle*. He had wanted to call him back, but his pride had stopped him. The final proof had come yesterday when he had noticed Monsieur Marcouf. He had seen the fisherman regarding him suspiciously from across a St Helier street, unable quite to place him. But he, Smith, had placed the singular-looking Frenchman instantly. In a way, he had been half expecting something of the sort to happen. And, of course, it had. Here was proof perfect that he was in for a stormy time. There is no such thing as coincidence! So what are the odds against my meeting in Jersey the very same man who ferried Berenice and I to Cancale? He had asked the Goblin that, quite flat. But the Goblin had not deigned to offer a reply.

He looked up now, one hand holding his hat, eyes slitted against the wind, breath steaming in the cold. The hovels and cottages hereabouts were shut up tight against the freezing blow, their whitewash weather-streaked, their chimneys bleeding grey smoke into a greyer sky. It was winter. Even so this Cancale was very different to the place he had visited during that scorching August which he had spent in paradise. Cancale had changed; he had changed too.

He asked the Frenchman what had been happening in his country, but either Marcouf knew very little, or he would not say.

They walked together up the slipway as soon as the boat was secured.

'I know that war is coming, monsieur. I can feel it in my bones.'

'I think your bones tell you the truth.'

'But they cannot tell me when. Can you, monsieur?'

Smith shook his head. 'Very soon.'

'That's it, then.' Marcouf said it like a man regretting the passing of summer.

Water dripped from Smith's hat brim. 'I need to hire a horse.'

'My brother can help you there, monsieur.'

In the stable yard he protested when they would not take a guinea from him. Marcouf asked him only to carry a parcel of children's clothes to his married sister who lived at Vire. 'The town is on your way, monsieur. She has been waiting for three months.'

'I will be pleased to do as you ask, but . . . three months? Why did you not send it to her sooner?'

'There are new laws. People are not permitted to travel to another district without papers.'

Smith shook his head at the devilishness of it. 'Extraordinary. You require a *passport* to travel a dozen leagues to Vire, a place in your own country?'

'That is so, monsieur.'

'Whereas I, a foreigner, may come and go as I please.'

'Monsieur, you do not belong to Paris.'

They entered the stables. The best mare was unclipped, but she looked sturdy enough and adequately well shod. They wrapped what baggage he had in sailcloth tarpaulins. As Smith mounted, Marcouf warned him, 'Be on your guard. The countryside is no longer safe.'

'Thank you, Marcouf. And God keep you.'

He left them without looking back. Ahead was the beach, grey skies full of icy drizzle, muddy sands revealed by the retreating tide. Under the mare's hoofs were worm casts and small holes that bubbled crab spittle, rags of seaweed that had been torn loose by the weather and cast up. Out to sea nothing moved, except the distant surf line and gulls knifing the sky.

He picked his way around the bay from which appeared the astonishing abbey fortress of Mont St Michel. It brooded there, a full mile from the beach, connected to the mainland at high tide only by a narrow causeway. Marcouf's brother had warned him that the Mont was garrisoned by the Guard now. The Revolution had expelled the monks. Now everyone knew it as the 'Sea Bastille' – those ancient dungeons and oubliettes, he said, had become home to the least fortunate of France's political prisoners, cold hells of iron and stone in the Abbey undercroft.

For a while the precipitous structure stood reflected in the wetness of exposed sands, a vision drained and colourless, the indistinct silhouette seeming to him like a ghostly mediaeval apparition, unable fully to materialize. He recalled the night some five years ago when he had climbed the stone stairs of that citadel, watched by a hundred gargoyles – monstrous, Gothic, intimidating. He had eaten in the ancient refectory, and the prior had told him how English armies had besieged the abbey in the days of Henry VI, until a vision of St Michael had appeared to Joan of Arc, saying, 'I am Michael, Protector of France. Arise and go to the aid of your country!'

The prior's voice echoed in his mind as he looked across the waste of water. The man had been proud, proud and elderly and full of mysterious regrets. When Smith had asked after God's opinion on revolutions, the prior had said simply, 'His burning eye sees all.'

Where are you now, St Michael? Smith wondered, melancholic with the memory, his face raw in the wind as he looked back. Where are you now, when your France needs you?

He spurred the mare on, and cut inland, galloping over the polders towards Avranches, covering the first of the miles of forest and field that separated him from Thury-Harcourt.

The inclement weather had ruined the roads, but it had kept such people as did not need to be abroad indoors. He wondered how he would fare if he should be stopped, but he took care to avoid the places where checkpoints might be found, and by late afternoon he had delivered his parcel in Vire, enjoyed for an hour the hearth and hospitality of the family of Marcouf's sister, drunk a little soup with them, and then taken his leave, coming as the gloom gathered to the rolling hills around Clecy.

He recognized the brown, loamy soil of the district. The River Orne cut through the land like a rusted ribbon in the day's last light. The river was rain-swollen and as turbulent as his heart felt inside his breast. He knew that he had only to cross the river by the bridge below him, then to follow it north for just a little way now to arrive at the château, and for the first time he allowed himself to think of what he would do when he arrived, what he would say, and how.

The sight of the river and the bridge triggered a flood of feelings, and his hand trembled on the reins. He knew that at the next bend he would see the roofs of that noble château, just a few more yards. He stopped the mare, made her stand a moment, breath steaming from her nostrils into the cold, still air, while he composed himself. But suddenly he was jolted by the realization that he was being watched.

He whipped his head round and saw two ragged men step out onto the roadway. One carried a musket, the other a cutlass. When he looked back he saw that the road ahead was also blocked by two men. These each carried a pair of cocked pistols.

The mare felt him tense up, and reacted to the fear that swept up into his belly. She began to stamp and sidestep under him, wanting to bolt, and he had to pull back hard on the reins to control her. Perhaps it's the Guard, he thought, then dispelled the notion as too wishful. For a split second the idea grew in his mind to spur the mare on, to run her directly at the two men ahead, but there were four pistols levelled at him, and if any one of them was primed he would be blasted at close range as he passed.

'What do you want?' he asked in French, trying to put as much authority into his voice as possible. He put out his hands. 'As you see, I am unarmed. I am carrying nothing that could be of service to you, save the clothes that I wear.'

One of the men came from behind and grasped the reins.

'Get down.'

He knew the moment of decision was almost upon him. As soon as the man with the two pistols lowered them an inch he would spur the horse forward. 'I told you – I have nothing for you!'

Then he saw a fifth man step out. He wore a heavy cloak and boots, but there was something about him that made Smith pause. He was tall and lean and fair, and to Smith's astonishment he caused the others to put up their pistols. Then he made a sign of recognition.

'Brother Smith . . .' He shrugged. 'I must apologize for the circumstances of this meeting.'

'Brother . . . Phelypeaux?'

The other inclined his head in acknowledgement. 'The same.'

Antoine Louis-Edmond le Picard, Comte de Phelypeaux, had taken him as guest to several Brotherly dinners, had furnished him with the letter of introduction that had gained him entry to the abbey. He had found the man to be intensely likeable, the more the pity because he had also been present at that fateful dinner in Thury-Harcourt when everything had come crashing down. It had been clear then that Phelypeaux's was the suit that Berenice's father had wanted her to accept.

But what complexities there might have been in meeting this man once more were drowned by Smith's relief and his amazement as the Frenchman politely introduced his accomplices. They were Brothers all, and proceeded, grim-faced, to shake his hand in turn.

'How did you know . . .'

'We have moved heaven and earth to intercept you. When a Brother asks a favour "on the Square", no Brother may refuse. You are wanted in London.'

Smith felt the remark burn him. 'Tell me, was this favour asked for the Sake of the Widow's Son?'

'Yes, Brother. It was.'

Smith stiffened, heartsick with foreboding. 'I have already given my answer.'

Phelypeaux approached him, a filtering of snow, starting from the darkening sky, settling on his clothing. 'Allow me to ask again, to implore you: go no further, but return instead to London. If for no other reason, then for the sake of a Brother's feelings!'

The devil in him suddenly suspected Phelypeaux. He married her, isn't that so? Of course it is! Yes, he married her. Oh, God! And now he's trying to—

'What Brother's feelings?' he asked, controlling his inner turmoil with difficulty.

Phelypeaux's grey eyes were steady on his. 'Why, Brother – your own.'

'Mine?' He felt the explosion inside. 'What do you know about *my* feelings, monsieur?'

'More than you imagine.'

'I must *know* about her!' He readied himself to kick the mare on, but he read something in Phelypeaux's face that prevented him. 'I *must*, Antoine. Don't you understand?'

'Brother, if I could, I would satisfy you that a lady of our acquaintance is not in jeopardy . . .' Phelypeaux looked away, trying to bite back his anguish, but when he looked back there were tears in his eyes. 'Since I cannot persuade you, you shall see for yourself. Dismount.'

Smith got down. He passed the mare's bridle to one of the others, and allowed Phelypeaux to lead him to the bend, so he could gaze at his heart's object.

Even in the deepening gloom Smith could see the devastation that had been wrought on the house.

'God above . . .' In an instant the golden memories of the place vanished, to be replaced by images of ruin and destruction. Now his fondest recollections could never be the same, and he felt deeply wounded.

'This is the sight your Brothers have tried to spare you,' Phelypeaux said softly, and Smith knew then the pain he, as a Frenchman, must be bearing in his heart every day he spent in his own country. When Phelypeaux continued his voice was coolly distant. 'The France we knew is no more. Thury-Harcourt is no more. The family du Fay are no more, and the lady of whom you spoke . . .'

'Where?' he asked, aghast. '*Where* is she?'

'No one knows.'

FIVE

NOVEMBER, 1792
The Bois d'Harcourt

She came awake suddenly in darkness. For a moment she thought it must be the pre-dawn, five or six o'clock in the morning, and the voices those of early rising servants, bringing hot water for the family's morning toilet. Then the geometry of the unfamiliar room resolved itself in colourless gloom, the illusion vanished, and the reality of her situation began to frost her with fear.

She sat up. The air in the room was cool. The fire had all but gone out; embers glowed red in the grate. She felt the cold on her cheeks when she went to the window. It was dark, a clear-skied evening outside, and the stars were bright among bare sycamore branches. Then, beneath the trees, a wash of lantern light spilled from the kitchen door, and three long shadows moved in the rays. She heard voices, they were distinct if she concentrated closely. The first was Adeline's, the second was a man's.

'Citoyen sergeant, you must be starved. Out on such a night as this. Why not take some refreshment before you examine the house? A bite of new bread? And a little wine to warm the inner man?'

'Don't mind if we do – how about that, lads?' The sergeant stamped his feet and rubbed his hands together. Berenice forced herself closer to the cold window pane and was rewarded. She glimpsed a scarecrow figure wearing an outsize bicorne hat and a coachman's cape belted over a tattered uniform. He wore wooden sabots on his feet, stuffed with straw. With him were two youths, maybe sixteen or seventeen years old, she thought. They wore only short coats and ragged trousers, and red woollen caps. Their breath steamed in the cold. All three leaned on long muskets, and the sergeant wore a big curved hanger besides.

'It's been a raw day, and no mistake. I'll be glad to see my own hearth again.'

'You've been out all day?'

'Ah, the Guard's been mobilized across the whole department. Mopping up such as remains of the Harcourt gang. We're under orders to be doubly vigilant after what happened today at St Siffren.'

At that Berenice felt a pang of fear in her belly. Her attention wavered as her mind fought down her rising panic. She saw the sergeant take a grateful draught of wine from his mug and wipe his mouth on his cuff. 'There was a report of a gang of Royalists roaming these parts. A dozen or more of them turned up at the house of the Commissioner and threatened his life.'

'You're joking!' Adeline sounded amazed, and it was strange to hear one so respectably religious lying. Berenice was shamed to realize she was the cause of it. 'You say that Citoyen du Plessis himself was accosted? Please, don't stand out there all night. Come in, come in.'

The sergeant grunted amiably and moved towards the door and out of view. The long shadows that were thrown across the courtyard cobbles fanned and moved, then the shard of light narrowed and disappeared as the kitchen door was closed.

Berenice stared into the darkness. Adeline has invited them in, she thought aghast.

At the same time a door opened, startling her, but it was only Davout, coming from the adjoining room. She stayed him to prevent the creaks that his weight drew from the floorboards. She dared not breathe, but remained poised like a statue, until Davout sat himself down carefully where he stood, and she did likewise. They waited in the darkness for more than an hour, then heard the Guard depart with Adeline's compliments following them.

Adeline appeared two minutes later. 'Sergeant Verdière and his sons,' she said.

'Don't they find it suspicious that you treat them with such indulgence?' she asked, awed by Adeline's calmness.

'Suspicious? Why, no.' Adeline pursed her lips. 'I treat them no differently now than I did when Jean Verdière was in my uncle's employ. Ten years is a long time to know someone.'

'But they're in the Guard. They're evil!'

Adeline left pause for thought, then she said, 'Sad are the prejudices that divide us, one from another. You don't know very much about ordinary people and the general workings of the world, do you, Berenice? It's to be expected, I suppose, with your privilege and upbringing.'

She stared back, unable to comprehend. 'I have tried to keep myself informed of events. I read the broadsheets whenever I could obtain—'

'Broadsheets are not what I meant. You must look behind events, to see people.' She shook her head, as if faced with impenetrable naivety. 'The Verdières are locals. From St Rémy. Not bad people, really. Just uneducated and easily led and, I think, quite scared. None of them are bad people.'

Berenice caught an underlying sadness in the spinster's words, as if her faith had been loosened after all. It must be hard to keep a belief in the goodness of men in these savage times, she thought. She could not stop herself asking, 'You think they'd hesitate to kill us if they caught us?'

'They would not want to kill you.' Adeline shook off

257

her regretful thoughts and was brisk again. 'However, that is no guarantee that they would not do so. And if they did not kill you you would certainly be handed over to some very wicked men.'

'Then you do admit that there are *some* men who are evil?' she said.

'Oh, there is evil in the world. Who can deny that? Fortunately those who have truly given themselves over to evil are a very few. Most who seem so are merely stupid or greedy, weak people who have been misguided or coerced.' She laid a hand on Berenice's knee. 'I advise you to, in your heart, forgive everything, save malice.'

Berenice allowed Adeline's hand on her knee, but inside she recoiled from the limitless forgiveness she found in the woman. It's easy to talk of forgiveness, she thought, but Adeline has not suffered at the hands of a wild and bloody mob. Her philosophy is comfortable and at one remove from real events. She is a person who would tolerate the intolerant. And she thinks me naive.

But the paradox, Berenice knew, was that without Adeline's kindness she would herself be in a terrible and hopeless strait.

They ate bread and cheese, and Berenice was surprised to learn that she had slept twelve hours, and that it was evening. At nine o'clock, after thinking over Adeline's various suggestions, they prepared to leave. Adeline's plan was that they try to reach the house of one of her uncle's estate farmers, the man Adeline had visited during the day, while they had slept.

'Remember, they are expecting you at midnight. Present this letter so they will know you for certain. There is no risk. It's a private sign that only Monsieur Larcher will recognize.'

She took the 'letter' – a simple note of thanks, but folded and sealed with the impress of Adeline's signet.

The journey of three leagues took them as many hours, through a dark and frozen landscape, a vale that lay wrapped in mists on the fringes of the Bois de St Clair. When they arrived at the isolated house, Davout circled around it twice and examined the outlying buildings before knocking.

Monsieur Larcher's eldest son, a boy of eleven or twelve, opened the door. His manner was suspicious until the seal was presented and recognized, and then they were welcomed inside. Larcher was a corpulent man with nose and cheeks reddened by years of red wine drunk from lead pewter. He offered her a piece of bread and an omelette, then he told her they could sleep in his barn overnight.

'The National Guard have already passed by,' he said. 'But I must warn you, it'll be impossible tomorrow night. There's been a running fight at Pont Erambourg. Paris has sent the volunteer levies here to crush the opposition. All Normandy is crawling with *gens d'armes*.'

Berenice considered the man and his household. He was pig-eyed and falsely courteous, a man she felt no inclination to trust. Look how he treats his wife, she thought, regarding the sullen, grey-haired woman who laboured wordlessly at the hearth. They have lived too hard a life, or there has been some tragedy that has made them bitter. Even their dogs' natures have been soured by the atmosphere of this home. I'm so glad that Davout came with me.

'Mademoiselle de Hergevault says you think it would be best for us to hide ourselves in the forest,' she said uncertainly.

Larcher shrugged. 'Since the uprising, the Guard have been beating out the Bois de St Clair for Royalists as thoroughly as we used to beat out pheasants for your father.'

'She says that each night we must change our location, and to tell you at intervals where to bring food.'

Larcher eyed her for a moment in a way that almost

unnerved her. Then he said, 'It may be necessary for you to move from place to place. The Revolutionary patrols continually go back and forth in those parts of the forest that border the old estate. Do you have any money?'

She thought of the pearls she had hidden in her clothes. They were currency, but something prevented her from admitting to them. Instead she shook her head.

Larcher saw her hesitation and pounced on it. 'Are you sure you have no money? It will make this very much easier.'

She stiffened, recalling how Adeline had lied to the Guard. 'Quite sure, monsieur. I don't have a sou.'

He eyed her again for a long, calculating moment, then grunted. 'I know of a charcoal burner's hovel. The woman died last winter. That will be a good place for you. It is sheltered and hidden, and not too far from here.' Then he cocked a thumb at Davout, who was warming himself by the fire. 'As for the big fellow, he'll be my cousin, come up from Orne. A good enough story. I hope he's used to farm work.'

Berenice searched Larcher's face. 'What do you mean, monsieur?'

Larcher's open palm flicked out at the table. 'Well . . . you want to eat don't you? This cheese – this wine – a knuckle of mutton – everything costs money, mademoiselle. You must be in hiding, but there is nothing to stop your man working for your keep. This is only fair.'

Her shoulders fell, and she looked to Davout. 'If you say so, monsieur.'

Larcher sat back, his eyes half-lidden. 'So you agree?'

'You had better ask him, monsieur. He is not my man. We are all citizens now.'

SIX

The vaulted chamber was deep underground. It was dimly lit by no more than a dozen candles. The stone floor, incised with the sign of two Knights riding upon a single horse. Four marks showed the four cardinal points.

Three Knights stood in their ceremonial stations, in niches spaced at equal intervals around a veiled central altar. Each wore mail and a white surplice quartered by a huge red Latin cross. A dozen others were gathered in the chamber. These wore black surplices bearing a white Maltese cross on the left breast.

It's a profound sight, the Seneschal thought with awe and pride. One that might have been seen in twelfth-century Jerusalem, or the fortress of St Jean d'Acre. There's a certain irony that thirty feet above our heads the commerce of modern London continues, ignorant of what we are about.

He put his hands together as if in prayer and returned them to his side three times. The rest replied with the Sign of Obedience. They knew what was coming next. It was his duty to consecrate the chamber.

The Seneschal felt the anticipation he always felt at this inspired moment. The spirit of St Bernard and King Baldwin and Jacques de Molay surged inside him as he recognized the pressure of his responsibility in the weight of his robe, and he took up his Wand.

'O Thou, Great Maker, Lord of Sabaoth, to whose fury the nations are but as dust, maintain Thy servant's right. Without Thine aid, the twisted mail and spear, and forged helm, and shield of seven times beaten brass are but the idle trophies of the vanquisher . . .'

He concentrated his mind on the words of the ritual of purification. By its mystical mind-calming power, he knew, this dark crypt, built under the ancient church of St John's Clerkenwell, would be transmuted for a space of a few hours into the semblance of the Immaculate Temple.

He stood at the station of the West, a few feet from the deep, unguarded well that fell away fathomlessly. The formulas he mouthed began to dissolve his real identity. His name, his nationality, his standing, his rank – everything about his life and station – was falling away; everything that made him what he was in the world, melting. Gratefully, he allowed himself to be absorbed into the role he was here to perform.

Tonight he must be Azrael. Already the brother Knights who were Israfel and Gabriel stood in the niches designated North and South. He waited in silence for them to step forth and give their knocks on the altar with their gavels.

They did so, in turn, then they all moved round and turned to face the East, himself in the middle, with Israfel on his right hand and Gabriel on his left. They went together, taking nine steps. At the third step they halted and bowed, and the Seneschal pronounced the First Key.

'Omnipotent.'

At the fifth step they stopped again, bowing a second time. Israfel said, 'Omniscient.' The Second Key.

At the ninth step they stopped for the final bow and the deep voice of Gabriel gave the Final Key, 'Omnipresent.'

Then the Seneschal knelt for the Dedication, and he

laid down his Wand. 'Great Maker, who sees into the true hearts of Men, to whom all secrets are known, and from whom no failings may be hidden, purify the desire of our hearts, and help us to our end, which is also Thine end.'

He heard the echo of his words die away. To either side of him, the Brother Knights said, 'So shall it be.'

The Bailiff came forward and handed an Old Testament to each of the officiators. They stood to order holding the Testament in their left hands, with their right hands clasping one another's bared forearms to form a triangle, and saying in unison:

Three Brother Knights do meet and agree – pledged in solemn secrecy – the sacred law to serve and see – and never to divulge the Key – unless when we – or such as we – do meet and agree – agree – agree.

They kissed the Testament in turn. Azrael kissed it twice, so that he was first and last to do so. He stepped to the West, and as Gabriel faced North, Israfel faced South. They raised their right hands and pronounced the secret Key.

The Seneschal picked up his oaken Wand. The kernel of the evening's business began to press on his mind. There was to be an admission to the Order. An initiation. A man who has passed the test, in ext aordinary circumstances.

He took his seat, the non-officiating Brothers saluted his Wand, and made the Sign of Obedience. Israfel and Gabriel unveiled the altar.

Then he said, 'Brother Knights, in the name of the Great Maker, I declare this place once more a Tabernacle. The Chapter is open.'

They stripped Smith to his breeches, taking away his overcoat and undercoat, his silk shirt and neck cloth and his stockings and shoes. But they gave him a pair of backless rope-and-canvas slippers to wear in their place. His hands were bound behind him. He still wore the silver ring on which the square-and-compasses were graved on the inside surface, but nothing else above the navel, except the black hoodwink that bound his eyes.

He felt the damp chill of the cellar on his skin, his other senses heightened by the blindfold. The place was ancient, a place of the dead, a dank, mediaeval hole that still seemed to have the breath of the Black Death about it. He had counted thirty-nine steps, twisting and narrow, going down into the earth.

The sole irons of their street shoes scraped on the sandstone flagging. A formidable door was hauled open by a ring. His left arm brushed the pattern of studs and his knuckles touched a cold, metal lock.

He had no exact idea of where he was. Somewhere in the City of London – so much was certain. They had brought him a couple of miles north and east from St James's in a phaeton, then into what had seemed like a churchyard, or at least an open space overset with trees and surrounded by tall iron railings. He had caught himself actively trying to decipher his position, but then had told himself that to do so would make a mockery of the oaths he had already sworn. Why do you feel on edge? he had asked himself sharply. You must trust your silent Brothers, as they must trust you. This is a great honour they are about to do you.

He had relaxed, and tried to think about something else, but even so he had recognized the street calls of Holborn and caught the whiff of the open sewer they called the Fleet, and it had been beyond his power to ignore when the phaeton had turned, lurching to the left. Then there had been the unmistakable rattle of West Smithfield cobbles under the iron tyres and the smell of sheep pens. It had been impossible for a naval officer not to know they were going north, or not to speculate that they were probably heading out of town towards Islington, when the phaeton had slewed left again into a yard and he had been bundled from it along a narrow defile and into some quiet place, open to the sky.

The voices Smith heard now were removed and echoic. One in particular struck him as powerful. Ritualistic, ceremonial, as one would expect, he thought. But more than that. Almost rhapsodic. And faintly . . . familiar.

'Hold hard, now, Brother. I am the Marshal of the Order. You are not yet fully prepared.'

He felt a sudden fear of confinement. The urge to struggle against panic swept through him, and he felt the oppressiveness of the atmosphere intensify unbearably. He swallowed, but his mouth and throat were dry. Demons leapt up from his childhood, from the dark corners of his memory, as he felt a cold, sharp blade pressed against his naked throat. The unmistakable feeling of a small trickle of blood running down onto his left breast.

They're all Brothers, he told himself, clinging to the only certainty. They've all taken the Oath. They will not harm you! But he knew the fright he had taken was very real.

'Bailiff, I have this night brought an Aspirant.'

'And has this Aspirant been selected and elected according to proper rite?'

'This I do affirm.'

'Then, Brother Marshal, bring the Aspirant hither.'

The voice enabled him to sense something of the geometry of the place: an ante-room and a chamber beyond, barrel-vaulted, doubtless with Gothic pillars and stone sarcophagi.

He heard footsteps approaching across the flagged floor from within the inner chamber. The air was dank, yet smelled of candlegrease, and it was cool and still on his naked body. He imagined the flames burning on long, untrimmed tapers, shedding an inconstant light. There were many men here, he sensed. Maybe as many as two dozen.

'Brother Smith, advance into the Ante-room of our Tabernacle in the Degrees of the Craft, and communicate to me the Keys of the Five Promises.'

He stepped forward alone and sightless, trustingly, making the signs as he had been bid. At each step he gave the Keys that symbolized Truth and Courage and Duty and Honour and Fidelity.

The Bailiff said, 'Do you pledge your honour that you have been raised to the Most Sublime Degree of the Craft, for at least a space of time that spans new moon to new moon, or full moon to full moon?'

He swallowed. 'I do.'

'Do you then pledge, upon penalty of a traitor's death, that you will maintain what passes here tonight, and all the secrets thereof?'

He knew that the implied threat, though couched in symbolic terms, was very real. No man of honour could break his vows then live untortured and with conscience clear. 'I do.'

He sensed the speaker turn and approach him, seeing absolutely nothing, but imagining more. 'Then I will entrust you with the Key that opens the Order to you.'

The Key was a mystical word. Smith listened to the three syllables. They sounded as if they must come from an ancient, eastern language. He repeated them.

The Bailiff said, 'The meaning of these words is: "The people shall have mercy." Repeat to me the meaning and let your mind dwell upon it.'

'The people shall have mercy.'

A moment was allowed for him to reflect on the mystery, then he heard another heavy door – one that must have stood half open – swing wide. The Marshal came up beside him, and a voice he could not identify said, 'Most Excellent Azrael, there is a report.'

The one named Azrael said, 'Brother Sariel, see who seeks admission.'

Sariel spoke to the Marshal. 'Whom have you there?'

The Marshal said, 'Brother Smith, who as an initiate of the Craft has been raised to the Most Sublime Degree. As a reward of merit he has been entrusted with the Keys of this Order into which he seeks admission, and for which initiation he is now duly and fully prepared.'

Sariel asked, 'How does he hope to obtain the privilege of our Order?'

Smith heard the Marshal answer for him. 'By the aid of the Great Maker and my Brothers.'

There was a pause, then Sariel said, 'You stated that Brother Smith possesses the Keys? Is this true?'

The Marshal said, 'You must ask him.'

Smith sensed Sariel turn to him. 'Give me, if you can, the Key of this Order.'

For a moment Smith thought he had forgotten the syllables. He wondered what would happen if he failed to pronounce them, then the words came to him and he spoke them clearly, just as he had heard them.

Sariel said, 'Now say what is the meaning of the Key?'

'The people shall have mercy.'

Sariel took a step back. 'I bid you wait here. I shall report what you have said to the Most Excellent.'

The great door was slammed in his face, and he felt the wind of it on his sweat-dewed chest. The loudness and closeness of it made him flinch, but he stood.

There must be an aperture in the door, he thought, because I can still hear them. The sounds of a heavy bar being loaded across the door were very clear. He tried to identify the faint sounds that accompanied it, to make a picture in his head of the scene in the inner chamber.

'Most Excellent Azrael, the Brother Smith, an attested initiate of the Craft, who has been raised to the Most Sublime Degree, has, as a reward of merit, been entrusted with the Keys of this Order into which he seeks admission, and for which initiation he is now duly and fully prepared.'

The voice of Azrael asked, 'How does he hope to obtain the privilege of our Order?'

'By the aid of the Great Maker, and of my Brothers.'

'Does he possess the Keys?'

'He does, Most Excellent.'

'Then, admit him.'

The door was unbarred and opened, and Smith commanded to step forward so that he stood between two others. Someone, the Bailiff he thought, unbound his hands and took up the right one.

The voice of Azrael said, 'Brother Smith, the Keys of this Order have been entrusted to you, and you have come among us. I must know if you have come willingly, and without compulsion or coercion.'

He said, 'I have.'

'Then, have you the sincere desire to improve yourself and likewise the lot of your fellow man?'

'I have.'

'Then, will you take our Solemn Obligation, and vow to keep our mystic rites?'

He felt a momentary hesitation. How can I give my word to something I still know nothing about? he wondered. My motives are sincere, though partly I'm craving this recognition, and partly I'm simply curious. That's the great paradox. I must promise before I am allowed to learn, but what happens if what I learn is repugnant to me?

The darkness pressed in on him, then he heard his mother's voice inside his head. She had a way of cutting through any Gordian knot. 'They're teaching you to trust your Brothers, William. You should know how to do that.'

He said. 'I will.'

'Kneel, Brother Smith.'

As he knelt there were three knocks, from three

different directions, as of three mallets being struck on wooden boards. He heard a concerted rustling, like a dozen men bringing their arms to the salute, or making a sign in unison.

Azrael's voice spoke an invocation. Still there was the rhapsodic quality, still the hint of familiarity that Smith could not quite place. 'Great Maker, at whose command the universe of Light was brought into being, grant that the Brother who now seeks to enter our eupractic Order may ever remember that our aim and object is the greater good of our fellow man, and that he may assist in the carrying forth of the world from the shadows and into Light . . .'

Smith's mind was trying to take in the meaning of what was being said, when twenty voices chanted together, 'So shall it be.'

It sounds like a hell-fire prayer, he thought uncomfortably. A rational man, a man of logic and science and worldly affairs, should find such sorcery as this a very laughable thing. Perhaps I would, too, were it not for the utter sincerity of those who are taking part.

The hairs on the back of his neck began to rise, and he felt the gooseflesh on his arms and shoulders just as he did when he listened to a particularly moving piece of Handel's oratorio, the *Messiah*.

His mother's voice came again, this time a childhood memory, another one of those thousands of bits of parental wisdom that had fallen on his childish ears and had made him what he was. *A man must feel as well as think, William. Feeling and thinking together makes the whole man.*

What does this Azrael mean by 'our aim and object is the greater good of our fellow man'? he wondered, thinking fleetingly of the ancient Order of Knights known as the Hospitallers. These were the Knights of St John, and their aim had been to bring succour to wounded crusaders.

But this unnamed Order sounds more like the Templars, he thought, excitement stirring inside him. Can it really be them? They were supposed to have been stamped out by Europe's jealous sovereigns in the fourteenth century, but what if they continue as a sect within the Brotherhood? And how can I 'assist in the carrying forth of the world from the shadows and into light'?

He felt a dryness affect his throat. Why must I be of the Craft before I can join them? The Craft is dedicated to charity and good fellowship beyond the limits of race, language or nationhood, aims I know I can applaud and contribute to . . . but the aims of this Order sound gigantic and apocalyptic, the very struggle of the powers of Good against those of Evil. What do they really want of me? And why do they hide behind the names of angels? Isn't Azrael the name of the Angel of Death?

His speculations were cut short by the oracular voice. 'Brother Smith, in times of difficulty and danger, in whom does your trust reside?'

He replied as he would to any Brother of the Craft. 'In the Great Maker and, after Him, my Brothers.'

Azrael said, 'Right glad we are that you have faith. You may rise.'

There were three more mallet strikes as he got to his feet.

Azrael said, 'Brother Knights, take notice that Brother Smith who is of Sublime Degree within the Craft shall now pass in view before you. Let stand and speak now any who can show why he is not an Aspirant properly prepared to our Order.'

Someone, doubtless the Bailiff, took him by both hands and began to walk backwards, leading him round the Tabernacle, then many hands spun him until he became disoriented. He staggered, no longer able to intuit which way was north. Absolute direction was a sense he had never lost since he had first studied navigation, he had always known which way he was facing, even in the absence of sun and stars, and the loss disconcerted him. He felt truly blinded now.

Azrael said, 'As you seek to participate in the Light of our mysteries, first you must advance along the Narrow Way in the manner of the Craft.'

He did so obediently, taking three measured steps, starting with the left foot, bowed, then two more steps starting with the right, bowed again, and finally four steps and the last bow.

Azrael said, 'You have now arrived at the World's End. Before you is only the Void. It is necessary that you should show your allegiance to this Order by discarding a jewel. Take off your ring and cast it from you.'

Something about the reflections of sound spoke of a tremendous danger, a chasm of water at the bottom, a deep well, inches in front of him. A fear of falling terrified him, swept sickeningly from his testicles.

He screwed the ring from his finger and threw it down in one motion. There was no sound, then a distant ringing as it struck off the walls far below, then, a count of three later, the sound of it entering a pool.

'Turn about to face whence you came.'

The command horrified him. He felt dizzy and bound to lose his balance. His trust and obedience had brought him to this place, figuratively the World's End, now he needed his courage. But he felt far from alone as he about faced and took a moment to steady himself. Sweat was dampening his whole skin now. The object of his terror, the pit, had moved from before him to behind his back, which was worse. He took refuge in pure thought. His mind continued to track the symbolic significance of the ritual, knowing that every detail would be crammed with multiple meanings.

A voice he could not identify began a reading: 'Happy is the man that findeth wisdom, and the man that getteth understanding, for the merchandise of it is better than the merchandise of silver . . .'

'Marshal, you will help him to find that which is before him.'

The Marshal caused Smith to get down on his hands and knees. He searched about, then a scroll was put into his right hand.

'It is found,' the Marshal said.

Azrael said, 'What is found?'

The Marshal whispered Smith's proper response and he repeated it. 'A parchment.'

Azrael ordered, 'Read, so that we may know what it says.'

Again the Marshal prompted him. 'For the want of Light I am unable to do so.'

Azrael said, 'Let the want of Light remind you that mankind is sunk in the darkness of ignorance. And that ever shall remain, except that he be Illumined. Prepare, Brother Smith, to receive the Light.'

Another extensive reading began, and he heard it patiently. Then Azrael said, 'Take the Testament in your left hand and place your right hand upon it.'

The mallets knocked three times as he did so.

'State your name at length.'

'My name is William Sidney Smith.'

'Then say after me, William Sidney Smith . . .'

He promised to keep the mysteries and rituals of the Order, and never to reveal its Keys or signs to any who was not a Brother Knight. Then he swore never to reveal the full aims of the Order, and acknowledged that the oath was binding on him so long as he should live.

Azrael said, 'As a pledge of fidelity to the Oath you will seal it with your lips three times on the Testament.'

He kissed the Testament.

Azrael said, 'Brother Smith, now a Brother Knight of our Order, arise.'

Azrael said, 'Having been in a state of darkness, what is the desire of your heart?'

Unprompted, he replied, 'Light.'

'Brother Knight, let that blessing be restored to the Aspirant.'

The Marshal removed his hoodwink. The sudden light was searingly bright. The chamber was smaller than he had imagined, and there were several bizarrely robed men. The officiators stood in order with sceptres forming a triangle, others stood against the walls, bearing lit candles in outstretched hands.

Azrael said, 'We congratulate you upon being admitted to the Light of our Order. We express our confidence that your future conduct will justify our having so selected and elected you. I bid you read the contents of the scroll you have brought with you out of the darkness.'

He recognized it as the first three verses of Genesis. 'In the beginning God created the heavens and the earth. And the earth was without form and void; and darkness was upon the face of the deep. And the Spirit of God moved upon the face of the waters. And God said, Let there be light, and there was light.'

Azrael said, 'Walk worthily in the Light which shines around you, Brother Knight, for you are now at liberty to retire.'

After the final address, Azrael said, 'Now let the Aspirant be shown the penalty of all traitors.'

His arms were seized suddenly and he was marched forward and held, his head thrown back and gripped. A cold blade was pressed into his flesh and drawn slowly across his throat from ear to ear. He felt the blood trickle from the wound. Then the blade was pressed to his breastbone and drawn down to his navel. Then across his stomach crosswise. He was paralysed, terrified, unable to cry out or resist or even to move as he felt drops fall down his skin and splash his feet.

The horror of it was total. They had scarred his body, with his tacit permission, but he felt violated, and was outraged. The calculating part of his mind told him that what was done was done, and that he would do best to go along. He was alive, wasn't he? The cuts would heal, wouldn't they? They were nothing so grim as the wounds he had faced many times in sea fights, and anyway this was a stern warning . . .

Azrael said, 'Release him, and tend his hurts.'

He felt the hands let him go.

SEVEN

Berenice looked up at the rooks' nests and shivered. The treetops above her were roaring eerily. Since daybreak, an hour ago, the wind had moved round to the southwest, taking away the dry cold, and bringing damper air, and now a steady rain.

Her home was a rough lair dug in the dry earth, an enclosure six feet square, walled in by stacked turfs and lined with moss and leaves. It was raftered with branches and roofed with a rotted piece of canvas. A blanket served as a door. For the first week she had not dared to light a fire for fear of discovery.

Water dripped from the awning of sailcloth under which she sat. She was filthy – her hands grimy, fingernails torn, her hair matted and dirty, her feet clogged with mud. She carried the marks of her passage through dense undergrowth. Thick brambles and thornbushes had scratched her and plucked the patched woollen stuff of the miller's coat and breeches. From time to time the tip of her tongue probed the sore on her upper lip. It itched where the skin had bubbled and dissolved.

She sniffed. At least my head cold seems to be going away, she thought. I must be grateful for every small mercy.

She fancied she could smell Atlantic salt in the air, and that made her think of Smith, and the joy of those happy times so long ago. That was another age, another country. Both had vanished for ever in a crisis that had shattered her inner life as the Revolution had shattered her outer life. She thought about the pivotal moment of her life, of the ticking of the great case clock in the dining room of the château of Thury-Harcourt in those vital seconds when Smith had looked from her father to her, and she had looked from Smith to her father, and the decision had been made.

The château was now desolated. That elegant dining room was destroyed. Everything was broken, burned, stolen, dispersed. Now it only existed inside her head, and there it remained clear and bright, as if it was yesterday. The table laid, her family seated for ever in frozen attitudes, watching Smith as he was betrayed and embarrassed. The memory was still there, and it was still heartbreakingly poignant. It was there, as sharp as the point of her knife, the great moment of decision. She had known, even then, that it was so.

'Father, how could you?' she asked. 'How could you have robbed me of him?'

The thought of her father's present horrifying predicament turned despair up in her belly, but still she was able to think of an alternative world. How different my life must have been had I defied him. What if I had eloped with my dashing English captain?

The cruelty of it made her cry, and she wept, not because she was unable to prevent herself, but because she was alone and no one could see her, and because it made her feel better. But then she remembered Smith's face, and the quality about him that he said was not his alone but a characteristic of the English. He had called it a very particular good humour.

'Nothing can hurt those who laugh, Berenice. And we can laugh at anything.'

Yes, she thought, and forced her tears into laughter. I

shall be like the English. I shall have a very particular humour too!

Rain dripped into the wooden bowl she was using to collect drinking water. She looked around at the broken turf kilns of the dead charcoal burner. The old woman was long dead but her spirit still seemed to inhabit the place, and Berenice wondered how long she had suffered life here. She began to laugh. For more days than she had been able to keep count she had been living like a wild animal. And now she was laughing alone. Like a madwoman.

But laughter was something. It was the first time she had dared allow herself to feel any emotion for weeks. Knowing that it was Christmas Day had been the worst. Then had come the family memories of New Year's Day. After that, she had forgotten to notch the pole for a day or two, and after that it was pointless trying to work out what day of the week it was, and anyway she could ask Monsieur Larcher should she ever again need to know.

It seemed the wind was changing direction again. She got up and used a smooth stone to whet the blade of her knife, then she began to whittle a stake with which to re-peg the awning. God help me if the weather turns freezing again, she thought as she carved a notch in the wood. It's bad enough now, but a freeze when everything is soaking . . . It's hard to credit there are people who live like this all the time. Poor souls.

The charitable thought sounded suddenly ridiculous to her, and she said 'Damn them all!' out loud, then felt ashamed that she was losing her humanity. She sighed, then said, 'Poor father. Poor mother. Poor sister.'

Since the shock of her initial escape had worn off, the bleakness of solitude had begun to press heavily upon her. She was not used to such a life. Her emotions had been made raw by being alone – frustration at her powerlessness, then hopes raised by deliberately sanguine reveries, then the blackness of despair at evil tidings. The only constant had been her bodily discomforts and the terrors of the nights spent alone.

Food had come every three days. For the first few weeks a bundle had been dropped at a place close by the nearest track. She had agreed to collect her provisions two hours after sunrise, but never sooner – to avoid meeting with the courier, who might be watched. Larcher had come himself to tell her of her father's capture near Condé. Three days ago she had crept from her hiding place to collect the bundle, when Monsieur Larcher had reappeared.

This time he told her many ill-tidings, and she had begged him for wider news. Only then had he said that the king was dead.

'So, they have murdered him?' she said. 'I always knew they would.'

The war had continued to intensify he said. Now the Revolutionaries had overrun the Austrian Lowlands, had declared war on the Dutch and also the English.

'Soon,' she had said, 'Spain will also become an enemy.'

It had seemed to her then as if all of France's thirty millions were being mobilized against the whole world.

She had screwed up her courage to say, 'I don't care if it takes foreign armies to come here and snuff out this evil. I'm pleased that the Convention has surrounded itself with foes.'

Larcher had regarded her with his pig eyes. 'You think so?'

'Can't you see that Paris is just using those foreign threats to the Revolution as an excuse. It wants to take up emergency powers. Now they have killed the king they will begin to beat the people into submission.'

Larcher had grunted, 'Well, they're certainly drafting all men of capable age into the army. There's hardly anyone left to work the land, and spring coming on.'

She had looked at him then, seeing his interests

clearly. He was not driven by any motive other than the cheap labour he could exact from Davout. My God, I could be here, stuck in this limbo for ever, she had thought, the realization sickening her. All it takes is that I do nothing.

Larcher had looked away from her stare, as if he had divined her thoughts. He seemed to debate whether or not to tell her more. Then, finally, he met her eyes, watching her to see how she took the news. 'The National Guard has commandeered your family's ancient seat as its barracks.'

She had laughed shortly. The knowledge of her father's arrest had been a thousand times more painful. 'A house is but a house, Monsieur Larcher.'

'There is more.'

'More?'

Larcher had waited, apparently sympathetic. He was a man who could break bad news very artfully. He had learned to satisfy his own tragic sense of the world's injustice by such a game. 'The official notice has been posted. I am sorry to say, that the Comte du Fay has been tried at Caen and sentenced to death.'

Despite herself she had started at what he said. 'He is *condemned*? My father? When?'

'Didn't my son tell you?'

She had shouted in her anguish. 'No! Nobody told me!' Then she had taken hold of herself, seeing the way he seemed to feed on her distress. 'Except you. Thank you, monsieur.'

It had been the worst moment of her time here, and she was astonished that she had felt the impulse to thank him for the receipt of such terrible news. For days the fact of her father's fate had made her mind numb, and that had been the only state of mind in which her sanity could bear it. Even so, it was amazing how the human body could endure. It had a marvellous capacity to adjust to new situations in a matter of days.

Now she got up and prepared herself to leave the clearing. She had made up her mind to lie in wait again for the courier, whom she suspected would be Larcher's son this time. This time she would follow him back, and she would set about reclaiming her family.

She had been crouching behind the earth bank for only a few minutes when she heard a gate bang against a post, and the rattle of chain. Then, moments later, to her inexpressible relief, she saw the giant form of Davout coming up the track. She ambushed him, but she thought that she must have appeared so wretched that he hardly recognized her.

'Davout! Do not recoil from me!' With tears in her eyes, she threw herself into his arms.

He knelt to her, then, and in a booming bass voice he lowed like a bull.

'Dear, loyal Davout, I beg you: go to Caen.' She heard her own voice tighten with suppressed rage. 'Find out about my father. And inform me as to the proceedings of these . . . these *savages*!'

'Auuuuung!' He looked at her stolidly, and she understood that his brain, which everyone took for a dullard's, was as sure as his heart.

After a while he made a groaning sound and began to draw pictures in the air with his hands. 'Soldiers? At Thury-Harcourt?'

He dipped his great shaggy head, and she saw the frustration he was feeling.

'I know that the Guard are stationed in the house.'

He shook his head, pointed to the sun and counted on his fingers.

'Not for five days?'

His groan of assent puzzled her. 'Where are they gone?'

He made another mime, failed in frustration. Then she heard words forming in his mouth. 'Orehaaaaooo.'

'Say it, Davout! Say it!'

He groaned again, an animal noise, but this time she could make it out.

'To the Forêt de Halouze!' She hugged him, her eyes filling suddenly. 'Davout, you spoke! You spoke to me!'

She stared at him, shaking her head, more proud of his tortured effort than she had ever been of anything. The feeling overwhelmed her, and she laughed and cried at the same time.

He grinned back, and she was awed by the freedom in his unpractised gape. It was the first time she had seen him smile, the first time he had allowed himself an uncontrolled human expression.

After a while, she said, 'Why, Davout? Why those woods?'

This time his mime was violent, and ended with a snapping motion.

She wondered at the news, filled with hope. 'A Royalist army? In the Forest of Halouze?'

He nodded again, grimly.

'Who is at the house now?'

He told her the answer silently.

'Our own good people . . .' She knew he meant the servants. So the commander of the Guard has solved the problem of how to dispose of the house servants by retaining them for his own needs, she thought. The Guard, like any company of men, would have use for cooks and porters.

'We must go there, Davout. Tonight. I cannot stay here any longer. But Monsieur Larcher must know nothing. Meet me here after sundown.'

They took to the road in darkness, so that a league's walk took them what seemed like an age. They went by unfrequented ways, and Berenice was in constant fear of being met and recognized.

Their way was blocked near the hamlet of Caumont when they were forced to lie low in the fields until a military convoy of ox-waggons passed. She watched Davout regarding a bearded, dishevelled Revolutionary officer. The man was foul-mouthed, a strutting little cockerel who used his speck of power over his subordinate without mercy.

'*Aujourd'hui, comme hier* . . .' she heard Davout whisper, as clear as a bell. Today, the same as yesterday . . .

Eventually they reached the meadow near the ash-grove gate, and she crouched down behind a wall. A single light burned in the house, in the kitchen, but she no sooner saw it than it blinked out. She sent Davout to look around the house, to find out if any strangers were to be seen. She watched from her hiding place as he went down. He must have found everything quiet, because he went to the kitchen door and knocked.

It seemed to Berenice that Madame Cozette had just gone to bed. She soon came out with her lantern, and a flinty hardness in her voice.

'Who's there?' Berenice heard the question clearly. Then, 'Lord of Heaven! Davout? Where have you come from?'

From behind the wall, she heard Madame Cozette scold him, but fondly. At the same time she enquired what had become of some of the other servants.

'Auuung!' Davout said, astonishing the cook, who had never heard him utter a sound until now.

'The soldiers, Davout? No, no, there is no danger. Come inside.'

When Davout would not move, Madame Cozette tried to reason with him. Her tone of voice showed that she had no idea how much Davout understood of the world. She spoke to him as she would to a three-year-old child. 'The Guard have gone into the country. They will not return for many days. Listen to me, Davout. This is now the soldiers' house, but they are not here.'

Berenice got up, with tears in her eyes. She could not

keep from her mind the many happy days she had passed here with her family – a family now scattered and in great danger.

Madame Cozette put her hand to her mouth when she saw her. All she could say was, 'Oh, child! Oh, child!' Then she heard a noise in the yard, and instantly she was on her guard.

Berenice was about to run from the house, when the cook pushed her and Davout both indoors and stepped out with her lantern.

'Who's there?'

There was another noise, then a gruff voice. 'Only me.'

'Who's "me"? Show yourself!'

'Confound you, woman! What's the matter with you – it's me, Jean Boyer.'

Berenice saw that the village farrier had certainly taken too much wine. Madame Cozette was unmoving. 'You're not coming in my kitchen,' she told him. 'You always smell of horse shit.'

He sounded wounded. 'Of course I smell of horse shit! I'm a farrier. I work with horses – I shoe them and care for them. They are my darlings. It's the smell of honest work, woman.'

'Don't talk to me about honest work, you drunkard!'

'Ahhh, give me a kiss, plump chicken!'

The cook bustled past him, cuffing up the sleeves of her nightgown. She brandished a big iron ladle at him. 'You see this? It will be kissing your ear, Jean Boyer, if you don't get off to your bed.'

'But I'm hungry.'

'So are we all. There is nothing for you here any more. Those days are over. Now, go on! Get!'

'You're a hard woman, Marie. A hard woman . . .' His voice trailed away.

When he had gone, Berenice looked around the kitchens and saw that they had been partly restored to order. The kitchen parlour seemed stiflingly hot, and she saw that the stove had been fired from a heap of wooden blocks in the corner. With a shock she realized that they had once been the floor of the ballroom. She steered her mind away from the door that led to the rest of the house, knowing that to see it would undermine her remaining strength. She closed her eyes momentarily and visualized it as it had been.

When the cook returned, Berenice asked her, 'Madame Cozette, is it possible that you have some provisions to spare?'

'Alas, there is nothing here but rabbit stew, some coarse bread and lard. I hesitate to offer it.'

Berenice and Davout ate ravenously from wooden trenchers, then she exchanged stories with Madame Cozette, the cook eyeing her all the while with purest pity in her eyes.

'The whole house is ruined,' the cook said, lowering her voice as if speaking of a holy crime. 'You know those bastard-pigs have ripped up the floor of the ballroom and burned it for winter fuel. They say they are going to turn the great hall into the people's grain store. A grain store with no roof? Have you ever heard of anything so foolish?'

'So what do you think can be done for my father?' Berenice asked, scouring her plate.

The answer came reluctantly. 'Your father is yet alive. But . . .'

'But what? . . .' The silence gnawed her nerves. 'Madame, I have to know!'

'It's terrible, Mademoiselle Berenice, Père Fournet told me about it yesterday. He was at Caen and went to the prison on the pretence of some trifling business. He met some public officers, men known to him, who said: "We have two of your parishioners in another prison, women who could give no account of themselves when they were tried by the Revolutionary Tribunal. They are with about three hundred other women, all condemned to be shot at the end of the week. The names of these women are the Mesdames Ronceray." '

The news hit her like a hammer blow. 'That's my mother's maiden name . . .'

Madame Cozette nodded. 'It seems the Guard do not yet know who they have caught. Père Fournet enquired where they were confined, and learned it is at La Precey, an ancient abbey for women, of which the abbess and twelve of her nuns have been shot.'

'Dear God . . .'

'The good father said he repaired immediately to the abbey, where he saw them. They were separated each from the other, and he said they were almost starved from the scantiness of their allowance, which was only bread and water. They had no means of getting anything else, so he gave them what little money he had in his pocket. They thanked him for it, saying it was sufficient for the supply of foods for the little time they had left to live.'

'Then they are for the executioner.' Berenice stared, numbed with shock. She began gasping for air, and when her senses returned she asked, 'Madame Cozette, tell me: who is head of the Revolutionary Committee in Caen?'

'The two biggest men are named Rethureau, by trade a confectioner, and Thierry, the innkeeper. The latter is very well-known to Père Fournet. He is not a Revolutionary through principle. Like most of them, he is a hypocrite. A man full to the brim with avarice. He sees advantage in shouting the cause.' Madame Cozette bent forward. 'I know from Thierry's daughter that he has always expressed his desire to have the good father come secretly to his house to hear vile confessions. Whatever godlessness he spouts to his Jacobin friends in the municipality, he is at heart still terrified of what awaits him in the Kingdom to come.'

Berenice forced herself to concentrate. 'We must ask Father Fournet to return with all speed to Caen,' she said. 'We must give him these pearls. They are all of value I have left in the world. Will you ask him to give them to Thierry as a present, and desire him to save the Mesdames Ronceray?'

Madame Cozette thought about it, her face set, then she nodded. 'I shall visit Faligan tomorrow.'

Berenice found the overheated kitchen had made her breathless. 'I trust he will act with – discretion?'

Madame Cozette straightened. 'Last month my sister learned that her only son had died in the Netherlands. Bernard was impressed into the Revolutionary army. They marched him to Jemappes. There was a big battle. So much fodder for Dutch cannon. Few outside our family ever knew that Bernard was Faligan's son also. We know how to keep secrets, mademoiselle.'

That night and the night following they stayed inside the house. Throughout the day Berenice hid in the empty pantries, on a straw mattress, trying to catch up on sleep. After dark Madame Cozette boiled water and Berenice washed and changed into fire-dried linen, and cleaned up her hurts. Only then did she notice the way her hands and feet had hardened and the way the skin had peeled from her lips. Later, they ate a pheasant that Faligan brought, but Berenice felt a numbness in body and mind that she knew she must fight. She knew it must be the natural defences of her mind combating hopelessness, by setting aside thoughts that were dangerous to dwell on.

Beware of this numbness, she cautioned herself, breathing deeply. Do not yield to it. You are a fugitive with too much time to give over to down-spiralling thoughts. It is a most dangerous leisure, and for the sake of your family you must not succumb.

After supper, when the hearth burned low, Berenice got up to fetch in more wood, despite Madame Cozette's protests that she stay by the fire. In the cobbled yard a waning moon, now in its last quarter, shone down. It revealed to her the orchard through which she had escaped from the Revolutionaries. She saw it had been mutilated – half the apple trees had been cut down for firewood by the soldiers. She wandered there to sit on one of the sawn stumps, not feeling the cold.

Everything was silent, frosted and fairy pale, and she sat very still. The thought came to her that this might be the very tree where Smith had carved a monogram of their initials. The scarred bark was gone now. Burned to ashes. She turned her eyes to the winter stars, saw the Great Bear, and followed the curve of the tail down almost to the eastern horizon. There she saw the bright star Arcturus, marking the constellation of the Herdsman. It was rising, and twinkling violently, an orange beacon that seemed to illumine the bloody road to Paris.

She kissed a tress of her own blonde hair and said a prayer, remembering that Smith had shown her how to find that same star one August night long ago. At that time of the year Arcturus had been in the western skies, following the sun down, and promising a voyage to England. Smith had pointed to a patch of sky midway between the Bear and the Herdsman and the Lion. 'Just a whisp of unremarkable stars,' he had said. 'Nothing much in the way of things, d'you see? It's called in Latin *Coma Berenices* – Berenice's Hair.'

'A particular good humour,' she said to the empty air.

And then she saw it. Carved into the stump of a tree were her initials. His also. She went to it, unable to believe her eyes. Stared at it, ran her finger along the grooves in wonderment. They were exactly like those that had been carved on the apple tree, only these were recent, and incised into the flat top of the stump.

This might be the very tree, she thought, marvelling. Is it magic? How can it be? It's as if the tree itself has preserved our names for eternity. What a miracle!

But then her heart hardened and she thought, there's

no need to believe in miracles. It must have been one of the men who cut down the orchard. No more than the idle carving of some illiterate soldier, copying the letters he saw on a nearby log. That's all.

A noise alerted her and she started. Instantly she moved for cover. Down below someone had entered the yard. She saw two pheasant feathers sticking from his hat band – Faligan. But Père Fournet was not with him. She stood up, her heart beating, and hurried down, knowing that the waiting was over, but Faligan's normally taciturn features remained unsmiling. He seemed pained by what he had to tell.

'Take courage, mademoiselle,' he said in a way that stabbed her heart. 'We must all hope for the best.'

'What happened, Monsieur Faligan?'

Faligan's life had been that of a lone creature, a fox haunting the copses and clearings of the du Fay lands. He began hesitantly, 'The good father said that on his arrival at La Precey he asked to speak with the Citizen Rethureau alone. To him he delivered the present and the message.'

Berenice put her hand to her mouth in horror. 'But he was meant to go to *Caen*.'

Faligan seemed unsure if he should go on. 'It seems the Citizen Rethureau received the present with a smile. He put the pearls in haste into his pocket, like so. Then Père Fournet says he hushed him out of the room, saying only, "Go about your business, old man." '

'Oh, no! The pearls were for Thierry! He's the one Père Fournet was meant to bribe, not Rethureau.'

'I don't know about that, mademoiselle. But Père Fournet is a clever man.'

Madame Cozette put her fingers to Berenice's lips. 'Let Faligan finish his story in his own way.'

'Madame – the good father says he went downstairs to that part of the abbey by which he knew prisoners were led to the place of execution. This is on the square

288

in the front of the abbey of La Precey, mademoiselle. Here upwards of two hundred people have been shot and thrown into trenches which are covered up immediately, though some of the poor creatures have been still alive—'

'Faligan, what *happened*?'

'Pardon, madame. Well . . . on arriving at that place Père Fournet found a large trench already dug. In a little time a long train of poor women appeared, coming towards that spot, when he saw among them the comtesse and her daughter. Rethureau, to whom he had given the pearls, came to see the executions. The good father stood a little way from him. As the procession passed, when the comtesse came up, Rethureau said to the gaoler: "Take those two women back to prison. I have received information that the rest of their family is still living concealed in the woods of Cinglais. We shall soon have them in our power, and then we will make a more striking example by executing the whole family together." '

A flood of gratitude poured from Berenice's heart. 'Then they are at least still *alive*?'

'Père Fournet saw them safely reconducted to the prison at Caen, where they are once again under Citizen Thierry.' Faligan nodded, and looked up from under his grey eyebrows. 'I am come in all haste to give you notice that the good father is now hearing that citizen's confession.'

PART 6

The Black Anvil

FEBRUARY, 1793
Paris

Well, they've finally killed the king, monsieur. *I cannot say I am surprised, your amazing prophecy notwithstanding. When Louis Bourrienne and I saw the mob overrun the Tuileries, it showed me that the kings of France, who had won power through strength, had forgotten how to exercise it, and so must fall.*

To add to that, we have gone to war with Britain and Holland. Six hundred generals of the old style have been swept away, two thirds of the officer corps cut down! And the nation at war on all fronts. What a time of unparalleled opportunity this has been for such a man as I!

Therefore, I say the time is ripe for me to return a third time to Corsica. This time I shall stamp Paoli's face into the dirt. And he will have the Revolution, or he will have Armageddon. It will be just as I have always desired. Think of it!

But you say that my destiny is not confined by that small island shore? I don't understand you, monsieur.

So, then? What is meant for me? Do I harbour personal ambition? No. I see Ambition as a demigod, with pale cheeks, wild eyes and a sardonic smile, a god for whom crimes are a sport, a god who speaks only lies and calumnies. What was Alexander doing when he rushed from Thebes to Persia and thence into India? He was ever restless; he lost his sanity. He believed himself a god. What was the end of Cromwell who governed

England? Was he not tormented by all the daggers of the Furies? I don't want that.

No! I will not listen to you this time, monsieur. *Surely I have witnessed, as you said I would, how much the so-called patriot Paoli has become corrupted. My family, brothers, sisters, uncles – staunch Jacobins all – saw through him as soon as I pointed out his true nature to them. I remember saying to myself: 'You've turned against me, Paoli; so I shall turn against you.'*

You know, Paoli's people never missed a trick to move against me. But I will give them more than they bargained for, I can tell you! I believe a man must meet intrigue with force. It is the only way. The coward wants to sell us to the English.

Do you know, it took me a long time to realize that he always saw me as a threat – ever since the first time we kissed one another's cheeks. Me! The most fervent patriot of all! You know, there was a time when I worshipped the very boots he stood up in. But no more. He took every opportunity to put me in a difficult position. Instead of protecting me he offered me up to the French authorities like a sacrificial goat. That's why I came to Paris in the first place.

But my days here have been a time fraught with excellent possibilities. Leadership is a commodity in short supply, and technical expertise in the art of war is rare indeed. You see, monsieur, *hard realities will out in the end. Those of my aristocratic colleagues who treated their army posts as sinecures, those who interested themselves in women and wine more than their duties, what has happened to them? They have bled across the border to join the Prussians or the Austrians. False soldiers. Useless men!*

But me. Ah, I am rare. For I have studied hard, and I have learned well, and I have true substance at heart, for what I don't know about the deployment of artillery is not worth anyone's knowing. You yourself have forti-fied me with your prophetic wisdom. So when the confrontation comes, monsieur, *we shall see who tri-umphs, they or I.*

Why do you still try to dissuade me? Answer me! I have told you that it is my family duty to return to Corsica. I must escort home my sister Elise. My applica-tion has already been approved, and so I shall go back to Corsica, whatever you say! I am officially a Jacobin; I have friends in high places in Paris. I have made sure that the deputies and représentants en mission *are all per-suaded of my ardent beliefs. They are in agreement with me, all fully convinced that my presence in Ajaccio will be of greater service to the Republic than fighting with my regiment in Savoy.*

I know it is your function to guide my destiny, monsieur, *but before you try to alter my mind again consider this: that of all the prophecies you have made to me, one alone has convinced me to be led by you – the prophecy that one day I shall be master of Corsica.*

I feel that day must soon be at hand.

But you will forgive me if I am presuming too much?

ONE

Smith looked at his dimly lit chart one more time, then straightened as much as the *Proteus*'s low-beamed cabin would allow. His servant, Gilmartin, had blacked out his cabin windows with heavy curtains; all ports were shut. No lights were showing on deck. A dangerous night lay ahead.

The Frenchman lay unconscious in his cot, fully clothed, and under one of Smith's mother's marvellous cotton quilts. Smith smiled at the familiar boyish features from which all care had been erased. As for himself, he felt a dull pain in his back, and an overall tension in all the muscles of his body, but the sense of expectation that surged through him at intervals was invigorating, maybe even pleasurable. Whenever he allowed himself to think of the fact that he had been given a ship and a mission it filled him with a kind of terrifying inspiration, and he knew he was fully alive. How Jacques de Tromelin could sleep at a time like this was something he could not explain.

It was time to go on deck.

The *Proteus* was a bluff-bowed, 370-ton bark. Originally, she had been the *Collier*, engaged in shipping coal from the Tyne to London, but she had been purchased by the Admiralty six months ago, and altered for special service. Her crew numbered seventy-one, including her captain. There were three passengers.

Smith heard the lone marine sentry on duty outside his cabin come to attention. He donned his hat and started up the companion. It was pitch dark, but the sky was a mass of stars, and as his eyes adjusted he saw that there were four men on deck: Barlow, the sailing master; John Hines, at the helm; Lieutenant Bellingham, the quietly capable officer of the watch, staring over the starboard rail amidships; and Cooper, the for'ard lookout, stationed in the bows. All of them were rugged up against the cold.

The sea was unseasonably calm, and they were carrying a full press of canvas, making headway at two knots or so. He saw with satisfaction that the topgallants were beginning to draw a little. The *Proteus* was tranquil. Not a creak nor a complaint from her; not so much as a snore from below decks, only the sound of water running smoothly under her new-coppered hull. There were hours to go before readying the boat.

'Coming abreast La Grotte now, sir,' Barlow said, as he acknowledged the captain's presence.

The sailing master's soft burr was in harmony with the mood of the quarterdeck. Barlow's a diamond, Smith thought, a man with half a century's experience of the sea, the kind of man who talked with me on Dover beach when I was a lad, the kind of man who filled me with a longing for the sea, and an admiration for those who go upon it. They may have given me one of the meanest three-masted vessels in His Majesty's Navy, but by God, she's perfect for this work, and she carries the most efficient complement I've ever come across.

La Grotte was an outcrop of rocks that stood less than a mile off the French port of Barfleur, rocks that dried at low tide, and could rip the hull out of any ship that drove on to them.

'Thank you, Mr Barlow,' he said, then he added, relaxing the usual formality of command, 'I daresay you've sailed this coast sufficient times to know how difficult the Point can be.'

'Aye, sir. In all weathers. In peace and war. There's Barfleur Race to beware out east and north-east of the Point in the rough. A man ought not to trust to fine weather here, but this is as well as I've seen it.'

'Do you think it will hold like this until sun-up, Mr Barlow?'

'Aye, sir. I do.'

'And I do, too.'

Smith grunted approvingly at the older man's judgement, enjoying those few moments' conversation, sensing the mutual respect. He clasped his hands behind his back and moved away a pace, letting the night close around him.

A solitary hand came up on deck and began to broadcast a mixture of salt and sand across the decks, to combat the ice formed there and to give grip. Smith watched him set the bucket down. It was Peter Cobb, a man with admirable pride in his work, which gave him a natural dignity. He was typical of this crew: responsible, amiable and prepared to go the extra mile unbidden. He wondered what they would be like under fire, then put up a prayer that he would not find that out tonight.

The air was very cold and crisp. The dew that had condensed on the tarry surfaces of the mizzen ratlines had frosted them white now, reminding Smith irresistibly of spiders' webs. Above the mastheads the winter stars blazed steadily: the Great Bear directly overhead, the Seven Sisters, pursued by Orion and his dogs, waning in the south, over the dark mass of France. Their familiarity reassured him as the dark sea slid silently under the *Proteus*'s keel.

He had laid a course south-east, taking them to a point twenty-five miles further along the coast. Now, he thought with regret, it is the enemy coast. That's the paradox, for I love France almost as much as I love my own country, and one of her children more than anything in this world. He thought of what Phelypeaux had told him at the destroyed château, a grim shaft of hope in the dark: 'She is not in their hands. Her father was taken, and is imprisoned at Caen. So, she is either at large, or she is dead.'

His charts and notebooks told him that there was a shelving, pebbly beach, backed by firm ground then low cliffs – ideal for the landing. Which is why he had selected it.

The meeting at the Admiralty had been secret. No record of it had been kept; Lord Grenville had told him the mission would never be admitted. The remembrance of Grenville's familiarity at that time made him smile inwardly – so much was possible now that had not been possible before, and all because of an ancient rite performed in a Clerkenwell cellar. Proposal, followed by acceptance, and suddenly everything was different. Strange how it had taken an act of defiance – when it was obedience that was asked for – to prove him true to his heart and therefore worthy to be a Knight.

He thought again of the moment he had undergone the terrors of initiation into the Order. The bloody cross incised into his breast while blindfolded had been painless, as promised, but the process had excruciated his mind. He had felt the cold fire of the blade as it was drawn very slowly, parting his flesh. The blood had issued from the two cuts, trickling down his skin, soaking his waistband. A deliberate agony inflicted, he had presumed, so that he might know the meaning and the solemnity of that into which he was entering. Perhaps it was done also to show the power of the Order, but he preferred to see it as his means of showing faith and trust in them, for his Brothers had sworn they were not hurting him as they cut.

And so it had proved.

At the time, his mind had been occupied with sticking

to his resolve – not to cry out or flinch – but he had opened his eyes to a miracle, for when the hoodwink was removed there was no wound to be seen – nothing except a faint pink scratch, where he had expected to see himself bloodily laid open.

In the carriage his Brother Knights had affably told him the secret. 'Ah! The Seneschal draws on you with a sliver of ice,' one had said, revelling in his reaction. 'The cold numbs the skin and fools the mind into thinking it a knife.'

'Good God!'

'And the melting of the ice into water by the heat of the body,' added his second companion, 'gives the illusion of bleeding. All quite simple. But it gets the point across, don't you think so, Brother?'

'Yes. It certainly does,' he had said, and they had laughed together.

Smith smiled now, and shook his head at the memory of it, bringing himself back to the matter in hand, relishing the uncertainties. The absurd plan he had volunteered for called for a particular week as the only time when a landing could be made.

Problems of wind and tide and the agreement to rendezvous with those ashore had reduced the possibilities to one of three moonless nights. One had passed in squally rain, one in fog, but tonight the glass was steady, and the seeing good, and Barlow, who had more experience of the Channel than any other man in the king's navy, had said that the weather would hold.

They had stood off a long way from land during daylight. He had not wanted to run the risk of the *Proteus* being reported. Since the declaration of war there had been little sea-traffic in the Baie de la Seine. The French navy was apprehensive of leaving port and perhaps blundering into a blockading fleet, and few merchant-owners were prepared to risk their livelihoods being taken by a British frigate, but it would only have taken a lone fisherman to multiply their risk ten-fold.

The landing had to be made where he had specified, between two cliff-top batteries, and it was essential that the Revolutionists were not warned of *Proteus*'s presence. Smith crossed his fingers under his boat-cloak, and settled down to a long night's wait. The thought of his passengers unsettled him. Landing them is dangerous enough, he thought, but their plan . . . their plan is pure insanity. And so, perhaps, is my own.

Proteus continued on her south-easterly course with no change in wind or weather. They moved once again beyond the range of shore batteries, then the land on their starboard quarter slid over the horizon. There was a slight veering of the breeze to east-south-east that had to be accounted for, but by the time Barlow's dead reckoning placed them five miles north-west of the village of Arromanches it was halfway through the watch.

Smith consulted his notebook again. Off Pointe de la Percée there was a bank extending three cables offshore, with rock ledges that broke the surface. When he had come here with Berenice he had recorded what the local fishermen had told him, that a race formed over the bank according to the tide, the eastward stream getting up to a knot and a half about five hours after high water at Le Havre. There was a westward current of equal strength about an hour after high water. The information was crucial if the *Proteus* was to heave-to on station at the arranged time, but still be able to get out of the range of shore batteries before the dawn or moonrise revealed them.

De Tromelin came on deck. He wore a dark cloak and looked even more boyish with his short hair and less-than-impressive moustache. He had made the crossing to England little more than a week ago, bringing news and information from the dissident groupings trying to organize themselves in France to their émigré friends in London. He had made it clear he had established confidential contacts inside the Revolution itself. It was not surprising, since more than a hundred of the Brotherhood were members of the National Convention.

He turned to Smith and said in French, 'A fine night. Almost windless.'

'It seems that way because we're running before it presently. But you're right; it's perfect for a landing.'

'You think we will succeed?'

'We'll get you ashore.' He paused, then said, 'But beyond that, my hopes and my expectations for your mission remain somewhat at variance.'

De Tromelin looked sharply to him. It was the last thing he wanted to be told, or expected to hear. 'If you think that, then why did you put yourself forward for it?'

'I don't know. The plan of rescuing *anyone* from the Temple prison is, to say the least, audacious.' He sighed, changing tack. 'And in this circumstance somewhat ironic also, what?'

He knew de Tromelin would understand the remark. The Temple in Paris had been built in the year 1222, and had served as the great fortress headquarters of the Knights Templar. Four huge round Crusader-style donjons and two lesser towers were connected by high battlements, forming the keep. Following the destruction of the Bastille, it had become the most feared prison of the Revolution.

De Tromelin drew a deep breath. 'However remote the chances of success, we must try. They call the Temple "the ante-room to the guillotine".'

Smith nodded. It has surely been that for France's late king, he thought, and is now for the rest of the poor fellow's unfortunate family: his wife, Marie Antoinette, and his eight-year-old son, Louis – the boy that Antoine

Phelypeaux and his die-hard Royalist friends were adamant in calling Louis XVII.

'As Frenchmen, we must try,' de Tromelin said. 'Who would we be if we did not try?'

'Who, indeed.' He turned, remembering that the Brotherhood had a debt to discharge toward Marie Antoinette. She had assured her husband all along that France's controlling Grand Orient lodge, a network of forty thousand Brothers, was no threat to the social order.

'Prepare to heave-to, if you please, Mr Bellingham.'

'Aye, sir.'

As the watch came on deck, Smith went below. In their cramped cabin Ponthieu and Ranir were silently checking their gear. De Tromelin was to get them to Paris, where they were to attempt the miraculous. Much more than that Smith had not been vouchsafed.

He knocked and entered. 'The waiting is over, gentlemen. The landing will be tonight.'

Ranir nodded shortly. As Smith closed the cabin door, he heard him mutter to Ponthieu. 'So . . . this is it.'

The *Proteus* hove-to a mile north of Sainte Honorine. Her tar-black longboat was called away. As it was being lowered Smith turned to de Tromelin, and said, 'Your night's sleep seems to have been extraordinarily sound.'

De Tromelin's smile was bitter-sweet. He said in English. 'A clean conscience, Captain Smith, result when a man know 'e 'ave done all that can be done in pursuit of 'is duty.'

'A fine maxim, sir.' Smith handed him his packed-up portmanteau. 'Which is why I have decided to go ashore with you.'

'But . . . you are the captain.'

'Quite so. Which makes the risk – and the decision – all mine.'

He glanced at Bellingham and said. 'Mr Bellingham is a most admirable officer but, alas, his local knowledge is nowhere near as detailed as my own. I'm sorry to disappoint you, Mr Bellingham.'

'Sir.'

'And remember that if fired upon, you will take *Proteus* out of range with all speed, and in any event before first light. Do you understand?'

'Yes, sir.'

'Good man.'

Smith reflected that the operational plan he had laid before Grenville called for a landing supervised by *Proteus*'s first lieutenant, whose orders would be to remain with Ponthieu and Ranir and de Tromelin until contact was made ashore.

It makes no difference to the plan if I go ashore, he told himself. *Bellingham is a capable officer. Added to which his spoken French is rather rudimentary, so he would be at a disadvantage ashore should anything go amiss.*

His thoughts rang hollow. He sighed, seeing through himself. *I'm feeding myself false justifications. That's so stupid. What's the matter with me? In London they already think I'm so eager to get my own command that I'll volunteer for any hare-brained plan, no matter how ill-conceived. And it is ill-conceived. But I don't care. The real reason I volunteered is that I'll take any opportunity to talk with Phelypeaux, to find out what news he has of Berenice.*

During the crossing Ponthieu and Ranir had prepared themselves as best they could, but something about them had made Smith's heart sink the moment he had seen them. Ranir, big and coarse-looking, with heavy brows and gross features and hairy as a gorilla, but also with delicate manners that sat very oddly with him; Ponthieu, a pale, nervous elf of a man, prone to intensity, hot flashes of temper and ill-concealed frustration.

But what had dismayed Smith was that they had the look of desperate men, fanatics, men prepared not only to die for their cause should it become necessary, but already dwelling in a state of mind far beyond that. They seemed almost resigned to death, perhaps even eager to go out in a blaze of glory.

He checked his tide tables again, and saw that it was just on the turn. One reason he had selected this spot was the steepness of the beach. He must make sure they were not left so high and dry by the ebb as to make relaunching the longboat difficult. Able hands Cobb and Eldridge were already unshipping the oars. Ponthieu climbed over the side and down the rope-ladder after them. The *Proteus*'s slow pitching had upset him. Ranir climbed down, then de Tromelin. As soon as Smith joined him on the stern thwart the boat pulled away towards shore.

'How old is the dauphin?' Smith asked, his hand on the tiller.

'He is the king,' Ponthieu said definitely. 'And, however old, he is of an age to sit on the throne of France.'

'Yes. Quite so.'

De Tromelin said, 'Do not forget that the greatest of our kings, Louis XIV, was but five years of age when he ascended.'

Smith decided to turn away from the subject. No purpose would be served by agitating de Tromelin's feelings, or upsetting the others. He asked, 'Would anyone like a tot of brandy?'

A glance astern showed that *Proteus* had already merged with the night. The shore ahead was black, the wind dead onshore, and a run of small waves was moving in towards a long, curving beach. The dip of the sweeps gave the night a steady rhythm. After a while de Tromelin said urgently, 'I can hear surf.'

'Yes. You might like to take off your shoes and hose. Nothing worse than salt stains to give the game away, hey?'

The black mass showing against the starry sky told

him how close they had come in. These were the cliffs they must mount, an easy climb, he knew, but they had come in a little too close to the headland. It was just the sort of place guns would be sited. A single bright maroon, sent up over them, and both the longboat and *Proteus* herself would be easy meat. The oarsmen brought them ever closer. Smith chose his moment, then put the tiller hard over, turning the boat parallel to the shore, where it heaved and wallowed. A few minutes' more pulling, and he swung the tiller the other way, bringing them in.

The oars scraped bottom, then the forefoot, then the surge bore them against the pebble bank. The rowers leapt into the foam, trying to beach the boat with timed heaves. But the bank was too steep, and there was too much weight in the prow. As soon as he saw them having difficulty Smith joined them in the numbingly cold water, shoes and all, pulling until the Frenchmen could climb out without wetting their breeches. They came ashore making unnecessary oaths.

'Quietly there!' he hissed. Everyone froze, and there was only the sound of the surf again. They assembled the gear and prepared to move off. Then Cobb's voice close to his ear.

'Beg pardon, sir – but I seen a light.'

'Where, Cobb?'

'Up there, sir.'

He looked along the beach, saw nothing, then after more than a minute a brief flicker of light. He ranged it at no more than a hundred yards away. Who are they? he wondered. They could be friend or foe. Whoever they are, they're close enough to pick up the sound of half a dozen men staggering around on a bank of pebbles. The sooner we reach firm ground the better. I hope to God it's Phelypeaux.

The tide was high, and the beach no more than twenty yards wide, but steep, and the pebbles were sized awkwardly underfoot. It ended abruptly in a little cliff of clay, waist high and topped with grass.

'Lie down,' he told them. They were slow and reluctant. His shoes had turned into loose, squelching puddings. He took them off disgustedly, wishing he had taken his own advice, as he emptied the water out and squeezed the feet of his stockings as dry as he could.

The sound of men approaching along the beach grew louder. They were talking in low voices. He listened for Phelypeaux's distinctive tones.

'Them's Frenchies, sir,' Eldridge breathed, awed by the suspense.

'Eldridge . . . shut up.'

The newcomers halted. They've seen the boat, Smith thought. The moment has come.

Then he heard the call. An owl call. Distinctive. Unmistakable. It had been arranged, and yet—

Suddenly Ponthieu was on his feet, Ranir heaving himself up after him. Smith damned them silently and laid a restraining hand on de Tromelin.

'Ponthieu? Ranir? Is that you?'

'*Mes amis*—' My friends—

Then there was a yell. Thuds and groans. The sounds of a struggle. Then a searingly bright flash and a report that echoed along the cliffs. Jesus God! Smith cursed them under his breath. The fools!

'They've nabbed 'em,' Eldridge whispered, mesmerized.

Smith's mind began calculating. The chance that a random patrol could have encountered them was negligible. Therefore the plan had been betrayed. But by whom? He thought of Phelypeaux, but discarded the notion instantly. No, not Antoine. Antoine was a completely honourable man. The image of the man suffering in some appalling torture dungeon sent a lance of horror through Smith; it also added to his concerns.

'Make him stand up first, then tie him. And the other

one. If he moves, break his arm. No, no. Behind their backs! You and you – look for others.'

Smith ducked as they revealed their lanterns. They were perhaps fifteen yards away. The light was long and grotesque. He counted eight men's shadows. All were carrying muskets with bayonets fixed.

And the ninth is the officer, he decided, to judge from his headgear. At least, he's the one giving out the orders.

So, they had seen the boat, and the boat had two oars. It was possible Ponthieu and Ranir had landed alone. Possible, but unlikely. Smith could read as much on the officer's face.

'Corporal! Render that boat useless. Knock a hole in it, imbecile! Look – use your musket-butt! And put out that lantern, unless you want to get us shot.'

As the sound of splintering wood reached him, Smith's grip tightened round the boarding pistol. They had given him a ship, and he had given it straight to Bellingham. And now he was stranded.

God damn them! The pistol was primed, but quite useless. Only one shot was available, and that, he knew, would get them all killed. Of course, there were two hangers, but what good were swords against muskets?

'How many came with you? Put him on his knees. Hold him.'

Smith heard a pathetic whimpering, denial and pleading, then a vicious kicking. It took all his will power to stop him from charging down on them. If de Tromelin had not been there, he would have done so, sure that Eldridge and Cobb would give a good account of themselves, but de Tromelin was too important.

Another agonized cry came from the darkness.

'How many, I said! Spit it out, or you'll be spitting out the rest of your teeth!'

There was coughing and incoherent mumbling from Ponthieu. Sobbing. So much for their blaze of glory,

Smith thought poignantly. They must think themselves in hell.

'So – three English sailors. You, you, you and you follow me. The rest of you take these pigs up to the village, and send Garamonde and his men down to us. I'll finish my little conversation with this scum later. Patrol the beach. Find them. They can't get away. Find them and kill them.'

The difference between hope and expectation had widened to a gulf now in Smith's mind. The mission had been halted before it had even begun, and he could not avoid the feeling of guilt. He had failed. He had lost his ship. He might soon lose his life.

He thought again of Ponthieu and Ranir, of what he had seen in the latter's eyes, and shook his head. They had been men who knew they were going to die.

TWO

Three days after leaving Thury-Harcourt Berenice returned to Mademoiselle Adeline's house. She was welcomed in, and went immediately to the bedroom to begin a tense vigil, interrupted two hours later, when Adeline brought her a glass of calvados – apple brandy.

She was barely able to take the refreshment, knowing the tremendous risk her host had taken on her behalf.

Adeline smiled grimly. 'The rules are being tightened all the time. The Department has ordered that anyone found so much as transporting provisions without a specific permit will be arrested and shot.'

'You must be terribly scared.'

But Adeline shrugged, a glint in her eye. 'Some of us don't respond as expected to threats.'

They heard an owl, and knew the signal had been given. Berenice went to the window, saw Davout make a circuit of the barn to see if all was clear before he ventured to knock. She came downstairs and saw old Monsieur Hergevault ruling the room from his arm-chair. His face was blotched and red as a boiled crab. His swollen legs were bandaged. He was over seventy years old, and quite deaf now. His gout had become worse in the last few weeks, 'Partly,' Adeline had said, 'because he insists on trying to flush the ailment from his circulation with draughts of home-made cider.'

He flourished a pair of walking sticks at Berenice, as if

311

they were pistols. 'Don't let them destroy all we built! Don't let them do it!'

'Monsieur . . .' She tried to smile at the old man, a little frightened by his unfocused wrath. Her nerves were stretched tight.

'Don't let them do it, Emile! That's what he told me. But it wasn't like this when I fought the English at Pondichéry. Monsieur Governeur Dupleix! Now there was a man of vision. Ahhh! A great man. Not like the fools we have to lead us nowadays!'

Adeline's cousin, a local boy of nine or ten, came in. He watched the old man's raving with fascinated eyes, until Adeline shooed him out, and sent him patrolling round the house to warn her instantly should he see the Guard. 'There, now, uncle.'

'The fools shipped him home! The man who had tried to give us an oriental empire! Shipped him home to die a pauper. And India was gobbled up by the English. What has happened to the spirit of Dupleix and of La Pérouse? That's what I want to know!'

Another knock came, Monsieur Hergevault seemed to lose his train of thought and subsided into muttering. Adeline went to the door and Berenice tried to control the surge of emotion she felt. The anticipation of meeting her mother and sister again had agitated her, but nothing could have prepared her for the sight she saw. The Comtesse du Fay's flesh was wasted, she was dressed in rags and she stank. When she hugged her, her body seemed insubstantial; she seemed to have aged twenty years. Celestine was in the same miserable state, her cheeks were hollow and there were sores on her lips. Both appeared unimaginably changed.

Berenice hugged them in turn, and they all cried together. Then Adeline sat them down by the fire and made them take a little food and warm their limbs, which were starved, but the frost on their shawls had barely begun to thaw when the boy came running in, shouting, 'The Guard! The Guard are coming!'

'Save yourselves!' Adeline said. 'Go the back way!'

The comtesse seemed too dazed to react. Somehow Berenice and her sister got her out of the house and into the yard. But the yard was walled, and the gate chained. She looked around desperately. The old carriage house had been turned into a barn. It was full of straw. If they've come in earnest they're bound to search it, she thought, if only for sleeping vagabonds to impress into the army.

'Celestine! Up there!'

They had to climb a ladder, and then to climb down the other side – a drop of fifteen feet. She knew there was a door that would let them out into the broom field beyond.

The sisters guided their mother up the ladder. When at the top, Celestine went ahead and tried to help her mother down, but Berenice lost her footing. She grasped handfuls of straw, and fell headlong into the darkness. A terrific pain exploded across the side of her head, filled her vision with false light. For a moment she lay, dazed and fumbling, not knowing what had happened.

Her head rang with the concussion. She pulled herself up, groping in the dark, until her fingers felt the iron rim of a barrel. The main impact of the fall had jarred her left shoulder. She struggled to her feet too swiftly, felt as though she was about to pass out, but the panic caused by the flow of blood from the wound seemed to bring her back to her senses.

Celestine was pulling at her, and with her sister's help she was able to crawl out of the yard and reach the field beyond. There they lay down in wet grass and waited, panting and weak, to recover their strength.

She heard indistinct whisperings and men beating about the place. The fear returned, impelling her. She tried to make them go on, to move on the other end of the field.

Her mother said, hopelessly, 'I can't.'

'You can!'

'Why?'

Her whisper was fierce. 'Dogs!'

'I don't care. Let them find us. I want to die.'

She felt fury at her mother's weakness. 'Well, I don't! Celestine doesn't! And we didn't save you from the guillotine to have you die here! For the first time in your life do something for someone else!' She slapped her mother's face to shock her back to reality.

Celestine flew at her. 'Don't touch her! You don't know how much she did for me in prison!'

Berenice seized her sister's wrist, then saw the madness of their situation. 'Use your anger, Celestine,' she told her sister. 'Use it to give you strength. Help me get her away from the house.'

They dragged their mother fifty yards then lay still and quiet. Berenice grasped the looped cross and held it tightly, filling her mind with a kind of prayer. If there is such a thing as a protecting angel, she told the sky, and if you can hear me now, please help me! She was terrified she would hear dogs, but eventually the lantern light subsided, and she dared begin hoping they had won through the crisis. She staunched the blood from her head with her handkerchief until the flow stopped. Her hand and face was sticky, her hair matted.

The three of them lay shivering, watching the steam of their breath rising. After perhaps half an hour, she decided the Guard must have gone, and she thought it safe to stand up again. She gave an owl hoot. From the yard where he had remained, watching, Davout made a reply.

Only then did she approach the house. Davout opened the yard gate. Once in the house they all looked at her as if she was an apparition – Mademoiselle

Adeline, Davout, but now also Faligan and the man in the officer's uniform.

It was too much. She felt her knees weakening, and the sensation of pins-and-needles crawling over her scalp just as she had the day of the balloon flight when she had seen the figure in black turn his grotesque face to her with the words, 'I am death.'

The blackness took her, and the next thing she knew she was lying on a chaise, and Mademoiselle Adeline was holding something intensely pungent under her nose. She heard Adeline say, 'She's coming round. Stand back.'

Berenice saw those who had been in the room before, but now also her mother and sister. There was an officer of the Guard and Père Fournet too. There was dried blood on her clothing; she felt it caking the side of her head. She struggled to sit up.

'Lie still, child.'

'I'm not a child.'

But her voice sounded childlike, lost, as if there was no strength in her. Mademoiselle Adeline squeezed her hand. 'How do you feel now?'

'A little cold.'

The spinster pressed a pad of wetted cloth against her forehead where it stung, then wrung it out red into a basin.

'When we saw you we thought the Guard must have shot you. Celestine told us what happened.'

She tried to struggle up again. 'It was a fall. But the Guard . . . I thought . . .'

'A false alarm,' Père Fournet said, leaning over her. 'The boy mistook our guests' arrival, but God is with us.'

Berenice's mother's eyes were glazed. She shook her head vacantly. She seemed utterly exhausted and without hope for her husband. Celestine, too, was infinitely weary. Berenice scanned the faces of the others, and saw the army officer, only now he was not an officer he was

Jacques de Tromelin, wrapped in a dark cloak and wearing short hair and an absurd moustache.

Berenice took a little calvados, and felt her throat burn, but when the burn subsided she felt better. Mademoiselle Adeline's vanity glass revealed a cut an inch long above her left eye, with a hard swelling that she thought would blacken into a bruise. Ludicrously, she felt embarrassment that Jacques should see her like this.

It's my useless upbringing, she thought. I have refinement, but it has done nothing to equip me for the sort of life I am being obliged to live now. Père Fournet says the Jesuits believe that we are all as potters' clay when we are young. Impressions are made on us, and then we are fired in the kiln, and all that we are is hardened in us. Pressure applied to us after that makes no mark, unless it shatters the vessel . . .

She shrugged off the idea. It was as foolish as a Revolutionary theory. Just a simple analogy. People were more complicated than clay. But even if human beings are only like pots, she thought, we can still be filled. We can still learn.

De Tromelin was telling her mother, 'I wish to come to your assistance, comtesse, however much the Municipality has taken care effectually to prevent it. There are road blocks, and the Guard are at pains to arrest all those they think may be abroad without good reason. They have laid an injunction on everyone not to stir out of their area. On pain of death.'

De Tromelin's formal way of speaking seemed to recollect the comtesse to her senses. It was a style of speech she had not heard for months, and it broke her heart. She said, 'I thank you for your attentions, sir. You have put yourself at great risk on our behalf.'

De Tromelin took it graciously. 'The law applies to us all equally now – except, of course, those on official business. Fortunately, I have such business.'

Berenice saw his eyes twinkling, like the old, reckless

Jacques de Tromelin she remembered. It lifted her soul more than a little.

'My regiment is not yet at full strength,' he said, 'and I am in pursuit of it. Even so, the system of passports is now so general, and so particular, as to make free travel from one town to the next quite impossible.'

He explained how he had come to Caen in the hope of discharging a debt and, Berenice heard with growing unease, to save part of his confiscated property. 'I'm here under a considerable obligation to the Commissary of my regiment. That man is my protector. He has important connections among the Jacobins in Paris.' Berenice saw them all look to one another aghast as he mentioned the name of the hated party of terror. 'The man may be trusted. I cannot explain everything here and now, but we have a method. In essence it works like this: he shows proof that he has advanced me money – which is perfectly true. Then, since he is my creditor, the goods confiscated from me have to be handed over to him to the value of the debt. We then split the amount.'

Berenice said, 'How much do you get? And how much does he?'

'We have agreed that my cooperation in this matter is worth a share of one fifth the value of all he should recover.'

There was silence at his eagerness.

'You say your protector is a *Jacobin*?' the comtesse asked, appalled.

De Tromelin was quick to explain. 'Madame, he does not believe any of that hellish creed, he simply uses it – as do all of them who have the wit to recognize what is actually happening.' He waved the matter away, but Berenice saw that he tucked in his chin like a man on uncertain ground. 'I . . . I suppose, madame, that this man is, after a fashion, as obliged to me as I am to him.'

Berenice took the bloodied pad from her forehead. The flesh around the the wound was warm, and that was good. 'It seems to me, Jacques, that the regimental Commissary must carry four times the obligation you do.'

De Tromelin's brow creased. 'What do you mean?'

'Oh, Jacques! Listen to yourself. You're delighted at the chance to redeem one part in five of your property. And for this you give up four parts of it to a scoundrel. That and all your honour. Is that also part of your business arrangement?'

De Tromelin's manner hardened. 'We are in a new world Berenice. There is no honour now. We all must do what we can to survive.' He seemed abashed, and quickly added, 'And I may say that my protector is far from being a scoundrel, as you shall know when you meet him.'

His words caused her a moment of doubt. Honour is not to be bought like a suit of clothes, she thought. Can there ever be convertibility between notions like duty, obligation, glory and honour, and these grand universal rights? The old values were never easy to define, but they are real. And they are important.

She recalled the old saying that those who lay down with dogs invariably got up with fleas, and told de Tromelin, 'Surely such a man as your protector would not help such as us. For we have nothing to offer him.'

But de Tromelin only said, 'If you desire freedom for your father I shall send my protector to the Department to concert measures for his release. If you do not desire it, you have only to say so.'

Her mother cried out, 'Is such a thing possible?'

'Madame la comtesse, I have already made application to the Municipality. Albeit so far without success. In the final resort, an application to the Convention may be necessary.'

Berenice saw her mother's fervent expression. The knowledge that the brave Lieutenant de Tromelin was prepared to help her husband by going to the highest authority available in this new poor and benighted country had rekindled a flame of hope in her.

De Tromelin's the one my mother always wanted me to choose, she thought. It would have made her happy if I had married him. But Jacques and I would have fought endlessly. I know that. I think she sees in Jacques a semblance of my father's own dash and impetuosity in the days of his youth. How strange, the way these things go.

The comtesse said, 'And if your protector succeeds in freeing my husband, what then? We have no passports such as you say we now require. Nor do we have any place to go.'

'Mademoiselle Berenice, if you will permit me: I have contrived the following stratagem. The wife of my one-time manservant has now a position in the house of the new mayor of Caen, where she assists in the washing. By her inquisitive nature, madame, it so happens that she has found the opportunity of borrowing certain blank passports from that official's desk. They are properly printed papers – that is so to confound forgers, you see? They require only to be filled in with particulars, and then signed by officers of the Department.'

Berenice thought it over cautiously. 'That's excellent, but . . . the signatures themselves are not insignificant details.'

De Tromelin turned the thought aside, and she detected his reluctance. 'We must cross one bridge at a time.'

'Jacques, you must tell me exactly what you intend.'

He sighed. 'My protector will know how we can proceed. Tonight I had planned to go into Caen to begin negotiations.'

'I will change my clothes and come with you.'

'That's impossible, mademoiselle, your injury would prevent—'

'Jacques, I have been living like an animal in the woods for months.'

'But—' He gave a small grimace of incomprehension which quickly changed to a shrug of acceptance. 'Mademoiselle, you have been too courageous.'

She took his hand. 'Courage, my dear Jacques, is like love. It feeds on hope.'

THREE

Smith closed his pistol's pan cover on fresh, dry grains of priming powder and laid the gun aside, satisfied now that it would do its duty if called upon. He wiped his hands on a rag, careful not to soil the suit of borrowed clothes he was wearing. Not exactly *à la mode*, nor the style I would choose myself, he thought, but they seem to pass for a rather less than well-to-do visiting merchant of Revolutionary persuasion. The question now is can Jacques be made to go along with my plan?

The garret was verminous, but comfortable enough – dry, roughly furnished with bed, table and a couple of chairs. It was very warm, even afforded light by a small window. He had made do with far worse accommodation for most of his time at sea. The room sat above a sympathizer's lodging that was itself above the man's bakery. It had a rickety stair that descended into a narrow alley behind the main square, and an ever-present smell of fresh bread hung about the place. He stepped to the window overlooking the Place de Greve, and watched idly for de Tromelin's return. He had gone out charged with the task of discovering what he could about Berenice. He might bring news that will change everything, Smith thought, feeling a combination of hope and excitement coursing through him. Please God that he does. Please God . . .

The square was a dismal sight. The grim walls of the

castle reminded him that Berenice's father was suffering in a stinking oubliette within. The comte had never been his friend. The truth is, he thought, I've probably suffered more from that man's opposition than I have from any other cause, but he did what he felt he had to do, and I must respect that.

The day of the comte's despatch had been decided for Thursday, the Tribunal having posted notice to that effect. We have four days to get him out, he thought. If only Jacques can be made to agree.

He considered again the complex game of bluff and counter-bluff that de Tromelin appeared to be playing, and hoped that the man's wits – and his honour – were equal to it. He's far too easy to toy with, Smith thought. And there's something not quite straight about him, something not perfectly 'on the level', as a Brother should be. He certainly has several highly placed contacts among the Jacobins, and many more among those pledged to counter them. It's true that without his help we could not have covered the twenty-five miles to Caen, nor found safe lodging here. But I sense that I must not let him play matters his own way.

The night of the landing, Smith had led de Tromelin, Cobb and Eldridge off the beach near Sainte Honorine. They had eluded the Guard, and lain undetected in underbrush throughout the day. From time to time he had scanned the vacant horizon with quiet satisfaction, approving Lieutenant Bellingham's capacity to follow orders.

'My ship was renamed with commendable foresight by the Admiralty,' he told de Tromelin, his teeth chattering in the cold. 'If you recall, Proteus was a son of Poseidon, god of the sea. Legend says that each day Proteus came ashore to sleep among the rocks of the shore, and that anyone who would know the future must catch him before he returned to the deep. Once caught, he would be obliged to tell the truth. But Proteus had the power to change shape at will in order to escape the necessity of prophesying, and was never caught.'

'Then, let us hope that we can do the same.'

'Yes. Let's hope so. I don't like the idea of being caught and obliged to tell the truth. At least, not as your unfortunate friends Ponthieu and Ranir are doubtless being obliged to tell it.'

The weather had been sunny but cold, becoming misty as the uncomfortable day drew to a close. It had given him time to think things over. *Proteus* would return to Portsmouth, report him gone ashore to an uncertain fate, and because the mission was secret his name would not be forwarded to the French governmental office whose task it was to arrange the exchange of imprisoned officers. So far as the Admiralty was concerned it was a far worse crime for a captain to lose a ship than for a ship to lose a captain. Naturally, there were those in London whose jealousies would be succoured by the news that the precocious Smith had failed so spectacularly, but that did not matter a whit. In personal terms, he thought, feeling encouraged, this is a wholly satisfactory situation, for I'm exactly where I wanted to be.

After nightfall they had gone inland, and made their way to a farm near the hamlet of Ryes where de Tromelin said they would be safe and find food. And so it had proved.

'What to do now?' he had asked de Tromelin once they had eaten.

'Tomorrow night you and your two seamen will be conveyed to a point on the coast. My friends will make sure that a boat is provided for you. The coast is patrolled more effectively now than it was when our two countries were at peace. It is difficult to make the crossing to England, and getting more difficult every day, but . . .' De Tromelin had moved his hands and nodded to show that work would be needed on his part.

'. . . I can arrange it. You will all be in Kent before sunrise.'

'Portsmouth,' Smith had corrected him. 'About a hundred miles, due north. Closer to here than Paris, and that's a curious thought. Though if I know Eldridge, he'll be persuading Cobb to make for Brighton.'

De Tromelin had turned, suspicious of his amusement. 'What do you mean by that?'

'Only this: you see, I've half a mind to stay in France for the moment.'

'That's impossible!'

'Excuse my saying so, my dear Jacques, but the idea of rescuing your boy-king from the Temple – now *that* was impossible. And if it wasn't impossible yesterday, it certainly is today. However, I have a rather more practical plan.'

De Tromelin had eyed him closely, unsettled by Smith's independence of mind. 'What kind of plan?'

'Phelypeaux told me that our old acquaintance the Comte du Fay is held at Caen, and that he was actively organizing against the Jacobins when he was taken. He is one of the few figureheads in this area around whom a movement of resistance might gather. We ought to try to release him.'

'Do you think the Jacobins are not aware of that? He is extremely well guarded.'

'But not so well guarded as your young king and his mother. And in this enterprise we would have a significant advantage.'

'Which is?'

'That the plan, my dear Jacques,' Smith had tapped his own forehead, 'resides in here, and nowhere else. No one is going to betray us this time.'

De Tromelin had looked at him for a long time then, his expression impenetrable.

Jacques' youthful features seem quite open on first acquaintance, Smith thought. They proclaim him to be a straightforward fellow, but there's a deeper current running in him, and the longer a person knows him, the deeper that current seems to get. He is certainly under an immense strain.

Smith heard a noise on the stair. He took up his pistol. When he heard the knock, he asked in French, 'Who is it?'

'A man from the East, Brother.'

He unbolted the door and let de Tromelin in. He was alone. He went straight to the table and ladled out a bowl of cold fish stew, ripping off a hunk of bread from the stick he had just brought. Smith uncocked the pistol and put it back on the chair.

'Well?'

De Tromelin shrugged, his mouth full. 'No news.'

The disappointment was bitter in him, but he hid it strenuously. 'Surely someone must know something about what happened to her.'

The other cast him a fierce glance. 'And the rescue you proposed is impossible. It can't be done.'

'That's a matter of opinion,' he said levelly.

'It's impossible, I tell you!'

'Nothing is that.'

'You're letting your personal feelings cloud your judgement. You only want to rescue the Comte du Fay because he disliked you and he embarrassed you, and because you think, in some vain English fashion, that you can make him eat his words and set your account to rights by becoming his saviour.'

Smith absorbed the insult on top of the disappointment that was simmering inside him. He felt his anger rising, but again he controlled it, crushing down his feelings as he knew a civilized man should. The moment was too important to jeopardize by reacting like a savage.

'My motives are as may be,' he said. 'But I was asking you about Berenice. She cannot simply have vanished.'

'She's gone. She could be in England by now for all I know.'

He made no answer, letting the man eat, which he did without looking up, his back half turned. Eventually Smith said in a measured way, 'Jacques. I want you to help me find her.'

De Tromelin whirled round. 'I did try to find her! I just told you! She's disappeared! Gone! Are you calling me a liar?'

Smith regarded the other steadily, until he resumed spooning up the fish stew.

'No, I'm not calling you a liar particularly,' he said, knowing his manner was infuriating de Tromelin.

'You think he knows where she is, don't you? You think the comte knows. That's why you want to get him out. Isn't that the truth?'

The remark lodged in him like a musket ball, but he put it out of his mind, just as he would have put a wound out of his mind. He tutted. 'Why, Jacques, must you be so eager to impugn my motives? Of course, I'll forgive you, since a man may believe whatever he likes. However, I shall tell you the real reason that I believe it's important to rescue Berenice's father, if you'd rather know the truth?'

De Tromelin stopped chewing, and turned.

'Phelypeaux told me that the Comte du Fay compiled a list of every dependable counter-Revolutionary in western France. Though the Jacobins have him in their power, they do not have the least suspicion of the hundred or so names he keeps in his head. If they did, they would have applied the means to get it from him, and this they have not yet done. London would very much like to have that list, but at all costs the Jacobins must not have it. Now, it occurs to me that to rescue him would be the way to achieve both objects.'

De Tromelin's gaze lifted slowly to meet his own. 'It's impossible.'

'Maybe not. Given a small sum of money, a quantity of gunpowder and some rope. I've been thinking about the problem quite a lot.'

'How do you know for certain that he has not been tortured?'

'I've been making certain enquiries.'

'I told you not to leave here!'

He laughed shortly. 'Surely you didn't think I'd be content to sit in an attic room, like a piece of furniture until you came back, did you, Jacques? I have a quite appallingly restless nature. And friends to see.'

'What friends?'

He hesitated, then said, smiling archly, 'The comte's unhappy lodging-house is currently shared by three brothers awaiting trial – brothers in the family sense, that is. Two of them were known to me when they were officers in the regiment of Roche Dragoons. The third was formerly the Grand Vicar of Deauville. He and I are Brothers – in a much more *exclusive* sense.'

De Tromelin put up his hands in a gesture of complete frustration. 'The Grand Orient has been fragmented by politics! Don't you know that? The Brotherhood in France is utterly compromised. Every shade of political opinion is held and few respect their oaths. You can't trust anyone. Anyone!'

'Yes, I believe I heard that there were Brothers among those who tried Brother Paine in his absence for having written his pamphlet *The Rights of Man*. Extraordinary turn of events, don't you think?'

De Tromelin's rage frothed. 'Listen! There are other operations running in Caen. Important operations – things you know nothing about.'

'Perhaps it's about time I did.'

'You must not interfere! You'll get us all arrested!'

It's what I've thought all along, Smith decided. He's unwilling to countenance any ideas except his own. I think he's keeping a great deal from me. He met de

Tromelin's eye and relaxed the superiority of his tone just enough to disarm the other's fury. 'It's not necessary to harangue me, Jacques. I'm not deaf. I'm not speaking about the Brotherhood at large. I've made no mention of you or your people to anyone – I say, you're not *worried*, are you?'

As he had hoped, de Tromelin had no defence against that kind of rhetoric. Part of him knew that his courage had been slighted, but it was hard for him to know in what way. The effect was crushing. De Tromelin resumed his seat and nodded. 'I'm sorry. I've had a very difficult three days.'

'No doubt.' Smith nodded back, his affability precisely timed. He began to peel the lead foil from the top of a bottle. 'Still, you'll be calmer once you've had a glass of wine, I'm sure. Now, here's what I think we should do.'

FOUR

They met at an isolated inn near St Sylvain an hour before dawn. It was deserted, except for the innkeeper, a small, balding man, who twisted his hands in his apron nervously. Berenice wondered what he had been told about the meeting, and if there might be any grounds for his fears.

Père Fournet had walked to Caen to fetch the man they were to meet. On the way to the rendezvous de Tromelin had asked her to let down her hem before they arrived, so they did not appear like travellers. He then explained to her that the man they were to meet was a military Commissary, or quartermaster-general, one of the few men in France who would be in a position to make himself rich in these difficult times. 'The feeding and equipping of an infantry regiment of two thousand men,' he told her, 'involves the raising and spending of great sums.'

'And the difference between the sum raised and that spent being the Commissary's living, I suppose.'

'Exactly.' De Tromelin's voice had remained bright with enthusiasm. 'That's why the Commissary is a political appointment.'

'A gift from those who have power,' she said bleakly, 'to their good friends who helped them get it.'

'And to those who they hope will help them keep it

whatever happens in the future,' he said. 'That is the way the world works. How it has always worked.'

She was put in mind of the time that Père Fournet had been parted from his living of twelve hundred livres per annum by the Revolution. He had explained the practicalities of priestly stipends and livings to her. She had never considered before who paid for priests. She had been quite shocked that the good father had revealed so shrewd a knowledge of worldly things, and had said so. But he had leaned towards her with tired eyes and asked, 'What good would a priest be, child, if he did not understand the nature of the earthly kingdom God has created?'

The Commissary arrived on horseback soon after sunrise. She saw him from the back, watched him dismount. On the way here she had imagined him to be a Paris dandy of some new kind; the glimpses she now had of him outside the window did not disappoint her. He was elegantly uniformed in Parisian black – superfine doe, stuff of the very best to judge by the way the fabric folded and hung – impeccable Revolutionary tailoring with deep collar and lapels, riding boots, soft yellow chamois gloves. He wore the tricolour rosette. The man was almost a Jacobin fop; he appeared every inch one of the new élite.

She remembered Davout's perceptive words: '*Aujourd'hui, comme hier . . .*' Today, the same as yesterday. How right he had been. Politics did not change, because human nature did not change. The deeper the anarchy into which a state was plunged the faster did the strong, the cunning and the ruthless rise up. How foolish of the people to believe that their New Order would be run by butchers and bakers and candlestick-makers.

She felt a pang of disgust at herself for having to go on her knees before such a man. Then she curbed herself with a warning not to pre-judge him. After all, he was offering help, no matter what his motive, and no matter how costly to Jacques de Tromelin.

He certainly knows how to ride, she admitted. He shows his command as he brings the animal round, and now he is tender, speaking softly. Perhaps I have done him an injustice after all. Perhaps the times have made me unduly suspicious of kindness.

She still had not seen the man's face, but something told her inside that all was not well. The way he moved as he held the bridle assailed her with a powerful feeling of *déjà vu* that made her shiver. She heard the latch rise, and tried to compose herself, but the man she saw come through the door astonished her enough to make her rise from her seat.

'Monsieur!'

'Yes, citoyenne, it is I.'

'But . . . *Gugnot*?'

The ex-groom laughed at her amazement, at the way she looked to de Tromelin for an explanation.

'I told Jacques not to identify me to you,' he said, enjoying the moment.

'Why?'

He shrugged, his manner glib. 'For fear that you would take fright.'

'You may trust Citoyen Gugnot,' de Tromelin hastened to say. 'Believe me. He is – one of *us* now.'

She remained silent as Gugnot pulled a tankard of cider from the cask on the counter and sat down across the table from her. There's a swagger about him, she thought. He's so pleased with himself. Look how he brushes a fleck from his sleeve.

'I've heard you need my help, so here I am,' he said, but his eyes were as unreadable as a fish's.

No, she thought on the edge of panic, he's enjoying my discomfort. Jacques, what have you done? You were never a very sure judge of character.

She said, 'You appear quite . . . different.'

'Thank you,' he said, looking her up and down. 'It's amazing how a painted flash gives fresh respect to the same old horse. I assure you, that's what I am. Even though our stations appear to be somewhat – reversed – citoyenne.'

Her eyes remained downcast against his gloating. 'So it seems.'

'Yes, as you can see, the Revolution has done well by me – and I've done well by myself. It's been a time of opportunity in Paris. I arrived there with nothing, within a year the famous Jacques David was sketching my portrait. Now he's imprisoned in the Luxembourg and I'm quartermaster-general of a regiment! What do you think of that? And that's not all . . .'

As he spoke, she appraised him. She found she could not easily put aside the anger she felt over what Agnes had revealed. Gugnot was the one who had spied on her.

Why should a man who was maltreated by the *ancien régime*, yet who has done so well out of the Revolution, want to help us out of our distress? she wondered. It seems to me he's too intelligent to have continued with Revolutionary ideals for long. He does not really believe the Jacobin creed. He certainly does not recognize 'equality', for it's clear to me he only wants to prove he is as good as any gentleman. Look at him! How he is at pains to show he has a gentleman's sense of honour, and a gentleman's aesthetics and a gentleman's sensibilities. Perhaps that's the key to him. For Gugnot the Revolution is purely a means of unfettering his ambitions, realizing his potential. He still admires us, for he believes that we have, even in our distress, the very qualities he would like to see in himself.

Père Fournet drew de Tromelin away on some trivial matter. A pretext, she suspected, to make the exchange between herself and the quartermaster-general private.

'You seem to have lost none of your nimbleness of mind,' she said, trying to keep any trace of irony out of her voice, trusting to his vanity that he would not detect any.

Gugnot said, 'I try to keep my wits about me. It's the best protection. That and money. I'm on the road to becoming wealthy now.' He smiled with obvious inner satisfaction. 'Perhaps that's why your cousin consented to be my wife.'

'My cousin . . . Marguerite? You're married to *Marguerite*?'

'De Tromelin's sister. Yes.' His eyes investigated hers intensely. 'Well . . . don't sound so surprised!'

She heard the dangerous edge in his words, and said instantly, 'I'm sorry.'

'Of course, until recently, such a match as ours would have been unthinkable. We were married six weeks ago at the Temple of Reason in Rouen.' He drank daintily, then put down his tankard and stared at her with a half smile. 'It was quite an affair. And expensive. No – I know what you're thinking – you imagine she saw her chance to take the easy way out, that she married me for the protection I can give her. Well, you're wrong about that.'

She found it hard to think of a suitable reply. At length she said, 'I hope good fortune attends Marguerite as it seems to have attended you.'

The words sounded thick with sarcasm in her own ears, despite her having tried hard to make the sentiment anything but ironic. Still, Gugnot appeared not to notice, or if he had, not to mind.

'I'll drink to that,' he said, leaning back and snapping his fingers at de Tromelin. 'Fetch Mademoiselle Berenice and myself a glass of champagne each, there's a good fellow. In fact, you can bring us a bottle.'

She saw de Tromelin's eagerness to please, and her heart fell as he unwired the bottle and popped it for them. The pale effervescence fell into Gugnot's tankard and another brought for her. He took a draught, smacked his lips appreciatively. 'Here's to the good life.'

'The good life,' she echoed emptily.

He leaned forward again, putting his elbows on the table. 'You know, I've been back up to Thury-Harcourt. I was told the Guard had been quartered in the house. I wanted to see for myself what the mob had done to it.'

She swallowed, but forced herself to remain placidly attentive to his words. She did not admit having been there herself. 'How did it seem to you?'

He shook his head. 'Most of the roof was off. If it's a wet spring the whole interior will have rotted away by the year's end.'

His regret seemed genuine, almost proprietorial. This time she said nothing.

'Such wanton waste. So many beautiful things destroyed. It's a crime.'

She looked away again, knowing now that the real reason Gugnot had gone to see the house was to lay to rest a cherished dream of one day becoming its owner.

'How disappointing for you,' she said.

This time he caught the tone of her remark and regarded her closely. The conceits were now fully stripped away.

'Why did you come here?' she asked.

He pursed his lips. 'To help you.'

She stared back. 'Why?'

'Why, Berenice?' Gugnot smiled a smile of such appalling insincerity that she almost recoiled. 'Because we're family now. And because I believe it is the honourable thing to do.'

'Oh, *do* you?'

He looked at her for a moment, absorbing her hostility, then his eyebrows lifted. 'You find it hard to believe that a groom should strive to be a man of honour?'

She took care to keep her voice neutral. 'You are a groom no longer.'

'Oh, you're wrong! I *am* a groom. Born and bred. My father was a groom, and so was his father. Let me say it clearly: the Gugnots are grooms. Grooms to the marrow of our bones. I never want to deny that, mademoiselle. I only ever wanted others to recognize that even a lowly groom may have dignity, may be a man of intelligence and honour and—' He stopped himself, and ran the tip of his tongue over his lips. 'Do you think I stole from your father?'

She saw the danger of straying any further than she must across Gugnot's sensitivities. His resentments were his own affair, but they had made of him a spring-trap, waiting to snap shut on her.

'I think it is – unjust to accuse anyone without proof.'

'Ah, bravo! But that is not what I asked.' He was as sharp as any lawyer. 'Do you *believe* I stole your father's watch?'

'Not now.'

'Did you *then*?'

'I didn't think much about it – then.'

He grinned in a way that sent a blade of fear through her. 'Because I was a groom?'

She sighed. 'No, because the watch was my father's business, and none of mine.'

His face hardened. 'I want to know: *did-you-think-I-was-a-thief*?'

She was aware how much hung on her answer, but she decided to gamble. Wearily she admitted, 'Yes, Monsieur Gugnot, I thought you probably were a thief. You were certainly clever enough, and . . . and I thought you had probably done what my father accused you of doing. I now know differently.'

He leaned back, still looking closely at her, making her very aware of the bandage just visible under her hat. His glance was altogether too penetrating. After a while he said, 'Good. That's honesty. I respect honesty. It's part of being a —' He hesitated minutely, and she thought he was going to say 'gentleman', but he actually said: '— an honourable man.'

He got up and looked out of the window for a moment, thinking unfathomable thoughts. Look at him, she thought, adopting what he doubtless imagines is the posture of an honourable man. He makes me sick!

He turned back. 'So, you think I'm clever, eh? You're right, I am. Cunning – that's what your father used to say I had. Cunning, as if I was one of those damned foxes he used to hunt.' He paused, looking at her for an uncomfortable length of time. 'Your English captain was a clever and honourable man, wasn't he? So you know the qualities I'm talking about. It's funny how things happen, isn't it? How they always come full circle in the end?'

She felt his eyes stripping her naked once more. 'What do you mean?'

'Just this – if your father hadn't forced me to spy on your affair with Captain Smith you might have eloped with him and ended up safe in England. And if your father hadn't accused me and thrown me out, I'd almost certainly have married Agnes.' A shrewd but private smile fleeted across his features, then vanished again. 'Whatever happened to her?'

Berenice drew a deep breath. 'I don't know.'

'Really?'

'The last I saw of Agnes was when the Revolution came to the château. Madame Cozette says she has not been seen since.'

'Oh, well . . .' Gugnot shrugged. 'I don't imagine it matters now, but – you see, things *do* come full circle – it was Agnes who stole your father's watch.'

She searched his face. 'How do you know?'

'Because she told me so. She said it would bring at least twenty-five *louis d'or* if we sold it in Havre. "Our little nest-egg", she called it. It would set us up in married life together, so she said.'

'And you said nothing about this to my father?'

He laughed shortly. 'How could I? I'd been entrusted with a secret.'

She looked at him again, this time for a longer space. She felt the brittleness of his personality then. 'Well, Monsieur Gugnot. It feels as if I'm meeting you for the first time.'

He smiled tightly. 'Perhaps you are.'

'In that case, let me ask you something: do you hold a grudge against my father for the way he treated you?'

He sat up. 'Mademoiselle, in spite of the risks I run, you can rest assured that I'll exert every means at my disposal to have the opportunity to speak with your father again.'

Gugnot rose. He slapped de Tromelin on the back. 'Jacques! Come! Let's go and see if we cannot account a count.' He chuckled at his own joke.

Berenice stood up. She felt Père Fournet's eyes on her as she joined Gugnot at the door. She wanted desperately to ask him if she should dare to trust Gugnot, just until her father was safe. She wanted that confirmation. Once Père Fournet's eyes had held all knowledge, all wisdom. Now they seemed uncertain. Suddenly she became aware of the sound of rain driving against the window panes and felt very much alone.

'Please . . . allow me to come with you.'

Gugnot turned in the doorway. 'To Caen? What for?'

'He is my father. This is my responsibility more than anyone's.'

'Very well. Meet me in three days' time at the Mountain. Jacques knows the inn I mean. Be his sister. You look the part. No one will recognize your true identity, that's a certainty. And in any case the Guard in these parts may be relied upon to yield absolutely to my authority.'

FIVE

Dark shadows cast by the sentry-house lantern rioted over the cobbles as the cloaked man alighted outside the prison. He got down from a fiacre, a small four-wheeled hackney-coach drawn by two horses, like those that waited for hire outside the Hôtel de St Fiacre in Paris. The sentry who watched it draw up stood automatically to attention.

The figure who presented his papers wordlessly had the hat and boots and the impatient bearing of a man of power. The sentry saluted him before taking the papers, glancing briefly at them before knocking on the huge iron-studded door.

'Citizen!'

A face appeared, regarded the newcomer from behind an iron grille. The papers were passed through, then the sound of a large bolt being slipped echoed, and the gate swung just wide enough to allow the visitor to pass inside.

'Wait here, if you please, citizen.'

'Hurry up, doorkeeper!'

'Yes, citizen.'

As the doorkeeper led the way up the long entrance court the prison stench grew worse than any animal byre. The shadows danced in the lantern glare. Barred windows, narrow and high, overlooked them as the visitor was conducted to the governor's house.

338

The visitor waited five minutes before the governor appeared. He was a man of some forty years, jowly, unkempt, suspicious. A day's growth of beard showed dark and silver on his jaw.

'You are in charge here?'

'I have that privilege.' He took the papers and looked them over, saying at last with reluctance, 'It's a very strange hour to be doing business of this kind, citizen.'

The visitor was curt. 'Because it gets a man out of his bed?'

'I didn't mean . . .'

'The road from Paris is long and uncomfortable. I consider myself honoured to be doing the National Convention's bidding at whatever hour, Citizen Cholet. Read this.'

The governor's expression changed when he read the two signatures that established the man's Revolutionary credentials. 'Of course, citizen. I . . .'

'Where is he?'

'In the Dark Walk. Please, this way.'

The night was damp. Dew greased the stone flags underfoot. The oppressiveness increased as the door-keeper admitted them to the central block. An aged turnkey got to his feet and opened the next door. The passageway beyond the iron door was utter blackness. When the lantern light pierced the gloom an oddly-proportioned lobby was revealed. Overhead, shallow vaults of granite bound six stout pillars together. Five channels cut in the floor carried seepage to a central drain, each ran from under a recessed cell door.

The visitor coughed. 'The place reeks!'

The governor's voice betrayed no compassion. 'It catches in the throat a bit, but a man gets used to it after a while. There're no windows in the Dark Walk. That's why we call it by that name.'

'Which is his cell?'

'Down at the end.'

The governor regarded the man from Paris as he would a viper. 'If you don't mind my asking, citizen, what's the reason for the urgency of this move to the Abbaye?'

'One does not question Citizen Robespierre's decisions. If he considers it important to transfer the prisoner immediately, then it is important.' The visitor unbent a fraction. 'Between you and me, citizen, he's not destined for the Abbaye, but for the Temple.'

The governor's brow creased. 'The Temple? My God. Then he is important.'

The visitor nodded. 'Yes. He's to be interrogated. We didn't realize how important until we received information that certain malcontents and opportunists are planning to break him out.'

'What?'

'Oh, yes. Sometime tomorrow. Have you heard nothing about this?'

Governor Cholet stiffened. 'They'll need a siege gun to get in here.'

'Apparently, part of your wall has been mined. They intend to blow it up.'

Cholet took the remark silently, but the revelation had shocked him. The turnkey handed his lantern to the visitor as the cell door swung massively on its great hinges. The man shaded his eyes from direct light as he advanced into the cell. An emaciated figure was chained to the far wall. His head had been roughly shaved and he wore rags of clothing. He was sitting upright in a mass of sodden and filthy straw, semi-conscious. He screwed his eyes tight and moaned as the lamp blasted away the foetid darkness. Rats feeding on the open sores of his calves fled.

'You are certain this is the *ci-devant* Comte du Fay?' the visitor asked the governor crisply.

'Yes. No question. He's not so grand now, is he?'

'Unshackle him.'

'I don't know about that . . .'

'Unshackle him. Sign him over first, if you will. I shall take full responsibility.'

'Surely you don't propose to take him with you now? Alone?'

'Citizen Cholet, I cannot impress upon you too much that, in this matter, time is of the essence.'

'I don't know that we can provide a guard to accompany you.'

The visitor cast a scornful glance at the governor. 'That's of no consequence, citizen. He's hardly going to run away.'

'Yes, but even so . . .'

'Have him brought up. We'll be halfway to Paris by daybreak, at which point you will post details of his transfer. Follow the usual form, but make no mention of the Temple specifically, if you please.'

Cholet was hesitant as he thought through the consequences, but then he nodded. 'Of course.'

The visitor turned on his heel and slapped the back of his hand into his palm sharply. 'Get a search under way at once for the mine. There's probably not much to worry about. These so-called "Chouans" are scum, counter-revolutionary vagabonds. I doubt they'll waste their powder on this hole once they learn the object of their attentions has left the vicinity.'

The prisoner could not stand. The doorkeeper took him under the arms, and the turnkey lifted his ankles and they struggled him outside and to the entrance to the governor's house, stopping each time to bolt and lock the doors through which they passed. At the governor's house, the Comte du Fay was laid on the floor, and the visitor called for a blanket to be brought for him.

'A blanket?'

'Yes, citizen, a blanket. It's almost certain that the gate is being watched. Therefore we must be as unobtrusive as possible.' He added as an afterthought, 'And it wouldn't do for him to die of cold on the way to Paris, would it?'

Cholet responded with a grim smile.

'Now, I need you to sign his release papers. Here, here and . . . here.'

A receipt was left, and a blanket brought. The prisoner was wrapped in it, then they carried him down to the main gate, and out to the waiting fiacre. At a signal from Governor Cholet the sentry stepped up to open the carriage door. He laid down his musket to help manhandle the prisoner inside.

When the visitor climbed in the sentry tried to close the fiacre door after him, but he was prevented from doing so.

'Thank you, Citizen Cholet. You have been most efficient. Citizen Robespierre will hear of it personally. Driver! Drive on!'

The fiacre lurched forward as the horses were whipped up, almost throwing the comte off the seat.

'Here, drink this. It's good brandy.'

The comte's eyes were dull. He turned his head aside as the flask was put to his lips, but some of the amber fire trickled into his mouth. He coughed, and that seemed to revive him a little. Then his eyes opened wide and he moaned.

'Am I dreaming? Is this madness?'

'No.' The other grinned, throwing down his hat. 'Nor am I a ghost. You *do* know me.'

'Captain . . . Smith.'

'At your service, my lord. And with any luck we'll be in England by this time tomorrow.'

Smith's heart was thumping; exultant excitement trembled inside him. The performance had wrung him dry, and the broken condition of the man he remembered filled him with concern and pity, but his plan had worked far better than he had dared to hope. Ingenuity had succeeded where a ton of gunpowder would have failed. He clenched his fist and grimaced in private triumph.

'Then I am not to go to Paris?'

'Monsieur, in a moment we will turn off the Paris turnpike, and instead take the coast road to a beach near St Aubin, where a boat is waiting for us. It is imperative that you recall to me now a certain list of names.'

The fiacre bounced over uneven streets as the driver did as he had been charged to do, and drove like the devil. The comte's ghastly face looked to Smith like that of a dying man who had been asked to reveal where he had hidden his life's savings. How many times must he have slipped in and out of nightmare in that foul place? Smith wondered. He can't believe in me. His world has been shattered. He can't believe in anything anymore.

'Monsieur, I need to know who are the Chouan leaders. Where they are massing their forces. What is their strength. The king's navy can help supply them.'

The comte's strength waned and he seemed to slump back inside himself. Smith tore off his cloak and bundled him up, pillowing his head. There was one question he burned to ask, but his first duty was clear. 'France is at war with England. Her insurrections must be encouraged. If Brittany and Normandy can be set afire the Revolution might yet be reversed.'

But the comte only stared back, stupefied by what had happened to him. He was like a sleepwalker.

Smith stared, wondering how he could break the spell, then, suddenly, an inspiration came to him out of nowhere. He felt in his pocket for the little silver charm and put it before the comte's vacant gaze.

'Do you remember this?' he asked fervently. 'Look at it! Do you remember seeing it about Berenice's neck? This proves I am in earnest. You must trust me.'

The comte's eyes focused; he recognized the worn silver figure.

'Oh, the Christ . . .' he breathed in faint rapture.

Smith could barely hear him above the clattering and bouncing of their ride, as he said, 'Look for the screech-owls in the woods of Fougère and Misdon and the Forêt de Pertre. The brothers Cottereau lead them. They are four in number. In the Vendée there are fifty thousand who will follow the Prince de Talmont, Jean-Nicolas Stofflet, Jacques Cathelneau and Gaston Bourdic . . .'

Smith roused the comte again as the man's concentration began to fail. 'Listen to me, monsieur! I must tell you that I've had news of your wife. I was told yesterday that she has been got out of La Precey where she was being held.'

A spasm convulsed the comte, and he cried out: 'My wife?'

'And also your younger daughter, Celestine. I don't know where they are, but I have this information from one whom I trust completely. A bribe was paid to buy their release. One day, sir, you will be reunited with your family.'

His wasted hand gripped Smith's own and tears welled in his eyes. 'Oh, my family . . .'

'What do you know of the fate of your elder daughter?' He braced himself in the wildly bucking carriage, squeezing the comte's hand, willing him to answer. 'Berenice, monsieur? Please. What has happened to Berenice?'

'Berenice?' the comte echoed distantly, his eyes rolling. 'She wanted to marry an Englishman . . .'

The fiacre slewed suddenly as one wheel jarred on a kerb, throwing him hard against the door. He felt impotent anger surge in him. 'Monsieur! For God's sake, what has happened to her?'

But there was no answer, even though he gripped the comte by the shoulders this time to shake him, until sense overwhelmed him. Four loud thumps reverberated on the roof, warning of trouble on the road ahead. The driver, a desperate fellow who had been a monk at Mont St Michel, showed no sign of slackening his speed.

Smith flung down the window and put his head out into the night. The rush of air was cold and damp. A branch clattered the side of the fiacre, lashed his face, making him flinch back, but not before he had seen that the road ahead was blocked. Three men, one with a lantern, were waving the carriage down. But the driver had determined to ride through them.

'No!' he shouted, banging crazily on the roof. 'I'll talk us through!'

But the three men were already leaping aside.

'Damn you, man! Why did you do that?' he shouted uselessly. The driver was so bundled up in scarves he could not hear anything. Smith heard a report ring out behind, but the shot missed. Then he was thrown violently to the left and skinned his hand on a sill as the fiacre shuddered to a halt.

He got to his feet and burst out of the door. The Guard were less than fifty yards away, yelling after them and running in pursuit. The two lathered horses stamped and whinnied anxiously. Smith saw that they had refused because the road was blocked by a great *chevaux-defrise* – a pine trunk, drilled at intervals and set with sharpened stakes, set across the road for just such an eventuality.

The driver had bolted into the woods. Smith stared around, and saw that the Guard would be upon them in seconds. He leapt back into the fiacre, and dragged the comte towards him, hoisting him over his shoulder. He was heavier than Smith expected, and struggling.

'Stay still, sir!'

'Leave me!'

'No!'

The first of the Guard was ten paces away when Smith drew his pistol and fired at him. The man collapsed, doubled over. The other two dived off the road and into the undergrowth, fearing that Smith had a second pistol. He wished that it was so.

Smith left the road also, carrying his burden into the darkness on the other side, crashing through the undergrowth until he could no longer hear the wounded man's groans. He laid the comte down on pine needles, breathing heavily.

The Frenchman's voice was weak, but lucid once more and distinct in the silence. 'Save yourself, I beg you. You have given me one last taste of freedom. I could not have asked for more.'

'That's really not the object of the exercise,' he hissed back.

'You are a tenacious man, but you must see that you have no alternative. Go, captain, you have done your utmost. I have already severed myself from this world, but you, whom once I misjudged, must live to fight another day.'

He collapsed inside himself again, and Smith shook him again. 'What happened to Berenice? Open your eyes!'

The comte's eyes opened again. 'They told me . . . my lovely girl had died in the Convent of La Precey.'

There was yelling. More men had arrived, summoned by the sound of his pistol. He stared at them, shocked by the old man's words. It couldn't be true. It couldn't! It was mere incoherent rambling! Then the terrible moment of decision was upon him. He knew there was nothing more he could do for the comte. To abandon him here felt like a monstrous crime, but the thought of avenging Berenice drove him to a choice. He saluted and with the words, 'I will live to fight again. I salute your courage!' he turned and plunged into the darkness.

SIX

Berenice and Jacques de Tromelin crossed the Calvados plain in driving sleet, taking the road first to Bourgebus, and then towards the Orne and the southern faubourgs of the city. Those few travellers they met coming the other way told them that Caen was in uproar, that there were road blocks up ahead, that the town was thick with soldiers.

Berenice felt sickly fearful as they came in sight of the inn. She scraped the mud from her feet at the doorway, entered and sat down. The main room was already occupied by a dozen or so people. It was spacious and light, with big windows and set with tables and chairs on a scrubbed wooden floor, but the decor sent shivers through her. The walls were painted with Revolutionary trophies – wallpaper depicted the Revolutionary 'Mountain' rising above the 'Plain', its summit sending out bolts of jagged red lightning to smite the enemies of France. There were tricolour swags and laurels, rosettes and Roman spears surmounted by the red bonnet. New souvenir porcelain, she saw, crudely depicting the triumphs of the Revolution, stood along the rack.

Gugnot had a devil-may-care air as he met them. Perhaps, she thought, it was to compensate for his bodily ills: his face was bruised, and there was an ugly gash on his hand. When she asked him about it, he

347

shrugged. 'Nothing at all. A fall from my horse, that's all.' But she knew he was lying.

He ordered the *traiteur* to prepare them a dish peculiar to the place. The fellow who came to them was obsequious, and Gugnot turned to Berenice well-pleased. 'I assure you, citoyenne, you will find it most delicious. Exquisite. Don't worry, I shall bear the cost. It's a dish composed of a species of salmon-trout, of which the river hereabouts produces an infinite number.'

Berenice bit her lower lip, then said quietly, 'I'm sure the menu is excellent, citizen, but may I remind you that we have important business in Caen?'

Gugnot leaned closer, his smile enigmatic. 'Let me tell you: the landlord here is quite new. He has taken the place over from his rival, a man who was not so – how shall I say? —' He made a clenched fist. '—*enthusiastic* for the Revolution. Citoyen Thierry turns his riverside situation to very good account, don't you think?'

The name sent a pang of anxiety through her. She felt the impulse to hide her face from the serving staff. It was Thierry who had made his confession to Père Fournet, and to whom therefore she had sent her pearls to ransom the lives of her mother and sister.

'Why are we here?'

'Because Thierry will meet us soon.'

Her heart almost missed a beat. 'You've arranged it?'

'Of course.' He touched his forefinger against the side of his nose. 'He's as good as his word. There are to be no executions today.'

As they ate, Gugnot chattered continuously and inconsequentially. Berenice felt increasingly unsettled by his behaviour. Her instinct was to make herself as transparent as possible in this strange and threatening place, but Gugnot was in expansive mood. He grew louder with each glass he downed. She saw him take every opportunity to flaunt his Revolutionary credentials.

After a second bottle had appeared she noticed a well-dressed man, apparently in his late fifties, come into the room. His coat was wet and he wore a wide-brimmed hat that he took off as he entered. His expression was vinegary and unamused.

Berenice's first thought was that this must be Citizen Thierry, but he lacked the bearing of the owner, and he sat down at a table like any other customer. He ordered a plain, one-egg omelette, and began to pick at it.

'Good afternoon, citizen,' Gugnot said and, raising his glass, added, 'The Republic – One and Indivisible!'

The man nodded back, coldly.

'What's the matter, citizen? The weather getting you down?'

'I have no wish for conversation at present.'

Then Gugnot took him a glass of wine and asked after his appetite and then his name.

The man looked up and replied with studied patience. 'Citizens, my name is Leon Fabius. I am a Walloon, born in Ghent, and a stranger to these parts, though I have been a physician in France these thirty years.'

Gugnot was still not satisfied. He resorted to more Revolutionary bluffness, and continued to play the over-hearty comrade. 'It's a free country now. Free and open. And we're all equal citizens together, are we not? So why not tell us what business you're about.'

The doctor stared back bleakly. 'The town is swarming with soldiers. I have had a difficult morning. I am quite certain you do not want to hear my tale.'

'Come, citoyen doctor, why do you say that?'

She saw how the doctor's hands tightened on his knife and fork. 'Because I know that what I have to say would only harm your conviviality.'

Berenice felt the man's hostility, as Gugnot continued to ply him with forced bonhomie. The doctor was disinclined to drink, but Gugnot pressed the glass on him. He made his voice loud enough to encompass the entire room. 'I'm sure we do want to hear your story, citoyen doctor. We'll have no strangers in our midst, so speak up.'

The doctor spoke in a low, controlled voice. There was something fierce about him now. The room had fallen silent. He said, 'I am just returned from beholding a most *unholy* spectacle. The execution of three brothers. Two gentlemen who were officers in the regiment of Roche Dragoons, and their brother, the Grand Vicar of Deauville. According to the charge, they were all caught in the act of emigrating at Havre. They were tried this morning, condemned, and – as I have just witnessed – executed upon the infernal machine.'

Berenice's stomach turned to ice-water. Gugnot had said there were to be no executions today.

The doctor had said what only a foreigner could say. But even so it was foolhardy to speak in such terms, and the atmosphere in the room had hardened.

Gugnot's voice filled the silence. 'I myself saw the forger Pelletier executed in Paris not a year ago.'

There was a look of utter contempt in the doctor's eye as he held his peace, but Gugnot would not let the matter go. He said, 'You are a doctor, a man of the same profession as the deputy, Joseph-Ignace Guillotin, the same who proposed our *humane* method. Antoine Louis, he who conceived its exact design, is also a surgeon. Therefore, citoyen, I am interested to hear your opinions of the machine.'

'I would rather not speak of it at present.'

'Oh, but I *insist* you give your views.'

Fabius put down his fork very deliberately. His face was pale and his lips narrowly pursed. Berenice saw that he knew he had already said more than was consistent with his own safety, given the sympathies of the locale, but still he went ahead. 'Very well. I shall tell you exactly what I saw. I was passing the Place de Greve when I saw a great concourse of people coming towards me. I stopped and was – as it were – enveloped by this crowd, and trapped so near the condemned men that I heard all that passed between them. They began by entreating the Almighty to receive their souls. As they put it, the sacrifice they made by their deaths was purely occasioned by their persisting in their duty to their God, their religion, and their king. At the same time they prayed that their murderers might be forgiven, and that they might be reconciled to their Maker.'

Fabius halted, but then to Berenice's horror he continued. All those in the inn had heard what dangerous talk was being broached. They looked at the heretic, aghast.

The doctor's voice grew more powerful. 'These men addressed themselves to the people. One of them said, "My friends, it is from this true Christian that you must learn how to die. You have been deceived by the Revolution! This is not the way to improve society. I pray you live long enough to discover your errors!"

'The executioners began with the youngest. The two elders encouraged him to meet his fate with fortitude. They reminded him that he would soon be beyond the reach of his enemies. Then he was laid on the bed of that gruesome machine, the blade was let fall, and his head was parted from his body.'

Berenice looked from face to face, but instead of the hatred she expected she saw only fear. They looked like so many churchgoers mortified by the sermon of a heretic priest, but one who had swept away a fiction. All present were willing the doctor to silence, but all knew very well the truth of his declaration. And it was significant that not one of them rose to shut him up. She now knew the meaning of what they called 'the Terror'. It was not the terror that had been inflicted on the aristos, but the terror inspired in their own hearts.

The doctor's impassioned voice rose again. He had been reluctant to begin, but now he was impossible to stop. 'If the first brother met his fate like a hero, so did the second. The Grand Vicar, with a calmness and placidity that made the strongest impression on all present, offered up a short prayer. Then he suffered like a saint in the silence that surrounded him. His fortitude in the face of terror, his bravery after all he had witnessed, the bloody deliberateness of it ... Citizens, they did not even wash the blood from *la guillotine* before they laid the last brother upon it.' His accusing eye encompassed them all. 'So – citizens of France – I must apologize to you all, for I cannot describe the scene to you. As for myself, the poignancy I was obliged to behold had such an effect on me, that I left the city with the utmost horror. I bid you all a very good day.'

The doctor's simmering passion had crushed his audience to absolute silence. He had made a visible impression on de Tromelin, who stared wordlessly at the vacant chair and the half-eaten omelette. But Gugnot showed his mettle. He stood up gallantly, and addressed the doorway as if the man could hear him. 'Citoyen doctor, we're all very surprised that you should feel so much compassion for three men who are plainly culpable towards the state. Come back and join us in drinking to the health of the administrators who in thus doing their duty do most essentially forward the interests of their country.'

The toast was ghastly, the sentiment vile, but Berenice noted that everyone in the room raised their glasses and drank to it. Then the noonday chime sounded.

She realized that the news that the executions were going ahead in Caen had thrown Gugnot on to the horns of a dilemma. Should he wait for Thierry, or go to Caen with all speed? She urged him to do the latter.

The ride into town was nightmarish. Gugnot took them through the road blocks, but she knew with a sick feeling that they had arrived in the rainswept Place de Greve too late to save her father. Gugnot left them –

going direct to the Municipality was the only way to halt the proceedings. She knew he would not be able to do it. She felt the certainty now, like lead in her belly.

A great number of people had gathered. On the orders of the Municipality, the shops had been closed. The crowd were huddled behind a line of bedraggled soldiers, all drenched by the downpour, but their curiosity remained undampened. The knowledge was an abomination, but there could be no explanation other than her father's celebrity.

Berenice moved among the crowd. They are not wild beasts, she thought, repelled by the general good humour. They are not hate-filled savages, but ordinary people – tradespeople and labourers and artisans. People such as these gather in the marketplaces of every civilized nation, to witness the execution of criminals. The only difference is that now they have come to see how a count of the *ancien régime* dies.

Her first sight of the execution ground appalled her so much that she could not prevent herself from gasping. There was her father, on the stage. De Tromelin tried to steer her eyes away from the bloodstained timber platform that had been built almost head high in the square, but she fought his hands off, and pushed foward.

The crowd were too thickly packed. She saw there could be no way through them, nor the soldiers with their muskets and fixed bayonets who formed the palisade around the platform.

De Tromelin grappled with her. He held her tight to his wet coat, and she yielded, realizing with depression that if there was no way to approach, there was also no way to make herself known to her father. To have that moment of intimate leave-taking was necessary. It was hers by right, and all that she wanted if her father was to die.

They have robbed me even of that, she thought in despair. Her father appeared, staggering on the stage.

She wanted to cry out, but de Tromelin's life, as well as her own, was hostage. She began to babble a prayer. Her hands were bloodless, shaking. Then her knees would no longer hold her. De Tromelin pulled her tighter to him, until his grip crushed her. He seemed horrified by the scene she was making. He shook her.

'This is insane,' he hissed. 'Come! We're leaving!'

She saw people nearby scowling at her as she screamed back. 'No!'

'If she can't stand the sight of a bit of blood you'd best get her home,' she heard someone call jocularly. She faced de Tromelin, feeling her rain-wetted features contorting. 'I'm staying! It's my right to stay! If you try to pull me away, you know what I'll do!'

His face twitched at the threat, and in that moment she saw a deep pain in him – as if he at last understood why she had never requited his love for her. There had never been any magnetism between them. He held her even more tightly, but it was without authority. He knew he did not have the moral right to take her away against her will.

All she could do was stare at the mesmeric stage backed by the brooding blocks of mediaeval stone. The pathetic victim – shorn of his hair, shorn of all his dignity – stooped and wretched. He was attended by three black-shirted executioners who went so matter-of-factly about their business.

Half a dozen Municipal officials appeared, then a man in a blacksmith's leather apron, and then an army officer. It was so casual, and so leisurely, like men gathered to perform some trivial mechanical task like the opening of a toll-gate, or the agreed butchery of an animal. There was no sense that anyone considered the event significant, as if it would not have mattered much either way if the Comte du Fay were executed, or escaped to England. The soldiers and officials were doing their duty, the artisans earning a living, the crowd had been coerced to bear witness in the dismal weather.

'Look at him!' she wanted to shout. 'Are none of you ashamed? Have none of you any pity in your hearts? Have none of you the heart to put yourselves in his place? You're blocks of stone! Worse than barbarian savages. Is this your *entertainment*? Are you so sated with vile sights that you are unable to see cold-blooded murder for what it is? Who amongst you has the least understanding of what you are doing? Let me take him away to England. Let me take him away . . .'

Her eyes roamed over the wooden machine that was erected in the centre of the platform. It was a monstrous sight – two upright pillars twelve or thirteen feet high, joined at the top by a cross-beam. The uprights stood a little more than a foot apart, with grooves to guide the moving part. To the nearer was attached an iron hook. Below was a sturdy plank with securing belts and a board with a hole to hold the victim's head immobile.

Gugnot's words in the inn rang unstoppably in her mind. This abomination he had called 'the humane method'. It had been conceived and designed by *doctors*.

She looked at the great iron weight which was riveted to a deep triangular blade from which rain dripped. The contemplation of that ghastly shining edge shot her stomach through with bolts of dread. The revulsion was made worse by the readiness with which her mind understood the mechanism as it was prepared.

The sound of ringing iron came from the blade as it was honed. A dozen rhythmic strokes of the whetstone, applied by the leather-aproned man.

The pulley in the cross-beam took the lifting rope, which was secured to a hook on one of the uprights. The biggest of the black-clad attendants hauled hand-over-hand on the rope, so that the heavily weighted blade lifted two feet, paused, lifted another two feet, paused again, on and on, until it was at the top of its travel. Then a loop in the rope was secured on the iron hook. The tautness of the rope and the difficulty the attendant had in lifting the weight showed her it must be forty or fifty pounds.

An official began to read from a paper that he had difficulty in shielding from the rain. His voice was reedy over the heads of the crowd. The rain smothered his words. She could not hear what he said, but it drew murmurs of abuse from the crowd. Then her father was brought forward. They ripped his filthy shirt, pulling it down around his elbows. Something made him reluctant. His hands were bound behind his back, and they would not release him.

There were a few desultory jeers as some of the crowd misunderstood what was happening.

'He only wants to be able to pray,' she whispered. But she saw her father obliged to step up to the plank and be helped to turn and lie face down on it. Two of the executioners – father and first son of the family Wirion – stood either side and lifted the *ci-devant* count bodily forward, so that his chin passed over the semicircular hole cut in the lower stock. Then the second son slid the upper restraining board into place above his neck and chocked it in place.

The steady, drenching rain poured down. It intensified, turning the platform to glass, haloing the infernal machine and the victim's bare white back in spray. Berenice watched it all, tears cascading unseen down her face. She heard the connoisseurs criticize something. The two restraining belts had been left unbuckled. A swelling complaint began to spread from the front. Whistles of derision, raised hands gesturing obscenely in the rain. There was a further delay as a section of the crowd pointed out some other lack to the officials.

A baker's basket was brought and placed under the count's face, and the dissatisfaction of the crowd subsided. Then the signal was given and the rope unhooked.

The second son of the family Wirion took the strain momentarily as a rumbling roll sounded from the drummer's rain-slackened skin. There was a moment of expectation, then the blade fell.

Berenice forced her eyes to see and her ears to hear, so that the crime would live with her, properly impressed on her brain and on her heart. She saw the blade travel and heard its scraping and the way it bit into the base block. She heard the momentary squeal of the pulley wheel, saw the head fall and jar the basket as it landed. She saw the horrific gouts of blood – pints and pints of it – pour from the apparatus and suffuse the pools of rainwater that had collected on the stage.

It was done. An irreversible act. There was no going back on it. No denying. The hoping was over. All the plans had failed. She would never see her father again. Never hear his voice. Never . . .

She watched the body's limbs twitching and moving for an astonishing space of time after as her father's death-white head was lifted from the basket. The vigorous Wirion strode the platform from end to end with it raised on high. The eyes were open and staring, the mouth hanging slack, tongue protruding because the strings of the throat had been severed. The people let out a jaded chant, extolling the virtues of their Revolution all around.

Berenice's mind was losing touch with the world. There was a tremendous and sickening sense of numbness. It was shock, a sensation worse than anything she had felt before. It was suddenly as if she was seeing herself from above, looking down from somewhere outside herself. She saw herself, fainting, pale-faced and bedraggled and falling back, yet some part of her remained conscious all the while. She wanted to know where the spirit of her father had gone; it was certain that he could no longer inhabit the waxen flesh that was being so loathsomely displayed.

When she came to, she was gasping and there was pain in her chest. The crowd was melting away from the square, and Jacques de Tromelin was holding her, looking at her with compassionate but uncomprehending eyes.

He tried to hug her to him, but she wouldn't allow it. The only thought she could resolve in her mind was a simple practical question: how would she ever be able to conceal what she had seen from her mother and from Celestine?

It seemed impossible, but she knew that it must be done – for she was resolved that no others of her family would be brought to the same fate. They were going to escape the nightmare that was France, or die in the attempt.

PART 7

The White Hammer

SUMMER, 1793
Aboard a French frigate bound for Toulon

Monsieur, *how pleased I am to see you once again! How can you ever forgive me for the grotesque crime I committed in disbelieving you? It will not happen again.*

Well – *you can see how abject I am. I have missed my fate. I am disgraced. Paoli is supreme, Corsica is his, and I am in exile once again. It is as before, only worse, for this time my family must go to France with me. Myself and my brother, Joseph, my two sisters, my mother and Uncle Fesch. Look at my proud mother, Madame Mère, Letizia! Forty-three years of age, a widow these eight years, her two youngest children still in Corsica, in the care of relatives. Everything she owned is gone. She possesses only what she stands up in. The mob ransacked our house and gutted it, but she does not complain. Nor does she blame me. She never blamed me once. For her, still, I can do no wrong.*

And you forgive me, too, do you not, monsieur? I may say that your presence is a great comfort to me, in this time of desperation. And how these dialogues with you encourage me. Without you, I would have given in to melancholy years ago. Instead, I have that strength, that fierce burning energy that you put into me. I have heard you say it twice now that you will make me master of Corsica. I know better than to disbelieve you, but as I gaze on that receding coast the child part of me wonders how it can be that I will ever return. What an irony, the homeland I have sought to liberate has now driven me out as a Frenchman! My heart tells me that I am done with Corsicans and islands. And you tell me so, too, monsieur. For the moment.

So, Paoli has won. He has declared Corsica independent. He says the Corsicans' allegiance to France was ended when King Louis was murdered, that the popular feeling in Ajaccio is against the Jacobins. He says that Corsicans are good Catholics, set in their ways, that they have no time for murderous French atheists. He believes everyone thinks as he does.

You know, on my return I was prepared to work with him. I tried to make him cooperate, but he never trusted me. It was the campaign to seize control of Sardinia that showed Paoli in his true colours. He and his nephew, Cesari-Colonna, together plotted my death. Despicable treachery, while we were engaged on a mission to take Caprera and the rest of the Madalena Isles. A mutiny aboard ship, they said – so sorry, but we cannot reinforce you – but it was all a filthy scheme, a deliberate plot to leave my battery exposed! To get me killed or taken prisoner. They must think I'm stupid to believe it was a mutiny. And they did not reckon with you, monsieur!

I only escaped by a fluke of fate. Four cannon and a mortar, lost. Ah, well, in Corsica now we are wanted. Like criminals. Banished. We only got away from that shore by the skin of our teeth. At night. Through the same woods that my mother negotiated to escape the French when I was in her belly four-and-twenty years ago. If it had not been for this French ship, I don't know what would have become of us. A stroke of fate. Or should I say, your agency, monsieur. Tell me true, did you provide for me? For us?

I thought so!

Well, now we are sailing for Toulon. The heart of me is a furnace, white hot; it shall consume all. You are *right: a great leader must learn to shelve all his vendettas at will, and to take them up again only when they are ready to bear a resolution. I learn so much from you. You are so wise; like the father I hardly knew. You have taught me that I must bide my time but work constantly towards my goal, that my faith in you must never falter, and that the taste of defeat is the bitterest gall.*

Believe me when I say I will not willingly taste it again, monsieur.

ONE

MAY, 1793
France

Berenice knew as the waggon pulled up in the clearing in the Forêt d'Ecouves that she must try to give herself courage. Courage to continue with the lie that could save them, courage to drive them on, across France and all the way to the free city of Lyons. They had to go south, for the coast was now so well patrolled that they would stand no chance of getting a boat, let alone reaching England.

Jacques de Tromelin jumped down. He was equipped as a lieutenant, and if challenged they were to respond as his family. The passports had been prepared, and the signatures of the different municipal officers imitated. The thought of the passes made her stomach turn over. It was incredible that these ridiculous pieces of printed paper – things of no intrinsic worth at all – were now absolute life and death to everyone in France.

Whatever happens, she thought, this will be the last time I will ever see two very good souls.

Three hours ago Mademoiselle Adeline had set before them a last good meal, and then, one by one, their faithful friends had taken their leave. She had found to her astonishment that each of them, no matter how poor, had brought her the present of a small sum of money. She had tried to refuse it, but it was pressed on her. As was a note carried to her by Faligan.

'To assist you in your journey,' Père Fournet had

written from Caen. 'I shall pray that the Lord, who has so far aided you, may give you strength to accomplish what you must, and preserve you from all harm. Bear your cross with endurance, my dear. And God bless you.'

Adeline had looked at her approvingly. 'You will be lucky. I know it. Events have hardened you, Berenice.'

'Yes.'

So they had parted with tears in their eyes, and this beginning to their journey – the real beginning – had been set for eight o'clock that night. She embraced Madame Cozette, then turned to the loyalest of her friends.

'Dear Davout,' she said hugging him. He stood stolidly, in his old lumpish style. He had, she knew, retired again from human contact. 'Won't you at least wish me a farewell?'

But he made no sound. Perhaps he's unable to make a true response while the others are in attendance, she thought. He has moved inside himself rather than take leave of us.

The sound of the irons of his clogs crunching under-foot was a sound of infinite sadness. She looked at his ox-huge shoulders for a moment, then wiped her eyes, thinking, for all his great strength he has no defence against the disappointment of losing people. Perhaps what drew us together was the loss of my family; I never discovered how he lost his own, but now I have mine back again, all except Papa . . .

'Come, Berenice. We must hurry.'

The dreadful lie hung heavy over her. She recalled the moment when she had seen her mother for the first time after returning from the Place de Greve. It was easy to decide what to do: there was not sufficient strength in the Comtesse du Fay to bear the truth. A description of her husband's fate would have killed her too.

What's been hardest is the bearing of that terrible

truth, she thought. And the lie that I had to put in its place. Jacques promised to say nothing. That is as it should be. The lie is to be mine alone.

'How is he?' That was the very first question her mother had asked. 'Tell me how is your poor father?'

She had bitten back her feelings, her fist clenched white at her side, so that her nails bit into her palm. There was no lie in her first reply. 'He sends you his fondest love.'

But then there had come more questions, questions tumbling one after another from both mother and sister. She told them that he was in good spirits, that she had seen him and he was not now in any discomfort, he was securely held, had sufficient for his needs, but he had ordered – had *begged* them – to make good their escape.

'We cannot leave him.' Her mother's head shook. 'I *won't* leave him! I'll never do that, Berenice. Never.'

'Mother, listen to me—'

'No!'

'You *must*!'

'Berenice! It does not befit a lady.'

'Mother – *you* are not a lady now!'

The venom Berenice heard in her own voice shocked her, and she instantly regretted crushing her mother's objections in so cruel a way. But then she rushed headlong into the vacuum. It must have been a divine inspiration, for an ingenious idea had appeared in her mind. Without warning. Without effort. The perfect solution, come as if from the air. 'Mother, you know they want to execute all aristos. But—'

'Berenice, I will not listen!'

She held her mother's hands, willing her to listen. 'But they will not execute father. Not until the whole family has been apprehended.'

Her mother stared back. 'What?'

In a blinding moment Berenice recalled the words Faligan had used when he told what had happened to her pearls, the ones that Père Fournet had used to bribe Citizen Rethureau: '*Take those two women back to prison. I have received information that the rest of their family is still living concealed in the woods of Cinglais. We shall soon have them in our power, and then we will make a more striking example by executing the whole family together.*'

She saw de Tromelin looking pointedly away. She saw her sister's upturned face, the way she hung on those terrible lies as if they were gospel. It almost unnerved her, but she forced herself to go through with it, even though her voice began to quaver. 'The gaoler says that father is to remain in his cell. He says he knows that the rest of the family du Fay are hiding in the woods of Cinglais. "We shall soon have them in our power", he said. "And then we will make a more striking example by executing the whole family together."'

'The devil said that?' Her mother was aghast. 'Oh, they are evil, *evil* men!'

Berenice had nodded, closing her eyes, but only to see her father's head falling into the basket again. She felt that terrifying dislocation of her senses, and wanted to blind her own mind's eye.

'So you see, mother, father is quite safe – until we are captured also. The only way we can save his life is by saving our own. That is our duty now.'

She looked at her mother in the dappled light of the forest clearing, and hid her true feelings. It was hard to suppress the disgust she felt at her own deception. It's a dreadful thing to do, she thought. But, in this case, the truth is so terrible that a lie *must* be better. It has worked on mother, hasn't it? Like a drug, energizing her, and driving her to a new resolve. She *will* leave Normandy. She *will* escape the Guard. She *will* cross all of France if need be, to save her husband. And that is all that matters.

Jacques smiled briefly at her. Yesterday he had said, 'We have all lied. It is well that none of us know the true thoughts of another.' And the look of loss in his eyes had troubled her. He looked like a man who had made too many difficult decisions, and was no longer the young, careless fellow she had known in the time before.

De Tromelin had laid plans to remove them from the district as soon as possible. They had not revealed to the comtesse or to Celestine the identity of the mysterious Jacobin Commissary who had helped them. De Tromelin could not go with them, but he had agreed to meet them at Roanne and provide a way to get them across the lines and into the Royalist-held city of Lyons.

There had been a great deal of rain, but Berenice thought the weather was warm. The May evening light was already fading. The plan was for them to arrive at their first destination by sunrise next morning. She knew that to do so they would have to walk a dozen leagues, and cross streams and rough country, avoiding robbers and the Guard – it was a difficult undertaking for anyone, hugely so for one in her mother's condition.

'Will we get to Lyons?' Celestine asked her in a quiet moment.

She hugged her sister. 'Yes. We will. And you must believe we will.'

But as she said it Berenice realized she had spoken out of hope rather than conviction, and that her sister would hear the hollowness in her voice. The entirety of the journey is too much to comprehend, she told herself strictly, pulling her shawl about her shoulders. The only way to succeed will be to take each day as its own individual challenge.

'I don't know if I can believe,' Celestine said.

'Don't let me down,' she said. 'Be strong for mother's sake – even if you don't feel it. There is no way to foresee what we shall encounter, so we must face whatever obstacles lie across our way with courage.'

They watched the waggon being led round in a circle, and Davout driving it back the way it had come, then they set off from the clearing themselves. De Tromelin conducted them first to a boatman's house along a series of quiet paths, bringing them eventually to a place of willow trees, and a muddy riverbank. There they found a boat ready, and the local people, who were not at all for the Revolution, provided some bread and cheese.

She asked de Tromelin what time it was. He opened his pocket watch. 'Not quite ten o'clock.'

They lost no time in getting off on the river. The Sarthe was swollen. Its surface was muscular and knotted, and seethed as black as lawyers' ink. The torrent of rain that had fallen in the past week had brought the water up, and the flow fascinated her with its promise of danger. They went swiftly upon it.

'Quiet now,' the boatman whispered. 'Guard boats are stationed up and down the river at every half-league.' But they went unchallenged, and in an hour he began to guide them in towards the left bank. When they were tied fast, he put his hands together and gave the owl hoot that Davout had used in the woods to signal to her.

'Such an eerie sound,' she said.

'It has become the cry of freedom in all the west of France,' de Tromelin said. 'How the men faithful to the Cause recognize one another.'

A guide appeared from the darkness, a small man with a weatherbeaten face and bright eyes, to take them over the common. One league from the high road to Le Mans their ways parted.

De Tromelin drew her aside, his face grave, and pressed on her a small kid purse. 'Take this.'

'Jacques, you have already proved yourself the most faithful and generous of men.' From the weight she knew it must contain at least fifty louis. 'I cannot . . .'

'I assure you, you will need it on your long journey. Please. For your mother's and sister's sake.'

'No, I insist. We have sufficient.'

'Then take this.' He produced his silver pocket watch. 'This time, I insist.'

He embraced her, and when he released her she took the watch and said, 'Jacques, such men as you are rare. I shall pray for your health and happiness. Through your kindness I already feel my destiny has turned. Adieu!'

He regarded her with a strange look then, strange and lingering, like a man who could not bring himself to a confession. Then he turned away to hide his face, but not before she saw his jaw clench.

'This way, mesdames.'

The guide was a mad-eyed man in his middle fifties, hunched and myopic. He took them on, chattering without pause. 'What a country they've made of France! A country where more than three persons travelling in company is a cause for suspicion. A country where everything is banned unless it is specifically permitted. A country where every honest man is driven to night-time escapades to earn a crust.'

Berenice tried to give him a coin to soothe his grievances, and to reward his services, but he surprised her by refusing it.

'No. I won't have gold from you.'

'Please take it, monsieur.'

'No, no. Not me!' He cackled. 'Not gold.'

'What then . . . ?'

'I tell you, I'm doing this work for love, mademoiselle. I am a button-maker by trade. The Revolution has killed off my best customers, so it has taken away my livelihood. It has impressed my three sons into the army. It billets soldiers in what used to be my home. So, you see, this is my way of setting the account partly to rights.'

'Surely a golden louis would comfort you better, monsieur?'

'What? Haven't you heard, mademoiselle citoyen? Golden coin is no good anymore.' He fell to a customary heavy irony. 'This is the new stuff!'

He drew from his pocket *assignats* of the French Republic to the value of a hundred livres and waved them. 'See this – it's the money of paradise!' His words were loud with scorn now. 'Paper! Soon everything will be done by paper. You just print whatever amount you like, and spend however much you want. That way everyone will be rich. A wonderful system, *hein*? Here, take it, if you will, *madame la comtesse*. It may bring you good luck, if nothing else.'

Her mother said. 'Monsieur, we are being forced from our native country by villains. France has fallen under the spell of wicked wretches, yet there are some left behind whose virtues are beyond compare.' Then, to Berenice's surprise, she embraced him.

'Oh-ho, madame! Fare you well, and come back to see us when times are once more as they should be.'

'We shall.'

Berenice rehearsed their directions once again, then set off over the meadows. After a minute she looked back to wave a last farewell, but the night had swallowed their guide, and she felt herself missing the protective aura the man had spread around them.

'We shall take our exodus one day at a time. One day's problems and one day's solutions are quite sufficient to think about. Remember that even a journey of a thousand miles begins with a single step.'

It's down to me now, she thought, and led the way with a strong heart. They had chosen a night that was moonless, and she found it nearly impossible to see where she was going. She had grown used to night walking. Celestine, she saw, was nimble enough over the uneven ground, but her mother stumbled time and again.

'How are you coping, mother?' she asked at last. 'Shall I take your arm?'

'Someone once told me,' her mother said, breathing

hard, 'that physical endeavour is something accomplished not by the body but by the mind. A person has only to keep the object in view in the mind's eye, and that is sufficient to give the legs strength.'

'*Bravo, maman*! That's the spirit.'

'I hope my informant was correct,' her mother said. 'For we have a terrible journey ahead of us. You are right: this is our exodus. We are like Jews fleeing from Egypt, except that we have no Moses to lead us.'

'Then we shall just have to do as they did, and put our trust in Jehovah.'

'Yes, and may God save us.'

Celestine chewed her lip, then, after a few minutes, asked, 'Do you believe we can reach the rendezvous at Roanne by Midsummer's Day?'

'There's enough time,' she said, showing all the confidence she could muster. But inside she sighed. The question had revealed Celestine's blind faith, and her ignorance, because the obstacles they must negotiate before they could reach Roanne were many. They had to get past Vendôme, and then Blois, it would be necessary to cross the River Loire, and go on from there as far as Bourges. And even when they had accomplished that, as much a journey again lay before them if they were to reach Roanne, and thence get into the Royalist city of Lyons. 'We have time and we have a little money.'

'But I heard Jacques say that for every five steps we took on our journey we would be obliged to take four back. Midsummer is only—'

'Celestine, the appointed rendezvous is in the future. It's best not to think about it yet.'

A little later, Celestine asked, 'Are you sure Jacques will be there? In Roanne, I mean?'

'Celestine, don't worry about him,' she said, but she was already worrying herself. How can I ever tell my mother about the execution? She wondered, her heart daggered by the memory. Why don't I have faith that

Jacques will meet us in Roanne? Perhaps that's what Celestine is sensing.

'Well, what if we can't get into Roanne—'

'Celestine!'

Her sister hurried along in silence, chastened by her sharpness, until Berenice relented. 'Listen to me, when I tell you we must take each day – each hour even – as it comes, I mean that.'

'I'm sorry, Berenice.'

'Don't be sorry. Be cheerful.'

She ignored her own device as she began to calculate the mountainous task that lay ahead of them, and set it against what they had already achieved. So far we've done well. We've managed two leagues by land and two by water. She told the others, 'If we can reach Lombron by midnight, then we'll have eight leagues to walk before we pass St Calais on the Vendôme road. After that we get beyond this Department. From then on our papers stand less chance of being noticed as forgeries.'

'How long do we have?' Celestine asked.

'We *must* reach Epuisay before daylight and that's not many hours away now.'

'In that case,' her mother said, 'we must think of your father. *Allons! Courage, mes enfants.* Celestine. Berenice. Stride out. We must exert ourselves tonight.'

Before long Berenice found herself thinking of Smith. He would have had no trouble deciding what to do, she thought. I wonder where he is now, and what he could be doing.

A little later she even dared to think of the day of their separation, and to recall the tragedy of it. She found it was as painful to her heart as it had ever been. Perhaps more so, she thought, because now Papa is dead, and so the little fantasy of reconciliation I so often played through in my mind can never now become a reality.

She allowed her thoughts to touch only lightly on these things, for she sensed the dangers of dwelling on them, and knew that, though she felt strong now, the rigours of the journey ahead might consume all her reserves of hope and courage.

They covered the first league in almost an hour, arriving on the high road by midnight at a little village called Souligne, three leagues away from Lombron, and eight from St Calais. They passed like ghosts through the village of dark and silent cottages. No one saw them approach, and no one saw them depart. Only a dog barked to wish them farewell.

TWO

MAY, 1793
Constantinople

Smith arrived at the square, at dusk, thinking of the importance of his new mission, but still devilled by unshakeable melancholy.

Raschid, his Turkish dragoman – interpreter-guide – showed him a favoured place, and so did him honour. The man has never seen me smile, Smith thought, feeling the knife twisting and twisting in his wound. Not once. Isn't that tragic?

The coffee sellers had already lit their modest lamps in the cold, still air. It was a place of peace. All around them, on benches and stools, turbanned dreamers smoked, talking little and always in low voices. The many hookahs made a fantastical sound, water bubbling in the flasks as the smokers took long inhalations, surrounded by their dying splendour, religious silence and prayer. It made Smith's mind reel just to look at them.

'England seems so far away, Raschid.'

The dragoman allowed a moment to pass, then he asked, 'What is it that troubles you, effendi?'

He looked up listlessly. 'Something that damages a man's honour and destroys his sense of self-worth.'

'What illness does that?'

'It's called guilt. Three months ago I was in France, watching a man being decapitated, a man whose life I

376

had sworn to save, but whom I abandoned to save my own skin.'

He told Raschid how he had made his way back to the baker's shop in Caen, and watched the execution from the window that overlooked the square. He explained how Jacques de Tromelin had managed to find a way to get him out of Normandy, but said nothing of the dreadful news that de Tromelin had confirmed, and that had made him agree to leave France – that Berenice was known to be dead.

Raschid asked, 'Why harbour guilt? When you did so much to save him?'

'Because I did not succeed.'

Raschid indicated the moon, doing so with the kind of gesture no Englishman could ever learn. 'You must let God worry about such things.'

'Must I?'

'Yes, effendi. Most assuredly.'

Raschid had become his devoted servant since he had arrived in the Sultan's astonishing capital. Together they had climbed up to the heart of the city, to sit in the stone-flagged space in front of Sultan Fatih's mosque. He sat now under the plane trees, where the hanging lanterns cast a smoky light. He wanted to dream here, in sweet Oriental peace, in the clear, dry, late-spring evening.

His journey to the edge of Asia had been at Lord Grenville's command. An inescapable commission to join his brother, Spencer, who had been appointed His Britannic Majesty's representative at the court of the Sultan. His mission was secret. It was also huge – something that, if it succeeded, would completely change the course of European political affairs. He could not have turned it down, no matter how much he might have wanted to.

The news of Berenice's death had shocked all the life from him. Jacques de Tromelin had even showed him the proof of her execution. The record of her having been shot and buried with a hundred other women at La Precey on Christmas Eve, 1792, had killed him inside.

After that, London had been just a misty dream. The meetings with Lord Grenville and their lordships of the Admiralty had been of vast importance to the future of Europe, but to him they had seemed dust-dry and pointless.

Nevertheless, he had left England and travelled by Dutch ship to the Lowlands, by river, canal and carriage into High Germany, from Cologne he had turned south, crossing the Palatinate, passing through the forests to Ratisbon. The Danube had carried him out of Bavaria and into the emperor's magnificent capital. After Vienna each league he had put behind him had taken him a step further into the past, until he had reached the border of Ottoman Europe at Peterwardein. There he had noted the final cessation of German speech, and the beginning of languages he could not understand at all.

He could recall a time when he would have rejoiced at all that, loving travel and new sights, but what good were new sights to a man whose spirit had died inside? A man who could still think, but who could no longer feel?

He was to meet Robert Liston, Spencer's hugely skilled political mentor and a man he had known himself in Stockholm. The Scot's remarkable career had meant that he was uniquely equipped to be plenipotentiary at Constantinople. In his younger days, in Paris, he had been friendly with the famous Scottish historian and philosopher David Hume. He had followed the Earl of Minto's second son, once his pupil, into the diplomatic sphere. The Honourable Hugh Elliot had made him his private secretary and taken him on missions to Munich, Ratisbon and Berlin. Later Liston had been appointed secretary of embassy in Madrid, after which he had succeeded as minister plenipotentiary there. His appointment as envoy extraordinary at Stockholm had been the turning point of Smith's own fortunes.

Now, looking out over the sultan's capital, he felt himself to be an intruder. Everything was in place for this to be a mystical, magical evening. The full moon shone plaster-white over the Sea of Marmara. It had risen two hours earlier from behind the mountains of Asia. As he watched he saw it reappear above the squat, massive façade of Sultan-Fatih. It crept slowly out of occultation, leaving no doubts in his mind that those about him who regarded it at all still imagined the world to be a stationary place about which the moon turned a daily path, just like the sun and planets and all the bodies of heaven. So much for truth and illusion. So much for what the unaided senses of a man may fathom . . .

He saw the lunar glow diffuse a blue evening vapour from the Bosphorus, a mist exhaled by the night. It had been diaphanous earlier, he thought, hardly visible as it seeped from the city. Now it's a pale miasma, enveloping everything. It makes the city walls, which in daylight are so weighty, seem so utterly insubstantial. He said, 'It's easy to see how the besieging armies of old might have been lured to their deaths by so deceptive a light.'

'Truly, effendi.'

They brought him his own pipe, with small, live embers glowing on leaves of Persian tobacco, and soon, like all around him, he felt a gentle semi-intoxication, relaxing and thought-inducing.

His attention had been captured that afternoon by a eunuch. The man, a pattern of his kind, had been tall, yet short-bodied, long in the legs and arms, yet flabby. A grossly oversized body with a beardless, withered face, void of expression, except an infinite weariness. He had worn a scarlet fez, and a long, dark frock coat over European trousers. In his hand had been a little whip, that Smith had later learned was of hippopotamus hide. The eunuch had walked in a distinctive way – there was a delicacy to it and a vigilance too. The least irreverence

379

shown by passers-by had brought an expression of ferocious anger.

A lady on horseback followed.

Smith's eyes followed her. 'Who are the ones that carry the whips?' he asked Raschid, knowing perfectly well, but wanting the dragoman to tell more of what he knew.

'That is the insignia of office of the eunuchs.'

'They certainly do not need to be pointed out by an insignia.'

'Surely, effendi, they are easily recognized.'

They were a presence in Constantinople, a factor. These semblances of men, secretly sad, displaced from nature, power brokers of an ancient city. They were sighted in every crowd, among the multitude who visited the Sweet Waters, seen in the bazaars, carried in the carriages and caiques, under the arches of the mosques.

'But what of them?' he had asked, intrigued beyond measure. 'Is their state not contrary to the formal precepts of the Koran? I have heard that holy book condemns the despoiling of nature.'

Raschid's eyes glazed with self-righteousness. 'Avidity for gold and selfishness dazzle brighter than God's law. This is the way of the world of men.'

He asked Raschid, 'So, do they *consent* to mutilation?'

'Oh, yes, effendi.'

He nodded, but he thought, they are all most surely victims, children of the poor, bought or stolen in Abyssinia or Syria, or brought from Albania.

'I have heard that only one in three survives the infamous knife.'

Now Raschid was sharp to the defence. 'Who pronounces thus?'

'I have heard. That is all.'

The old oil lanterns that hung in the trees cast a discreet light, and the moon hung too, enlarged in the haze of blue light, insubstantial and delicate. Beyond the square the night blurred. Moon shadows bathed the wise, devout smokers, and they sheltered in the protection of those massive sacred walls. And the darkness seemed more meaningful than anywhere on earth. It was, he supposed, the peace and mystery of an ancient city that must have seen every kind of woe and joy a thousand times.

He gazed out now over the threshold of the Ottoman Sultanate, seeing the citadel of the imperial realm, his mind too distracted to decipher what the sultan was offering.

When he returned to the Residency he was unsteady on his feet. His brother was severe.

'You're very late.'

'I know.'

'Where have you been?'

The demand made him balk. 'Raschid has been showing me the Bosphorus by moonlight.'

'The reflective qualities of the Bosphorus are hardly the kind of—'

His temper broke and he sneered back instantly. 'I already know you think I'm an appalling romantic with no moral fibre. One of the damned.'

Spencer's fists balled. 'Pull yourself together. You are a Brother Knight of the Order, an Illuminatus. You must stop behaving like this.'

He felt suddenly imprisoned by what he was, what he had striven to make of himself. Somehow, part of him had hoped to be liberated by the East, not further confined by it. Ever since he was a boy the same message had been drummed into him many times, a great and unquestionable truth in its several guises: 'You are an initiate.' 'You are an officer.' 'You are a Briton.' 'You are an élite representative of the ruling class of the most powerful, most advanced nation on God's good Earth.'

'Yes, I know,' he said airily. 'We are the heirs of Greece and Rome. It is ours to shape the world for the benefit of all Mankind. All this I know very well.'

'Then address those responsibilities. Like a man.'

'Oh, the very world would stop spinning if we should cease to twirl it, wouldn't it? Well, so far as I am concerned, it can all go to hell in a handcart!'

'What on earth is the matter with you?'

He broke down. 'I don't know, little brother. I don't know.'

Spencer controlled himself and deliberately softened his voice. 'For good or ill this is *our* time, Sidney. The flame of civilization has been given into our keeping. It is our responsibility now, and for centuries to come. It is our bounden duty to keep it alight.'

Smith thought about France, the hugeness of what they were attempting to arrange, untouched by Spencer's appeal. What if the light of the world was indeed going out? The perverted revolutionary fervour of the Jacobins had certainly stamped out the light of liberty and humanity in France. What if they should rage their monstrous Terror across the rest of Europe? It would plunge the world into a new Dark Age. As Brother Gibbon had pointed out to the world, such a thing had happened before – the inundations of Rome by the barbarian hordes had stamped out progress in Europe for a thousand years. He thought about the rest of the world – the tribal savages of Africa and the Americas; teeming, decadent Hindustan; vast China, that slumbering, xenophobic dragon of the East, crushed under its Manchoo conquerors; and here Islam, whose strict fanaticism had blazed like a meteor across the centuries, but which now slumbered also, dreaming devout dreams. There's no denying it, he thought. At best, nine tenths of the world has barely become mediaeval, let alone what we would make it.

Spencer said, 'Liston has received a message.'

'He makes an excellent job,' Smith said, 'of playing that transparent role "the Power behind the Throne".'

'He's an extraordinary manipulator, one who appreciates the difference between power and influence, and a very skilled applier of the latter.' Spencer coughed delicately. 'He's heard from Wright.'

The name made Smith sit up. John Wesley Wright was one of Robert Liston's talented young men, trained up in a Baltic merchant's office in London. The Russian tzaritsa Catherine's secret policemen knew him and watched him as an agent of the British Crown. They almost certainly had not the least understanding of his actual mission in Russia.

Smith asked, 'So Wright's left St Petersburg?'

'Yes.'

Spencer's tight-lipped answer irritated him. '*Well*?'

'The design "Grand Signore" is to be put into effect immediately.'

Smith felt the urge to draw a deep breath. Here at last was the news they had been waiting for. 'Grand Signore' was a term used to describe the Ottoman sultan. It was also the code name for what they hoped to achieve here.

'I see.' He turned, looked out of the balcony to where the eternal moon was lighting a morass of tumbled dwellings.

'You can't deny that decadence has a certain charm to it.'

'Charm?' Spencer laughed derisively. 'Are you telling me you would prefer to do without the modern material fruits that our enlightened condition has brought into being? If you are, then there are plenty of rude places about the Earth where you can go to live.'

Spencer's austerity of soul chilled him, but his logic was faultless. 'You're quite right, of course.'

'While you're here, Sidney, you would do well to keep one fact well to the fore of your mind: if our light should go out, then a darkness visible would fall across the whole world. As of three hours ago, we have an important mission to accomplish here. Do not be the cause of its failure.'

'Yes,' he said, looking darkly into infinity. 'I'll try not to.'

THREE

They had come in sight of Roanne a bare two days ago. Two days before the appointed time of the summer solstice. They had arrived at a mean lodging with the passports almost expired and their money all but gone. Now the early morning sun was shining, and the last part of the first stage of their journey was about to begin.

Their weeks on the road had been nightmarish. By night thieves lurked in the woods, waiting to waylay unwary travellers who happened along. By day the traffic was almost exclusively official, and the chances of their being stopped and examined by the Guard were multiplied ten-fold. Towns and cities were especially dangerous. It was a matter of last resort to take refuge in an inn. Inns were costly, and full of people who asked awkward questions. Bureaucratic checks were made at every city gate, on all turnpikes, on every bridge, and at every milehouse and major crossroad.

Often the roads were closed, or cleared for columns of marching men. They saw many ox-trains, military supplies going south, first along the road to Vendôme, then on the highway to Bourges. They were obliged to backtrack and make detours across country they did not know. Many times they had lost their way, many times a supposed short-cut had led them into rough or water-logged country. And to arrive in an unknown village in the cold dawn and start asking after the name of it could have been fatal.

Their watch-word had been 'stealth'. Since it was not possible to say who could be trusted, it was wise to shun *all* human contact. With the warming of the season they had eaten from the land, and sheltered under hedges, or in ruins, or where they could. But the coming of summer also meant shorter hours of darkness.

Occasionally, as at Blois, they had had no choice but to try to cross the river by the bridge.

'We must avoid it by making a circuit,' she had told them, an intuition of dread stirring in her.

'But there is no ferry across the Loire and the bridges north and south are closed.'

'Then we'll just have to try to pass the Guard.'

They were stopped as they tried to squeeze past the barrier. The man's uniform was a tattered jacket, a *bonnet rouge* and a pair of striped trousers. When he first looked at them he was half asleep, but he quickly roused himself. He got down off his high stool and sauntered over.

'Where d'you think you're going?'

She tried disguising her voice. 'Lyons.'

'Where?'

'Is there something wrong?'

He looked at her, sucking his teeth. His glance moved quickly to her mother and then to Celestine, then back again. 'What's your name.'

She presented their passports. He was young, she saw. Maybe eighteen.

'It's written there,' she said. When she realized he could hardly read she added quickly so as not to embarrass him. 'Pauline. Pauline de Tromelin.'

'Pauline.' She recognized the interest in his voice and manner – the interest men had for pretty women. It was not what she expected, feeling herself to be in a wretched condition. It was the last thing she wanted from this man. 'And these?'

'My sister and mother.'

He nodded. 'Hmmm. You don't sound like you're from around these parts.'

'We're not.'

He looked her up and down, his thoughts clear enough. He pinched the chain round her neck between finger and thumb and revealed the looped cross. He looked at it, then asked, 'Where, then?'

She was poised to sneer, but controlled herself. 'Cancale.'

'Cunca? Never heard of it.'

'We're not Orléanais. Nobody can understand us around here.' She put a note of impertinence in her voice and took the cross from his fingers, tucking it back into her bodice. 'We've got a long way to go. Can we get on, now?'

He thrust the papers back, knowing his languid charm had been rebuffed. 'Go on, then.'

They picked up their bags and prepared to move on.

'Wait.'

'What?'

'This isn't Orléanais,' he said. She saw the way his eyes narrowed at her, a young man proving something. 'The old province names are banned now. This is the Department of Loir-et-Cher. And don't you forget it.'

'I won't.'

Her heart had thundered as they had passed the barrier. Then they had been out on the open bridge with its stone parapets, crossing the sparkling silver waters of the Loire, and she had felt more elated than she had ever felt in her life.

That had been a month ago. The forced march that followed had taken them halfway across France. The journey had swollen her mother's ankles, but she had not complained. Berenice's own feet had been blistered, but she found the pain only came to mind when they rested, and while they kept up their march it was no more than an annoyance. Even so, she had known that the pace she was setting was too much for her mother, and as they had pressed on through the summer sunshine she had often had to lend her arm for her mother to lean on.

Now, despite everything, they were here. Her mother's spirit remained buoyant. 'Berenice, we may say the Almighty has worked a miracle in our favour. The last three leagues were accomplished in less than three hours.'

Berenice knew that was because they had travelled on the highway this time. Since they would have to enter Roanne, she had afforded them that luxury. They were now beyond the boundaries of the Province of Bourbonnais. There was no risk of their being recognized, and she might have felt content if the memory of her father's death did not present itself before her eyes every time she relaxed her grip on her thoughts. She had had ample opportunity to think about the dilemma set before her. If Jacques did not arrive at the rendezvous, they would be stuck in a strange city, penniless and without a valid passport. If he did arrive, they would be completely in Gugnot's hands. The thought made her shudder.

An hour later they arrived at the west gate. They negotiated the main street of the town and stopped at the last inn before the east gate. It had no board, having once carried, she supposed, a name like the 'Sign of the Dauphin' or 'the Cardinal', but the place fitted the description that Jacques de Tromelin had given them. It had been agreed that if he arrived first he would wait for them, otherwise they should wait for him until nightfall. But then, if he failed to arrive, they should go on alone to a second place, the next inn they would find on the road to Feurs.

She arrived at the door feeling anxious, but as she

looked around she saw that de Tromelin was not inside. Her mother seemed to take this as a bad omen, and Celestine began to worry.

'What if this is the wrong place?' she whispered. Berenice assumed a confident expression. 'This is the place. It just means we have a little more time to rest ourselves.'

'I don't like it.'

She snapped, 'I'm sorry about that, mother.'

When they went inside they saw there were a few locals, mainly elderly people or youngsters, who kept themselves to themselves. The leaded windows were closed tight. The cheap glass was uneven, some panes were foamed with bubbles and gave a greenish tinge to the view. Outside the back of the inn the rocky hills extended to an overcast sky. They were the Monts de la Madeleine, the start of the rugged hill country that was the heart of France.

Instinct made her choose a corner, away from the gaping blackness of an empty fireplace. She called for something to eat. Her mother unlaced her shoes and Céléstine pulled them off for her. Rumbles of thunder rolled in from the Bois Noir. The air was humid and oppressive.

The landlady came to serve them soup and bread. She was a fat shrew, busy-minded, chattering with gossip and criticisms of her ineffectual husband. She had a gossip's practised capacity for asking penetrating and impertinent questions. Berenice felt she must give some answers, for fear of being seen to evade the questions, but then she fended off further enquiries humourlessly, until the woman lost interest.

They ate, then, still sitting around their table, they drifted into sleep. She awoke with a start, troubled still, but a little refreshed. Her body was comfortable – her tough peasant clothes of wool and linen were perfect for the travelling life, warm in cold weather, yet comfortable in summer's heat. Her mind sprang from its rest instantly. It had been raining. There were puddles in the street, and sun brightness.

She asked the innkeeper for the time, not wanting to be seen bringing out Jacques de Tromelin's watch. He went to the door and squinted towards the town clock. 'The tower says coming up to three o'clock.'

They had been in the tavern for three hours and de Tromelin had still not arrived. She began to grow increasingly uneasy. Maybe they were in the wrong place, after all. Celestine went to the door a dozen times, until Berenice spoke to her. The chastisement made her sister sigh and drop down on the bench in a sulk. They were all restless, and Berenice wondered if she should try to explain that it was Gugnot whom they were ultimately depending upon. She decided against it.

The chimes of five o'clock came without an arrival, and Berenice began to realize they would have to work out what to do. Her eyes followed Céléstine to the door once again. It was then that she noticed for the first time a figure clothed in black, seated alone on the far side of the room. Berenice started at the sight. Her hand went to her breast. The figure had been hiding in her blind spot. She recalled instantly to her mind the black-swathed figure she had seen in the crowd the day of the balloon ascent, and, again, the fleshless Black Friar she had glimpsed in the Church of St Etienne at Caen. Both times she had taken the apparition as a presage of disaster.

But this was no apparition seen out of the corner of her eye. He was quite real, a young man, just a young man who had slipped in quietly in the last quarter hour, and who was sitting at a table near the door. Still, something about him struck her as odd, but she could not decide what it was. He was watching her between sips. She allowed herself only the briefest glance back at him, not wishing to engage his eye. He was fair-bearded and he wore black travelling attire. A walking staff stood propped beside him with his hat on top of it. He seemed more than a little absorbed in his speculations.

I know what seems so strange about him, she thought after a minute or two. It's his age. Twenty or twenty-one, and he's not in uniform. There have been so many call-ups to the army that very few men of his age are to be met with. Who is he? And what can his story be?

Her suspicions grew when she saw him engage Celestine in conversation. She got up and intervened quickly. First she excused herself, then she spoke quietly but brusquely to her sister, ordering her to check the road again.

'Citoyenne, your sister – or is it sister-in-law? – says you are the family of a soldier.'

'Monsieur, I do not know you.'

She turned, but he grasped her arm, lowering his voice. 'I have been observing you. From your refined manner, you seem to me to be—'

'You may imagine whatever you wish.' She cut him off, pulling her arm away.

He started back at her, but there seemed to be a kind of pleading in his eyes. 'I am tempted to believe that this with you is only an assumed character.'

She felt a pang of fear that made her shallow. 'That's no business of yours,' she said, knowing his obvious education was no guarantee of trustworthiness. 'In any case, it's time for us to take our leave.'

'Citoyenne, excuse me the suspicions I have entertained, but . . .' His voice was confidential now, his eyes seemed to search to make contact with her. '. . . believe me, had they proved true, then you would have found in me one more ready to assist than to apprehend you.'

She looked back at him, saw his inner bitterness, appreciated the risk he was taking in speaking this way if he was indeed genuine. On the other hand, what if he was one of the men Jacques had warned her about?

What if he was one of the legion of spies sent out by the Revolution to pose as Royalist sympathizers, and so to entrap and betray all those they found who did not love the Revolution?

He doesn't look like a spy, she thought. But then, what does a spy look like? How should I know one? Clearly it is the first business of a spy not to look like what he is.

For a dangerous moment she was tempted to indulge her desire to confide in him, but the temptation passed.

'Citizen, I am astonished on what circumstances you could have grounded your suspicions.' She said it as if she was puzzled, giving nothing away. Then she made light. 'But I'm resolved at least to wash them all away with another charge of wine for your cannikin before I go.'

'I am no beggar, mademoiselle.' He said it angrily, deeply cut. 'What are you looking at?'

'A cat may look at a king, monsieur . . .' she said, her voice trailing away. Suddenly she knew that under the hat she would find not a walking staff, but the T-piece of a crutch. His left leg was missing below the knee. 'I'm sorry, monsieur. I . . .'

His false brightness was hard to bear. 'Oh, you may blame the emperor of the Austrians for that.'

She excused herself again, feeling torn. Good manners demanded that she hear his story out, but that would be dangerous. Keep yourself to yourself, the tough part of her mind warned her. It could be fatal to show good manners now. The poor and the hunted must learn to be ruthlessly inconsiderate.

'I didn't know you were a cripple.'

She hated to do it. She saw the pain she had caused him. The pervading atmosphere of suspicion crowded in on her, making her feel breathless. You do not know him, she told herself. Who knows what will happen if you allowed yourself to be trapped into sympathizing with him.

'I'm sorry my condition upsets you, mademoiselle.' His words were delivered with bitterness.

She moved away. The callousness of what she was doing went against her upbringing and her nature. She whispered to Celestine. 'I'll try to find out where the other inn is. And how best to go from here.'

She smiled at the innkeeper and asked to settle her bill with him. He was a frail-looking man with sandy-grey hair and blotchy skin. He was quiet, his voice soft and hesitant, as if he was unused to being spoken to kindly by a woman, as if his personality had been crushed down by his wife's dominating manner. Berenice saw that he seemed to like her, so she encouraged it.

His wife gave her a hard, inquisitive look as she pumped him for information. We'll need to head for Feurs tomorrow, she thought, if we're to make it seem we're doing as our passports say. We must try to fall in with the regiment to which my 'husband' has been assigned.

'And do you suppose it will be easier to get provisions on the Feurs road?' she asked, turning the conversation.

'Well, citoyenne, that's been designated a military road. Soldiers' routes are so fixed that at certain depots they're furnished from the general stock of grain, hay, and straw. Everything along them is in requisition for military consumption.'

The innkeeper's wife came over, unable to bear Berenice's conversation with her husband any longer. The woman's manner was gleefully unhelpful. 'That's why business is so bad. You name it, they take it. And at a fixed price. The commissaries don't use gold, either. I have worthless pieces of paper coming out of my backside. So you're on the road to Feurs, are you?'

Berenice wondered with an inner shudder how any

man could stand to live with a woman so wilfully pessimistic about everything. 'Yes, we—'

'Only, your sister has been going to the door all day. I thought you must be expecting someone.'

'No—'

'What's the matter with your mother? – she is your mother, isn't she? She's hardly said anything all day.'

'She's tired.'

'If she wants to sleep, we have a room. At a very reasonable price. She doesn't eat or drink much, does she? None of you do.'

'My mother's not in the best of health.'

The shrew recoiled. 'Oh, nothing catching, I hope?'

'It's an old illness. Brought on again by the journey.'

The other looked her over again, her eyes glassy and utterly without compassion. 'Yes, well, it's a terrible time to be travelling. And three women alone . . . well.'

Her husband said nothing, but his manner showed genuine regret at their situation.

Berenice agreed. 'We've found it difficult to get provisions along the road.'

The wife cocked her head. 'You'll find that everybody has only a certain number of bushels of grain for their own use. I can't imagine what *you*'ll do.'

Berenice heard the stress that gave away what the innkeeper's wife thought she was. Despite herself, it shocked her. 'We'll rely on – good fortune.'

'Yes, I suppose you'll have to. And, of course, things'll get worse the further south you go. The bigger the town the worse it'll get. Where did you say you were going?'

This time the truth was as good as any lie. 'Feurs.'

'That's where the army command post is, isn't it? That'll suit you.'

She let the remark pass. 'I don't know.'

'So. Didn't you hear about what happened at Lyons, then?'

Berenice's heart came into her mouth. 'Lyons?'

'The town declared for the Royalists. Bloody fools, if you ask me. That's why the army's going there. General what's-his-name's surrounded the city already.'

'Completely surrounded? You mean, cut off?'

The shrew made a face at what she conceived to be a piece of stupidity. 'You can't *part* surround something, now, can you? It's either surrounded or it's not. At least, in a siege that's so. I heard they're going to starve the place into submission. Kellermann. That's his name. Citizen General Kellermann. He's got a reputation, they say. Lyons' gutters'll run with blood worse than Paris's ever did. And there's a prediction for you.'

Berenice went back to her mother and sat down to tighten the cords of her shoes.

'What did she say?' her mother asked in a fearful whisper. 'Must we go—'

'Berenice!'

She looked up. Celestine was at the door, her hand pressed hard against her mouth. In her excitement she had blurted her sister's real name. Now she was stealing glances at the innkeeper and his wife, to gauge if she had given them away.

Berenice went across smoothly and joined her at the door. All seemed well. Despite the blaze of anger she felt at Celestine's lapse, she squeezed her sister's shoulders, reassuring and calming her, then drew her outside and down the step.

'Look!' Celestine indicated the road they had come along. Berenice followed her eyes, and saw in the middle distance a double column of mounted soldiers – they looked like hussars. There were twenty of them, a carriage and pair and then twenty more. It was an extravagant way to travel, and at odds with the times.

'Soldiers!' Celestine was fearful. 'What shall we do?'

'Wait and watch,' she whispered. 'We must see if this is who I think it is.'

Celestine looked up at her in amazement. 'Could it be Jacques?'

Berenice narrowed her eyes. 'Yes. It could be.' She hardened her voice. 'You must be more careful in future, Bébé. My name is Pauline now. A slip like that and we could all be . . .' She ended the warning with a grimace.

'I'm sorry. But look!'

The leading horsemen were well equipped – gorgeous blue and silver uniforms, shakos with red cockades, sabretaches dangling at their sides, with insignia she did not recognize. When the carriage passed she saw the elegant profile of Marguerite de Tromelin, and a feeling of great piquancy welled up inside her, so that she felt like crying. She thought about the balls and levees that had taken place at Thury-Harcourt. She had always known how to create a wonderfully disdainful air, an enviable mystique, an exclusivity. They had been great rivals. There had been a time in their teens when she and Marguerite had been the most desirable, most eligible young ladies in Normandy. They had been beyond compare.

Gugnot sat beside his wife, imperious as Caesar. He made a slight sign of recognition as the carriage passed, then indicated the road ahead. Berenice nodded her head to show she understood. She turned to see Celestine gawping at the carriage, astonished to see Marguerite and the family's erstwhile groom sitting in it. Berenice made a reassuring gesture, then put a warning finger to her lips and indicated their mother.

'Not a word to her. Do you understand?'

Celestine nodded readily.

The gear of the hussars jangled as the following escort trotted past. Berenice swept a loose strand of hair back over her ear. Her hands were grimy, her nails damaged. The sun had tanned her complexion so it was like that of a peasant. She was suddenly aware of a mark on her cheek where a bramble had scratched her. She looked down at her dirty, patched clothes, and felt ashamed.

She went inside to pay the bill. The innkeeper's wife spoke as the tattered *assignats* were counted out. 'You're going, then?'

'Yes.'

'At this time of day? When it's getting dark?'

'We have to get on.'

'What's the matter?' She jerked her head dismissively. 'Can't you afford a night here?'

There was a quality to the other's voice – half false humour, half innuendo – that angered Berenice. 'I said we have to get on.'

'Yes. I'll bet. You'll probably find good pickings among those cavalrymen.'

She flashed the shrew a deadly glance, helped her mother up. 'Come, mother. It's time to be moving from this stink-hole.'

They left the innkeeper's wife muttering good riddance at the door and sweeping dust after them with her broom like an insult. Berenice led them along the route the carriage had taken and out of the town. The checkpoint was manned but the sentries were not checking people going out of town. They walked on for a mile, and Berenice felt the pressure of her sister's curiosity. To her credit Celestine said nothing, perhaps sensing that an important secret was being kept for her mother's sake.

At a distance from the last habitation, on a deserted stretch, Berenice felt the first pricklings of disquiet. It was muddy under foot; the road was studded with hoofmarks. Gloomy pine forest crowded the road on either side as it rose into the hills. Water-filled pot-holes reflected the dying light. There were midges. The air was warm and smelled of pine resin and fresh horse dung, and she felt the stiffness in her limbs as she pressed on. Already the rough leather of her shoes had become sodden, the soles caked with clay. She heard furtive-sounding birdsong as she scanned the road ahead. There was an overwhelming feeling of foreboding in the air, as if they were walking into some kind of ambush. Seeing the one-legged man at the inn as the black-swathed phantom of her fears had shocked her, conjuring in her mind a premonition.

She set her thoughts on her objective. There was the road and the carriage. They were the only things that mattered. The feeling intensified. She felt hairs thrilling on the back of her neck. It was as if evil itself was walking the road close by. It's irrational, she thought, feeling that she was giving in to foolishness and betraying a trust. But it's true that a sixth sense comes to travellers, and how many of our decisions are truly rational in any case? She stopped.

'Mother, Celestine.' She spoke very deliberately. 'I want you to hide among the trees there. You must wait for me to return. I'm going on alone.'

They protested fearfully, but she would not hear them.

She went on, seeing no one, but sensing the powerful presence crescendo and then diminish. She crested a hill and found the carriage waiting in the last grey light. The driver and escort had been ordered to a position a hundred yards away. As she came up, she noted that Gugnot stepped down first. His formality of expression and manner seemed at odds with the look in his eyes, which was both amused and supercilious. He offered no apologies, saying only, 'Where are the comtesse and your sister?'

'They're hiding.'

He inclined his head. 'Hiding? Why?'

'We have learned not to take unnecessary risks. Where is Jacques?'

It seemed to her that he was irritated by her answer,

but that also he moved to cover his feelings. 'Mademoiselle, may I present my wife?'

Marguerite got down from the carriage and embraced her warmly. She felt in the contact a moment of sudden relief. As they clutched one another in the last light of day it felt as if a dam was breaking in her chest, and her doubts rushed away.

Marguerite said, 'I have been so very worried about you. How is your mother?'

Tears welled as she thanked Marguerite. 'My mother and sister still know nothing of my father's death.'

Marguerite nodded slowly. 'Yes. I understand.'

'I've heard rumours that Lyons has been surrounded by Revolutionary brigades.'

'That is so,' Marguerite eyed her curiously.

'We were expecting Jacques de Tromelin.'

'His regiment has been delayed,' Marguerite began, but then Gugnot cut in. 'Mademoiselle Berenice does not appear to have heard about the coup d'état in Paris.'

Her interest surged. 'A Royalist coup?'

Gugnot snorted. 'Hardly. Three weeks ago all the Girondins were rounded up – like Brissot and Pétion – they're all locked up in the Luxembourg now. Roland is at large, but his wife has been arrested, so they'll get him too, sooner or later.'

Berenice knew that the Girondins were the less radical, less extreme, party of the Revolution. Despite hearing news that France had plunged deeper into misery and chaos, Berenice felt a stab of satisfaction. 'It is as I thought,' she said. 'At least some of the dogs who have brought my country this far towards ruin have in their turn been eaten by wolves.'

'And wolves with sharp teeth.'

'So, the Jacobins are supreme now?'

Gugnot gloated. 'Nothing else was possible right from the beginning. I certainly chose right. Not bad for low cunning, eh?'

And you even hedged your bets by helping aristos, she told him silently. But why are you helping us now? She turned to Marguerite. 'What about the risings in the south?'

'Many towns and cities are up in arms.' Marguerite seemed to be quite sincere. 'You'll have difficulties going on, but I promise we shall do our best for you.'

She looked to Gugnot. A dreadful suspicion about him began to form in her mind. 'You are going south also?'

He took Berenice's arm, and at the same time gave Marguerite a significant glance. 'Please excuse us, my dear.'

They walked a little way back along the track as Marguerite climbed obediently back into the carriage, then Gugnot said, 'Read this.'

She took the paper. It was a decree:

BY ORDER OF THE NATIONAL CONVENTION

Commissioners of the National Convention will go without delay to the various departments of the Republic to instruct their fellow citizens of the new dangers which threaten the nation, and to assemble sufficient forces to disperse the enemy.

The Commissioners will have the right to take whatever measures they may consider necessary to raise immediately a contingent of 300,000 men, and to seek out all citizens capable of bearing arms.

The Commissioners will have the right to take whatever measures they may deem necessary to restore order in any case of disturbance, to suspend temporarily and even to arrest any whom they consider suspect, and to make use of armed force if necessary.

The decree handed down despotic powers. Berenice felt an unbearable loathing for Gugnot crawl over her as he took the paper back. She knew, as she had known in Caen, that he could not resist boasting to her of his spectacular rise, and that was one reason he was relishing the meeting.

'I suppose an escort of forty hussars means that you are one such commissioner?'

Gugnot held her glance, laughing. 'No! Not me. I've been appointed by the Committee of Public Safety to accompany the *Représentants en Mission*. The post I hold is that of political commissar.'

'What does that mean?' She breathed the words.

'Simply this: Paris must have some way of making sure that the officers of General Carteaux's army stay on the straight and narrow and put down the rebellions as they're meant to do. It's my job to keep an eye on Augustin Robespierre and the Corsican representative, Saliceti, as they play their parts.'

She knew the name 'Robespierre' very well. The hated brothers were rabid Jacobins. Maximilien was a despicable apologist for murder, his brother Augustin, a fool. In the white heat of anarchy, she thought, it is scum like Gugnot who rise to the stop. This groom, this little man who by rights should have married a maid and lived an uneventful and unremarkable life on the estate of Thury-Harcourt – he has been shaken out of his niche by the Revolution. Now he is free to roam the country using his ingenuity to whatever despicable end he desires. There must be hundreds like him, thousands, men driven by jealousy and revenge, who cloak their evil in the glib slogans of idealism.

She humbled herself, knowing that neither the vulnerable nor the compromised could afford themselves the scruple of perfect honesty. Still she loathed the charade. 'You are the only one who has come to help us.'

He looked to his wife, then glanced at her again, quickly, almost furtively. 'I will confess that, when I pondered over the hazards of this understanding, I hesitated whether I should attempt it.'

'What made you decide to fulfil your promise to help

us?' she asked, phrasing her sentiments carefully. She expected him – had almost invited him – to say 'Honour'. But he did not.

'I was decided by the solicitations of my wife. She entreated me not to desert you. You are one for whom she entertains the most sincere affection. She said that if I would not come to meet you she would do so herself.'

'May I ask, what is your plan for us?'

Gugnot told her. 'As we travel south along the valley of the Rhône you will follow us. We must never appear to belong to the same company.'

She nodded toward the cavalry. 'What do they know of me?'

Gugnot shook his head. 'Don't worry about them. I told them that you were one of my informants. A spy. I'm sure that you will be able to get to people that I cannot. If you understand me?'

She looked back blankly, unwilling to understand.

He added, 'Being a woman. And one, as we both know, with a certain *appetite*.'

She felt a barb of ice lodge in her belly: hard, cold and unmelting anger. She was disgusted, and wanted to slap the smirk from his face, but she dared show no reaction. Instead, she spoke tonelessly, like a beggar, ashamed. 'We have no money left.'

'I daresay you'll have enough to get by.' He looked at her with his penetrating stare. 'I shall pay you a sum of *assignats* each time we meet. If you can think of other ways to make a little more that will be good too.'

Her manner remained completely passive. How far will he go if I show myself helpless or gullible? she wondered. But I already know the answer to that.

'We have no passports. What if we're stopped?'

'Papers can be arranged.'

'If I could have an advance of money—'

'I think it's better that you don't. This way you won't arouse suspicion if you're searched.'

She asked, 'What if something disastrous befalls us? What shall I say?'

He looked at her sharply. 'It will be your responsibility not to involve me. On no account must my name ever pass your lips. The dangers I run on your account are great enough to make you value my safety. Nor would my being exposed at all reduce the danger for you. On the contrary. Anyway, no one would believe you.'

'What has happened to Jacques de Tromelin?' she asked. 'He was meant to come here, as you must know.'

'I suspect you won't be seeing Jacques again,' he said, and the tone of his voice stabbed her with fear.

He gave her a piece of paper. On it was an address in Vienne where she must go to get new papers, then they parted. She went back the way she had come, and he went his way.

FOUR

It took half an hour for them to arrive at the entrance of the Seraglio. Spencer seemed impatient, Smith thought, Liston too, though both took pains to hide their feelings. The rest of their embassy, perhaps a dozen in all, seemed similarly ill at ease.

Smith had made an effort to adjust to the rhythm of the place. He saw quickly that he must do so or suffer enragement at every turn. Forgive everything, except malice, he remembered. Yes. Here the maxim applies. And the diplomatist especially must be gracious, no matter what turmoil he may be feeling within. Weeks were passing – months – and still he had been unable to fill the void inside.

The mounted entourage was met by a foot escort. For the first time the vast importance of the day's work possessed his thoughts. The huge goal that had been set for this mission overwhelmed his mind. He felt the presence of his Tutelary Genius almost palpably now. The little silver figure that it normally inhabited was in his dress-coat pocket, its arms still cast wide, implacable, expansive, reassuring, despite everything.

Before them now was the Bab-i-Humayun – the Sublime Imperial Gate, brooding and solid and three storeys high. Beside it the many-domed roof of Sultan Ahmet's fountain thrust its crescent-tipped spires into a violet sky. Inscriptions carved on its walls bade the thirsting to come and drink at its gilded basins in accordance with the charitable precepts of Islam.

From his saddle Smith merely glanced at the edifice where once he would have marvelled: it was as big as a house, all of white marble, like a square-built temple, and ornamented with inscriptions in coloured and golden letters. Curious how diverse is the human species, he thought. The world is a marvellous stew of distinct cultures, and yet here's a paradox, for we're all rather the same under our skins.

He smiled cynically. 'One supposes that Sultan Ahmet thought he was laying claim to the pleasures of the hereafter by demonstrating his piety so publicly. Just like any of our archbishops, what?'

Spencer met his humour coolly. 'I believe they disembowelled the last infidel for supposing as much.'

'You don't say so.'

Liston grunted. 'Do you doubt it?'

'This is a place that reeks of struggle,' he said, sensing the djinns – demons – that watched him from the shadows.

Spencer looked straight ahead, his black cocked hat sitting fore-and-aft. 'This citadel has endured centuries of violent politics. These stones have been bloodstained countless times by coups and dynastic assassinations, revolts and high intrigues of every kind. Don't forget it during the meetings that are to come.'

The ghosts spoke truthfully, then, he thought. I'll bet that struggles over wealth or power have left many an adventurer stabbed through the heart, many a pretender with his throat cut. But for all that, the empire they have is still a great power, and there are special reasons why we need to persuade the power of Turkey on to our side.

They were shown into a ruined kiosk on the left hand of the porch. It was dark and cramped and it stank. It affronted the ambassadorial party's dignity, but there seemed to be no intended insult in it. He glanced at his brother and saw Spencer nod tautly.

'What is this place?' Spencer demanded of Raschid. 'Why do we pause here?'

'Bey effendi, it is the executioners' lodge. We must wait.'

'What for?'

'You will see.'

He received no other answer, but the officials conducting them seemed agitated, and concerned to keep them from going on for the moment. Spencer took off his hat and put it under his arm. Smith did likewise, and so did the junior officers and the civilian gentlemen present. The order of precedence among the English, he saw, did not go unnoticed by the Turks.

Smith tuned his ear like a fiddle string. The habit came easily after years of shipboard life. He perceived the hum of subtle communication among the Seraglio staff – messages sent, protocols adhered to, orders given and received, an attention to procedure that reminded him of a man-o'-war. It was the same with this vast stone ship, a complexity of hidden but well-understood rules operated to regulate the lives of many men, and woe betide the one who by his slackness or misapplication of those rules caused such sublime coordination to break down.

After a few minutes a man appeared, urgently waving, and they were ushered towards a second court, one much smaller than the first. It was colonnaded on three sides, with a lawn in the middle and set with cypress trees. The fourth side was an open promenade.

I have it, Smith thought suddenly. It's a surprise. Our arrival is being timed to coincide with some great event, something got up to impress us, a changing of the guard or . . . He saw a fountain and the hall of the Divan, and buildings he guessed were the Seraglio kitchens, for a huge quantity of rice had been portioned out in thousands of little pewter dishes.

Then the sound of a striker being rung against an iron plate signalled an amazing sight. Thousands of janissaries – the soldiers of the palace guard – appeared as if summoned like djinns from an unstoppered bottle. They were barefoot, dressed in white smocks, running from all corners for their pilaus. Smith's mind began automatically to estimate the number of them as they filled the square. There must be four or five thousand, he thought, wondering at the apparent chaos of the system. The food's being scrambled for and seized on by them as if . . .

He said, 'There's not enough to go round.'

'It is tradition.' Raschid's eyes drank in the disorderly struggle. 'It is to instil an instruction in them: even food for the belly does not come free in this life. In this life nothing comes as right. Everything must be fought for.'

Smith nodded as if approving, but privately he thought, how very immoral . . . it's obvious that their generals feel they must show their power by careless abuse. Someone of rank delights to see a demeaning spectacle.

One of the Turks, the leader of the escort, turned to him, showing his delight. There was a certain nobility in his face, but the character of that nobility was notably cruel. Smith returned no sign. He wanted to say the obvious: 'But *any* fool can use position to crush down an underling.'

But he did not.

He thought instead of his first commander, Captain Ford of the *Unicorn*. Ford had applied a rule of his own devising to sharpen his crew when drilling his hands aloft. The last man down from each mast received a half dozen lashes at the following day's punishment. But since there was always a last man down, and most often the same man, it did little to improve performance, although probably a great deal to gratify the austere and embittered personality of an autocrat.

They waited until Raschid led them on, past the third gate, the Baba-Saadi, or Gate of Happiness. Here the walls of the interior palace fronted the entrance to the court. He saw that the Divan – the audience chamber – was a vaulted saloon. Three small windows were set in the dome, insufficient to illuminate the inside. As he passed into the gloom within Smith began to feel himself nearing the living heart of Ottoman power.

There was a sense of sinister grandeur pulsing here. High officials were present in faded splendour. The *kaimakam*, the grand vizier's deputy, was in his seat. To his left two more dignitaries sat, and on the other side was a man Smith took to be the *Tefterdar Effendi*, accompanied by two lesser officers of the Treasury. Smith recognized the robes of a *kazi-askar*, or judge, though of what province he could not discern. The cushioned bench on which they sat spanned the width of the kiosk. It reminded him of the one in the Court of Chancery in London, except that the grand vizier himself sat in the middle of this one.

Smith appreciated that the vizier's place was slightly raised and more prominently decorated, as befitted the sultan's chief minister. It also stood before a small latticed opening, and he suspected that these must be the apertures through which the sultan himself occasionally inspected the transactions of the Divan.

He looked around, noting the rich ornament: intricate wainscoting and walls of veined pink marble, screens of rosewood and brass. He saw that to their left was a cushioned bench, and to their right a lower plain bench that was attached to the wall. A second vaulted chamber stood to the left of the main saloon. It was sectioned off from the first by a breast-high panel, and was manned by a dozen court clerks and their attendants.

There was a certain amount of obligatory ceremonial to be observed: the exchange of presents and the presentation of Spencer's credentials. He watched it with a weary eye. Nevertheless he could feel the sense of a once-enormous power, a tremendous vigour that had settled into an infinitely slow decline. Ever since the failure of the siege of Vienna a century ago, they've been withdrawing from their glory, he thought. Half their Arab provinces are controlled by nominal viceroys who are really more or less independent rulers. They've lost the Crimea to the tzaritsa Catherine, and left Hungary to the imperial Austrians, but now the war is over, and while the ink of the Treaty of Jassy is hardly dry we have got to make our case. Events in France have swung the whole world aback. How shall we make the counterpoise that will bring Europe to an even keel, if the sultan will not listen to what we have to say?

Formality followed formality. The air was hot and humid, the season uncomfortable. As they waited there was a moment when he caught the scent of jasmine, and glimpsed shapes, veiled and fleeting, through a screen. Slave women. The flutes of their voices as they passed stirred him. How long had it been since he had troubled his mind about women?

Thoughts of Berenice had begun to make him angry. He could not prevent them coming to him. There were too many triggers that touched off the charge of memory, too many smells and sounds and sights. The associations were precious, but the pain that came a split second in their wake was like an assault. He was utterly tired of it and so he had decided to distract his mind with urgent matters, some problem or other, anything to put away from him that which was now patently unobtainable.

But lately he had begun to notice that this blotting out had affected him in other ways. He had ceased to feel the intense, indiscriminate desire of his youth. That was perhaps understandable, but then he had ceased to feel desire at all. His celibate state was a secret shame to him. It has been like some part of me is living in exile, he thought, and in a place from which there is no way back. There is nothing to be done about it, so why are you allowing a thwarted love to all but destroy you?

The image of Lilliehorn's gaping leg came into his mind, and he thought: Like him, you dare not acknowledge the seriousness of a wound. And until you do, it will not heal. It cannot.

He came to the dining room feeling that this maze of a city and its alien ways had affected the unknowable machinery of his mind. How, he could not say, but the ways were deeper than he had yet dared to comprehend. That there was a hugely more complicated world out there – more complicated than a simple set of English morals could possibly cope with – was quite evident. The thought troubled him, and also, he realized, excited him.

There was not long to wait for the evening meal. The dinner began at ten. Spencer, attended by Prince Mustafa, sat at table with the *kaimakam*. Smith was placed at a second table with the gentlemen of the embassy and the *Chelibe Effendi*. He watched two more tables and some seats brought into the terrace, but was surprised to find most of the company obliged to stand. A huge crowd of people had materialized, simply to watch, it seemed.

The table was spread with a coarse cloth, on which wooden spoons and cakes of unleavened bread were set, one for each guest. The first, he saw, looking around, was for the soups and sherbets; the bread was to serve instead of a plate. He copied the local manner, tearing off the meat with the fingers of his right hand.

As he ate Smith was amazed to find beggar boys capering for morsels at the table.

'Who allows beggars in here?' he asked quietly of Raschid.

'Any person may beg at a new ambassador's table, effendi. That is law.'

'Extraordinary.'

'Oh, no, effendi. Quite normal.'

These ragamuffins have been admitted purposely to disgrace the embassy, Smith thought. But then he brought his suspicions under control, realizing that his displays of discomfort were only making his brother's task more difficult. After a few minutes the thought occurred to him that his first impression had been wrong, and the conviction grew. The manners of this moribund empire are unimaginable only because they're foreign and ancient, he thought. I see now that it's foolish to jump to conclusions, and the height of folly to imagine insults. This is the East, he heard himself say silently. The East. So wait and see.

He was reminded of the tales he had heard in Stockholm of the barbarous table manners of the Russian Cossacks and the incredible sexual excesses said to be a commonplace at the court of the empress Catherine. If the stories that Liston told of her doings were only a quarter true then the tzaritsa had packed a great deal into her sixty-odd years.

And now the Great Empress has made peace with Turkey, he thought. But has she done so to allow her to concentrate on the tearing apart of Poland, or in order to join the grand strategy against France? Our Mr John Wesley Wright has made mention of that. No one has convinced me either way yet.

A doe-eyed boy who could not have more than five years old approached the table, his nose streaming. He watched Smith eat with close attention, until the Englishman felt himself quite unnerved.

'Hello . . .'

'*Afiet olsun, Bey effendi.*' The boy muttered in a gritty little voice, then indicated the wedges of meat. '*Olur?*'

'He wishes you good health, sir,' Raschid explained.

In some matters the Turks are quite right, Smith thought, encouraged by his insight into the seemingly incomprehensible ordering of their ancient society. I must indeed remember my charity. As a Brother, I cannot eat and drink when others present are in a state of hunger.

'*Olur*? *Olur*?' The child kept repeating the word, until Smith put a choice piece of lamb into the boy's mouth.

He raised his eyebrows comically and asked, 'Now, little man? What do you think of that?'

The child grinned up at him like a cherub, his small mouth working on the meat.

Those among the Turks who saw it smiled at one another, Prince Mustafa and the *kaimakam* among them, and he nodded back at them. It was a small thing, but it seemed to break a spell and the atmosphere soon became marvellously affable.

Twenty-two courses were served up in quick succession. Smith tasted some of them, but many appeared and disappeared from the board so fast that he was hardly able to notice them. He showed more charity to the poor by giving to all of the beggar boys, allowing himself to appreciate the charm in their eyes and their girlish movements as his reward, and also to remind himself of the delight there was in giving.

And when the meal was done he was served with a silver ewer to wash his hands. He rose at last, feeling replete, and found himself sprinkled with jasmine water. He had found, for a little while at least, an oasis in his pain, but still, for some reason, he couldn't get what de Tromelin had said about Berenice's death being on Christmas Eve out of his mind.

His bedroom was hung with embroidered draperies, and the mirror traced around in gold and enamel and emblazoned by the arms of the Turkish Empire.

He stood at the open windows, dwelling for a moment on the framed view, as if listening to a visual music that had the capacity to soothe his mind. The ambassador's apartments were spectacular. Everything was gorgeous, gilded and highly furnished with every luxury, but more important by far, he realized, were the sublime proportions of the building itself. The art of correct proportion is an essential ingredient of civilization, he thought, appreciating the way the builder had done his utmost for the comfort of the eye.

Inside his bedroom the divans were of brocade and embroidered velvet. There were marbles from Italy and Persian carpets in the principal saloons. He flung open the shutters and revelled in an atmosphere that was added to by the dazzling glories of the parterre garden spread out beneath the windows. It contained fountains and magnolias and orange trees and the scent of them perfumed the air.

He had explored the residence, and wherever he went he found evidence of the love that Islam showed for water. A desert faith, he thought. What else would they find so precious as the stuff of life? On every side were graceful fountains of white marble. Their flashing waters fell with a musical sound into sculpted basins.

He paused at one of exquisite design, where the stream trickled from a feather so marvellously wrought in alabaster that it seemed to bend under the weight of each sparkling drop. At another, two swans, life size in pure white marble, poured water from their beaks.

Such a lot of trouble to go to, he thought. And to what end?

Raschid entered and said, 'Smith Effendi, your brother comes . . .'

Smith followed him into the concourse.

'Sidney, you'll excuse my barging in on you, but it seems my humble request of an audience has been communicated to the sultan by an officer of the Divan. The Grand Signore has sent a message intimating that he will receive us today.'

'That's really very good of him.'

Spencer looked quickly at him. 'For God's sake! You

act as if you had no idea of the man's power. He's like the pope and the tsar put together. God's mouthpiece and an absolute despot all in one. Thank God they have no idea of subtle English irony here, or your irrevence would lose us everything.'

Smith felt taken aback at his brother's sudden blast. He said with galling calmness, 'My English irony was so subtle, brother dear, that I wasn't even aware of it myself.'

An hour later they entered again the incredible Palace of Topkapi, this time in eye-aching brightness. The party, mounted and all heavy finery, were conducted towards the third gate of the Seraglio – the Threshold of Felicity, and there entered a mysterious and terrifying world.

A chaotic crowd of people waited inside. There were perhaps a hundred of them. Suppliants? Petitioners? Whoever they were, they came forward in a rush as the ambassadorial party entered the gate. Smith was buffeted. Anxieties grew on the hollow faces of the crowd that they would again be ignored. They wailed and clamoured and surged forward like souls trapped in Purgatory. He saw that those who were not wearing fur-trimmed pelisses were pushed back by the guard.

Once inside the inner court the guard became more attentive. Smith found two men escorting him closely, and Spencer and Liston and the others from the embassy each had guards at their shoulders. They were White Eunuchs. He saw a group of them standing within the gate, milling around with the kind of busy idleness that characterized the whole city. He was reminded of slack crews he had known, men who had learned to appear falsely occupied when under the eye of their commander, but who fell dormant as soon as their officers' vigilance was relaxed.

Is it inevitable, he asked himself with ghastly foreboding, that such an atmosphere of mistrust and frustration must attend the slow decay of all empires? Was this how Rome ended? Or was that glory overrun by Vandals in almost a single season, in sudden violence from without or within, as has happened to great France?

They went through a large saloon that was open on both sides. It was attended by rows of Solak guards – men in white robes and pointed caps of gold. The way forward was by a flight of shallow steps into a passage that was floored with rich carpets. Smith's eunuch guard ushered him to within ten paces of the throne, and held him strictly by the right arm all the time.

'It is merely tradition,' Raschid explained when Smith reacted to the guard's touch. 'We have not forgotten the assassination of Sultan Ibrahim a century and a half ago.'

It's incredible, Smith thought, how readily a practical usage becomes an inflexible tradition. Since I can do no other than permit the formality, I will not show bad grace by treating it like an insult.

The kiosk was cramped and gloomily lit, but as his eyes grew accustomed to the stifling light he saw that the walls and ceiling were completely smothered in silver and pearls. Spencer had told him that the throne itself was by far the richest in the world. He now saw it was a thing somewhat like a four-poster bed, but utterly dazzling and splendid. The lower parts were made of burnished silver and pearls, and the canopy and pillars were studded with hundreds of large gems.

Sultan Selim, the third of that name, sat in the middle of the throne, very still, his feet on the ground, composed in an attitude of utmost ceremony. His hands rested on his knees. He was a slight man of thirty-two years. He wore a robe of yellow satin, with a broad border of black sable. His dagger and the ornament at his breast were both crusted with diamonds. The front of his white and blue turban also shone with a diamond clasp that buckled a high straight plume of bird-of-paradise feathers – the *chelengk*.

Smith recalled the briefing Liston had given him: 'Selim's the son of Mustapha III, whose brother, Abdul Hamid, succeeded his uncle nearly five years ago. He's lived in the Seraglio all his life – studying the Koran and the history of the Turkish empire. They say he's ambitious of being a reformer.'

He had said half flippantly, 'That sounds like a dangerous thing hereabouts.'

Liston remained intense. 'You're quite correct. Especially since he's in favour of the *Nizam Jedid*.'

Smith raised his eyebrows. 'What's that?'

'The reorganization of the army. Of course . . .' Liston said with a tentative air, 'the wars with Russia and Austria have prevented his attempting that task.'

'Until now.'

'Correct. And straight away the revolt of Passwan-Oglu broke out.'

'I can well imagine the idea of reform has excited a certain dread among some of the fellows hereabouts.'

Liston had nodded. 'You mean the janissaries. The Grand Signore's empire is a rotted stump. He might seem secure here among his jewels at Stamboul, but there have been rebellions and insurrections in his provinces. He needs us as much as we need him.'

Smith noted how the sultan's eyes moved restlessly from face to face. His features were pale. His bejewelled hands also, as if he spent all his time in the semi-darkness of state, a creature of the labyrinth. He fingered his goat beard with an air that was unnatural, but which, Smith thought, added to the indescribable majesty of an Oriental potentate.

An embroidered cushion rested on each side of the throne. The one to the sultan's right supported a silver satchel that contained, so he had been told, a letter from the Grand Signore to the king of England. Beside it a silver inkstand stood, adorned with more jewellery. A sabre, partly drawn from a diamond-encrusted scabbard, was placed nearly upright against the cushion on the other side.

Liston was alive to the proceedings. 'It was once the custom for foreign ambassadors and their suite to kiss the sultan's hand,' he murmured. 'My predecessor said the whole reception used to be a more courteous affair than it is these days. It was usual for the sultan to address a word or two to the minister, which he now never deigns to do . . .'

Spencer stood nearly opposite but a little to the left of the throne. On his left was Prince Mustafa, who was acting as his sponsor and interpreter.

On the right of the sultan the *kaimakam* stood to the side with his head bent, his hands crossed submissively in front of his vest, a posture that Smith noted with interest.

Spencer also put his hand on his breast and inclined his head as he addressed the sultan. The speech was delivered in a low tone, interpreted still less audibly by the prince. The sultan then said a few words to the *kaimakam*, who replied to Spencer. Immediately afterwards the ambassador extraordinary bowed and withdrew, and Smith realized that the audience was over. It had lasted less than a quarter of an hour, and nothing of importance had been said.

The thought suddenly struck him on the way out: if I am to be in this ant-hill until the embassy is thoroughly accomplished I shall be here years!

On leaving, Spencer's eunuch led him back, then he dismissed him, showing him down the steps of the antechamber. The rest of the embassy followed, and passed out through the third and the second gates of the Seraglio where they remounted. They were made to wait for an hour under the scorching sun until the *kaimakam* and his suite had gone from the Divan and retired to the

417

Porte, and all the janissaries had issued from the second court. They came out, roaring and running, and a part of Smith envied their mindless riot.

He was pleased to hear that the British would land at Uskudar in comparative splendour. His Britannic Majesty's ship *Crescent* had dropped anchor in the Bosphorus yesterday morning. She was dwarfed now by the dozen triple-decker ships-of-the-line that were the pride of the Turkish navy, but the neatness and efficiency of the British frigate spoke of a formidable power.

There had been a time when Smith could not have regarded a frigate of the king's navy with anything other than an envious eye. The *Crescent* was exactly the kind of vessel he had so often hungered to command. Captain Skynner's immaculate thirty-six-gun frigate was as orderly and precise as her captain appeared to be. She had been detached at the last moment from Lord Hood's fleet, and sent with urgent despatches for the embassy in Turkey.

But Smith's sense of shiplessness was in abeyance. At dinner last night the cabin had stirred up a hundred memories, but none of them had touched him. His fortunate, fair-haired host had been eager to pass on what he knew of the war, especially the daunting news of Toulon, France's main Mediterranean naval base, but Skynner had not raised Smith's interest. The dinner proved that his longing to take command of a frigate again was gone.

'There's now a very powerful force at Toulon,' Skynner had said. 'The French have seventeen sail-of-the-line ready for sea, mostly seventy-fours, and with them is the biggest warship in the world, the *Commerce de Marseille*. She carries a hundred and twenty guns. What do you think of that, Sir Sidney? And there's another hundred-and-twenty-gun vessel, the *Dauphin Royale*, refitting in the port. She's in company with an eighty and a couple of seventy-fours. Nine more are repairing in the inner harbour, and there's a further seventy-four building on the slips, and a number of frigates and corvettes to boot.'

Smith had shrugged at the vastness of the naval power. 'It's especially alarming,' he said without conviction, 'knowing that the Jacobin, Robespierre, has all but made himself dictator of France. Why so many ships at Toulon?'

Skynner pounced on the question. 'Ah, being out here you won't know much of what has passed in France, but it seems that a Revolutionary deputy by the name of Jean-Bon St André has dismissed all the old-style officers at Brest, and a fair few of them have lost their topmasts, if you take my meaning.'

Smith received the news with a sigh. Those men had been his late enemies in the American war, and fine hosts during his time in Normandy. First he had respected them, and then he had grown to like them, and to hear of their ignominy gave him no satisfaction at all. He thought fleetingly of the noble Antoine Phelypeaux and sighed.

Skynner went on. 'The Jacobins have appointed some fellow called Dalbarade as their Minister of Marine, a pirate by all accounts.'

'It doesn't surprise me.' Smith shook his head, ghosts of the past clouding his mind. 'Their whole country's in uproar and led by monsters, Skynner. Why should their navy be any different?'

'Quite. Well, at any rate, a full seven of those seventy-fours in Toulon belong to the Biscayan ports. They've come in since the start of the year.'

Smith looked up. 'You know what that must mean?'

Skynner's face brightened. 'Exactly. The Revolution hasn't yet got their hands on them. The good news is that the Toulon fleet's under the command of Rear-Admiral Trogoff.'

Smith sat up. 'The Comte de Trogoff de Kerlessy?'

'The same, I'm sure. Do you know of him? Toulon itself has declared against the Revolution, along with a dozen other towns in the south.'

Smith shrugged. 'Well, that's something. From what I remember Trogoff's a sound fellow, too much a Monarchist to fire a shot in the cause of Republicanism.'

Skynner showed himself unconvinced. 'Perhaps, but a spirit of disaffection is growing among the men of Trogoff's fleet, despite the scale of rebellion in the south. Most of Toulon's inhabitants carry Royalist convictions, but they're all presently dreading the arrival of Republican armies from the north, and that fear is making unreliable allies of them.' Skynner shook his head. 'The finest thing the comte could do for his country would be to hand all those fine ships over to Lord Hood's care. But I don't suppose he will do it.'

'Of course not, my dear Skynner, no more than you would surrender *Crescent* to the French – or to me, for that matter. Those ships're Trogoff's only bargaining counter. And he's a Frenchman first and last. So tell me, what has our Admiralty done about the situation?'

Skynner told him how an English fleet had been hastily brought into being to give succour to Toulon. The first division of the fleet, under Rear-Admiral John Gell in the *St George*, had sailed from Spithead in April. Later that month a second division, under Vice-Admiral Philip Cosby, in the *Windsor Castle*, had followed. A third division had sailed under Vice-Admiral Hotham in the *Britannia*, and finally, in late May, a fourth division had departed, under Vice-Admiral Lord Hood, commander-in-chief, in the *Victory*.

'They're throwing everything into the pot.'

Skynner nodded. 'Also, we have common cause with the Spaniards now. Naples and Piedmont and the Kingdom of the Two Sicilies are with us, too. If only we can defend Toulon successfully, then we stand a chance of halting the infection before it spreads into Spain and Italy. How are things here?'

Now Smith breathed in the salt air, gazing out over the space of water that separated Europe and Asia. His mind was replete with half-digested thoughts. The ship moved, creaked, was alive to him. The deck boards were holystoned almost white; he could feel the pitch seams beneath the soles of his shoes. There was no smell on earth like the one he tasted now. His eye ran up the ratlines to the tops, along the lower yards and down the shrouds. Ropes were flaked out on deck. The crew were busy with a hundred tasks. There were navy faces to be seen and navy accents to be heard about him. Why then, did he feel so indifferent to it all?

Last night, the once-sweet shrills of the bosun's pipe as they had climbed down in an alcoholic haze to the gig had grated on his ears. This was just a ship. What he had been trained to all his life, but still just a ship.

Now, as he looked around him, he saw a suite of officers and gentlemen assembled in full-dress uniform. They stood in the ship's waist, aware that some conspicuous show was necessary from them.

'This is not England, where a man may wear a plain broadcloth coat at Court and not be thought the less for it,' Liston told him. 'The Osmanleys respect pomp. That is how they judge prestige. See there, on the point – they've erected marquees for us. That's where they'll dress us as they please after we're eaten.'

Smith bridled. A moment later, as they were waiting to climb down into the longboat, he asked, 'Did you say *dress* us as they please?'

'Auch, to be received by the sultan,' Liston said, his eyebrows raised at Smith's ignorance. ' "Feed and clothe the infidels" – that's the ancient expression, and the custom they stick to. One supposes it was once some kind of insult, but it is nowadays considered an honourable and indispensable formality.'

The pull to shore was a matter of ten minutes. Smith's hand went again to his waistcoat pocket, as it often did when he was in a small boat. But his fingers did not locate the silver trinket, and the shock of not finding the Green Goblin in its accustomed place recalled to him the fact that he had lost it. The loss was very disappointing. He had grown accustomed to touching it in times of stress, and had loved it more than any of his other personal possessions.

Liston said, 'My God, I almost forgot to tell you. This arrived aboard *Crescent* among the despatches.'

He handed over a personal letter. The envelope was sealed, and addressed simply to him by name. He did not recognize the handwriting, and so tucked it into his pocket to await a less pressing moment.

As he looked up they came alongside, and the passengers stepped out of the boat onto a stone-built mole where richly caparisoned horses waited for them. Skynner had arranged for the party to be escorted by the frigate's marines, a drummer, a fiddler and a fifer playing at the head of their column, and the men singing 'Heart of Oak'.

Urchins and beggars who had come to watch them pass were driven away by the violence of the Turkish guards. Smith tried to shrug off the formless anxieties of the last two days, and deliberately turned his mind to the ancient vows that he had taken. To serve the interests of mankind was his duty. His only possible duty now that his love was dead.

It's a duty higher than that of both nationhood and religious creed, he reflected. The Knights Templar and the Knights Hospitaller and all the other chivalric orders that have been incorporated into the Brotherhood as higher degrees – these exist for only one purpose: to impose order on the chaos of history, to drag all humankind towards the light of civilization. And how?

Through example, through membership, through charity, all of these, of course – but also through the medium of a steering hand applied to critical events.

And who shall steer? he wondered. And who shall salvage the wreck when, as must happen at times, the ship goes aground?

'*For evil to triumph it only requires that good men do nothing.*'

The maxim came unbidden to his mind. Where did I hear that before? he wondered. But wherever it was, it's true. Aye.

Dust rose at the periphery of his sight. The cracking of whips over the heads of the people made his blood boil. Consider the poor, he thought. There must be order, for it is the great mass of the poor who suffer most at every Apocalypse. It is their children who die in their hundreds of thousands in plagues. It is their flesh that starves in famine, their bones that war grinds to dust. It is the poor who are enslaved by barbaric laws, the poor who are forced to drudge without rest or rights, who are denied justice and education. Doesn't the Great Book say that the education of the poor is one of the foremost responsibilities of good government?

Soon the procession crested the hill and approached the main tent. It was open, and Smith saw that the *kaimakam* sat alone on his divan, flanked by two men whom he knew were the *kazi-askars* of Romania and of Anatolia.

The *kaimakam*'s eyes slitted in a smile as his guest approached. He motioned towards a low stool.

Spencer disregarded the assumption of superiority and, still within the bounds of Ottoman etiquette, chose to sit down on the divan beside the *kaimakam*.

Smith watched with interest for the *kaimakam*'s reaction, but he showed no hostility, and the stool was quietly removed. Then the dragomans knelt on the carpet beside their respective masters, and a mandatory exchange of compliments began. Smith clasped his hands behind his back and listened to the *Crescent*'s little band as they played, distantly but lustily, a series of familiar naval airs. From where Smith stood he could see the marines drawn up facing the imperial tent, a dead straight line of disciplined scarlet and black and pipeclay white. His eyes inspected them discreetly.

A gratifying contrast, he thought, comparing them to the slouching, ill-dressed men of the Porte guard. Who can say what impression it makes upon the Turks? But it certainly speaks volumes to me.

Water pipes and coffee were brought, then lunch followed, and a good deal of nodding and smiling between opposite numbers. As Liston had predicted they were then shown to a second tent to be clothed. Spanish mantles were brought out: scarlet, red or yellow, according to the rank of the wearer. Smith burned inside at the grotesque transformation.

'Now I understand why the Turks insist upon it,' he told Liston. 'It must be very much easier to conduct diplomacy with men who fear they look ridiculous.'

'Ah, Smith,' Liston said, raising a finger. 'Looking ridiculous is, after all, a relative condition.'

When he had got over the shock, Smith heard the boom of cannon, and felt irrationally uncomfortable on that account until he went to look for the cause. As he cleared the tent a tremendous firing and cheering broke out from the Turkish fleet in the strait. He saw that all the Turkish ships were now dressed with their people, their yards manned, and all bunting flying, to announce the sultan's departure from Therapia.

As he watched, a twelve-oared caique sped across the sapphire-blue strait. The mile of water lying between the Palace and Uskudar took the vessel a few minutes. Then the gilded eagle in the prow glinted in the sun as it came alongside the jetty.

He saw the sultan gather his robes and mount the

jetty. A superb Arabian waited for him, its trappings covered with jewels. The pallid figure, shaded under his mushroom of headgear, advanced slowly to his tent. Turbanned pages walked on each side with high peacock plumes to conceal his face from profane view. The guard salaamed to the ground as he passed along. The drummer and fifer struck up again at a signal from Liston, but their strains were drowned by cries of 'Live a thousand years!' from every Turkish throat. It seemed to Smith like something brought up from the days of the Plantagenet kings.

The English party were made to wait one hour. Then a *kapiji* – messenger-secretary – informed Spencer that the sultan was ready to receive his visitors. It was staged as if the sultan's entourage had happened to meet here by chance, a peculiar fiction, Smith supposed, to satisfy the greater fiction that the meeting was between the Lord of All the World and some supplicant or another from a land that was of little consequence. Such was the Asian method.

There's a balance to be struck, he thought, recalling the day he had visited St James's Palace and delighted in the archaic ceremonial. Tradition is essential, but it must be allowed to evolve to suit new times, or things become absurd and unworkable.

He entered the audience tent third and last, following Spencer and Robert Liston inside. As before they were each accompanied by a dismounted cavalryman with drawn sword who gripped his charge by the arm. To expect honourable diplomats to tolerate such manhandling, he thought, disliking the custom intensely, is quite incredible. What on earth do they imagine we're going to do?

Selim received the embassy with great simplicity; his two pages and the guards were the only individuals present. Now, instead of the robes of golden tissue in which he had made the procession, he wore a plain blue military cloak and trousers, with no other ornament than his diamond *chelengk*. Smith saw with satisfaction that the Sultan wore steel spurs on English riding boots. This man needs to do business, he thought. Perhaps he also *wants* to do business. But has he come ready to answer our central proposal?

That proposal was crucial. The encirclement of France by cooperating powers was essential if they were to contain the Revolutionary pressure that had boiled up to a head there. Such a vast explosive force would seek to escape across all of Europe, and no single nation would be able to oppose it.

Smith brought his mind back to the bizarre audience in which British government aims and the aims of the Brotherhood were so intimately twined together. Interpreters converted their words almost instantly, so that none of the conversational quality was lost from the exchanges. There were a few pleasantries; but after five minutes' worth Selim's face set into a death's head as he addressed Spencer.

'You speak of France. How fares that country?'

'It is in ever greater turmoil. France is, as it were, a hexagon sitting at the heart of Europe. She has six borders across which to bedevil the rest of the mankind. She has three land borders: to the north, the Low Countries and Germany; to the east, Switzerland and Italy; and finally south, across the Pyrenees, into Spain. Also she has three coasts – the English Channel facing Britain; the Atlantic coast, from which she has access to the wider world; and then the Mediterranean, from which she has access to you.'

'We have heard there is a war.'

'Since the French cut off the head of their king, there has been a general muster of arms across all Europe.'

'This is to be expected, is it not?'

Now Liston answered. 'Alas, the capacity of the French for war is not diminished by their internal

426

upheaval, for they have always maintained a very great army and a most numerous navy, and their interest in faraway lands is as keen as ever it was.'

Smith understood the references that were being made, and how pertinent they were to this meeting. In the latter half of the century French forces had been smashed and smashed again in North America and all across the East. They had been forced to give up their American colonies, and lost the struggle to inherit the crumbling Moghul empire. The British East India Company had been left with the lion's share of that, and a virtual monopoly of the immensely rich Asian trade. Last year the war in Mysore had come to a climax with Lord Cornwallis's great victory over Tipu Sultan at Seringapatam: there would now certainly be no French empire in the subcontinent of India. Unless . . .

'So, too, the British are keen to travel afar,' Selim said, his voice reedy and forlorn. 'I have heard that your countrymen range where they will about the globe. Perhaps it is that they believe it is their duty to remake the whole world in their own image?'

'Yes,' Spencer said flatly. 'We do. As the Romans were once the leading civilization in Europe, so we intend that Great Britain shall become the pre-eminent light of the world. It will be no bad thing for all mankind if the world is taught as our children are taught.'

Smith was astonished by his brother's bluntness. Spencer's brilliant, he thought, but he has a regrettable bullishness of mind. The sultan received the interpreted answer like a stab in the heart. No one had dared come to Constantinople with such vast and threatening language. His voice rose higher. 'This is a terrible arrogance.'

Liston tried to moderate the crisis. 'By no means, my lord. Empires rise and fall. It is simply that we are presently rising. And, since the French won't yet admit their days of greatness are over, certain steps must be taken to correct their view.'

Selim's reply was delivered calmly, but his amazement at them was plain. The interpreter said, 'What mandate have you to say this shall be here and that shall be there the world over? Who are you? I do not know you.'

Spencer smiled at the quaintness, but Liston said, 'We are, my lord, like the look-outs aboard a ship. Someone must point out the dangerous waters into which the world is heading, or we should all be sunk.'

Selim's eyes drifted away, returned to his main tormentor tiredly. 'The French ambassador claims this also. What makes you suppose that your way is more fitting for the world than that of the emperor of China? Or the tzaritsa of all the Russias? Or the mamelukes of Egypt? Or . . . whomsoever?'

Spencer inclined his head indulgently. 'You talk of despots. What the world needs is an industrious and ingenious nation to give it material benefits. As I hope my presents to you have shown, there are many examples of our industry and our ingenuity. We have invented iron work-machines that are driven by the power of steam. We have made timepieces so accurate that we can steer a ship anywhere in the world. We possess looms that can spin thread and weave it into cloth as if by magic, a hundred times faster than any man can do it. We have even found a way to prevent a person from catching the smallpox. Now, can the tzaritsa, or the emperor of China, accomplish any of these marvels? Or are not these proofs that we are greater?'

'Disease is merely the measure of God's displeasure.' Selim pulled back his cuff elaborately and snapped his fingers. Smith thought it seemed a curiously incongruous gesture. 'And *so* much do I care for looms that weave a hundred times faster, or the power of your work-machines, when I have ten thousand looms and ten thousand men to do my bidding.'

'Would that we were all so fortunate.' Spencer cleared his throat with an air of suppressed irritation. 'But I see that I am not yet making myself quite clear to you—'

Selim's finger shot out in sudden accusation. 'You have eaten sinfully of the Tree of Knowledge. This is of no use to the world!'

The audience was not going well. Spencer's smile was withering now. He said, 'Well, no matter, because the French have eaten of the same tree. Whereas, fortunately for us, my lord, they have of late spat out those fruits.'

Smith winced inwardly, knowing that his brother's remarks would probably not translate, or, if they did, they would be more likely to irritate the sultan than to win him over. So what does it matter? he thought. What does anything matter? As I told Spencer, the whole world can go to hell for all I care.

As the oblique talk proceeded, Smith's attention began to wander more and more. He began to look around the tent, yawned into his hand, and wished that he was outside and walking alone, or with Raschid a few paces away, through the streets of the old city. After a few minutes he remembered the letter in his pocket. He drew it out surreptitiously, tearing off the end of the envelope as quietly as he could. It was just one small sheet, and he slipped it out to satisfy his curiosity.

He began to read, and the words on the page jolted him so violently that he almost jumped up. His mind was racing. He read the letter again. Then again. And once more, trying desperately not to let his agitation show. I knew it! he thought, clenching his fist. I knew it all along! Oh, my God . . . I *knew* it!

In a moment the grey sense of worthlessness and futility in which he had lived for so many weeks had vanished. It was as if a chronic pain had suddenly ceased, or the sun had come out, saturating the world with vibrant colours.

By the time he could bring himself to refocus on the

proceedings, Spencer had brought the audience to the brink of disaster. His manner had become cool, lofty and logical. What was worse, he was lecturing the sultan.

'You must know that the Jacobins are terrorists. Fanatics. Dogmatic intellects, untempered by the slightest human feeling. They've killed their king. They've wiped out their political opponents. And they are going to cause a great deal more trouble before they're done. Make no mistake: they will run amok in Europe tomorrow as they are running amok in France today.'

The Koranic scholar rocked a moment, then said darkly, 'One must never trust government to intellectuals, for they love their theories and principles better than they love people.'

'Quite so . . .'

It was as if Smith's mind had come suddenly alive. He saw at once how things stood. It appeared to everyone else that the sultan's subtle personal jibe had gone unrecognized by Spencer. Of course it had not. Spencer had certainly picked up the remark, but it mattered less than nothing to him, and he behaved as such.

The jeopardy of the moment was vivid to Smith, as he heard Spencer ploughing on regardless. 'To return to the matter in hand, it is our belief that if the French may not have India then they will try to have somewhere else. And I think you know what I mean by that.'

Selim appeared fatigued. He said with a bone-deep weariness, 'Christians would govern the whole world.'

Smith felt the sweat starting to bedew his face. He could see that Selim understood exactly what Spencer meant, but because of the Englishman's brusque, arrogant manner he could not consider the problem without a loss of prestige. Smith knew he must try to rescue the moment, and when Spencer paused he made a reckless move.

'My lord sultan, is it not true, according to ancient

lore, that Egypt was the granary upon which the might of Rome was built? And that presently the province is the main glory of Ottoman possessions?'

Selim shifted his gaze, interested in what the man who had not otherwise made a contribution had to say. When Spencer tried to cut him off, Selim waved him to silence. He then looked to both Prince Mustafa and to the *kaimakam*, who nodded back approvingly. When the sultan levelled his gaze once more he said, 'That is quite true. Egypt is an ancient jewel.'

'And is it not also true, my lord, that there was once a canal connecting the Mediterranean Sea with the Red Sea? A great canal built thousands of years ago, in the days of the Pharaohs?'

'That is also true. I have read that in antiquity a canal connected the Nile, Wadi Tumlat, the Bitter Lakes and the Red Sea.'

'And two centuries ago one of your own Turkish engineers proposed that a new canal should cross the isthmus, did he not? And three times in his reign the French King Louis XIV recommended to the Sublime Porte the building of this waterway?'

'Again, what you say is doubtless.'

'Then, my lord sultan, may I clearly say what our embassy has been meaning to lay before you?'

'Say.'

Smith glanced at the others. Spencer's expression was furious, Liston's merely tight-lipped.

'Egypt controls the direct route to India. And the Indian trade is presently the main source of British wealth. Our vessels must sail from London thousands of miles around the whole of Africa to reach Bombay. If a canal were to be built across the isthmus of Suez then French ships could sail from their base at Toulon, where they have an impressive navy, and reach India in less than half that time. They could embark troops and reinforce those armies at will.

'My lord sultan, we know that it has long been the design of French foreign policy to seize Egypt from the Ottomans. The Revolution has not changed that. They will try to take Egypt from you just as soon as an opportunity presents itself. And this is why Turkey may wish to join with us in opposing them.'

Sultan Selim considered, then stood up. 'The audience is at an end.'

Smith stared as the sultan stood up, fearing that his gamble had failed. They all bowed, and straightened to find Selim had gone.

Spencer turned to him when they were out of earshot. His hand was flexing, a mannerism he affected only in moments of extreme frustration. 'Thank you for that contribution,' he said tightly.

Smith appealed to the Scot. 'Liston, do you think it was my fault that he's left?'

Liston said, 'Good God, no.'

Spencer looked at him. 'I suppose it's permissible in this decadent culture for adult men to give free vent to their most childish impulses. The fate of the world rests on his decision, so he has decided to sulk. Extraordinary!'

'What do you suppose?' Smith asked, striding away with his brother. 'Will he join with us and the Russians against the French?'

Spencer was bleakly angry. 'The man's an intransigent maniac, so I have absolutely no idea.'

Smith clutched his letter, unfolded it again and looked at it for the sheer, unimaginable joy it gave him. The signature at the bottom belonged to Antoine Phelypeaux. His friend was alive after all.

And so too, Phelypeaux had reported, was Berenice.

FIVE

They crossed the River Rhône on a hot morning in late October. Berenice saw the guard post and knew instantly that her feelings about today were correct. It was just a pinch-point in the bridge road, an open door and a small windowlet in a wall of ruined grey masonry, but it worried her. She saw that they would have to pass it; there seemed something repellent about it, some quality that tensed her stomach and warned her.

Living so long as a fugitive had sharpened the cat senses within her. She thought of it like that – the danger instinct that wild animals relied on, but that civilized human beings had lost.

They had starved for days on end in the hill country to the north-west of Lyons, snaring rabbits, raiding farms at night, stealing chickens and vegetables from the fields, until they had become savages.

It had been impossible getting beyond Lyons because of the siege. The dangers of being seen had driven them from the roads. According to a proclamation she had seen posted at a deserted crossroads, the Convention had announced even more hellish powers of seizure. Now, without papers they could be arrested and executed within twenty-four hours, without trial, merely on the whim of a military commission. The address at Vienne that Gugnot had given her was their only recourse.

She knew the siege was over by the columns of men marching south. She had not realized how the character of the country would change; three hundred thousand men moving south left a void. The land was suddenly desolate. Yesterday she had brought them out of hiding and set off on the road that bypassed Lyons. The day had been hot, the road parched. They had reached Givros at seven o'clock in the evening, and pressed on through the dusk.

'What's the matter,' her mother had asked, seeing her uncertainty as they came in sight of the walled town.

Berenice had bitten her lip. 'I'm getting worried that nightfall will prevent us from getting into Vienne.'

'Do you think that's likely?'

'There'll be a curfew.'

'How do you know?'

'I just do.'

She had offered her sister a warning glance, and drawn her aside. 'I'm going to try to scout the way. I want to find out if we'll be able to get inside the town at night. Wait here.'

Her mother's fears had seemed to grow. 'What are you two whispering about? Tell me.'

'Nothing important, maman.'

Berenice set off alone. The stench of Gugnot's evil remained in her nostrils, even now, months later. Her instincts had told her the truth about him. The evidence was there also. But still her thinking mind had been unwilling to believe that a man whom she had known all her life could want to degrade and humiliate her for the sake of his own satisfaction.

She had said nothing at all to the others about what had happened on the Feurs road. At first it had seemed simple enough to palm off Celestine's questions with an insistence that the carriage had vanished. Her mother had accepted the disappointment easily, but Celestine had known she was lying.

'What really happened with Gugnot?' she asked, when they were alone together. The question had been eating at her.

'Nothing. I told you. I couldn't find him.'

'What did he want? Why was he with Marguerite in the carriage?'

'I said, I couldn't find him.'

'Why did you make us hide in the forest?'

'Stop asking questions.'

'Berenice, tell me!'

Her anger had flared. 'Don't raise your voice! It's hard enough for me, without your being deliberately stupid all the time!'

It was another lesson she had learned about poverty then: that no one needed patience more than a penniless fugitive, and no one found it more elusive.

She had repaired the rift with Celestine quickly enough, but the haunting questions about Gugnot had chased round and round in her mind. Whichever way she thought it through the answers always came up the same: it is not enough for him that we are fallen and that he is risen, he wants to see us crushed down completely. He deliberately brought me to the Place de Greve to see my own father die. I understand that now. He wanted to take my mother and sister from me, and turn me into a whore that I might spy on his behalf. He is insane for power over others. How completely is Marguerite under his sway? How much poor Jacques? Oh, God!

After a brief detour she had satisfied herself that a curfew was in place in Vienne, and that a watch was being kept on its walls. She knew they would not be able to find a way into the town, so they had slept in a barn a quarter of a league outside the gates.

Now the morning had dawned, and they were trying again. Her presentiments of disaster had been growing ever since they had woken up, but she had tried to put

435

them out of her mind. If they stop us now, she thought, it'll be because we look like vagrants.

'Hoi, you!'

Her prediction was coming true, just as she had known it would. Two fusiliers in equally beggarly uniforms came out, a young man in a red cap, the other, older, leatherfaced, and wearing a black bicorn.

They stopped.

'You. Where're your papers?'

She produced them, hoping that neither would be able to read, but her heart emptied as she saw the suspicion on the soldier's face.

'Stand still!' The soldier in the rat-eaten bicorn looked her up and down. His manner was menacing. She imagined some hellish committee giving out measures of authority willy-nilly to bitter men who should never have had the slightest power over others. 'What do you call these, eh?'

It was not a question that could be answered. She felt panic seize her. 'Are not the passports in good order?'

He snarled at her. 'Move!'

'But why? What—'

'Just move!'

She felt numb as she was prodded in the kidneys. She hoped that neither soldier would notice the expression of terror on the faces of her sister and mother. She asked again, but was given no answer, so she asked a third time. Then she stopped asking, aware that her voice was betraying her fear, and that fear would probably imply guilt to men such as these.

Far better a dignified silence, she thought. They were taken to a narrow cobbled alley, and the suspicion burgeoned in her that they were being taken to a quiet place to be raped. For a moment, the fear filled her mind and the joints of her knees loosened, making it hard to walk.

It can't be, she told herself. Today is such a pleasant

day; it's warm, the sky is so blue and clear. There is moss between the cobbles, and the weeds in the gutters are in bright yellow flower. Everything is so ordinary.

They were conducted almost past another open door, then called back to it. The wood of the door frame was old and wormy. She saw old nail heads embedded in it. Her eyes seized vivid detail. Fear did that. The building was mediaeval, two or three hundred years old. It must have seen many things.

They were made to wait interminably in the half wood-panelled hallway. There was a strange smell in the house, unpleasant and complex, like stale food, body odours and, under it, the hint of bad drains, but after a few minutes she ceased to notice it. Two men came by, one after the other, looked at them with incurious eyes, showing exactly similar reactions. They followed one another into a side door with armfuls of paperwork.

Then the man in the bicorn spoke. 'Give me all your papers. Everything you've got.'

Berenice complied immediately. At a nod from the older, the younger soldier took the precious papers away. He knocked at a door and entered. There was a short wait, then an old officer, who was alone, asked for them to be brought in.

Berenice saw that he was a severe-looking man – skull-faced under a black toque, like the worst sort of *ci-devant* cleric. He had spread their passports out on the table before him like the cards of the Tarot. He examined them minutely then looked at them. 'You know that these are not worth a *sou* beyond the extent of your own Department.'

The gravity of the man's demeanour speared her, leaving her in no doubt that they had been found out in a very serious matter. 'I . . . I don't understand.'

A moment passed as his unblinking gaze looked up at them. 'These ought to have been approved by the Department of Allier, which they were not.'

Berenice felt his eyes accusing her. Mustering as much humility as she could, she said softly, 'Citizen, you have me at a disadvantage. I have not even been told what is this place, or whom I am addressing.'

He was shocked. 'You have an education?'

'Of a church-school kind.'

He considered that for a moment, appraising her. 'My name is Kluger. I am the principal officer of the Committee of Surveillance of the Department of Isère. Now perhaps you can explain why your passports have been found to be defective?'

'I don't know how it could have happened.'

Kluger sat back in his chair. 'It says here you're from Sarthe. It happens that I myself come from that quarter originally. I am very pleased to see one from my own Department. Tell me, I pray you, what news of Le Mans? Is the city now free?'

'I know nothing of what has passed there,' she said, terror freezing her belly. 'We had scarce arrived there to see our relations when my husband was recalled. In consequence he immediately returned to the south. The state of our feet may show with what expedition we have followed him.'

'Bravo,' he said faintly. He put his finger to his chin thoughtfully.

Berenice knew this was the moment of decision, and that she must make the one remark that would cause Kluger to decide they were not to be imprisoned, but she could not say anything. She knew that once she mentioned Gugnot's name she would be in his power.

Kluger grunted, a cynical light in his eye. 'So . . . you are all zealots for the Revolution, are you? Well, I wish all were as warm in the cause as you. And because of that I will not detain you. Mansard!'

She stared back, unable to believe their luck. A clerk came in. Kluger ordered their passports to be registered, and told the fusiliers to conduct them to the Municipality. But then Berenice's hopes of release faded again. They were conducted across the town to offices where they were made to wait all through the sweltering afternoon.

'You're from outside the Department, aren't you?' a rudely inquisitive woman who was also waiting said.

'How do you know?'

The woman tapped the side of her nose confidentially and laughed. 'That's why you're here. They always give outsiders the run-around. Have you got any money?'

Berenice put on her hardest face. 'No.'

'Shame. How do you lodge on the road, then? You're a liar, aren't you?'

'Then mind your own business, citoyenne.' Strange how those most trodden down are always the ones most keen to tread down others, she thought. But if the bitch lays a finger on any of us I'll slap her, I swear I will . . .

The woman gave her back a wounded glance. 'Don't worry, chicken, I'm not going to take your *assignats* off you. But you'd better keep what you've got well hidden from those grasping thieves in there. The mayor owns all the eating houses hereabouts. If he thinks you've got money he'll detain you here a week and strip you bare before he'll set you on your way.'

The warning was clear enough. The old bitch probably only means to make me worry, she thought.

She heard herself called, and went past the guard into a room with a trio of men at a table, a bench of inquiry. They were ordinary-looking townspeople, whose lunch had just taken up the first half of the afternoon, judging by the smell of them and the way they belched. The one in the centre was obviously the mayor. He asked her for their passports.

After examining them he looked up. 'These are not valid.'

She sighed. 'So I've been told, citoyen. We have departed from the route for which they were made out.'

Another muttered darkly, 'It's the business of the Committee of Surveillance to examine passports.'

The third said, 'I'm surprised they should attempt to transpose their work to the Municipality. They know we are quite fully employed.'

'Unless,' the mayor said, looking up, 'they've sent them to us as a means of detecting their falsehood.'

Berenice looked from face to face. She could see that, to them, she was no more than a piece of human trash, too much of which was swilling around the country these days. They were refugees, the sort who must be kept away from quiet little towns.

She boiled inside. To have officials like these discuss their case as if they were not present and able to hear was the greatest insult.

'Falsehood?'

Berenice was aware of her mother's face, white as a linen sheet. Fortunately, she saw, the mayor's eyes were fixed on her. He said: 'Are you travelling alone?'

'My husband has been on leave of absence. This has been at his own expense. Upon his recall his wish was to resume his duties to the nation as soon as possible, therefore he has gone ahead of us.'

'How happens it that your passports have not been revised to this effect by your own Department?'

'Maybe my husband did not think it necessary to lose so much time by attending to these formalities,' she said. 'Should the family of a master gunner obtain vouchers from every district and Department?'

'The law is clear. It is the same for everyone, citoyenne.'

'Well, I didn't know.'

The other tutted. 'Ignorance of the law is no defence.'

She bit back her anger, thinking: all opposition to this monstrous state is punished with severity, but perhaps they have not yet learned how to cope with simple compliance. She said, 'In that case may I not now charge the state with the business of setting these papers in good order? If you think it proper to detain us until these matters can be cleared up we shall not object. Naturally, you will have to answer to the nation for the loss of my husband's services during the time when he comes to enquire after us.'

The mayor laced his fingers. He's one of the most dangerous kinds of men in the world, she thought. A cautious and unimaginative man. A coward in his ordinary dealings. The sort of man who by his negligence of duty creates great suffering for others to avoid a slight inconvenience to himself. Look at him! His horizon is petty rules and paper tokens. He cannot see us as people. He cannot be sympathetic, for he dare not put himself in our place.

He said, 'I applaud your husband's zeal, and I do not doubt your own good intentions, but ... has your Municipality given you a Certificate of Civism?'

'You mean this?' She took out a fabricated paper. The signatures were well counterfeited. It seemed to satisfy the mayor, and he passed it to the others on the bench, who looked at it with incomprehensible interest.

She said, 'Citoyen, to clear up all your doubts, there – read that letter.' She laid on the table an exact copy of the paper that Jacques de Tromelin had received from his regiment. 'You will find that it contains a recommendation of my husband to the major of the Fifth Regiment of Isère, in consequence of which he is now going to serve the nation and to reap laurels for France.'

The man to the mayor's right sat up. He took the paper with excitement. 'Ah, but this changes everything. You see, I know Major Abelard. We were at school together.'

Berenice saw the way her sister looked to her. She thought, for God's sake, Celestine, you always were

441

hopeless at deceit. I must see something to distract them.
'Monsieur mayor, we are very short of cash. I was
wondering therefore if you would do us a great act of
kindness by giving us a passport direct to Orange,
instead of obliging us to go back via Lyons?'

The mayor looked up sharply. 'There is no such
place.'

A sense of surreality overwhelmed her suddenly. 'No
such place as *Lyons*?'

The mayor's face changed, as if evil magic had
suddenly been invoked. 'Don't say that word, citoyenne.
That city is now renamed Ville Affranchie.'

'Whatever you call it, sir, I have heard it is nought but
a ruin now.'

He rapped out the answer like a formula, 'Royalist
and Girondist dogs rebelled there, but the city has now
been brought under control and cleansed by Generals
Kellermann and Doppet.'

'May we go direct to Orange?' She made her appeal
again, sensing it was the best thing to do. 'Monsieur, the
road is dangerous, and we are in great need. Will you
give me your name in writing? That I might use it as a
recommendation, just as Major Abelard has? And you,
sir, since you are a personal friend of the major's perhaps
you could see your way clear to making a small subsidy
which my husband will gladly repay once we arrive.'

That's it, she thought, looking at their confusion. If
the first reaction of the petty official is to cover his own
personal position, and the second is to process out of his
jurisdiction anything that looks like trouble – and what
is more trouble than someone who begs for money? –
then what better to put the cramp on them? Look at the
fat bastard scribble, she thought.

Now he's making out our new passports as fast as he
can write!

When they were completed, she put out her hand for

the three passports, but the man on the mayor's left held them.

'First you must pay the fee, citoyenne. Three livres.'

'But that's . . .' She recognized the pervasive feeling of injustice eating at her. 'That's a lot of money.'

'You must pay.'

She shrugged. 'We *can't* pay. If we did we would starve before we reached our destination.'

'Ah, so you do have the money.'

'Yes, but not enough. We'd starve!'

The bench regarded her with a stony silence. 'That is the law. Three livres each.'

'*Each*?' The feeling of injustice turned to anger, and she lost control of her temper. 'It's a racket! You tell us we need these damned papers to travel the nation's highways, then you try to soak us for your damned signatures. What do you think we are?'

'You must pay.'

'We don't have enough money!'

The mayor took a deep breath, and began as if explaining something simple to a deliberately difficult schoolgirl. 'Our time must be paid for. These papers cost money to print. Do you think you can get them for nothing?'

'We-don't-have-enough-money!'

She saw that they had reached an impasse. Then the mayor got up and drew her aside. 'Perhaps,' he murmured, 'something can be done, after all.'

Stiffly she permitted him to finger a lock of her hair. Fear seethed up inside her. Fear and also loathing for the kind of despicable creatures who had won power over the lives of their fellow man in this provincial market town.

'What are you doing, monsieur?'

'Please come this way.' He stepped towards a door at the back of the room. 'Come!'

An alarm tocsin was ringing in her head. What else

can this mean but another filthy proposition, she thought. What else can he want from me? She glanced back at her sister and mother. They were gaunt-faced. They stood together, forlorn and utterly careworn. Without her they would die. She knew that. Her mind had been made up long ago. She must do – she *would* do – whatever it took to get them to safety.

The other two members of the bench were looking into their laps, their thoughts hidden. She looked away from them and followed the mayor, thinking that she could still change her mind.

Once in the back room, the mayor closed the door. He told her to be seated, and to wait. The place was old and bare. Just a table and a chair, worn boards and an empty fire grate. A shaft of bright sunlight came through the windows on the southern side. It was hot on her neck and face and blinded her. The mayor had gone away for a few moments, and when he returned there was a second man with him. The other was more than fifty years old but with the tread of a dancer. He walked around her, looking her over appraisingly.

'Very nice,' he said. He sounded like an Italian. 'Very nice indeed. Pure gold. Oh, yes, you have a deal, monsieur.'

'Who is this man?' she asked frostily. She saw him pull something sharp and shiny from his coat. She turned her head to follow him, but he was behind her, and he took hold of her head and made her turn her face forward.

'Sit still,' the mayor grunted.

She complied. 'What do you want to do to me?'

She jumped as she felt a comb being pulled through her hair, and the strands being gathered into a pony-tail.

'When did you last wash?'

The humiliation of the question. 'Yesterday.'

It was true, the stream had been clear and inviting.

'That's good. You have looked after it remarkably well. Keep still. I will not hurt you.'

Now she felt the cold touch of a razor against the nape of her neck. She grasped the arms of the chair. The blade was drawn upwards in deft motions, scraping the hair from her scalp. She struggled, aghast at what was happening. They had not even asked her permission.

'Oh, no, please, not my hair . . .'

'Do you want the passports, or not? Hmmmm?'

She nodded. 'Yes.'

'Well, then.'

Fingers tilted her head and peeled back the top of her ear. She heard the sound of the razor magnified as it moved over bone. Loose wisps of hair fell onto her shoulders.

It took a few minutes to shave her. The razor was worked all around, to the crown. A couple of times the blade nicked her skin. Then she felt the terrible moment as the last tress came away. When the wig-maker stepped away her hair was in his hand. He coiled it carefully and put it inside a little muslin bag.

Her hand went to her cropped head. It was a wilderness of patches, some shaved completely bald, some not so. There were smears of blood on her palm. 'What have you done to me?' she whispered.

But they were ignoring her. The wig-maker counted out fifteen livres into the mayor's hand. As she stood up she caught her reflection in a window pane and the sight made her gasp. The pool of sunlight showed up her skull very white, her face and neck were comparatively tanned by the road. There was revealed an old scar from childhood, a fall from a horse she had taken when she was twelve . . .

She remembered the night of the ball at Thury-Harcourt, the shooting star she had seen with Smith as they had stood together in the dark. The meteor had seemed like a sign from heaven. 'The place crossed is betwixt the Virgin and the Herdsman,' he had said.

'*Coma Berenices* – the Hair of Berenice.' Then he had looked into her eyes, and kissed her for the first time.

She wiped the trickle of blood from above her brow with a grimy hand. The girl in the reflection looked like some kind of lunatic beggar. She turned away, feeling her eyes brimming with anger. It was as if her identity had been taken from her.

'It will grow out in a few weeks. You can go now.'

'Six livres are mine,' she said, holding out her hand.

'What are you talking about?'

'Nine for the passports. He gave you fifteen.'

'The rest is my arrangement fee.'

'I want the other six. Now!'

The mayor's face hardened. 'You can get out, or I'll have you arrested.'

She spat in his face. 'Bastard!'

Back in the interview room she was unable to hide her appearance from her mother and sister. Celestine's hand went to her mouth. Her mother looked stunned by the sight.

'Oh, no!'

She snatched up the passports and ran out, her family following.

On the way through the waiting room, the harridan burst into cackling laughter. 'I told you, didn't I, chicken? I told you they'd take you for something!'

As soon as they got into the street she rushed them along after her. People stopped to stare at her. Neither her mother nor Celestine said anything, and they lost no time in getting out of the town and finding the road that led south.

PART 8

The Ringing Steel

WINTER, 1793
The heights above Toulon

Ah, breathe deep, monsieur! Do you taste powder on the wind? Ah! There is no taste like that. It is the taste of life and death.

Do you see my face? How ghostly pale it is, and how sunken? Do you know what has caused this darkness under my eyes? I have not slept for a week. It is true that the autumn rains have brought a fever upon me, but the furnace still burns white within.

There is so much to do. I have sent trusted men to Lyons, to Briamon, and to Grenoble. The Army of Italy will send me guns from Antibes and Monaco. And I have established an arsenal at Ollioules. Despite the fever, I feel your gift of tremendous energy coursing through me. It is like a drug that allows me to do what other men cannot. I rest a very few hours by night, which sleep I take on the ground, wrapped in my cloak. I am always to be found among my men. The fierceness of my energy fascinates them. I have found it is an easy matter for me to conquer the hearts of soldiers.

Half a year has passed since you last appeared to your faithful servant, monsieur. Half a year since I stood on the deck of that ship bound for France, and you told me that one day I would be Emperor of Europe, and all my brothers and sisters will be its kings and queens. For six months, you have let me face that impossible prophecy alone and in poverty. Was it to see if I would break my promise, and begin once again to doubt you?

But what marvellous use have I made of the time! Let me tell you what I have done. You once explained to me that human beings are only pieces on the chess board of the world, and that human affairs are no more than a series of systems, and that it is necessary only to learn how to work them to advantage to succeed. You said: 'The cunning will not remain in need for long.' So, straight away when we reached Marseilles, I found the relevant committee and had my family officially classified as 'persecuted patriots.' As a result they were immediately given the top floor of a house – a place that was confiscated from some guillotined aristo.

Then also I used marriage. It was my design to set up my brother Joseph in the silk business. He is, as you know, a year older than me, and something of a peacock, but he lacks the knack of guiding his own life successfully. So I helped him. When Marseilles' most prominent silk merchant died, I realized that his two eligible daughters were left with no political connections upon which to continue the business. I saw immediately that Joseph was the answer to their prayers. Uncle Fesch – once a priest, you remember? – I have made him a silk merchant too. I thought that would please you.

For myself, there was the regiment. I was at Nice, serving in General Carteaux's army, then on the Rhône. Carteaux is a bumbling fool, a former court painter if you please! He knows little of war, except how to dress a line of dragoons. Without exception the officers that were put above me were all more-or-less incapable; not one of the ignorant dilettantes knew the range of a twenty-four pounder, or what such a weapon can do at short range to a column of infantry. You see, even when the Revolution turns everything over, nothing really changes. You have no idea, monsieur, how galling it is to one such as me to have idiots and weaklings set above me.

But I surely saw greater fools than Carteaux – in Lyons and all over the South: there were those who proclaimed the ex-Dauphin Louis as their king. Imagine, monsieur! An imprisoned waif as king? Don't they understand what it means to be completely in the power of the Committee of Public Safety? They will never let the prince go. The old king's brothers are at large in the south and calling themselves regents, but who in their right mind would join the standards of the Comte d'Artois or the Comte de Provence?

As you have so eloquently said, monsieur, *these are very strange times*. Times when men such as I may seize the chance to come into their own.

ONE

Smith sat on the balcony of a lodging-house as dusk fell. He was in the company of John Hill, a fresh-faced naval lieutenant of twenty-three years. Together they marked time, waiting for the savages they had come here to find.

Smith drummed his fingers on the balcony rail, his plans already laid. Out in the bay a small *felucca* – a lateen-rigged vessel – rode at anchor, a vessel of two masts, her sails brailed up to diagonal yards, possessing a keel about forty feet in length. He and Hill had been aboard her this afternoon, then he had bought her. In his mind he had already started to call her *Swallow*.

Down below the tribe had started to gather. They had come to the waterfront in ones and twos, drifting in as darkness fell, to the square, and the coffee house across the street, until they were a couple of dozen strong. They came as if returning from scavenging missions. Their tanned arms were tattooed, most sported beards, some of them carried cheap metal adornments, others head-bands, all wore an assortment of Arab and Turkish attire. There were several turbulent women with them too – not Turks, maybe Greeks or Italians, it was hard to tell without hearing their speech more clearly.

Smith watched the biggest of them with a mixture of disbelief and satisfaction. He shook his head slowly and murmured, 'You know, Hill, there's no such thing as a coincidence.'

'I beg pardon, sir?' Hill asked.

'Oh, nothing, Mister Hill. Go and find Raschid, please. Use the back way. When you catch him ask him what he's found out. And question him especially regarding the governor's immediate intentions. I need to know as soon as possible.'

'Yes, sir.'

Smith settled back, his legs outstretched, Hessian-style boots crossed one atop the other. He felt something small and hard lodged in the hem of his waistcoat. When his fingers located the object and he identified what had fallen through a hole in his pocket, he smiled to himself. It was the Green Goblin.

He continued to watch the big man down there from the remove of his shadowy balcony. Raschid the drago-man would have found out all there was to know about this tribe of beachcombers.

Down below the men had taken possession of a couple of tables and produced bottles and loaves. At one point one of their number had placed his hand on the table. He took his knife and began to stab the spaces between his splayed fingers as another counted through the dextrous procedure with glee and two younger men looked on. Most were getting drunk and had begun to gamble on a game of backgammon – half a dozen of them, disputing with one another, their noise growing louder.

Smith knew they were drinking the potent arrack spirit that could be had for very little money locally. They were drinking it like ale. A surfeit of arrack would make a bevy of admirals shout and dispute among themselves, but their behaviour was stupid, because the men below were Englishmen, and therefore, to the Turks, despicable infidels.

Back in Constantinople, aboard the *Crescent*, Smith had ticked off the strengths of his idea to Skynner. 'The Foreign Office furnished me with fifteen hundred pounds sterling to defray the expenses of my journey to Constantinople, my residence here, and the cost of examining the Black Sea, Bosphorus, Sea of Marmara, the Dardanelles archipelago, Ionian Islands, and so on . . . but, since I have not had time to embark on that ostensible mission, a clear thousand of the advance still remains. So, here's what I thought I'd do . . .'

When he had told Skynner the rest of his outrageous plan, something about it had appealed to the man. When he had privately made and received the sign of recognition, Skynner had offered to lend him his fourth lieutenant, John Hill, presently an apprentice of the Brotherhood, to help him carry it through.

'But what of the embassy?' Skynner had asked. 'Doesn't your diplomatic responsibility trump your duty even as a naval officer?'

'I had rather hoped the two duties would become complementary, but . . .' He had paused significantly.

Skynner had given him a conspiratorial smile. 'Brother Smith, is yours – what shall I say? – a mission that goes beyond both the naval and diplomatic spheres?'

He had looked Skynner in the eye. 'Well, it does concern the Brotherhood.'

'Is it, then, a matter into which I shouldn't enquire?'

He had smiled, relieved that Skynner had made it so easy for him. 'Brother, you're too kind. Let me say that it's plain to me now there is nothing more I can achieve in Stamboul, diplomatically or otherwise. My brother Spencer agrees that I should apply myself to my other duties. I have a pressing reason to want to get to France.'

The vastness of what he had left unsaid had reverberated like an empty cavern. It had ended as all conversations must between Brothers of high and low degree. It would have been impossible to tell Skynner the nature of his brief in Constantinople, impossible even to mention the Empress Catherine's son, Paul, and the moves being made simultaneously in St Petersburg by Brother Wright to gain access to the Russian heir in his carefully imposed seclusion. And if that were impossible how much more so the fact that he and Liston had been charged with offering the spiritual leader of half of Islam the invitation to become an initiate of the Brotherhood.

But Liston's efforts to shore up the world against impending chaos had met with a brick wall. Smith had sensed it ever since that day at Uskudar. Then he had thought Selim still too suspicious that the Brotherhood was a Christian entity. And that, politically, he was too insecure to throw the power of the Ottomans into the alliance against France. He had thought that Spencer was dealing with a man who could not be swayed, who *would* not be swayed, until such time as French troops were seen to be storming the gates of the Topkapi palace itself.

But later Liston had told him otherwise. 'Selim did not reject the Brotherhood. He has simply delayed his answer, which I hope will be an eventual "yes". This is not because he is a Muslim, or because the Russian heir Paul has embraced the Brotherhood so enthusiastically. Selim is a good man, but he is standing upon a tightrope.'

'Meaning?'

'He has no power.'

Smith had shrugged in perplexity. 'If the sultan has not, then who does?'

'Selim is in thrall to his corps of janissaries. They are the Praetorian Guard that chooses who shall be emperor. If, one morning, he should make a move they do not like they will spike his eyeballs upon a dagger by sundown. Selim knows that.'

'In which case,' Smith had said, 'my continuing here can serve no further purpose.'

'That's quite true.'

Smith recalled his joy at that.

They had gone back to the Residency and Liston had turned his departure into a startling interview. The revelations had been made privately after an exchange of Templar signs. When everything was arranged they had gone walking together for one last promenade along the Bosphorus shore.

'It's time you knew the truth,' Liston had said.

'The truth?'

'Aye, Brother Smith. The whole truth.' Liston had skimmed a flat pebble into the silver waters. 'It's a truth that will never be made generally known, for it is something that only Illuminati may hear.'

'So – it concerns the Brotherhood?'

'You might say so. Just as Brother Wright has been seeking to reconcile the Russians and the Swedes at St Petersburg, so we have sought to reconcile Russian and Turk. That much you know. What you have not yet been told is the reason why the Brotherhood has been so active with respect to the Revolution in France.'

He had given Liston his full attention. 'Why has it?'

'Because ours is the blame for it.'

He had stared at Liston, aghast. '*What*?'

Liston's expression had been as grave as he had ever seen it. 'It's quite true. For almost a century and a half the Brotherhood has been dedicated to an undertaking of a quite titanic scale.'

Understanding of the idea hit him with all the force of a great gun. 'Brother Liston, I have long fancied it was the aim of the Brethren to craft the Ideal State, but . . .'

'Auch . . . our forebears began that process in earnest many years ago. They promulgated the Formulas in 'sixty-seven, to mark the fiftieth anniversary celebrations of the Great Lodge Unification. By then, America had been chosen. It was all decided.'

Smith knew the significance of the date. It was the healing of the Brotherhood's great schism. He stared at the Asian shore, marvelling at what he was hearing.

'You mean to say that the American colonies were to become . . . ?'

'The notion was not particularly original. There have been all kinds of naive groups – Quakers, Levellers, religionists and visionaries of every persuasion – who saw in the New World an opportunity to start society afresh.'

'Innocent plantations of men . . .'

'Aye. They wanted to make Utopias. But the colonies grew up too fast for them, and their ideas were lost in the great struggle.' Liston shook his head. 'How many years have we *not* been at war with France this century, Brother Smith?'

'Too precious few. But surely . . . all modern war is fought over trade and—'

'Hear me out, Brother. It was not until the *Annus Mirabilis* that the Craft could move.'

Smith understood the Latin reference – the Wonderful Year – originally Dryden's year of 1666, when the English had smashed the maritime power of the Dutch, but lately used to signify 1759, the year that Admiral Hawke had destroyed the French fleet at Quiberon Bay and General Wolfe had vanquished the Marquis de Montcalm at Quebec.

Liston went on. 'Until that year, Britain's American colonies were under constant threat from the French. But not after 'fifty-nine. By the time the Seven Years' War finished in 'sixty-three the Union flag was flying over the entire span from Hudson's Bay right down to Florida, aye, and all over the Caribbean and across most of India too. As soon as it became clear that the French were beaten, the then Grand Master and his Council put the plan into effect. Naturally, there was a great deal of political opposition from factions that were not of the Craft, but we succeeded in disbanding all British infantry regiments junior to the Seventieth Foot and all cavalry above the Eighteenth Light Dragoons, so that shows you.'

Smith shook his head in astonishment. He felt a little foolish. Why did none of this seem apparent to me before? he wondered. 'You mean the losing of America was *prepared*?'

Liston nodded. 'Because of our influence British forces were withdrawn from America until there were just eight thousand men there. Then a *casus belli* – a cause for war – was manufactured in Boston in 'seventy-three. In the intervening time Brothers Franklin and Jefferson and others had undertaken to alter the opinions of the colonists. Brother Washington was elected to lead their forces. On this side of the Atlantic Brothers North and Sackville were responsible for preventing the crushing of the initial rebellion. Almost every regiment fighting on either side had an active lodge. Almost every colonel was a Brother.'

'My God.' Smith was awed by the scale of it. 'And the king, who was never a Brother, called upon the Hessians for help . . . And certain elements in France, again men not of the Brotherhood, saw their opportunity . . .'

'Correct. Ever eager to confound the English, the French came in on the side of the colonists. Which we were rather pleased about.'

'So General Burgoyne . . . ?'

'A Brother.'

'And General Clinton?'

'A Brother.'

'Good God . . .'

Liston smiled. 'Yes, the United States of America was not created to be just another country, but to be put to a higher purpose. The destiny of Mankind has to be guided.'

Smith put his hand to his chin, considering. 'Of course. Now it all seems so . . . obvious.'

'Such is the nature of revelation.'

'And the essential nature of America?'

'There is no secret about that. The signs are there for all who ask to see.' Liston took from his pocket a small book of blue morocco. His fingers found the page, and he spread it open, inviting Smith to examine an engraving of a medallion. The legend read, 'Great Seal of the United States'.

'First, look at the obverse. You see thirteen stars – the colonies – contained in the Glory – our symbol of Godhead. Below, the eagle – our symbol of the spirit of Man – carrying upon its body the "form" or shield, in its beak the banner, on which is writ "*E Pluribus Unum*".'

' "From out of the multitude, unity"?'

'Correct. Thus is symbolized how our Brotherhood has designed a government for one nation, under God. In the eagle's left talon you see the Arrows of War, and balancing them, in its left talon, the Laurel of Peace.'

Smith's eyes moved to the left-hand page, his finger tracing the message. 'The reverse of the Seal is straightforward. I see the Four Levels completed: the Great Pyramid – the Nation – founded in the year seventeen seventy-six – rising from its wide base toward a single point – the enlightened Eye – again, the Creator. And "*Novus Ordo Seclorum*" – a New Secular Order.'

'Brother Jefferson, a lawyer, took the Formulas and framed them into the American Constitution. As you will easily see, it is based on the three columns of the Tracing Board of the First Degree. Powers are separated threefold into Judicial, Legislative and Executive branches. A government of mutually balancing agencies – as befits the Ideal State.'

'And it worked.'

'Auch, aye, it worked. And very well too. For a decade the United States functioned so successfully that we became enthusiastic to transplant the model back to the Old World. But, I may say, we were rather blind to the dangers of so doing.'

Smith nodded. 'All that was required was a corrupt, mouldering monarchy that had begun to fall apart?'

Liston had pursed his lips. 'Aye.'

'And where better than France?'

'Aye. Where better than France. Brother Lafayette was intended to be its first president, and—'

Smith came out of his gigantic reflections with a start. He looked up, sensing someone in the passage. There was a knock and Hill entered. The lieutenant took his seat, casting a cool eye over the men in the square below. They were roaring and roistering uncontrollably.

'Listen to the bloody fools.'

Smith let out a lingering breath. 'Unlike ourselves, Mister Hill,' he said, indefinable regrets pervading him, oppressing him, 'the lower orders live for the moment. We cannot. That's the difference. Presently they are carefree and happy. In a short time I will have them in a state of anxiety. I regret that such a thing is necessary, but it is.'

Smith realized instantly that he had broken one of the great unwritten rules, and chastised himself for it. Revealing personal inner thoughts to a subordinate, especially one like Hill, could do no good. Hill was Skynner's creature, a straight-up-and-down, bread-and-butter officer, a Brother of sorts, but one made in Skynner's image.

To his credit Hill allowed a pause so that the momentary embarrassment seeped away. 'Well, sir, your dragoman appears to have been quite a busy man. According to his intelligence this tribe of villains has been gathering on the coast all summer. Apparently they've built themselves a cluster of driftwood and canvas hovels on a beach a league south of the town. Their whores make scarcely enough money for them to all get drunk, so their situation is worsening.'

'A little whoring, a little fishing and doubtless a little

thieving too. What did Raschid say of the Turkish governor's mind on the matter?'

'Sir, he says that, given a sufficient cause, his men would be called out.' Hill regarded the group with cold disdain. 'What do you think, sir?'

'I think they'll do quite admirably, lieutenant. Let's hope the women aren't too badly poxed.'

'I've seen worse, sir. I'm not certain about the big fellow. The one who's so handy with the knife.'

Smith wondered if he should tell Hill the truth about the big fellow, but decided against it. Instead he said, 'Oh, he's clearly a natural leader of men, Mister Hill. I especially want him.'

Outside there was a flare of violence that quickly settled again. It was probably time to go.

'They're certainly tossing down the liquor. The bottles are draining at a rate of knots, sir.'

Smith got up, and Hill started to rise too, but he stayed him.

'No, I want you to stay here and keep watch for me.'

'But, sir. Don't you think—'

'Are you questioning my orders already, Mister Hill?' he asked mildly, donning his sword.

'No, of course not, sir. I . . .'

'Good man.'

If anything should go wrong, Smith knew, Hill would be able to make a report of the matter to Spencer.

He left the lodging, cloaked in black, and with an Anatolian sheepskin hat on his head. The coffee shop was lit by four or five wicks. They burned in oil-filled bowls that were hung from wall brackets. As Smith moved into sight several of the men turned to stare at him. As the warning spread the hubbub quieted. Smith knew that his Hessian boots, cloak and hat were of a quality that would mark him out as a gentleman. He also knew they would be mistaken for the garb of a Turkish officer.

He stood there alone, feeling the dangerousness of the moment and relishing it. He could smell the salt from the surf spray in his nostrils. The men were tense with suspicion, unsure what to do. Most of them would be hands from ships chartered to the Turkey Company and other merchantmen that plied the eastern part of the Mediterranean, but many would be naval hands, ship-jumpers and deserters, men blown like flotsam to this backwater; he could feel the fear and the hatred of authority struggling in them. The drink might make some of them foolhardy. It would only take one misjudgement, just one of them, to launch a tankard at his head. Then the situation would be irrecoverable.

He approached them steadily, his eyes passing from face to face. Silence intensified the atmosphere. Only the sound of the waves pounding and dragging back through the pebbled beach could be heard. He picked his moment to say, 'Which of you is going to sign on with me?'

They stared back at him open-mouthed. The question was astonishing to them. It had been posed in perfect English.

He gave them a second to dispel their shock, then said. 'Well? I asked you – which of you lads wants a ship?'

The first to recover was the big man who had performed the knife trick. He was lean-faced, and there were pronounced shadows under his cheekbones, emphasized by the flickering light. The point of his weapon was jammed in the tabletop so that the handle stuck up invitingly.

'Who wants to know?' the man demanded, his voice hard but edged with bravado. His face was a perfect mask of mistrust.

Smith ignored the question. 'Speak up!'

The knifeman struggled to bear down Smith's clipped accent of command. He resorted to fury, got up with a sudden movement and plucked the blade from the table.

The others fell back as their leader moved at last to take control of the situation.

'I bloody well asked you who you was!'

Smith thanked God that the man had come to the fore. He raised his hand, his finger outstretched. 'If you don't know me, John Skrimger, I surely know you.'

The other stopped dead at the mention of his name.

Smith turned fractionally, so that a glimpse of his uniform and the hilt of his sword was revealed. 'You were foretopman aboard the frigate *Alcmene* in 'eighty-five.' He raised his voice, announcing himself to them all now. 'My name is Smith, captain, His Majesty's Navy.'

Some of them were ready to scatter now, but none dared. Skrimger had recognised him. Both he and the woman beside him stared back as if at a venomous snake. 'All Awk-meeney's hands was paid off!' Skrimger's voice betrayed panic now. 'I'm no Sahf Sea deserter!'

Smith saw that the news of how the king's navy had hunted down the *Bounty* mutineers in the South Seas had reached them. The three exemplary hangings carried out aboard the *Brunswick* less than a year ago would be looming large in their minds.

He said, 'Quite right, Skrimger. *Alcmene* was laid up in ordinary. When the American war ended, His Majesty had no further need of the likes of you.'

Skrimger's eyes were huge, his voice brittle – such was the power to terrify, such the authority that Smith's uniform represented. 'What you want wif' us?'

'Skrimger, how you came here is no business of mine. My interest is where you think you're going now.'

There was muttering and oaths. Some had begun looking for the press that must be nearby.

One of them shouted, 'You ain't got no roight!'

Another added his say-so. 'Yeah! This ain't Englan'.'

Smith raised his voice. 'Yes, but England's at war. Your skills are valuable. And so you are required by His Majesty. Such must be better than languishing here.'

A hail of scorn came back at him.

'We're bloody happy here.'

'You ain't taking me back to no piss-bucket!'

'He ain't taking none of us. Where's his men?'

'An' I'm American. What you goin' to do about that – captain?'

'You all find yourselves stranded here in Smyrna by some unfortunate happenstance, no doubt.' He gestured towards his recent purchase. 'My ship is at anchor in the bay. A two-masted *felucca*, which you have all no doubt wondered about. No questions will be asked of you, save your skills as a seaman, and your names – which you may choose as you will.'

Skrimger had recovered his spirit. 'I said, we *ain't* going with you, and that's flat!'

'Oh, I think you *are*, Skrimger.'

'I ain't joining no king's navy again. And you can't make me!'

'It's the only way you'll live to see England again. Because I happen to know that in –' He broke off to pluck his watch from his pocket. '– in a little under one hour, the governor of Smyrna, who is a notably humourless fellow, intends to descend upon you with a great many soldiers. Have any of you the least notion what would become of you at the oars of a Turkish slave galley?' He regarded them for a second with raised eyebrows. 'No. I imagine you have no idea whatsoever. Suffice to say that men are routinely sodomized to death at the bagnio of Constantinople. I can at least promise you an easier time than that. Skrimger will tell you that I am a fair-handed captain who doesn't approve of excessive flogging. I shall allow two minutes for you to decide your preference, and then I shall walk away.'

He consulted his watch and drew apart, sitting down on the end of an empty bench. Though he stared out into the inky blackness of the bay he could see that they looked at him with consternation. There were arguments, which they tried to guard from him, but their mood was veering. There was no trust in them still, but they were not fools. Skrimger was a good seaman, a natural leader. He had come from some stinking prison, but he had served long enough aboard *Alcmene* to know what sort of captain he had had. When exactly two minutes were up Smith went back to them.

'Now, Skrimger, the *felucca* is called *Swallow*. You'll be her bosun. She's a sound hull. Her sails and rigging appear to be in good order. She will need to be watered and victualled, however. Tonight, those that will sign papers may sleep aboard.'

Skrimger asked. 'What papers?'

'We shall use the land breeze to work her off, so that if a blow comes on in the night we shall be secure in reasonably open water. Tomorrow I shall put the lading and provisioning in hand at a place a little way along the coast.'

Skrimger repeated himself. 'What papers? We ain't give our word to nothing.'

'Why, volunteers' papers, man. You shall have the privileges due those loyal men who have heeded their nation's call.' Skrimger spat, but said nothing, so Smith laid a packet on the table and unwrapped it. It contained three sheets of paper, each ruled into columns, that were neatly headed up. 'Once you are officially signed servants of the British Crown any molestation of you by a foreign power will constitute an act of war. You will be entitled to His Majesty's protection, a right upon which I am prepared to insist.'

He sat down, flattened the paper out before him and looked up at Skrimger, offering a lead pencil. Skrimger hesitated, then took the instrument and wrote laboriously: 'John Skrimger, boatswain's mate'.

One by one after Skrimger they signed, and those who

could not, he signed for them: Thomas Clarke, carpenter's mate; Thomas Knight, quartermaster; John Wilson, able seaman, Robert Coulson, Charles Beecroft, John Carrall, James Boxer, Edward Morris, William Harvey . . .

He gathered up the papers and put them into his pocket, then rose in preparation for leaving. 'All hands will assemble on the foreshore in ten minutes.'

One of the women began to wail. As he turned, she ran at him, caught up the knife, but one of the men – John Wilson, he saw – grabbed her and took it from her.

Skrimger faced him. 'How did you find me?'

He laughed shortly. 'I didn't *find* you, John Skrimger. It's your fate to be found.'

Hill met him at the lodging-house door, his face beaming with admiration. He said, 'If I may say so, sir, that was the most amazing sight I have ever witnessed.'

He smiled. 'Lieutenant, you are as yet a comparatively young man. But thank you, all the same.'

'Whatever did you say to them?'

He grinned. 'I'll let you into a secret, Mister Hill. The man with the knife is called John Skrimger. He's an old shipmate. I knew he could not kill me.'

'But, sir. How could you be sure of that?'

'Because, Mister Hill, one day, aboard *Alcmene*, Skrimger approached me in an agonized state. He was plainly near to tears, and so I allowed him to come aft and speak his piece. He told me he had a matter of conscience besetting him. When I asked him what it was he said, "Captain, I killed a whore." I told him he had not killed a whore. And he insisted that he had. So I again told him otherwise. And this time he shouted it out at me. "Captain, I'm guilty, I tell you! I killed a whore!" '

Hill's eyes were rapt as Smith paused. 'And then what did you do, sir?'

'When he'd quietened down I said, "You did not kill a

whore, John Skrimger. You killed a *woman*. And I want you to understand that." '

Hill sucked in his breath. 'Good grief, sir!'

'Yes, Mister Hill. Good grief indeed. After that, I believe the man, Skrimger, was able to reflect on his crime with accuracy. I believe he came to a proper state of remorse, and that now he may be relied upon. Now, we must get aboard without delay. Tomorrow, as discussed, we shall complete our watering and victualling at the isle of Mitylene. Then we shall be ready to join Lord Hood at Toulon.'

TWO

The three barefoot women continued their struggle southward.

For days there had been a cold north-easterly wind blowing out of the Alps and down the valley of the Rhône. It blew at their backs, sending dust ahead of them along the road. The locals called it 'le Mistral' and closed their windows against it. For the sisters Berenice and Celestine du Fay, and their mother, the *ci-devant* Countess du Fay, the wind was inescapable.

Berenice's lack of hair had made her an outcast. She had tried to adjust her behaviour to take account of it, but that had only made her seem more furtive. In the suspicious villages along their way the people looked at her as if she was diseased or insane. Old women crossed the road to avoid them, children threw stones to drive them away. No shopkeeper or innkeeper would allow them into their premises. Even the beggars sensed they were different, and would not willingly know them.

Since Vienne, Berenice had become increasingly concerned for the condition of their mother's legs. They were ulcerated, so she had bandaged them as best she could with strips of cotton torn from her own shirt.

'How are they today?' she had asked as they had readied themselves to leave the village of Sarras at daybreak.

Her mother had taken to walking with the aid of a

469

staff like a mendicant pilgrim. She made a hopeless gesture. 'They are so stiff I can scarce move one in front of the other.'

'Our passports are not franked.' Berenice's voice sounded hard in her own ears. 'From here we still have a dozen leagues to accomplish. We might manage that by eight o'clock tonight, if you can stand it.'

A few miles further on she tried to find her mother a place to rest, but troop movements dominated the main roads south, forcing them to use indirect routes that doubled the journey. Her mother's agony had been terrible to see. For the first two leagues her sufferings had been extreme, but, as they got on, she had moved with greater ease.

Eventually they had reached Avignon, and passed over the bridge across the Rhône in company with a mass of other folk.

Her mother had said, shaking her head, 'Avignon was once a rich city. It was personally owned by His Holiness the Pope for almost four hundred and fifty years. Now look at it.'

Berenice looked about, taking in the ruined state of the properties she saw with little emotion. 'Revolutionary troops were sent to wrest the city from the papacy three years ago. There have been tremendous battles here.' She began thinking again of the simpering triumphalism of the broadsheet that she had found in Valence. It had told her that the city of Avignon had recently been incorporated into the new Department of Vaucluse.

'Political changes mean unrest,' she told Celestine. 'And unrest means vigilance on the part of the authorities. We will have to be especially careful.'

There was no obvious way to avoid the city. The checkpoint was guarded by two uniformed men, and Berenice felt her heart pounding as she passed under their lazy gaze. Most things get easier with practice, she thought. But approaching the Guard never does. I get closer to panic every time. I don't know why, but things have a way of going wrong just when a person comes in sight of their final goal. How these so-called men of the Guard stir me to fear and anger! But I must keep calm and show nothing, for all our sakes.

'I hate them,' she muttered as they cleared the danger. 'I never thought I would ever say it, but I have no doubt that I could kill such as them.'

'Who is looking to arrest us?' her mother asked, her voice an exhausted monotone. 'There's more to fear from other beggars than there is from the Guard.'

It was true. Berenice's mind went back to the robbery three days ago. It had terrified her. The man had sprung upon them as they had prepared soup in a quiet grove outside St Peray. He had stolen their shoes, then he had laughed abuse at them before running off. At the time she had felt only anger, but the more she thought of the knife that had been held to her throat and the baseness of the man who had robbed them, the more she understood how easily they might have been murdered.

'When no one will protect us, *maman*,' she answered just as tonelessly, 'we must protect ourselves.'

It was an essential truth. Just one more of those essential truths she had had to learn. None of those truths was pretty. She looked at her sister's dirty feet and shabby rags, the way her mother hobbled. The scabs matted her scalp where she had scratched at the lice. The straps of her own makeshift pack bit into her shoulders, and she resettled it. It was an old rushwork basket patched with canvas. Inside were more rags of clothing, a black iron pan, tinderbox, needles and thread, and whatever else of use they had been able to scavenge. Her most prized possession, the knife, she kept tucked in her skirts. She took it out to hone its edge on a stone when they were alone.

At such times she would reflect on what had happened

to them. It does not take long to turn people into criminal savages, she had thought. No matter who they are. There was a time when I would not have believed it possible. I would not have wanted to believe. But that was then, in the time before. The time before . . .

The question now is: can we survive? And, if so, is it possible that this filth can ever be washed away?

It was necessary to go through the market place to get on the road to Aix, which was partly fortunate because the market place held a number of possibilities. They would split up and loiter, meeting no one's eye as they moved through the crowds, but always staying on the lookout for something. There were often discarded cabbage leaves to be had, and occasionally a piece of rotten fruit. Or an egg or an apricot could be snatched from a stall in a moment. These days many of the stall-holders were old people. They saw nothing, or could do nothing but raise a feeble cry even if they saw the crime. Such opportunities were theft, but it was a fact that hunger undermined fine principles. And what did it matter in practical terms? – the threat of imprisonment hung over them whether they stole or not.

Berenice looked around, watchful, calculating. The towns of the south kept different hours to those of northern France. Soon the market would finish. This afternoon, she thought, Celestine might pick up a *sou* or two playing on the little wooden whistle. The first time that her sister had put on a red woollen cap and played the carmagnole, Berenice had almost cried. That zealots' tune had been seared into her mind the day the château had been wrecked. Its gay notes had seemed to crystal-lize their woes, and she had found it an infinite sadness to see fingers that had played the sublime inventions of Herr Mozart dancing out a mean little Revolutionary song for the benefit of coarse-minded conscripts. That was weeks ago, and the sense of humiliation had faded. Now, she could only think of the food that could be bought by the copper coins that were thrown by those same stinking soldiers.

The market place was crowded. Since the *levée en masse* – the mass conscription – it seemed as if the whole country was on the move. She watched the street furtively, then approached a horse trough, and leaned over. Her face was a dark reflection against the blue sky, a grimy, weather-darkened face, straw-stubble hair like a convict. She cleared the scum from the surface with the back of her hand, and spooned up a handful of water to her mouth. It was not too badly tainted, she decided. She had drunk worse. Then she looked up to the sky and saw the spires of the church soaring there, and felt the deserted cross that still hung inside her shirt. It was the last real possession she had left. The last thing that she had known in the time before. The abjectness of her condition came suddenly into focus in her mind like pain.

The handful of water disgusted her. She flung it down. 'What has become of me?' she murmured. A wave of desperation ran through her like a tremor. Facing hardships had stripped the refinements from her, but was there more to it than that? Will I ever be the same again? she wondered bleakly. Or is it like innocence? Lost for ever?

She saw half-a-dozen of the Guard approaching. They were mean-faced and looking for trouble, rapping on doors with their batons and shouting out. Thugs – nothing more, only now officially sanctioned. Another, harder self inside her took control. She ducked into the alley of a riverside inn. 'Look where such weakness gets you,' she muttered under her breath. 'You almost got yourself picked up.'

The Guard passed by without noticing her, and she looked around herself, to see steam issuing from a vent at the bottom of the alley. It dampened the air, and made her conscious of the rumbling in her stomach. She clutched her waistband to dispel the pangs. The smell of cooking was irresistible to her. Superbly savoury, like – fish soup. She closed her eyes and lingered to breathe in the odour, and was drawn towards it.

The kitchen was steamy. She saw a wooden chopping-board with fresh herbs, a great colander and copper pans boiling on a range. A greasy-jowled cook in a stained apron was tumbling peeled potatoes into a great pan. One potato bounced onto the floor and rolled into the drain. The cook appeared not to notice it. He put the basin down, and disappeared into the scullery.

She stepped inside the doorway, alone in the room. The swill bins stank, but she was so hungry that even the smell of kitchen waste had a peculiar attractiveness. She looked around. No one came. It was as if she was invisible. Two large carp stared glassily back at her from the counter. She was struck by their size.

A shaft of intrepidation went through her as she considered making off with one of them. They were huge. She imagined herself in a forest clearing, beside a little fire, serving helpings of delicious baked fish to Celestine and her mother. Such a fish would keep all three of them going for days.

She heard a noise and looked up. The cook appeared in the doorway so suddenly, and she was so lost in her daydream about the fish, that he saw her. For some reason she did not try to flee. He came past, glancing at her, but said nothing.

She tried to look nonchalant. 'These are fine fish. Did you catch them on the lines hanging from the bridge?'

'I don't know about fine.' His accent was Marseillaise, his manner surly and very knowing. He continued with his tasks. His hair was tied up in a rag and he carried a huge wooden spoon stuck in his belt like a pirate's pistol. The stubble on his cheeks was red, and he had cold, dead eyes. 'They're big, ain't they? The smaller one's eighteen pounds – too big for a skinny little thing like you to carry, eh?'

She made no answer, but looked them over distantly. 'What price do fish like these fetch?'

'You want to buy them, do you?' He laughed shortly, and turned his back on her. 'You can have one of them – for a sol.'

'Only one sol? That seems very cheap.'

'Cheap?' He coughed the word out, turned, looked at her more closely. Then he seemed to dismiss his suspicions almost instantly. 'Is that what you think? You're a laugh, ain't you, Lady Muck?'

She muttered. 'I mean they're less costly than usual. Where I come from—'

'You're from somewhere up north, ain't you?' He paused a half-smile on his face. It was a cynic's smile, full of the bitterness of life. 'I'll tell you why the fish is so cheap. So many enemies of the state was killed and thrown into the river at Lyons that the fish caught here gives dysentery to any Jacobin who eats them.'

The vivid images thrown up by her imagination revolted her. 'Oh!'

'What's the matter? Gone off the idea of eating fish that's eaten human flesh, have you? Too close to being a cannibal?'

'You shouldn't joke of it that way, citoyen.'

'It's no joke,' he said, shrugging. 'Since last month it is forbidden to eat fish from the River Rhône. Don't nobody read out the proclamations to you?'

'But – you're cooking them.'

'The citoyen boss says cook fish, so I cook fish. I know where my bread's buttered, see. These is hard times.'

'What if you poison someone?'

'It's an inn, ain't it? Who knows what they eat when they dine at an inn? Travellers are here today, gone tomorrow. If I don't like the look of them I piss in their soup.'

She made a face, but he caught sight of her reaction and he made a violent gesture towards her and showed pleasure when she flinched. 'Go on, Lady Muck. Come begging round kitchen doors, then start acting like you own the place? Not here. Think I didn't see you eyeing them carp, you thieving little bitch?'

She spat at him. 'I wouldn't eat your fish, if it was the last food in the world!'

'Well, you'd die then, wouldn't you? Go on, bugger off! Before I slit your gizzard.'

'Bugger off yourself, bastard!'

He jumped at her, and she fled, leaving the fish behind her, but a peeled potato was in her shirt, and a stolen fish-knife in her sleeve.

Serves the filthy swine right, she thought as she ran, feeling triumph, and not admitting guilt about her crime. It's natural justice: I'm hungry and I have needs. I must levy my own taxes on society.

By the time she reached the horse trough again she had calmed down. She admitted to herself that she had descended to the same level as the cook – worse, because he had only insulted her, whereas she had stolen from him. But it's only a temporary state with us, she told herself, knowing she must cling to the hope of a better life to come. We are educated and cultured, and we have sensibilities. One day we shall be respectable again, and our sins will all be forgiven.

She saw a pair of soldiers ambling in her direction. She pulled the shawl round her and moved on. The hard voice in her head said, 'Anyway, my girl, if you'd tried to make your way according to your genteel upbringing you'd be dead. And so would your sister and mother.' Then she felt her conscience satisfied, and she dismissed the debate from her mind.

A little further along the street she caught sight of a man reading aloud from a Parisian broadsheet. He was surrounded by a group of half a dozen idlers. He read the news out in halting snippets: the destruction of the former Lyons is proceeding with all speed ... two thousand Royalist and Girondist necks have been bared to the guillotine so far ... General Doppet declares that no two bricks are to be left standing one upon the other in that city of traitors ...

A little later, she found part of a broadsheet headed *Moniteur*. A glance confirmed what she had heard. She carefully folded it up, and hid it to read later. It was Jacobin propaganda, but it might reveal some fact or other important to their survival. At the very least it would serve to light a fire.

When she rejoined Celestine she noticed an odd look on her sister's face. It was a look she had never seen before, a sort of smirk – ashamed and yet pleased with herself all at the same time.

'What did you get?'

'This.' Celestine pulled out a large onion.

She took the onion and looked at her sister closely. 'What's the matter with you?'

'Nothing.'

'What do you mean, nothing?'

She searched Celestine's face. 'Don't lie to me. What's happened? Where's mother?'

'She's all right. She'll come back soon.'

Panic rose in Berenice's belly. Something had happened. She could sense it. 'Where've you been?'

'Playing for some soldiers.' Celestine wiped her mouth with the back of her hand and flashed her a glance that was meant to warn her off. It did not.

'I didn't hear you.' Berenice looked at the onion, and then saw that something else was clenched in Celestine's hand. She seized her wrist suddenly, and prised the object loose.

'What's this?' It was a question that required no answer. She could see it was a coin. And that it was silver. 'You didn't get all this for playing the carmag-nole!'

Celestine faced her, defiance in her eyes. 'No! I didn't get it for playing the carmagnole! But at least we shall eat today. Now – are you satisfied?'

THREE

6 DECEMBER 1793
Toulon, France

'So, you see, Sir Sidney. If it is your wish to impose upon the admiral's valuable time, I'm afraid you have appeared at a rather inconvenient moment.'

Captain Knight was a man in his late forties, grey-haired, slim, and with a bloodless complexion. His manner was short. Smith had come aboard *Victory* the moment he arrived. The great flagship, Knight's command but also the flag of Admiral Hood, had been anchored in Toulon's outer harbour, along with dozens of lesser vessels, since August.

'I've come at a very opportune time, I should have thought.'

Smith sighed inwardly. *Swallow*'s voyage across the Mediterranean had been accomplished without incident. During the weeks it had taken to navigate the Mediterranean from end to end he had come to know and trust his small crew, as they had come to know and trust him. In all his musings he had never expected to be received at Toulon as an unwanted interloper.

According to the information he had been able to glean so far, the past four months had seen a catalogue of solid but uninspiring moves. Hood had ordered fifteen hundred sailors and marines on shore to man the forts that covered the ships in the harbour. In particular he had directed Fort Malgue to be occupied, and had made Captain Elphinstone of the *Robust* its governor. A few days later the Spanish fleet had turned up to complicate matters. It had comprised the flagship *Concepción* and six other ships-of-the-line, under Admiral Langara, who had his own views about how the balance of power in the Mediterranean should evolve. By now the Revolutionary armies had advanced to within four miles of Toulon, and they had begun to tighten their noose on the port. Clearly, Smith thought, it was time to make a decision.

'I take it this whole operation is down to Grenville, what?' He turned, waiting for a reply. 'Well, sir? Am I right?'

Knight put down the printed proclamation, and met Smith's eye icily. 'This operation, Sir Sidney, has been occasioned by the monster Robespierre and his band of cut-throats, whose infliction of atrocities and inhuman cruelties upon the best and most respectable portion of the French remains even now unabated.'

Smith took the valueless reply soberly. From what he had heard so far, Knight thought it sufficient merely to repeat Admiral Hood's views, which he had done to the letter, like a parrot. Those views appeared on the surface to be remarkably uncomplicated: all France had fallen under the mesmeric influence of a nebulous evil called the Revolution. The populace had been gulled by high-sounding pledges and the promises of idealists. Englishmen had found themselves unable to believe that a country as stable and civilized as France could ever fall into such bloody chaos . . .

It was the same unsophisticated analysis he had heard so often during his time in London. But this time it was not the result of cosy thinking; the obfuscation seemed quite deliberate. At every stage, Smith thought with disappointment, there appeared men of little talent who preferred to regard information as privilege, and who treated those about them as if they were lesser beings. That's how they seek to maintain their position, he thought. And I suspect Samuel Hood is one such. I notice there are plenty of men about him who are satisfied with that – which is why, one supposes, they remain where they are.

'When are we, I wonder,' he asked Knight lightly, 'going to stop ignoring the precedents of history?'

'I'm sure I've no notion what you mean, Sir Sidney.'

He sighed. 'Oh, come, Knight. You know that so long as we continue to imagine that events in the world can never reach such an inhuman pass as this, or such a wretched state as that, they will continue to do so. It's no good our shaking our heads and saying that things cannot possibly get any worse. They can always do that.'

Knight attempted to be withering. 'I'm sure His Lordship will be obliged to you for your critique of the situation.'

'Complacency in the face of evil is no remedy. Remember: all it takes, is that good men do nothing.'

'I hardly think we are doing that.'

He laughed shortly. 'Well, if I didn't know better, I'd begin to suspect that His Lordship actually has no grasp of the ease with which human affairs can spiral into vileness.'

Knight stiffened. 'The capacity of Johnny Frenchman for despicable behaviour is very well known. They're a completely immoral race.'

Smith folded his arms, and asked with a show of innocence, 'Know many Frenchmen, do you, Knight?'

'Thankfully, none.'

'Thought so.' Smith couldn't resist looking up impishly. 'You know, they're really quite like us inside – only not quite so perfect, of course.'

Knight's icy politeness only just remained unbroken, and Smith decided to skate quickly across it. He looked again at the declaration Hood had made. 'His Lordship issued this on his arrival, you say?'

'That's correct.'

He surveyed the paper again and smiled wanly. 'Good God, there's really no mistaking His Lordship's style, is there?'

By the Right Honourable Samuel Lord Hood, Vice-Admiral of the Red, and Commander-in-chief of His Britannic Majesty's squadron in the Mediterranean, &c., &c., &c., to the Inhabitants of the Towns and Provinces in the South of France.

During four years you have been involved in a Revolution which has plunged you in anarchy, and rendered you a prey to factious leaders. After having destroyed your government, trampled under foot the laws, assassinated the virtuous, and authorized the commission of crimes, they have endeavoured to propagate throughout Europe their destructive system of every social order. They have constantly held forth to you the idea of liberty, while they have been robbing you of it. Everywhere they have preached respect to persons and property, and everywhere in their name it has been violated. They have amused you with the sovereignty of the people, which they have constantly usurped. They have declaimed against the abuses of royalty in order to establish their tyranny upon the fragments of a throne still reeking with the blood of your legitimate sovereign. Frenchmen! you groan under the pressure of want and the privation of all specie; your commerce and your industry are annihilated, your agriculture is checked, and the want of provisions threatens you with a horrible famine. Behold, then, the faithful picture of your wretched condition. A situation so dreadful sensibly afflicts the allied Powers. They see no other remedy, but the re-establishment of the French monarchy. It is for this, and the acts of aggression committed by the executive power of France, that we have armed in conjunction with the other allied Powers. After mature reflection upon these leading objects, I come to offer you the force with which I am entrusted by my sovereign, in order to spare the further effusion of human blood, to crush with promptitude the factious, to re-establish a regular government in France, and thereby maintain peace and tranquillity in Europe. Decide, therefore, definitively, and with precision. Trust your hopes to the generosity of a loyal and free nation. In its name, I have just given an unequivocal testimony to the well-disposed inhabitants of Marseilles, by granting to the commissioners, sent on board the fleet under my command, a passport for procuring a quantity of grain, of which this great town now stands so much in need. Be explicit! and I fly to your succour, in order to break the chain which surrounds you, and to be the instrument of making many years of happiness succeed to four years of misery and anarchy, in which your deluded country has been involved.

Given on board His Britannic Majesty's ship *Victory*, off Toulon, this 23rd day of August, 1793.

   Hood.

By command of the Admiral.

J. M'ARTHUR, Sec.

'Absolutely calculated to make friends, I should say.' Knight passed him a paper, newly dried. 'Here's your authority. You may now draw stores for yourself and your crew whilst awaiting the admiral's orders. Quite how the Admiralty will view the rather irregular procurement of your craft is not something I should like to comment upon. Good day to you, Sir Sidney.'

On the pull back across the bay Smith watched the encircling hills with his feelings in turmoil. Phelypeaux's letter had said that the family of the Comte du Fay had been recognized at Roanne by a young soldier of his acquaintance who had returned from the wars after having lost his leg. The report had been uncertain, but it had given Phelypeaux some hope, even though he had worried that the family must have been trying to reach the shambles of Lyons.

Then, some weeks later, to Phelypeaux's joy, a very definite report had come to him that three ladies had been interviewed at Vienne by a Brother occupying a senior Revolutionary office in the Department of Isère. The man had had a clear recollection of the comte's elder daughter from his attendance at a balloon ascent made from the grounds of the château Thury-Harcourt, three years previously.

Vienne is south of Lyons, Smith thought, daring to hope. When Lyons fell, they must have headed down the Rhône valley. There is an excellent chance they are coming this way.

Once aboard the *Swallow*, Smith showed the proclamation to Lieutenant Hill.

'Brave words, sir,' Hill said proudly. 'It does a fellow's heart good to see the forces of our nation setting about a mission of mercy, does it not, sir?'

Smith regarded Hill for a moment, then said, 'Yes, Mister Hill.'

'Famously brave words.'

'Absolutely, Mister Hill.'

Skrimger detected the irony in his tone, and tossed his head. 'Aye, brave, sir, but still we have a brave fleet to back them up.'

'You'll speak when spoken to, Skrimger,' Hill said.

Smith grunted. 'The disparity between us should prevent me from saying so, Skrimger, but what His Lordship has done is almost perfectly calculated to enrage the Revolutionaries. To compel a great army here that will not rest until Toulon is razed and the young Louis murdered.' He turned back to Hill. 'You know where the lad is presently, don't you?'

Hill took the rhetorical question like a fish taking bait. 'I'm afraid I do not, sir.'

Smith scratched the lobe of his ear, thinking grimly of the ill-starred mission to free the ex-queen and her son. Now Marie Antoinette was dead, gone to the same fate as her husband, but, horrifyingly, the royal orphan was still awaiting the blade.

'As a matter of fact,' he said, 'the lad's imprisoned in the Temple prison in Paris. A place known to infamy as the very ante-room of the guillotine.'

'There you have it, sir,' Skrimger said blithely. 'He's in the monster's power, and there's nought to be done about that. But His Lordship's still in possession of the town and harbour, and all its shipping.'

'For how long, though, Skrimger? How long? My God, how I hate to see things mismanaged so.' Smith clenched his teeth and shook his head tightly. A conviction was growing in him. Berenice *must* come to Toulon, he thought, half knowing it to be wishful thinking, but not caring. There's no other place for her to come. Not now. So it follows that I should search for her. I need to find a duty that will permit me free passage about the town. But how to do that? Where even to start?

He crushed down the thoughts, unanswered, and said, 'Mister Hill, I think I'll go ashore again. Tomorrow, or perhaps the next day, I'll see if I can't find Captain Elphinstone. He's a Scot, so he must know what's going on.'

'You're no yet thirty, are ye, Smith?'

'Twenty-nine, George.'

He and Elphinstone had climbed, at Smith's insistence, to the Poste de St Antoine, a mile north of Toulon and six hundred feet above the sea, where there was a redoubt of seven field guns, manned by Piedmontese troops.

'I was given five pounds for my pocket, and told to make my fortune.' Elphinstone breathed deeply, looking out over the panorama. 'That was three years before ye were born, Smith.'

'And did you?'

Elphinstone was a humourless man, a Scot, in his late

forties, fifth son of the tenth Lord Elphinstone of Stirling, a career sailor. Smith weighed him: Elphinstone had a strong face, and prematurely grey hair, a long, straight nose, emphatic eyebrows and a gritty, accented voice. He was ruddy-cheeked and clear-eyed. He had a dimpled chin, but the set of his head reminded Smith of a bull terrier, as did his manner.

Elphinstone ignored his question. He has no time for flippancy, Smith thought. Nor anything else he chooses to categorize as trivial – that much he has already said. I have the greatest difficulty in liking the man, which is a pity, because he served on shore at the reduction of Charleston, in the Carolinas, and he's been Member of Parliament for both Dumbartonshire and Stirlingshire, so he's an achiever after his own fashion.

'Quite remarkable,' Smith said, extending the brass tubes of his glass. Privately he thought, yes, quite remarkable that after all his experiences Elphinstone remained so amazingly small-minded. He's convinced that I've come here just to be in competition with him. He's been worrying about me since I arrived, and it's killing him to work out my motivations. That's certainly why he invited me to come up to the Heights in his company.

Below, the Petite Rade contained a row of French 74-gun ships, all moored in line-astern, and all ready to put to sea. He made out *Centaure* and *Commerce de Bordeaux*, *Destin* and *Hero* and *Heureux*, *Lys*, *Pompée* and *Scipion*. With them were the huge 120-gun ship *Commerce de Marseille*, and the 80-gun *Tonnant*. Then, moored separately, were the seven 74s that had arrived from the Biscayan ports: *Apollon*, *Duguay-Trouin*, *Entreprenant*, *Généreux*, *Orion*, *Patriote* and *Themistocle*.

On the climb he had noted four more sail-of-the-line: the other 120-gun ship *Dauphin Royale*, the 80-gun

Triumphant, and two more 74s, *Puissant* and *Suffisant*, all of which only required a little refitting to make them seaworthy.

Earlier, with Hill, he had rowed round the harbour and counted nine more ships repairing: two 80s, *Couronne* and *Languedoc*, and seven 74s: *Alcide, Censeur, Conquérant, Dictateur, Guerrier, Mercure* and *Souverain*, and one more building on the slips. It was a powerful fleet that had been built purposely to dominate the entire Mediterranean: a weapon that must not fall into the hands of the Revolution.

Smith had already scrutinized Toulon dockyard from another vantage point, the eminence of Missiessi, which he had climbed with Captain Edge of the sloop *Alert* yesterday as a pretext to go through the town once more. Besides the inner harbour, which enclosed the arsenal, there was an outer harbour and a road. The inner harbour was a work of art, formed by two jetties, hollow and bomb-proof, running off from the east and west sides of the town. They embraced a space large enough to hold thirty sail-of-the-line, the ships being stowed in tiers very close together. That would still leave room for thirty frigates, and a variety of small craft, as well as a sizeable mast-pond.

Elphinstone clapped his hand against the muzzle of a cannon, still lost in his own past. 'At the age of twenty-one I signed on as mate of an East Indiaman and made the voyage to China. 'Twas my brother William's ship. There's amounts to be made in the East, a'right, Smith.' Elphinstone's grey eyes locked on him, assessing him. 'Silver and gold such as ye'd hardly credit.'

'You don't say, George?' he drawled, affecting to be interested instead in some detail he had seen in the basin of the Petite Rade that glittered below.

'Aye, I do say.'

He looked at two of the closer French 74s that were

moored in the roadstead – the *Hero* and the *Themistocle*. They were superbly well constructed, quite beautiful to his eye.

'The French build their largest and best ships here,' Elphinstone said, coming close. 'I see ye're appreciating all that prize money lying at anchor down there.'

He lowered his glass and looked at Elphinstone, showing a querying face to his close scrutiny. 'You forget, I'm a half-pay officer, George. I'm acting as a volunteer.'

'You're under the admiral's authority and orders, are ye not?'

'Yes . . .' He shrugged, showing he had been confronted by a *non sequitur*.

'You're saying, ye're not entitled to any share in the prize money?'

'I have no interest in recompense. Prize money means nothing at all to me.'

Elphinstone narrowed his stare, then grunted derisively. 'Now, is that so?'

'Yes, George. That is most certainly so.'

'Then yer family are wealthier than I thought.'

'Not so. We have very little. I'm not interested in money. It's just a means to an end, but not a means to any end that I want particularly.'

'Ye expect me to believe that?' Elphinstone's accent was much harsher than Robert Liston's pleasant lilt. Everything about Elphinstone was harsh.

'Believe what you will, George, but I'm not in the habit of offering my brother officers lies.' He said it very mildly.

'Then perhaps ye'll tell me why ye've been nosing about in places ashore where ye have no permit and no proper business.'

He laughed, irritating Elphinstone. He had no intention of explaining to the older man about his searches for Berenice among the pauper bakehouses and the churches full of the thousands of destitute refugees. 'You make me sound like a bloodhound.'

'I don't know what ye are, Smith.' Elphinstone's stare pierced him. 'And I don't know what ye're after here. I can't work ye out, and that worries me. But I'll tell ye this: it worries other officers, too – officers senior to me. Ye might remember that when next ye look for a command.'

Smith lifted his glass, suspicious that some whisper had perhaps reached Elphinstone of his standing within the Brotherhood. Maybe he's got wind of the missions with which I've been entrusted, he thought. Maybe he's just worried about preferment. But there's something else, too. He's trying to tell me that Hood's got a definite down on me. I can hardly tell him that Admiral Hood's opinions don't bother me in the slightest.

He made no comment, but smoothly changed the subject instead. 'The governor told me yesterday that the engineer who constructed the dock at Toulon encountered all manner of problems. Apparently the ground was full of springs, that constantly undermined his foundations. But the man persevered and persevered. I admire perseverance, don't you, George?'

He played his glass over the harbour front. There was probably half a mile of it, counting the slips and repair yards. The arsenal was on the west side, and the ships 'in ordinary' or fitting out lay with their bowsprits or their sterns close in over the quays. The storehouses were crammed in together on one another, and within fifteen yards of them. He paced the distances out mentally between the rope-house, sail-loft, *boulangerie* or bake-house, mast-house, ordnance store, and other buildings. A glorious plan was forming in his brain.

Those dock buildings are all capacious and good, he thought. They could do us a great disservice in the years to come. And the model-loft is probably worth attending to as well. He moved his glass left. The east side of the dockyard was occupied by the victualling department and the gun-boats. The north quay was overlooked by a tower, and extended from the dockyard to the victualling office. Immediately in front of it was the mouth of the basin, between those two fifty-foot jetties. On the eastern, he saw, a pair of sheers had been erected for masting the ships.

Behind the dockyard, the town spread out a jumble of pantile roofs. She's out there, he thought, somewhere in that mass. I know it.

He had spoken with a Captain Edge at dinner ashore last evening, after his second search for the family du Fay in the area between the Faubourg St Antoine and the meanest dockside districts had proved unsuccessful.

'I understand they put a boom across the harbour entrance at night, to stop boats getting in.'

Edge, a bluff, sanguine personality, had nodded, clattering his cutlery down to gesture in explanation. 'Yes. And another boom runs from the jetty to the town, to enclose all the small craft and timber on the west side of the harbour. The harbour's well protected from the wind from whatever quarter it may blow. The basin's always calm. You saw the outer sides of the jetties? There's two tremendous batteries there, "*à fleur d'eau*", as the French say.'

'Presumably because they're nearly level with the water's edge?'

'Quite so. A disagreeable business to get in past them when they're in hostile hands. They're the very worse species of fort for a ship to encounter. More chicken, Smith?'

He had watched the succulent breast being carved onto his plate, then he had said, 'I thought I saw a couple of galleys tied up at the quay on my way down.'

Edge wiped chicken gravy from a silver knife onto the white flesh of the morsel he had cut. 'Handy craft in a near-tideless sea like the Med, what?'

Smith recalled the Russian galleys he had seen in action in the Baltic, and the poor devils – Turks mostly – who had been made to row them. 'Do the French use them?'

'Not much now.' Edge shot him a dark glance. 'Can't get a ready supply of villains to man them, I shouldn't wonder, not with the Paris government monopolizing that commodity. They have a large dry dock that uses convicts. When a ship enters it's pumped out by them.'

That conversation had laid down the keel of his plan, and since then his enquiries had added to it. His soundings had revealed the Petite Rade to have a rocky and uneven bottom. A safe anchorage, secure from Levanters – winds that could throw in a heavy sea from the south and east. The Grande Rade was a good anchorage, but again, he thought, a little confined. He could see why Lord Hood had anchored half his fleet there, but the later arrivals in the vicinity of Hières Island further along the coast. The bay to the east was open and the water deep – not to be relied on as an anchorage in bad weather. The outer road was defended on the south side by the peninsula of St Mandrier, an island almost, only connected to the mainland by a thin, sandy spit, and used by the French as a quarantine hospital or lazaretto.

He turned to Elphinstone now, zig-zagging his finger along the star-shaped fortifications of the town below, his mind calculating, calculating. His need to find Berenice was becoming an obsession, and he needed to work out how long he had left. 'Toulon may be protected by walls, but they'll not prevent guns sited here on St Antoine, or on Artigues, or St Catherine's, or any of the other hills that surround the city, firing down into the town.'

Elphinstone glanced at him as if he were a man who had missed the obvious. 'That's the reason we took these

Heights. I was doing hot work four months before you arrived here, Smith.'

'I don't doubt that, George. But when these positions fall to the French – and one must assume they will – then the Revolutionaries will command Toulon.'

The Scot turned away, barely brooking Smith's company now. 'They've to take these Heights first.'

'Surely the extent of the works, their temporary and detached nature, the number of our troops, and its multinational charact—'

'The possession of Toulon is important to Great Britain. It will not be abandoned until every effort, on the part of the British at least, has been exerted for its preservation.'

Smith lifted his glass. 'Well, in my opinion it is not possible to hold the entire perimeter.'

'And who do you think cares about your opinion, Smith?'

'Come now, it must be fifteen miles long, and manned by, what? – *in toto*, twelve thousand troops? Set against seven or eight times that number of Revolutionaries? The port is obviously doomed, George.'

It's a shame about Elphinstone, he told his Tutelary Genius silently. If only he was a little more intelligent, or possessed a slightly more subtle character I might have had an effective fellow pleader. It's only to be expected, I suppose, that a man like Hood will have laid his trust in men who possess even less talent than himself. But the admiral will be guilty of a great negligence if he leaves the French fleet to the Revolution, will he not? So we can't let that happen, can we?

They went down together, and all the way Smith endured Elphinstone's continued investigation of his motives without giving anything more away. Finally the Scot told him, 'I advise ye to keep out of the town, Smith. The admiral doesn't want ye there.'

'I hear what you say, George. Thank you.'

They parted company at the quay, and Smith turned in the direction of the town. He felt satisfaction that he had heard Elphinstone's views. They're bound to be the same as Admiral Hood's, he thought. But they are not mine.

He looked at his watch. It was twenty minutes past four. If I hurry, he told himself, I can lodge a description of Berenice with the sentries on the North Gate. Then I might be able to make one more circuit of the Old Town before curfew descends.

FOUR

They had lost no time in getting out of the city of Avignon. With the silver coin that had cost Celestine's innocence they had obtained food and passage on a little boat. It had carried them east up the Durance to near Peyrolles. There they had disembarked, and taken to a road that wound up into the hills.

She had known that the last fifty miles would be the hardest, travelling through rough, rock country in a land scoured clean by the locust army that had come to obliterate the last stand of the Royalist cause. They had come a long way south, and the bones of the country had changed. Here the trees and wildflowers were different, as were the noises the insects made.

They followed the road as much as they could, then a column of soldiers came by, and they got among the rocks and waited to see them pass. Several times on the way she had fancied she had seen a lone horseman. He had appeared briefly, but had seemed always to hang back, so that it seemed to her that he must be following them.

By the time they had gone a dozen miles her mother's legs and feet were in a terrible state. She looked at them, and bathed the sores as best she could in a pool of water, then she looked up and down the road, a strange fancy half making her expect to see Gugnot. Why did she think

494

he would appear once more? It was inexplicable, so she began to think it might be a real premonition.

'It's strange,' she told Celestine, 'how relying on your wits to travel a hard road awakens in you a dependable understanding.'

'What do you mean?'

She shrugged her pack higher. 'Don't you feel that it's sometimes as if your guardian angel is with you?'

'I have no guardian angel.'

Her sister's answer sounded so forlorn that she put out a comforting hand. 'Don't say that.'

Celestine allowed the touch, but returned no warmth. 'Why not? It's true.'

'Everyone has a personal spirit.'

'If they do, then mine's a very evil one.'

Berenice let the exchange go at that, but still she felt that her sister's Tutelary Genius must have been offended by the insult. As for her own, she could feel the invisible but nevertheless almost tangible presence informing and confirming her decisions. She found herself superstitiously touching her looped cross to summon the spirit to watch more closely over her, or perhaps it was just to strengthen her hopes. In the darkest times she kept despair at bay by reminding herself that she had been awakened to the protective power of sincere wishing. 'Ask and it shall be given,' she had told Celestine more than once. 'This little cross makes it happen.'

'Berenice, it's just a piece of yellow metal. If you sold it we could buy something to eat.'

'If I sold it, we would die.'

'You're losing your mind.'

'No. I'm very sane.'

Ever since lying hidden in a barn when the Guard had been searching the district, she had made a prayer of the phrase 'so far, so good'. For as long as she could remember the journey ahead had seemed too great an undertaking to contemplate in its entirety. Lately she had begun to see its end, and to dare to hope. But the road beyond the horizon was still a mystery. It was impossible to know very much of what they were walking into. It was only possible to feel. Already she had learned that the ways of *thought* led to hubris or taking things for granted and were fantastically dangerous. When travelling in a perilous land intuition was far more reliable.

Her guardian angel began to stir warning feelings in her again in the mid-afternoon on that lonely road to St Maximin. There was nothing to see, nothing pointing to danger, only a cool swirling breeze passing over the land. The sight made her stop. Suddenly the sense of foreboding had grown unbearable.

Celestine had seen her wariness. She sighed. 'What is it?'

Berenice looked up and down the deserted way. 'I think we must get off the road.'

Without argument, they had followed her a little way into a pine copse, to a dry spot where they were concealed, yet where they would still be able to watch the road.

'Who is coming?' her mother asked.

'I don't know. Somebody we would rather not meet.'

'What makes you say that?'

'It's a strong feeling.'

After a quarter of an hour, her mother had pressed her to go on.

'No. Not yet.'

'But we must get on before dark.'

'I know, mother. But I'd rather we trusted to my feelings for the present.'

They all knew very well that if they were discovered by soldiers this far south, without residence papers or knowledge identifying them as camp followers, they would almost certainly be bayoneted as spies.

After a few more minutes a lone horseman appeared, approaching at a walk. She made them lie low. She could not make out anything about the man, she only waited until he had got a long way ahead before coming out.

'Is that him?'

'Yes.'

Her mother looked at her queerly. 'But . . . *who* is he?'

'I don't know, but I can feel the evil in him.'

The figure was that of a young man, mounted on a black horse. His hair was shoulder length, lank over a fashionably deep Revolutionary's collar. He was swathed in a black cloak, his face ghostly pale, his eyes dark and shadowed. He made no demonstration except the slow turning of his head from side to side, like a blind man scanning the country through which he passed. When he came abreast of them he paused, and as his gaze swept over the place where they hid the sensations of dread that Berenice felt became almost unbearable.

Her vision seemed suddenly confined to a scene at the end of a long tunnel. Waves of ringing assailed her ears, like the all-consuming, sourceless booming that comes just before a fit of fainting. It passed away as the figure moved on, subsiding like a danger passing, and when he had gone she stood up, her heart pounding, to look at the bright evening light, and the grey dust of the road.

They had rejoined the highway, and pressed on for an hour longer, and nothing had been said between them, for they had seen the way the terror had touched her soul, and so drained her.

That night the accommodation had been uncomfortable. They had camped among rocks, and Berenice remained sleepless almost until dawn, waking dew-spangled and stiff in the first rays of the new day. For that and the next two nights they had kept no fire, for fear of attracting discovery. The pitiful scraps of food they had brought with them had run out on the second day, but there had been recent rain here, and there was

497

plenty of fresh water to be found running in hillside streams.

Now Berenice found herself thinking over ways in which they might trap one of the mountain goats that were occasionally to be seen, but without at least a bow and arrow it was impossible. The animals were too wary to allow any human to approach them, and too nimble to be pursued. But still the idea of how a goat might be caught exercised her mind as she fixed her eyes on the next ridge and prayed that the cresting of it would bring them a sight of the sea.

Instead they found signs that a monster had been stalking the land. They came upon a roofless cottage, a pool of stench where an old man's blackened body lay, stripped and stiff. All around was a ravaged orchard. But they were in a country of stumps. All the trees had been hacked off at waist height in the groves, like the columns of antiquity shattered by the Cyclops. Blond wood chips jagged at their toes. Twigs littered the road. There were white feathers near an empty chicken coop.

'What did this?' Celestine asked, dread thickening her voice.

'Men,' she said. 'Only men.'

Then they saw the main house a little way off, and as ever Berenice wondered if it would be safe to approach. She took her mother's staff to ward off any dogs that might attack her, and started out. The weather had cleared up, and the mist was gone. A shaft of sunlight enabled her to see the house distinctly. Something was amiss with it. There were several strange heaps or mounds nearby, and as she drew closer she began to smell the same horrible stink.

The place seemed to have been subjected to a bombardment. All the windows were smashed out. One door lay flat on the ground, the other hung by a single hinge only. She had no difficulty in entering.

The body of a huge man lay at the foot of the stairs. He

was nearly naked, and much decayed. She could not tell if he had been owner or servant. The whole place was in utter confusion. There had evidently been hand-to-hand fighting in the rooms. She made a wad of the corner of her shawl and pressed it to her mouth and nose, fighting nausea.

Upstairs were the remains of about a dozen men and women heaped together. All were blackened and bloated. They must have been dead several days, maybe even weeks. The horrible fetor of the place was unendurable, and she was driven out into the fresh air with tears blurring her sight.

Perhaps there's been fighting all over the district, she thought. Perhaps this was the Royalist territory we've been hoping to find.

Later, as they followed the road they found perhaps a hundred bodies scattered about. More were lying in two heaps in a farmyard. The building itself was completely ruined.

The sight was more dreadful than any they had yet witnessed. Many of the dead were already skeletal, or nearly so. Animals, maybe dogs or pigs, had been at work on others. All were bloated in the last stage of putrefaction. Many retained the positions in which they had died and stiffened. One man, with no eyes left in the sockets of his skull, was holding one arm straight up in the air, and to Berenice's shocked mind the thought occurred that his surprised pose would have been comical, if it had not been so vile.

Soon after she felt the horror of the desecration, and anger kindling in her again. No dignity had been accorded the dead. Worse, dignity had been deliberately refused them. What insane hatred could leave human remains unburied and at the mercy of the crow and the raven, let alone the host of curs that ran wild and ownerless hereabouts? That the perpetrators of the enormity would almost certainly go unpunished added an extra dimension of injustice to an already evilly inhuman crime.

Her mother hobbled bravely on through the hellish landscape, and Berenice thought again of the time at the Hergevault house when she had lost her temper and accused her mother of weakness and selfishness. When she had slapped her mother's face, Celestine had sprung at her like a cat, and only since then had she come to know how their mother's selflessness in the prison of La Precey Abbey had saved Celestine's life.

She had found resources of strength and courage that she had never suspected, and Berenice promised her guardian angel that if they ever reached safety she would do right by her mother, and admit the terrible lie she had invented. It's bargaining, she told the spirit silently, touching her cross. And I know you do not permit bargaining, especially when it comes from guilt, but I pledge to tell her the truth just as soon as we reach safety . . . if you will get us there.

As the evening of the third day arrived they came over another brow, but this time Celestine looked to her with alarm. She heard the unmistakable thud of gunfire. The sound knotted her inside, and made her forget her gnawing hunger. She narrowed her eyes at the brown land, looking for musket flashes among the dusk shadows.

There was no doubt about it, there were soldiers down below, shooting for food. Military camps were scattered in the valley. Seconds later she heard the noise of horses, and they took themselves off the road, as they had a thousand times before. Darkness came down as they crouched in the rocks. Berenice saw with awe that there were lights glowing all around. They were surrounded by the Guard, and it was their fires that could be seen in all directions. They regained the road and pressed on, horrified, fording a stream, then they had to stand still as statues, almost stumbling upon a pair of soldiers who had been detailed to fill their company's water bottles.

As they descended, the hillsides were dotted with fires and the dimly seen outlines of tents. Every nerve in her body cried out alarm. They could not stray from the road and they could not remain upon it. They could go neither to left nor right, yet to go back was equally impossible. The only way was forward. If, by some incredible miracle, they could pass the encampment in the darkness, then the way to Toulon would be opened.

The night was moonless, and she saw by the stars that the road had been heading west of south. The blue-white stars of Orion stood high above them in the south. The Hunter and his Dogs, fixed and immortal, beckoned them on. And the pearly path of the Milky Way, brighter than she had ever seen, overarched the world of cares. At the next junction there was a milestone. She ran her fingers over the inscription. It read, 'Vallée de l'Ubac'. The name meant nothing to her.

The next thing she heard was Celestine's catch of breath and the brief flurry of shapes moving near to her. She froze, heard men's grunts. Soldiers. Then her mother cried out and fell down in blind darkness. Next she felt herself gripped and pushed down to the floor, and a sharp knee shoved into her spine to hold her there.

She struggled, but the soldier knew his trade. The knee bore down on her, squeezing the breath from her, and the heel of a rough hand pressed down on her neck, so that her cheek was pressed hard into the grit of the road. A dagger of pain shot through her where the hand pressed, and so commanding was it that she tensed and cried out, then she submitted, to relieve the grinding pain in her neck.

False, fantastic colours exploded in her vision, then the pain started to subside. When it had died sufficiently she peered up, one-eyed, at the black spaces that blotted out the three stars of Orion's swordbelt. Other soldiers came up, their boots crunching on the bed of the road, dark silhouettes against the starbright sky. They were breathing heavily from some exertion. The steel of bayonets glittered star blue. There may have been a dozen of them. Too many to escape. She grunted with a reprise of pain when her arms were hauled up behind her back and her elbows locked painfully. There was some discussion, but her mind was full of panic as she began to admit to herself that the fatal error had been committed at last, and now they were probably all going to die.

Who would know if we are raped? Who if we are murdered? Who would ever care? Out here on the dark hillside, three beggar-women's torment is nothing, she thought, despairing. Our deaths are insignificant.

She was dragged to her feet again, and one man pulled hard on her left wrist and another on her right, as if wanting to pull her apart; a third man walked away from them with a terrifying nonchalance. Others came up, wary at first, then with eager, curious gestures. In the dark her imagination painted in the details of their devil faces.

'No! Please! Please!' she begged. 'We are camp followers of the army of liberation.' Then, wondering in terror and panic what magic formula could win their attention and save their lives, she screamed, 'Long live the Revolution!'

She screamed it again, and then a third time, her voice becoming increasingly incoherent with fear, until it broke. Suddenly, she became intensely aware of the terse communication between the men. It was the talk of men who had lived and worked together in each other's company for many months. A language of grunts and monosyllables, heavily inflected. They must be Provençal. She couldn't understand their words, but they were discussing her.

There were cries and wails, noise jangling her nerves, then she heard her mother's voice, protesting, pleading.

Celestine began screaming. She imagined her sister's face, ugly now, in the knowledge of what was about to happen.

Berenice knew their leader at once. He was a bull of a man standing with his back to her. His voice was a growl. From the way he held himself and the way he disposed of the others' objections, she could see he held some kind of sway over them. She had grasped at the hope of finding someone at whom to direct her pleas, but now she felt only fear, because this man was a brute. There was no doubt in her that he was cast in the mould of men who must continually outdo their own acts of callousness or cruelty to maintain their place.

Nothing brings men like these to violence so effectively as woman's voices, she thought. She was horrified to watch the leader plucking up the guts to kill. Is it that? she asked herself, paralysed. No. Even this man could not murder in cold blood. He was searching for something to trigger his anger. Then she sensed the violence coming to a crescendo and a fresh thrill of terror ran through her.

The soldiers were getting more agitated, worrying about the commotion bringing the enemy down on them. Her mother's fervent appeals were inflaming them. She realized that in a few moments the bull would turn, and run his bayonet into her heart, just to be done with the noise.

'Mother!' she raged, now. But her mother continued to wail and plead for her daughter's life, and she herself was adding to it. Words were no use here; no one could understand words. Her impotence made her struggle, but the more she struggled the more her captors held her, pulling at her, bracing themselves like two hunting dogs tearing at a hare. 'Mother!'

Please make her shut up! she prayed. Make her back away! Make her stand still! Oh, God quiet her tongue!

She wanted to hug her mother and explain that

nothing would do any good now. There was no way to win. These men had made up their minds what was going to happen. They were soldiers, waiting to witness their leader's act of affirmation. Suddenly she was filled with a vast sense of injustice, and it outweighed her terror. Anger welled up inside like a volcano, filling her.

'You can't kill us!' she shouted. 'Not after what we've been through! You can't! You can't! I won't let you! It doesn't make any sense!'

But there was no reaction from the men. Just the methodical preparation for her murder, and she felt herself lose control. Urine coursed down the insides of her thights, soaked the ragged hose that were rolled down around her ankles, spattered the ground beneath her skirts.

As the bayoneteer turned, she threw her head to one side and the pain in the bones of her neck made her gasp again. She heard her mother's voice screaming: 'Le prego, signori! Non uccideteci! Siamo tre signore! Abbiamo viaggiato a Toulon per scappare la morte. Avete pietà!'

PART 9

Crux Ansata

WINTER, 1793
The heights above Toulon

You were right again, monsieur! *Things have started going my way ever since I dedicated myself – mind, body and soul – to our enterprise. I am encouraged by recent political developments, and I believe that now, with your tutelage, I am beginning to get the measure of great events.*

As you suggested, as soon as I heard the Jacobins had become supreme in Paris, I began to look for a suitable conduit of influence. The man who attracted me was the one they call 'the incorruptible' – Maximilien Robespierre. He's the key now. It surprised me how easy it was to reach him, but I discerned your hand in this, monsieur, *did I not? Now, tell me true.*

Well, at any rate, you were right that a climb to power requires patronage. I decided it was time I tried my hand at political dialogues. What do you think of my pamphlet, monsieur? *Here – read it. I had it printed and circulated at no cost to myself. I call it 'A Supper in Beaucaire'. It's a sort of parable, a story of the bourgeoisie and of a soldier – a cautionary tale, you see? – to show the middle classes the futility of supporting the House of Bourbon. It lays out my political credentials quite nicely, don't you think? You see how it was written to match exactly the Jacobin party line? I supposed the party's faithful would love it – and, of course, I was precisely right in that supposition.*

I made sure that I gave the pamphlet to a fellow Corsican exile, his name: Antoine Salicetti. Do you remember him? I've talked of him before, monsieur, *in the days when he was Antonio. I had dealings with him when I was in Paris, and lately again in Corsica in my battle against the filthy traitor, Paoli. I knew Salicetti would do what he could for me; it was in his interests, you see. He promised to show the pamphlet to a man named Jean Gugnot, one who had no official position that I could discern, but who carried himself with such watchful disdain that I knew he must be reporting back to some very important connections in Paris.*

Again my well-schooled instincts were right, monsieur, *for Gugnot passed my writings to Commissioner Barras, and he to Augustin Robespierre, who is the younger brother of 'the Incorruptible'. I was coming back from Avignon with a requisition of black powder, when the same Gugnot secured for me an introduction, and then an invitation to dine with them. At that dinner I gained the confidence of them all. Robespierre particularly began to fall under the spell of my eyes. I charmed him exactly as you taught me,* monsieur, *so that by the end of the brandy he was nodding in recognition of my technical knowledge. By the end of that week he was sending my recommendations on military matters to Paris.*

Some may succeed by peddling the semblance of ability, but in extremity, as when chaos comes to the world, there is no substitute for what I possess. They need me, because they need what I can do for them. So — there you have it, monsieur. *That is how I became known in high places. That is how I put my talents before the faces of those who could raise me up.*

I suppose you saw the decrees of the Committee of Public Safety? All through the summer they have come gushing from the pen of Robespierre's lieutenant, Lazare Carnot. Carnot has conscripted everyone, hurled every last man, woman and child into the effort to rid France of her enemies.

Look down there, monsieur. *Can you see them? The old enemy: those filthy islanders, the English. Money-grubbing merchants. Tea traders. No doubt they will try to charge the Royalists for their services – take title to one of the French West Indies no doubt, or more likely to my Corsica. You see their great yellow and black ships, crowding the outer harbour? I hate them. They appeared this summer like a cloud of wasps. Their mission: to give those Royalist maggots succour.*

They are rightly called our natural enemies, don't you think, monsieur? *In all history perfidious Albion has never missed a chance to confound us. They take their damned ships where they please the whole world over, and swarm in the Channel round their hive when it is threatened. You promised me there will be a war all across Europe. 'War the like of which has not been seen since the Sun King fought Eugène and Marlborough.' That's what you said. One day, if you prophesy it* monsieur, *I'll lead a grand army into London to snuff out their arrogance, and thereby redress the honour of France. That is my sincerest wish.*

Did I tell you, monsieur? *I wrested command of Carteaux's artillery a few weeks ago. A hundred and twenty pieces of ordnance! And once they were mine I gave our commanders a winning strategy. It's very simple. You see there? Yes, where I'm pointing. You see how the inner and the outer harbours are separated by a promontory of land? They call it l'Eguillette. A child could see that it is essential to take that point in order to drive the English from the town. I told Carteaux that our fire must be concentrated on l'Eguillette. If we could breach the wall of the fort there, then Toulon would be ours.*

A child could have seen it, monsieur, *but Carteaux argued with me. I had to finesse him. I intrigued hard* against him, stirring it up until Carteaux was made a laughing stock and transferred out to the Army of Italy. Then they brought in General Doppet, another imbecile. Two weeks ago he failed to take Fort Mulgrave through his rank cowardice. You see this cut on my forehead? It's still not healed. That was down to his indecision. After that I dared to dress him down in front of his own men, because I knew they loved me, and that it would make his position untenable. This time the Deputies did as I requested and put Jacques Dugommier in charge. He's a man who knows a little something. We also have Claude Victor and young Muiron, both of them recklessly eager, so you can see that a real army is coming together at last.

Of course, I wanted the Committee to appoint me commander, but one cannot very easily recommend oneself, monsieur, and that fellow Gugnot knew the game. You see, if the Committee had given me command I'd have taken all the credit for my ideas myself. As it was, Gugnot and Barras were drawing their share of glory from my inventiveness, and my efforts. But this is a strategy that will eventually bear me fruit. One day both of them will pay me what they owe me. One day they will work for me.

A month after getting command of the artillery, Dugommier made me chef de bataillon. Better still, he told me he had adopted my plan of attack. So – there it is, monsieur. Look at Toulon, laid out below us like a map! It is waiting for me now. Fifteen hundred traitors, supported by two thousand British, four thousand Spaniards and a few hundred Neapolitans and Piedmontese. They can't hope to hold out against us. We are only waiting for the siege guns before taking up a position whence we may reach the English ships with red-hot cannon balls. Then we shall see how well tar and wood and rope will burn!

It is artillery that takes fortresses, and I know how to

use artillery. At last, the time has come to seize my destiny with two fists. Soon everyone will know the name of Napoleone di Buonaparte.

ONE

DECEMBER, 1793
Toulon, France

Smith made his way to the eastern shorefront, the only part of the town of Toulon exempted from the curfew. Here he searched out the rooms that were frequented by Spanish officers, where the dining was vigorous and the wine good. He had offered to return Edge's compliment in style, but there was another agenda in his mind. There was very little time left, and his anxieties were growing.

Lieutenant Hill was waiting to greet him, along with Edge and another officer, by introduction Captain Hare, of the *Vulcan*, a friend of Edge's, one the latter suggested might well become a recruit to the plan Smith was about to put to them.

Edge had also brought with him a half case of excellent Burgundy wine, and after a meal of pleasantries he turned the atmosphere conspiratorial amid the din of Spanish toasts. They fell to discussing the admiral, and Smith confessed a burn of impatience at Hood's ponderous style.

'He's a naturally cautious man,' Smith said, ignoring Hare's discomfort. 'Thorough enough, but he's faced with a situation that's unsuited to his intellect. Caution is not required here.' He lowered his voice to deliver the kernel of the evening. 'Those French ships out there are going to have to be sunk. And soon.'

Hare stood up and looked out of the window. When Smith enquired after his health he said, 'I daresay, Sir

Sidney, that the exalted reasoning of those of flag rank is rarely apparent to their subordinates.'

Smith wanted to say, Hare, you're a complacent and unimaginative ass, unfit for independent command. Instead he enquired politely, 'Do you *really* imagine that admirals are born with greater powers of reasoning than the rest of us?'

Hare's shocked at my presumption, he thought, amused. That anyone can think to question orders is barely conceivable to him. That a mere post-captain might get himself up on the same level as minds that formulate policy is quite beyond him. Maybe I'll bait Hare, for the sake of winning round Edge's opinion. It might work.

When Hare had sat down again, Smith said, 'Admirals really have no monopoly on intelligence, you know, Hare. In fact, it has been my observation that rank and ability are not often closely correlated. In this fleet in particular.'

Hare regarded him frostily, as if the remark had been deliberately directed at his own person. 'Your impertinence astonishes me, Captain Smith.'

Smith put down his knife and fork, making a show of keeping his patience intact. 'Hare, it's not a question of impertinence. I long ago learned that great enterprises will succumb to bumbling incompetence quicker than to any other disease.'

'You're being deliberately provocative.'

'But what if I'm *right*? Hmmm? We are lost, once we start to place comfortable lies ahead of hard truths, are we not?' He smiled candidly at Hare, an impish challenge. 'All men have their faults, isn't that so?'

Hare blinked back at him. Crescendos of Spanish merriment erupted coincidentally nearby. 'That is most certainly so. Admirals must consider higher matters. There are doubtless factors of which you have no knowledge.'

'Oh, come, captain. Faulted though we may be, we're none of us blind men. We can see what's happening ashore and in the harbours. The evacuation of Toulon is inevitable. It's already happening. You know that as well as the rest of us.'

'I know my duty. And I know yours, too. Rather better than you seem to.'

'Oh, indeed?'

'Yes, sir! Your duty is to obey orders. That's all. They say you've been touring the town, looking for French-women, instead of attending to—'

His fury got the better of him. ' "*They*", Captain Hare? Who are "they"?'

Hare got to his feet. 'I'll not stay here in this company longer.'

Smith smiled up at him. This time it was with unveiled scorn. 'Balls, sir! I'll choose to ignore your pathetic insult, and still the fact remains: I have not the slightest doubt as to the rightness of my conclusion. And what's more, unless I am given direct orders to desist I shall make an independent attempt to destroy at least some of those ships as soon as the evacuation begins.'

He watched Hare go and turned to Hill, who was trying to look as if he had heard nothing of what had passed.

'He's a limited man, Hill. Narrow little thin-piss sort of mind. Narrow vision. We don't need him.'

'Yes, sir. I thought so, sir.'

'Quite right.'

As he sat down he saw that he had offended Edge too. The wine they had drunk had made him boorish, but he did not care. He shrugged. 'Well . . . the bloody man's no good for us.'

Edge just sucked on a hollow tooth and stared at the tablecloth. He was on the point of making excuses too, so Smith refilled his glass, and was about to raise it in a cajoling toast when he became aware of a figure watching him from a little way across the dining room. He was a lieutenant in his early twenties, quite dapper and thoughtful looking. There were two others with him, but he was definitely their master.

Smith was unprepared when he met the man's eye. His tone was tinged with temperament as he called out, 'You have some *business* with me, sir?'

But the other took it as an invitation to approach. He saluted Smith's uniform. 'I know you are Sir Sidney Smith. I . ∴. couldn't help overhearing—'

'Overhearing, did you say?'

His response had been sharp, and the other hesitated. 'I also heard what you said to Captain Knight last week. We all did, actually.'

Smith regarded the others. There were two of them, one the far side of twenty, the other not. Smith dropped all trace of humour from his manner. 'What are you saying to me?'

'Just that – we thought you were right.' He offered his hand. 'Lieutenant Charles Tupper, sir, of the *Victory*.'

Smith saw the gesture, got up from his seat and shook, feeling the subtle pressure exerted there, as he had expected.

'In that case . . . well met, Mister Tupper. Perhaps you'd care to join us?'

Tupper indicated the men who flanked him. 'May I introduce Lieutenant John Gore, sir? And this is Midshipman Eales.'

'Captain Edge of the *Alert*. Lieutenant Hill.'

'If you should need any help, Sir Sidney, in . . .' Tupper indicated the harbour. '. . . in leaving Jean Crapaud high and dry, then I hope you will remember us.'

'Ha! Well, I like your style, Mister Tupper. I do believe we're of one mind on this, you and I.'

'Yes, sir. I believe we are.'

'In that case, we'll have to see what can be done about it.'

He smiled up at the lieutenant, his outward self, he knew, appearing composed and full of confidence. Inside, he was wondering just what he had got himself into.

TWO

DECEMBER, 1793
Toulon, France

Berenice lay on the pavement of the town square waiting for the doors of the pauper house to open. Celestine lay propped against her, and she cradled her mother's head, stroking her grey hair. A tear of shame came to her eye as she remembered what Smith had taught her about the strange ways of fate and the paradox of giving and receiving. Those who chose to behave selfishly cut themselves off from their guiding spirit, and those who were generous were repaid in unimagined and unimaginable ways. There was no rational way to account for it, but it was true.

So true, she thought. How many times on the journey have I silently damned my own mother as an encumbrance? How many times was I impatient with her stupidity and her weakness? There were times I wished myself free of her. Yet for all the terrors and hardships I was not ready to give up the life she had given me. In the end it was she who saved my heart from the bayonet.

She remembered the struggle in the darkness, and the cruel blade that had been levelled at her breast. Her mind had seized up. She had thought the troops were the same through whose midst they had passed that night: Revolutionary troops, Toulon's besiegers. But her mother had understood their words, had known them for who they were.

'Please, sirs, don't kill us!' she had said, in Italian. 'We are three ladies, who have travelled to Toulon to escape death! Have mercy upon us!'

And that had been enough to surprise them, and drive them to seek the opinion of their officer. And he had interrogated them, and seen instantly that they must be who they said they were.

The troops had withdrawn to their post, and had given them a little bread and sent them down to the city. On arriving, they had been told to gather with all the other destitutes who had come seeking relief. An issue of bread was made each morning at a bakehouse near the church.

At five o'clock lights appeared in the tall windows overhead. At six o'clock they began to smell the wonderful aroma of baking bread. A tiny window in the door opened, and rations were handed down to those who headed the queue.

When their turn came the woman she glimpsed through the window said, 'Bread is finished today. Come back tomorrow.'

Berenice felt a surge of anger at the injustice. They had waited hours, and thereby earned the right to have what was being given out. 'But we're hungry! We've just arrived from the north!'

The woman's voice was hard. 'You've come here without considering that it requires money to live in Toulon just as much as every other city of France.'

'We came here to be released from our persecutors and our fears. But you're no better to us than the villains outside!'

The woman's face showed no compassion. 'When you've been here longer you'll learn to show more gratitude.' Then she shut the window.

As they lay huddled together now, Berenice listened to the distant booming of cannon. It rolled like summer thunder.

She asked her mother, 'How did you know they were Neapolitans?'

'Piedmontese.' Her mother produced one of her archest expressions, reminding her of old times. 'My dear, a lady must be able to comprehend Italian opera. It's absolutely *de rigueur*.'

Berenice broke into husky laughter. They were filthy and ragged and starved, their cheeks were sunken and they were infested with lice. Only her mother could have said such a thing lying on a cold pavement with an empty begging bowl before her.

'Yes, of course.' Her laughter was close to tears. 'Of course, a lady must be able to comprehend that!'

'You once told me we were not ladies any more, Berenice. You were quite wrong. Once a lady, always a lady. Never forget that, whatever we may sink to.'

She caressed her mother's hair, seeing her as she had never seen her before. I have still not given her the credit she deserved for looking after Celestine in prison, she thought. She was stronger and wiser than ever I was prepared to admit. So much passed unsaid between us in the time before, because then it had always seemed unsayable. There was never a right moment, and always too much distance between people in that great house. The château had not been built as a home; it had never become a place where it was appropriate to broach personal questions.

Such a thing would have threatened etiquette with indelicacy, she thought dismissively. But our long nights and days together on the road have made up for all that. I wish our family could have been this close in the time before . . .

She felt the warmth of that thought suffuse her, but then a familiar dread stirred in her again. It was her conscience: guilt about the secret, and now also the pledge she had made to her personal angel. I must speak about papa . . . but not yet. I can't. Not yet.

She looked at Celestine and noted the tracery of mauve blood vessels in her white eyelids. She was sleeping, her head back, her pretty mouth open, her hair swagged over one shoulder. She seemed very young and delicate and vulnerable, despite her filthy state.

'I . . . I have never said so before, *maman*,' Berenice whispered, 'but . . . I love you very much.'

Her mother squeezed her hand and pressed it to her temple. 'And I love you, too, my darling firstborn girl. The Revolution has dispossessed us, but I think we have also gained much more than anyone could know.'

Everything seemed perfect for a moment, but then the pangs in her stomach came again. Hunger brought a strange kind of listlessness with it, an almost narcotic sense of resignation. The weaker a person became, the easier it was to give up the struggle to find food. That way lay death.

After all our struggle, she thought, we have reached a place beyond the Revolution. But still we are starving and in utter need. Revolutionary armies have surrounded us. Where can we go from here? Whatever will become of us?

Somewhere a clock chimed eight. She counted the bells, then summoned together the iron in her soul and forced herself to her feet. 'Time to get busy. Where there's a square there will be market stalls.'

It had been a great discovery for her that the poor starved, not because there was no food around them, but because they had no money to buy it. People died most often of want right in the midst of plenty. She had never understood that in the time before, but it made perfect sense to her now.

The realities were very simple: there was food in Toulon, but the price was impossibly high, so they must do as they had done before – forage and steal, or die.

'Wait here,' she said. 'I'm going to see what I can find.'

She saw many foreign soldiers in the port, and the

sight dismayed her. They were Toulon's protectors, but they were not the fresh-drafted peasants of the Revolutionary army; most of these men looked like professional soldiers, brutish veterans with foreign-looking uniforms and foreign-looking faces, and speaking languages she could not understand.

An officer in Hessian boots strode along the street. She automatically flinched away from him, like an animal, hiding her face and looking up only after he had passed.

She saw him discard a half-eaten peach, watched it roll along the pavement and pounced on it, unable to believe her luck. She bit into the luscious, sweet flesh, looking about warily. There was something uneasy about the troops she had seen that morning. It was just an intuition, but it was dominating her thoughts. She could not put her finger on it, then she saw a column of men pass her and she understood. It was a matter of pride. These men had seen action up on the Heights, but now they were down in the town. They were soldiers in retreat, and soldiers in retreat had that haunted look about them.

You can tell with reasonable certainty how a Frenchman might behave, she thought, gnawing the peach stone. But these Spaniards and Italians and British troops – who can tell what they will do in their thousands in the town? But what is it that my Tutelary Genius is really trying to tell me?

She knew that something else, something important, was trying to find its way into her conscious mind, and again she sought it.

Celestine?

What if Celestine was tempted to try to renew her whoring? The thought sent an unpleasant sensation through her. Perhaps that's what's under my thoughts and worrying me. Here it would be very dangerous to go with soldiers . . . but I'm sure that's not it. What is certain is that it's more important than ever that I find us something to eat.

She explored the streets until she came to the main square. It was dressed with granite cobbles and had a stone fountain at one end. Impressive buildings formed three sides, the fourth side retained an older façade of large merchants' houses, built, she judged, in a previous century. But there was no market.

Is it Sunday? she wondered. My God, I don't even know what day of the week it is! Or what day of the month.

She saw a decrepit old man loitering near the water pump. He was unkempt and very shabbily dressed, but she noticed the quality of the cloth from which his clothes were cut. The iron pump was sited over a grid and the handle was up high. Whenever the old man placed his cup down and worked the handle the force of the water gushing down knocked the cup over. She heard him ask a passer-by if he would help, but the man had a surly manner and went on without a word.

'I'll get you water,' she told him. 'Hold up your cup, and I'll work the handle.'

He readily accepted, took the water and drank it, afterwards thanking her in an exaggeratedly civil manner. She accepted his thanks, but saw that he kept his ancient blue eyes on her all the time.

'Why are you looking at me like that?' she asked, finally unnerved.

'Excuse me,' he said. He was very well spoken. 'But may a man not look at his own daughter when he likes?'

She stared back at him, shocked, thinking this was some trick of hearing brought on by hunger, or a quirk occasioned by her Tutelary Genius. After all, she thought, I have wronged my guardian angel, have I not? For I broke my promise.

'What did you say?'

'Ah, Hélène. Little one!'

She looked again at the wizened man, and saw that he was indeed a complete stranger. Just a confused old man whose mind was lost in a tragic past.

'Maybe I *am* your daughter, papa,' she said, thinking him more than a little mad now. 'But I must go.'

'So soon?' He rolled his eyes. 'Hélène, you are a naughty girl to have been away so long!'

'Never mind, papa. At least you know I'm safe and well now.'

She was about to leave him, when he said, 'But, you are so thin! You must come with me and eat breakfast.'

She felt his pull on her sleeve, his insistence, and she allowed herself to be directed towards a side street. A few minutes later they reached a little door, where the heavenly smell of warm cooking oil made her stomach spasm with expectation. The old man went in ahead while she hung back fearfully. The aproned owner came forward and remonstrated with him, but the old man insisted, and motioned her inside. He made her sit down at one of the tables to rest herself. She chose the seat nearest the door and remained poised on the edge of the chair as the old man told the owner to bring a bottle of wine, while an omelette was prepared for them.

The owner was in his fifties. He eyed her closely each time he reappeared, barely concealing his opinion of her. She had seen the look so many times, and knew well that it was always followed by the order to get out, but this man said nothing, and soon he put before them a basket of bread, and two glasses.

She drank off what was put before her straight away. It was a cheap red wine, with an acid taste and a good deal of sediment, but it was the best wine she had ever tasted. The alcohol went immediately to her head. All the time the old man kept up a rambling stream of one-sided conversation. He continued to call her by the name Hélène, but he was good-natured and solicitous of her welfare, and she replied in kind, calling him papa whenever the owner came near, stroking his hand and humouring him for more than two hours.

In that time two generous plates of soup were brought. Then an omelette and a good piece of ham. Berenice tore off hunks of bread and ate ravenously, cleaning her dish completely. She tucked as much of the bread as she could into her shirt, and pocketed three of four slices of ham, while the old man encouraged her with a toothless smile.

'Yes, yes! Eat!'

'Thank you, papa.'

When the owner asked her, 'More soup?' she could not help glancing up at him with astonishment, but he only shrugged, and said, 'Why not? I don't know who you are, and I don't want to know, but you're the third daughter my father has brought here this week.'

She stared back at him, letting go the old man's hand. 'He's your father. I didn't know. I'm . . . sorry.'

'No need. You've been kind to him.' He looked away and back again. 'My sister, Hélène, drowned in the harbour thirty years ago, and, as the proverb says, blood is thicker than water.'

THREE

DECEMBER, 1793
Toulon, France

Samuel Hood watched the turbulent, disputing officers seated around his cabin table. He disliked having to deal with foreigners, especially when the situation over which he had been given responsibility was reaching an unsatisfactory climax.

He was in his seventieth year, with half a century of distinguished service behind him, and a series of great battles, all fought against the same implacable foe. More than thirty years ago he had first made his name by capturing a French frigate in a fiercely fought duel with his own *Vestal*; ten years ago he had outfought De Grasse on the North American and West Indian stations, but now he stroked his long chin, his thin lips pursed; all his guarantees to the Toulonese were in tatters, and doom fast approaching.

Last night, as the Revolutionaries descended the Heights of Balaguier and took control of the western shore of the inner harbour, he had ordered all his ships out. Now they lay at anchor in the Grande Rade. There's nothing more I can do, he thought. If only I was thirty years younger. If I was that I'd be bold as brass. I'd know how to proceed. I'd be far less wise, but at least I'd have fewer doubts.

The great cabin of *Victory* was luxuriously appointed. There were portraits and his favourite Dorsetshire landscapes fixed to the panelled bulkheads, silver candelabra, a cushioned bench seat running athwart the stern, and behind it a row of nine great windows. The deck had been spread with a canvas cover painted in black and white diamonds to resemble a marble floor. *Victory*'s comforts rivalled those of the drawing room of any English country house, with the difference that here most of the fine furniture was collapsible. Even the partition walls could be removed, when need arose, to reveal two brace of 32-pounders, and to transform these palatial quarters into an extension of the warship's gundeck.

Damn it all, Hood thought bitterly, thinking of his likely detractors in the House of Commons. Like other enterprises of fair promise but unfortunate issue, these proceedings are bound to be found fault with at home. They'll say that Toulon should have been entered by force of arms, and not after a formal agreement with the inhabitants. They'll say that all the French ships should have been manned and sent to England, and the town garrisoned by reliable troops. And I can answer them only with this question: what can twenty-one ships-of-the-line, with two regiments on board, be expected to achieve against the Devil himself?

His eyes darted from face to face. Look at them all, he thought, arguing among themselves like geese. They know we're finished here, and they're all desperate to avoid the blame.

'Gentlemen!' Sir Gilbert Elliott sought to ease the tense web of national rivalries that had stretched the coalition to bursting point. 'Our line of defence was fifteen miles in circumference. Points of it only communicated by water. Once it was broken in the two most essential posts, there was nothing else but to fall back.'

Hood looked around them again, the diplomatic side of his nature barely in control. He asked, 'Are we all determined, then, on the impracticability of restoring the posts that have been lost?'

They looked to one another. 'Yes, my lord.'

'Then I must recommend to their lordships of the Admiralty the speedy evacuation of what has become an untenable town.'

Lieutenant-General Dundas resettled his spectacles and consulted his jottings. 'As to what measures have already been taken, my lord. Troops have been withdrawn from the Heights of Balaguier without much interruption from the enemy. Such posts as depended on the possession of the redoubt of Faron have also been given up and the troops drawn in towards Toulon. The forts of D'Artigues and St Catherine still remain, together with the posts of Sablettes, Cape Bran and Malbousquet, from which last the Spaniards, I believe, withdrew last night?'

The Spanish second-in-command, Gravina, nodded, as Dundas went on reading from his paper. He flashed a dark sidelong glance at the Prince Pignatelli. '... in consequence of the supporting post of Neapolitans at Missiessi having left the battery there, and abandoned it without orders, every attention has been given to ensure the tranquillity of the town.'

Hood turned to Sir Gilbert. This was a foul duty, and it stuck in his throat. 'You have, I believe, considered what further measures are required?'

Elliott said, 'Milord. The sick and wounded, and the British field artillery should be sent off tomorrow morning as a matter of priority. In the course of the day the post of Cape Bran will withdraw into La Malgue. The post of Sablettes will also retire, and the men be put on board. The arsenal and dockyard will have to be strictly guarded. Measures should be arranged for the final embarkation of the British, Piedmontese and Spaniards who presently occupy the town, about seven thousand men.' He cleared his throat. 'I think, milord, this would best be done during the night. Every care must be taken to conceal our intentions from the, ah, inhabitants.'

There was an embarrassed silent, full of regrets. They were sneaking away from broken promises under cover of darkness, and they knew it.

Hood's gaze drifted out through the stern windows and extended over the calm waters. He could see a mist lying over the grey hills, lit as if by lightning. It was, he knew, the muzzle flashes of enemy cannon.

Smith, hatless and wrapped in his boat-cloak, watched the high ground of Lazarette and the Croix des Signaux through his glass. He chewed a flake of dry skin on his lower lip. Below him in the *felucca*'s waist his men were manning the sweeps and looking at the shore anxiously.

'Hell and damnation!'

He said it half under his breath, but Hill turned a questioning face to him. The bombardment had grown more and more ominous during the last two hours. Flat echoes of the cannonade came across the easy blue water of the Grande Rade. Blossoms of grey smoke appeared here and there on the scrubby crags around Fort Aiguillette.

'Cat's really among the pigeons now, sir.'

'Yes, Skrimger, I fear you're absolutely right about that.'

'Whoever's in charge of them Republican artillery pieces sure do know his trade.'

'How long would you give the fort?'

'This afternoon, sir.' Skrimger shrugged morosely and sucked his teeth. 'Maybe.'

Smith glanced over his shoulder at the great black-and-ochre-banded hull of the *Victory*, her masts, spars and mooring cables reflected in the dead calm. There was something vastly reassuring about the sight of the flagship and the other ships-of-the-line that rode serenely at anchor. The thought came into his mind that the loyalist French of Toulon would share that sentiment.

'You think it will fall so soon?'

'Well . . . maybees, sir. And after that the town'll be wide open.'

'Then Vesuvius engulfs Pompeii, eh?'

Skrimger's forehead creased. 'Beg pardon, sir?'

'Just history repeating itself, as it so often does.' He sighed, wanting Skrimger to understand. 'The Roman town of Pompeii was destroyed by a volcano during the first century. Pliny the Younger wrote about how their navy tried to take off the people.'

Skrimger absorbed the information without comment. Despite his obvious capacity he had been convinced at some early stage that learning of that kind was none of his business, and he therefore kept it at a distance.

Smith fell silent. His imagination began to embroider the scene in vivid colours: the final abandonment would be like something out of Pliny's account. Only this time the agent of evil would be human, and not the blind force of nature. A hundred thousand troops were converging on the town, and when they appeared thousands of people would start fighting over one another to reach the departing fleet. It would become a little hell on earth. He knew he must find Berenice before then.

Last night, tossing and turning in fitful sleep, he had remembered another little hell from his past, a nightmare of bad organization and bad planning and worse leadership. He had sweated the night through, visited by demonic dreams of frustration, feeling his limbs bound or powerless, as if he was swimming in molasses. Fragmented memories from his youth had come spinning at him like the shards of a shattered mirror. Each had carried an image from that terrible shameful time when the *Sandwich* had been sent to the Caribbean isle of St Vincent . . .

He had woken with palpitating heart, had sat up in his cot, knowing that to talk the incident through rationally was the only way to unshatter the glass and reshackle the demon. So he had dressed and gone on deck.

'We arrived with ten sail-of-the-line,' he had told Hill. 'There were frigates, marines of the fleet and troops on board the men-of-war. On landing we found the French strongly situated upon a hill within a fort. Our light infantry and grenadiers got halfway up the hill that night, then had a skirmish with a party of Caribs that the French had stirred up against us. I was on shore in the boats, landing the men. I had a hundred well-trained seamen under my command ready to land the next morning. Every other ship was the same. But when morning came, instead of orders to land, we were told to embark the troops with all possible speed.'

Hill had nodded and listened sagely. He was a good listener.

'It came as a thunderbolt. We got all our crews off the island before noon the next day, without molestation, and just sailed away. The Caribs, led by some appalling French lieutenant-governor, went murdering in the most shocking manner. Every Briton – man, woman, and child – died. Their houses were burned down. I was among the last boats that came away. As I left I saw the beach covered with them – people crying, begging, to be taken off. Begging *me*, a sixteen-year-old boy. Some we did take off . . . but many more we could not. And I swore then . . . I swore that if ever . . .'

After a while, Hill said, 'Let's hope it doesn't happen again, sir.'

He had sighed, and said, 'Oh, history always repeats, Mister Hill. Because people don't really change through the centuries. We're so slow to learn, you see. This is going to be worse. Much worse.'

Now, as he looked at the town of Toulon, he felt the cold perspiration on his face. He recalled that he had spoken of that shameful time at St Vincent only twice before. Once in a letter home and once during a dreaming summer in Old France. He remembered telling Berenice all about his hugely responsible adolescence. He had wanted to sound brave and therefore equal to her obvious worship of him. And so he had made small of the pain and frustration, and the idiocy of it all. He had succeeded in making most of his experiences of war sound quite jolly to her. Jolly, because how else should a man make war sound to one with no idea of what it was? A profession such as his was hard to explain. Fighting, using main force, death and maiming and the threat of the same to police the world into a state of comparative peace. You could not force people to be good, but it was at least possible to force them to behave as if they were, and that was an improvement.

But Berenice had been an innocent girl, without any knowledge of how the world really worked. And so he had not loaded her mind with a full account of his trials. That was the day we made love five times, he thought. How they had rolled and pitched on top of that haystack, ruining it for the poor farmer. How vile to think that all France has fallen prey to the darkness, as much as ever St Vincent's Isle did. She's out there in that town somewhere now – unless she never came here, which is entirely possible. It's ridiculous. I should have married her then and there, but I let her father chase me away. Well, then, I'm the greater fool for I did as he told me when I knew that I knew better. A man must always try to do what he thinks is right, and damn the consequences.

He knew the way Hood would arrange things. He cannot take everyone off, but he'll certainly take his pick. They've been coming aboard for days, those who are valuable to the allies. The rich with their families, those with relatives or property abroad, military offi-cers, any number of deal-making politicians . . . but never the hapless poor.

He recalled with a troubled mind an incident that had happened yesterday. It had been an event of no great consequence, but it had stuck in his mind as poignant. He had been going through the town, on his way to check the official refugee registers, and happened to be eating a peach. But it had been a little dinged and so he had thrown it down. At the same time he had passed a beggar huddling in a doorway. He had paid no attention to the young woman, but he had seen how she had snatched up the peach almost as soon as it had touched the ground.

The poor are starving, he thought, knowing for certain now how near the end was for the port. Toulon is about to fall, and may God have mercy on them when it does.

Another troubling thought struck him. Perhaps Berenice is already aboard the fleet . . .

How can I find out?

It's impossible.

So what do I do now?

Hope that she is, and assume that she is not, he told himself, holding to his plan. But perhaps I can lay things more squarely open to chance. Do something she will be sure to see wherever she is in this damned town. I must light a beacon that everyone will see, and realize the time has come to get out if they can. But what?

He took the silver figure from his pocket and kissed it gently. Then he stood up, resolved. 'Come with me, Clarke. And you too, Carrall.'

The two men followed, exchanging mystified glances as Smith got down into his cockboat and told them to row him to the *Victory*.

Victory had weighed yesterday to be towed further out. She had come to with her best bower anchors in twenty-five fathoms of water. Captain Knight met him as he stepped on board. He was still refusing to behave properly, his attitude still of the '*I'm-damned-if-I'll-pipe-the-side-for-a-half-pay-officer*' kind.

Around them the watch was busily employed in all kinds of mending and repairs. He looked aloft and saw hands bending sail and working free the stunsail booms. There was no doubt they were getting the flagship ready for sea. He looked to starboard. Other ships of the fleet were warping out too – *Terrible, Robust, Courageux* . . .

'Sir Sidney?' Knight's expression was that of a stickler who had discovered an irregularity. 'I don't recall His Lordship making to you.'

'No. The admiral sent me no signal.'

'Then perhaps I may enquire why you take it upon yourself to come aboard *Victory* uninvited?'

The loftiness of Knight's manner invited attack, but he restrained his nature. 'I've come to volunteer Admiral Hood a special service. I should therefore be grateful, Captain Knight, if you would have his secretary informed to that effect as soon as possible. It is a matter of some particular urgency.'

'Had I known that, Sir Sidney, I certainly should have sent a boat for you.' It was said with naked sarcasm.

'You're far too kind, sir.' Smith clasped his hands behind his back, stared up at the main-top and assumed the pose of a man preparing for a long wait. Knight was captain of the flagship, but there were prescribed limits to how he must behave towards a fellow captain. He can't order me off, Smith thought. Not without creating an incident. And he knows it.

Knight's attitude hardened. He looked down his long nose. 'His Lordship is presently in discussion.'

'Yes. I thought he might be. I'll wait.' Smith lifted himself on to his toes, then rocked back on his heels, an impudence that infuriated Knight. 'Who's he talking to?'

'He is with Admiral Langara and his staff,' Knight said icily.

'With the Spaniards, hey?'

'Yes.'

Smith recalled Admiral Langara's arrival at the port. His squadron of seventeen ships-of-the-line had arrived on the very day Hood had first dropped anchor in the Grande Rade. Don Juan de Langara would never have consented to Hood's bringing away all the French ships to England, even if the Toulonese had, he thought. And, in any case, where were the men to sail them? Hood has had to employ fifteen hundred Maltese to work his own ships. The emperor of Austria promised him five thousand men from Milan, but of course they never arrived.

'Where's the rear-admiral?'

'Sir Hyde Parker, Sir Gilbert Elliott and General Dundas are all aft—'

'A veritable council of war. I take it they've finally decided to order the withdrawal, then?'

Knight's self-control deserted him. 'I would certainly not presume to guess at the admiral's decisions.'

Smith crooked an index finger and tapped it twice on Knight's lapel, as if knocking on a door. He winked. 'That's why you'll never be one, hey, Knight?'

Knight's fists balled. 'You may wait, if you are pleased to, Sir Sidney.'

'Thank you. I shall.'

Knight disappeared under the break of the quarterdeck, past the wheel where a red-coated marine stood stock still, his stare fixed glassily ahead. Smith turned on his heel, studying the view through the gap in the hammock netting. Toulon was a doomed place. It cowered now under the encircling hills, overlooked and indefensible. It was now closely surrounded by at least sixty thousand Republican troops, and the bombardment would soon give them entry. There would be terror and screaming chaos there tonight as the place fell to a looting army, and the inhabitants were systematically raped and massacred.

Most of the warships he had seen whilst on the Heights with George Elphinstone remained at anchor. By any calculation they represented a huge and lethal naval force. Worse, the French crews were still confined aboard. The word was that they were, to a man, supporters of the Revolution, and on that account they had not been permitted ashore. The situation was poised on the very edge of disaster, and there was probably nothing he could do to ameliorate it.

Smith licked his salt-dried lips thoughtfully. He had learned that to forestall any mutinous action Admiral Trogoff had ordered the ships disarmed, their guns taken off, and all the French powder – above a thousand barrels of it – concentrated aboard the frigates *Iris* and *Montreal*. Both had been captured from the British in the last war, though the larger of the two, the *Iris*, was originally American built. They had become a main objective of Smith's carefully worked out plan.

As the precious minutes ticked by, the flat reports of cannon could be heard quite distinctly. They added to Smith's sense of unease, but there was not long to endure. He had waited a little over half an hour when the council of war broke up. The marine stamped and presented arms as the august retinue issued onto the main deck. They gathered there, a confusion of gold-laced uniform coats of different colours, cocked hats in hands, filling the space abaft the main companionway as they waited for their gigs to come alongside. Some of them eyed the basin anxiously. The enemy were closing in.

Smith steeled himself, and when the admiral appeared

he stepped forward. 'My lord, may I ask you: what do you mean to do with all those fine ships of the enemy?"

Hood ignored him with the kind of pointed disregard that was designed to crush insolent young officers. Smith raised his voice. 'Sir, do you mean to leave them behind?'

The atmosphere on deck solidified. Hood turned to him, and Smith thought he saw the man's amused disdain for what it really was: a cover to conceal anger, itself a reaction to Hood's own deep uncertainty.

He may have been made a Lord of the Admiralty Smith thought, but he's so jealous of his command that he's trying to hold on to everything himself. It's the sign of a man working beyond the limits of his capacity. Well, to hell with him. I'll say what I came to say, and there's an end to it.

'Admiral, I must have your answer.' The remark, and the tone in which it was delivered, went well beyond the bounds of naval discipline. 'Sir, what's to be done with the enemy ships?'

The admiral's attempt at nonchalance failed. Hood faced him, rage trembling in his knotted jaw. He could only grunt and turn away, as if the young man had said something foolish. It took every atom of Smith's persistence to say, 'But, consider, my lord, suppose it *is* possible to destroy their ships.'

Hood took two steps towards him and put his face into Smith's own, growling in a voice the Spaniards were not meant to hear, 'God-damn your conceit, sir. I'll deal with you later.'

He was aware of Langara's eyes on him. He waited until Hood turned away, and used the moment. 'My lord, I am volunteering to *burn* the French fleet.'

'*Burn* it?'

'Yes. Along with the docks and arsenal. While we yet may.'

Hood tried to laugh him to scorn. 'That is an absurdly hazardous undertaking!'

Smith allowed him no escape. 'Then, sir, I am surprised you do not consider me eminently suited to it.'

FOUR

DECEMBER, 1793
Toulon, France

They had survived for six days thanks to the refugee's bread ration and whatever else they had managed to find. Two days ago she had found a hapless chicken that had got out of the byre beneath one of the houses she passed. She had launched herself at it, and caught it without anyone seeing or hearing her.

Wringing its neck had not stopped the bird fluttering, and when its throes had finished, blood had dripped from its beak, leaving a trail after her. Her mother had taken the bird gratefully and started to take off its feathers. They had long ago learned that it was best to pluck a fowl as soon as possible after it was killed; feathers came away more easily from skin that was still warm.

It was late afternoon when they arrived outside the offices of the provisional government, the place where Berenice's mother had listened to a rumour and was insisting they must register their identities. The building was surrounded by an iron railing. Red-coated soldiers with bayonets fixed to their muskets were stationed in the grounds. Outside, a mass of anxious people pressed up against the gates, hundreds of them, with papers in their hands, clamouring to be admitted in the last minutes before the office closed.

'Mother, I told you this was a waste of time.'

'But we must register!'

'We'll never get in! Look at it!'

'We must!'

'Why? To get an ink stamp on a piece of paper to show we're really persons of quality? It doesn't *mean* anything any more!'

'Then, what? Tell me! Oh, Berenice, what have we come to?' Her mother seemed to lose her will to fight on. All around the tall houses of Toulon's most expensive residential faubourg stood silent and grave, their windows hidden by louvred shutters.

'Celestine, take her arm. This way!' Berenice whispered the instructions fiercely. 'We must get there before the others do.'

'Where?' Celestine asked. 'Where are we going?'

'Out of the city.'

'What?'

'We have no choice,' she said, hurrying them. 'This place is going to become a killing ground.'

Her mother looked back at her, aghast, wordless. For a moment all they could hear was the sound of cannon banging hollowly on the distant hillsides. All day it had been gradually getting closer.

'Come along, mother! You must try to help yourself. We will not leave without you, but we must leave.'

Berenice had realized the first day they arrived that her mother had been sustaining herself on the journey south by imagining what a haven Toulon would be. The comtesse had told herself that their condition would be restored immediately they reached a Royalist city, that it would only take a declaration of their noble status to the proper authorities for a secure living to be provided. It had been a useful dream, but a dream all the same.

She really came to believe that *idée fixe*, Berenice thought, which is why the truth of our plight is now so shocking to her. I know that survival means not only being determined and strong and listening to intuition, but also confronting things as they are, however bitter that may be. Otherwise, how can even a clever person decide what's best to do?

They followed the road that led back to the market square, and from there chose one of the streets that led south towards the harbour quarter. A little while ago Berenice had realized the significance of what had been troubling her mind. She had understood at last why the faces of the soldiers had made such an impression on her. All week the assault on Toulon had been intensifying. One by one the ring of hills that backed the port had fallen to the enemy, and though the gathering army outside was made up of raw conscripts they were obviously in overwhelming numbers, and she could not doubt that their ideologue commanders would hurl them relentlessly at the city, not caring how many died.

Soon an effective attack will be made on the defences of the city itself, she thought. Perhaps tonight. The walls will be breached and the Revolutionaries will pour in to devour their enemies without mercy. It will be just as it was at Lyons.

She imagined the panic that must ensue, and shuddered. But the fear drove her on.

'Why are you hurrying us so?' her mother said breathlessly.

'Because Toulon is going to be abandoned by the allies,' she said. They came to a halt in the lengthening shadows. 'It may happen tonight. We have to find a way to escape.'

'But we've been here less than a week!' her mother said hopelessly.

'We must get out before everyone else realizes what is happening. Or it will be like it was back there.'

'How do you know Toulon's going to be abandoned?' Celestine asked.

She had felt her patience dissipate. 'I just know.'

'That's not an answer!'

She threw her hands out from her sides angrily. 'The allies will run because they can no longer fight!'

'That's why they came here, isn't it? To fight. They won't just abandon us.'

'Do you suppose foreigners will fight to the last man to hold a French port?'

'They've been here five months.'

'Celestine, open your eyes! They've been secretly pulling their forces out for days!'

'What do you mean, "secretly"?'

'They don't want to create a panic among the people. Yesterday I watched empty boats coming in, and full ones going out. Early this morning I was in the Faubourg St Antoine, where the governor's family live. There were handcarts piled with valuables outside his house. They were leaving!'

Her words had a jolting effect on Celestine. Suddenly she seemed fear-stunned.

'So we made our journey for nothing?'

Berenice could not keep the cruelly ironic tone from her voice. 'We should be glad! The whores and beggars of Toulon are going to be liberated by the glorious Revolution. We should come out to cheer!'

Celestine clasped her mother's arm harder. Her mother groaned, wrapped up in her private agonies, but she still managed to put one foot in front of the other, and so they hurried on.

This part of the town was quiet. Most of the artisans had completed their labours and returned fearfully to their homes to shut themselves in for the night and to pray.

After a while Berenice stopped, unsure which way to take. Celestine said, 'Maybe we should stay. Even if we could get out of the city, and then managed to avoid the Revolutionaries, we would have to walk for weeks to reach Spain or Piedmont. And then what would happen to us? We would die, Berenice!'

'That's why we must get aboard a British ship.'

Celestine searched her face, looking for a sign that she, at least, believed it possible. The British ships had moved out of range of the shore cannon, they were now anchored far out, in the Grande Rade.

'How?'

'I don't know!'

Soon they came in sight of the sea, and saw the defences of the dockyard. High brick walls sealed the naval supply depot off from the town. It was almost a separate town, a huge site with bakeries and roperies and warehouses and all that was necessary to supply a large navy. The gates were well guarded by sentries. It was impenetrable.

Last night Berenice had dreamed of Smith, but the dream had been horrible. He had come striding past her while she was begging on a street corner. She had recognized him, and had jumped up in joy to put her arms around his neck. But he had not recognized her at all. He had thrown her off, and dusted himself down. Her earnest claims to be the girl he had known as Berenice Sainte Honorine du Fay he had laughed to scorn.

In the west a blood-red sunset had made the Petite Rade into a cauldron of fire on which two lines of great black ships stood. They were the French Mediterranean fleet. And it was rumoured that some of them were moored there with Revolutionary crews still aboard.

'Wait here,' she told her mother and Celestine.

She decided to walk by the dockyard gates, to see what she could learn. But the only thing of significance she saw was a white Royalist flag flying from the staff. The sentry did not even seem to notice her.

She went towards the fish dock, her dismay gathering all the while. People were gathering now in great numbers on the foreshore, but to what end it was impossible to say, for the strands and jetties were empty of boats. All vessels, of whatever size, had been requisitioned by the military.

A little way along she saw a walled, guarded place where soldiers were drilling prior to embarkation. Some civilians had been admitted through a gateway and were being marshalled into line to await a lone boat that was labouring toward shore. People were milling about beyond the wall, their expressions vigilant, anxious, but uniformly sick with hopelessness.

As she approached she saw a small mob picking over a patch of waste ground. As she got closer she saw heaps of possessions being sorted through by many hands. Nearby was the handcart she had seen that morning in the Faubourg St Antoine, lying on its side.

Mother can barely walk, let alone swim, she thought ludicrously. Her own knees were starting to give way now.

It's already too late, she thought. We're trapped.

FIVE

Smith sat in the stern of one of *Victory*'s boats as they entered the tiger's mouth. They rounded Grosse Tour, and in the dusk light he made out the arsenal, the masthouse, hemp-house and the other key stores that they had come to destroy.

When he had left *Victory* he had grinned at Hill and given a small gesture of triumph. 'At least the Terrorists shall not have ships to export their insane idea to the rest of the world,' he said.

'How did you do it, sir?' Hill had marvelled.

'I simply took the opportunity of urging my request. I asked His Lordship for gun-boats. I told him I'd have less reason to be apprehensive of being set on fire by the enemy's red-hot shot than did larger ships. I said I thought that nevertheless we could keep station so as to awe the town to the last, and cover the troop embarkation.'

'And the burning, sir?'

Smith decided to say nothing of the part the Spanish admiral had played in forcing the decision. Langara had thought only one prospect worse than the French keeping their ships, and that was that the British might take them.

'When I urged the burning upon His Lordship, Mister Hill, I found it had already been resolved in the council,

545

but . . . being everybody's business in general, it had become nobody's in particular. If you see what I mean.'

Hill had blinked with amazement that so renowned a group of worthies could have been prey to so huge an oversight. 'It's hard to credit, is it not, sir? They're all such eminent men.'

Smith had chuckled. 'Oh, you'll learn about eminent men, Mister Hill. In time, you'll discover that all your idols have feet of clay.'

Now Smith watched the shore grim-faced. He had failed, and the knowledge of that had brought a bitterness to his soul that he found hard to bear. For a few brief weeks he had maintained hopes, but now there could be none, and he felt empty once more. Despite all his efforts he had not located Berenice. Now he knew that he would go ashore just one more time, and that would be to fulfil a mission not of mercy, but of destruction.

He consulted his watch, his attention absorbed in the evolving details of his plan. He knew that the operation depended on many things, not least of them the protection afforded by Fort La Malgue. It had been built to command the neck of the peninsula that enclosed the Petite Rade, or inner roadstead. Its cannon were worked by Major Koehler, and two hundred men, whose task it was to see the last man off the shore, and spike all guns.

Toulon's defences had been breached. The town had been entered and the fight was even now raging through the streets. Captains Elphinstone, Hallowell and Matthews were to superintend the embarkation of the last remaining troops, and Smith felt the doubts and fears that every man feels when approaching a situation so dangerous that everyone else is trying to escape it.

In the waist of the boat forty seamen strained at the oars under the coxswain's growling encouragement, making it surge. He could smell the seamen's bodies and the odours stirred from the calm waters by their sweeps, and he caught the tang of powder smoke from the bombardment of the town. It was a piquant smell, one he had tasted many times. It made him tense, and the associations it awakened sent a dagger of excitement through his guts.

Three tartans – small, single-masted gun-boats – and three Spaniards, one of them a mortar boat, were all that Lord Hood and Admiral Langara had spared him to carry out his plan. It was understandable; the task of embarkation was huge, and every vessel was required, but the efforts of Tupper and Gore had succeeded in adding two other vessels to his force. He looked over his shoulder and saw anchored, outside the harbour and away from the batteries, the *Vulcan*, in company with the sloop *Alert*, the five-gun boat *Wasp*, and three other small gun-boats that had been taken from the French.

As soon as they passed Fort l'Eguillette and entered the Petite Rade, he signalled Don Pedro Cotiella, officer commanding the Spanish contingent. Cotiella acknowledged his order and took two of his boats towards the anchored French hulls. They sheered off to starboard, their sweeps propelling them across the still waters toward the majestic ships of France's Mediterranean fleet.

He looked away from the invaded town, keeping the compartments of his mind separate, refusing to think the thoughts that had come to him so often in the darkest hours.

All around him the Petite Rade was crammed with huge ships-of-the-line. Some rode at anchor, while the bowsprits of others nosed the quay of the Darse as they jostled together like suckling piglets. He counted a dozen more, and perhaps an equal number of frigates and corvettes.

They were fine ships, very well constructed, with raked masts, and showing superb proportions. Good sailers and good fighters, he thought. They were more heavily armed than British 74s, too, and they carried far bigger crews.

He looked about and identified them again, one by one in the failing light: there was the 80-gun *Tonnant*, a dozen or more 74s: the *Heureux*, the *Centaure* . . . over there the *Commerce de Bordeaux* . . . and lying together close in, the *Hero* and the *Themistocle*.

The vast shapes loomed larger and larger as the little gun-boats pulled shoreward. The oars were lifted as the boats came alongside the quay. Nearby two ominous-looking slave galleys rode, unmanned. He directed his men to follow him ashore, and they swarmed on to the mole, along with the Spaniards under Lieutenant Don Francisco Riguielme.

It was essential to find out what was happening in the immediate vicinity before attempting to seize the dock-yard. He detached three scouting parties and sent them off in three different directions, setting the rest of the men to unload the combustibles.

The first obstacle they found was the dockyard gate. It was secured, and Smith saw the tricolour flying in place of the white Royalist cockade over the port governor's residence.

Hell, he thought, that means the yard commander's gone over. I hope he spiked the guns before he did so, or we'll never get out of here alive.

'Shall I prepare to blow the gate, sir?' John Wilson asked.

'No. We don't want to be occupied in exchanging shots with a few turncoats, Wilson. That's not why we came here. We'll try the back way.'

It's not safe, he thought. Our force is too small. Any contest that breaks out will pin us down, and the whole plan will fall apart.

'Sir!'

He turned to see Midshipman Matson of the *Britan-nia*. He had been ordered to take a party of men to reconnoitre the quay in the other direction, and was breathless.

'Sir, round that building – there's five or six hundred men on the dock.'

As they reached the corner he saw they were galley-slaves, French convicts condemned to long terms of servitude in place of prison. Someone had decided to unchain them, doubtless the same dockyard governor who had ordered the tricolour hoisted.

The rumour of immediate pardons for all those imprisoned under the Bourbon regime had been spread by Republican pamphlets in Toulon, Smith knew. The sweet promise of freedom will be warring in their breasts with the fear of dying before they may enjoy it, he thought. He read their intent instantly, and saw they were desperate and therefore dangerous. But they were also unarmed, and so he stayed his men, who were preparing to receive them with musket fire.

'Mister Valliant, take thirty men and confine those people back aboard their galleys. They must be kept out of harm's way, where they cannot interfere with our preparations. Have Skrimger direct the *Swallow*'s guns, and also those of Number Two gun-boat on them. Tell Skrimger he must direct his guns in such a manner as to enfilade the part of the quay they would have to cross in order to come at us. How's your French, lad?'

'My mother's French, sir.'

'Good man. In that case assure them that no harm shall happen to them if they remain quiet.'

The midshipman swallowed hard. A part of him was clearly appalled at the task he had been given, and the weight of responsibility that had suddenly been loaded onto his shoulders. But he did as he was told with commendable willingness.

As Smith finished speaking part of the top of the dockyard wall thirty feet away exploded into brick fragments. An iron ball had hit it. As one, every man on the quay ducked. Two seconds later another shot from the same battery smashed into the ropery roof, throwing pantiles into the yard below. A third, too long by twenty yards, ploughed into the water.

Ensign Ironmonger said, 'It's coming from Malbousquet, sir!'

It was a fortified redoubt half a mile to the west of them.

'I can see that. They've got command of the Heights and can drop shot on us almost at will.' He quickly surveyed the scene, and raised his voice. 'Their gunners have seen us and worked out what we're about. They're good, so spread out and keep your eyes open. It'll be dark soon, and that'll scupper them.'

'Yessir!'

And the galley-slaves, too, he thought, seeing the way the incoming shot had cowed them into accepting Midshipman Valliant's orders. They're repairing aboard like men who know where their best chance lies. With a bit of luck those in the town that are keen to show Republican zeal will be kept in their houses, too. The last thing we need is a mob disputing the foreshore.

He ordered gun-boat Number One to fire her four-pounder, and blast open the doors of the three store-houses that fronted the quay, and then they were in. He detailed three parties of men, two English and one Spanish, to the work of preparing and placing inflammable materials where they would do most damage, packing kegs where explosive force was most needed, and laying powder trains into them.

'Remember, not a faggot nor any train is to be lit until I give the command,' he warned them again.

At the final planning he had called Captain Hare of the *Vulcan* and Captain Edge of the *Alert* to join Adjutant Cotiella and Ralph Miller of the *Windsor Castle*. Each of them he had chosen to command a separate part of the enterprise. Hare, because he had volunteered, following a dramatic change of heart, had brought with him Lieutenants Matthew Wrench and Thomas Richmond, his master, Mr Andrews, and two midshipmen, Jones and Mather.

'It's not a job to be done piecemeal, or after the fashion of a mob,' he had told them. 'It must be thoroughly prepared, and then – and *only* then – put into orderly execution. Timing is the key, gentlemen.'

He had explained to them the chaos of doing otherwise: parties of men might easily be cut off, others prevented from reaching the places they were detailed to destroy, still others would be driven from their work by heat or smoke. And the urgency given to the enemy, he had reminded them, was another consideration to be borne in mind. The first flames would drive the Revolutionaries to attempt to save what they could of the dockyards. Fire would outline the work parties against the flames, making illuminated targets of their men. It was all easily predictable, and his logic had carried them, nodding at his words and openly grateful that he had taken the care to make a detailed explanation of his plan.

'Yes,' he had told them. 'That's why the firing will have to be simultaneous, begun only after all preparations have been concluded, and our people got out.'

The men, Spanish and English alike, worked on around him, relentlessly, methodically. A thrill of pride went through him as he recognized the steadiness of the brave seamen who had been put under his command. It gave him courage as he lent a hand in the moving of barrels of tar and paint and kegs of powder from the boats, to know the kind of people he was among. An indescribable feeling came over him. The commonality of a mutual purpose, hundreds of men labouring together in a dangerous situation, created a fellowship that was almost palpable. It was a bonding of spirit that a man rarely felt in ordinary life, but which was hugely manifest in this work.

Carpenter's mate Thomas Clarke came up. 'Them slaves on the galleys've filched hammers from somewheres, sir. They're freeing theirsels as fast as what we can chain them up. Most of the fetters'll have already gone over the side.'

He went to see for himself. When he heard hammers knocking on board the galleys his humanity welled up fiercely. He imagined the feelings of the convicts chained there, men not knowing what was to happen to them, but with eyes to see and minds to imagine. They want the liberty to save themselves when the conflagration begins around them, he thought. They don't even trust us not to burn them alive. What a state humanity has sunk to in this damned nation!

'Leave them be.'

'But what happens when we set light to the powder trains?' Clarke protested. 'What if they come swarming ashore—'

'Just tell Midshipman Valliant to keep them covered, Clarke.'

'Aye, sir.'

'Jeysas, would ye look at that, sor!'

He followed master's mate Lenahan's gaze.

Hundreds of Republican troops were cascading down the rocky slopes of Missiessi towards the dockyard as the night closed in. They came close enough to pour an irregular, harassing fire on to the work parties from the vicinity of the boulangerie and the hillside that overlooked its chimneys.

Smith ordered Lieutenant Riguielme to have the Spanish gun-boat brought wide so her two pieces could rake the wall on the outside and the watercourse and stone bridge across which an assault would have to come.

The situation gave Smith pause. The boats' guns

would have to keep the enemy at bay for up to two hours with occasional discharges of grape if a determined advance in the dockyard was to be halted.

'Can you do it?' he asked Riguielme in French after explaining the requirement to him.

'*Bien sur*!' Certainly!

'*Très bien.*' Very good.

The preparations continued as harassing fire rained in on them. Shouts and tumults came from the galley-slaves from time to time, and he knew that the balance of hope and fear must be carefully kept to prevent them rising on his people. I hope Midshipman Valliant is able to live up to his name, he thought, looking at the galleys with disquiet. He wiped the sweat from his forehead, then flipped over his watch again. Eight o'clock. He ran back to the quay, and peered into the gloom. Almost immediately he saw the white strakes of Lieutenant Gore's boat, towing in the fireship across the tideless Petite Rade. She was an old hulk, a ship not worth the dismantling. She had been packed with combustibles and would be fired at the critical moment to go up in a blaze of glory.

Good man! Smith's right fist clenched, and he allowed himself a brief smile.

Everything was proceeding according to his plan. He watched for a few minutes as Hare, the fireship's commander, began to manoeuvre his deadly craft athwart a tier of French men-of-war tied up at the Vieille Darse. As he turned his attention back to the storehouses he noted that the appearance of the fireship had caused the murmurings and cat-calling from the galleys to die away again, and his worries on that score began to subside, to be replaced by another worry.

'Where's Lieutenant Pater?' he asked, looking at his watch again. 'There's not long left.'

'Not back yet,' someone said.

'Aboard *Britannia* he's known to be particularly thorough, sir.'

The remark made Smith grin.

The parties came in one by one to the quayside to report their work complete. Lieutenant Middleton, whose responsibility was the mast-house; Lieutenant Tupper, who had been charged with burning the general magazine, the pitch, tar, tallow, and oil storehouses; and Lieutenant Hill, who was to fire the ropery and hemp magazine . . .

'Hell, where *is* Pater?'

They all knew that a signal would go off at nine o'clock and, on seeing it, those deputed to inflame the trains were to set steel to flint – no matter what. As he waited anxiously he took the still air, silently damning Zephyrus, the god of the West Wind, for his lethargy. The usual dawn and dusk breezes of the Mediterranean coasts had not materialized today.

'A near calm, sir,' quartermaster Thomas Knight said, almost reading his mind.

'And, as such, unfavourable to the spreading of flames, Knight.'

'Aye, sir. Sorry, sir.' Knight braced himself and made a face. 'Ne'er mind, sir. I 'spect the two hundred and fifty barrels of tar what we put among the timbers'll spread 'em well enough.'

Five minutes before the critical moment Smith turned to Midshipman Matson. 'Tell Lieutenant Riguielme to withdraw his men. Ensign Ironmonger of the Royals will continue to give covering fire at the gate.'

'Aye, sir.'

He surveyed the harbour, and saw that Captain Edge had stood the sloop *Alert* close in, ready to take off the detached parties.

He saw a trail of sparks rocket up from the gun-boat *Wasp* and arc across the heavens. A distant but loud boom sounded just after he saw the signal maroon explode. The ships of the Petite Rade were illuminated for a moment in the sudden meteor of white light. That was it. He gave the general order to commence the burning.

'Signal from *Alert*, sir: All His Majesty's ships, with those of Spain and the Two Sicilies are out of reach of the enemy's shot, except the *Robust*, which is to receive Captain Elphinstone and his men.'

Elphinstone had acted as governor of the fort of La Malgue, a strongly fortified position of a hundred and forty-eight cannon that covered the Grande Rade and protected the harbour from attack from the south and west. If the *Robust* was standing in to take Elphinstone's men off, it was time his own people pulled out.

'Very good, Matson.' He disregarded the midshipman. 'Hell! Come *on*, Pater. Where in God's name are you?'

He peered back into the gloom, scanning the storehouses, tight-lipped, annoyed that his perfect operation had been marred.

They're officers, he thought, men of duty, the best men picked from all those who volunteered. I can't complain if they take their tasks more seriously than their safety. But I'm responsible for them. I'm a man of duty, too, by God!

He collared John Skrimger, a man he knew he could trust absolutely, and said with emphasis: 'Tell Captain Edge to have *Victory*'s Number One boat remain at this quay until half-past. Then, if no one shows, he's to leave. Half-past, no later. Is that understood?'

'Aye, sir.'

Tinder was being kindled, and dips lit. The incendiaries took their lights and ran to their stations, to ignite light-fizzing powder trains. Magically the entire dockyard began to seethe with trails of light.

The harassing musket fire coming sporadically from

darkness on the far side of the dock wall intensified suddenly like a summer shower of hail.

'Step lively, there!' he shouted, seeing his men aboard.

He hesitated, then headed back into the now deserted dockyard as the last groups of men began to head rapidly toward the boats.

The storehouses were lethal bombs now. He stepped over a powder trail and bolted through the shed to the inner doorway. The dockyard road opened out to him, and he saw a gaping hole in the perimeter wall where a ball had hit. Bricks were scattered across the road.

The first of the explosions shook the dockyard, sending a plume of fire and smoke up into the night, throwing his garishly outlined shadow across the cobbles.

John Wilson, the advanced sentry, was falling back. He grabbed Smith, tried to block him from going on.

'They're coming, sir! A whole host of townsfolk, trying to get down to the water's edge. They're desperate that we shall save them! I heard Jacobin songs, and all!'

'Where's Lieutenant Pater?'

Another powder explosion drowned Wilson's answer. His face was a gaunt, imperative mask.

'I said I ain't seen him, sir – No, sir! You can't go thataway! Sir! . . .'

Wilson's voice died in Smith's wake. He made for the sail lofts and, as he turned the corner, he ran slap into a high, chained gate. Fifty yards behind it he saw Pater braving the flames, dancing along with a firebrand like a maniac to complete the work where the fire had caught imperfectly.

He called him off, but it was useless. A series of explosions concussed the air, and the whoosh of a tarpaper shack catching into a fireball meant his shouts could not carry. Several of the warehouses were burning fiercely, packed as they were with combustibles. Still, it was amazing how quickly they had become engulfed in flame, and how high the flames towered after so few minutes. The radiant heat Smith felt on his face as he watched drove him back. Burning debris was raining down all around. Then a hail of pantiles that had been blown off the ropery roof made him protect his head and flatten himself against a wall. It was hot to the touch.

Smith allowed himself an ironic smile. His plan had worked to perfection: the entire dockyard had become a blazing hell. He attempted to find his way back, but turned away when the heat on his back grew intolerable. He saw the singe marks on the arms of his coat and, seeing a horse trough, he ran towards it, meaning to douse himself from head to foot. The water was cold. It soothed and stung the burns on his face and neck, and helped him to focus his mind again.

He knew it was impossible now to go back the way he had come, even if he could have scaled the wall again. He was lost and almost certainly cut off, caught in the same trap about which he had so insistently warned his men.

Another explosion sent him up a dark alley. It led to another, and then another, before opening out on part of the perimeter wall. He skidded to a halt at the top of a stone stair, dripping water, breathing heavily, and saw the floor of the narrow alley ahead. He heard a chilling, high-pitched sound he could not identify. It reminded him of starlings flocking at dusk, but infinitely more menacing. He peered into the gloom and saw the alley floor seething in a ghastly way. There seemed to be black water flooding from the mouth of a drain, but the shrill noise made his flesh crawl and he shaded his eyes from the glare, staring hard to see what it was that blocked his escape. It looked as if the cobblestones had sprung to life: the entire alley was filled by huge black rats, thousands upon thousands of them, deserting their holes in the foundations of the dock.

Smith recoiled. He had always nursed an unadmitted disgust for rats; the thought of them living among the stores aboard *Alcmene* had led him to fumigate the lower decks with sulphur more often than the navy considered strictly necessary.

Now, seeing no other way, he hitched up his sword scabbard and leapt over the nearest wall, not knowing what was on the other side. There was a breathtaking drop, twelve or fifteen feet of free fall. He landed soggily on a grit incline, then slithered off it a further ten feet on to hard flagstones. He landed awkwardly, waited for the pain to pass from the soles of his feet and his jarred ankles, then crossed the street, looking this way and that. His plans had come to full fruit now. The whole sky was lurid with flame. The scorching roofs trailed incredible plumes of white smoke from their eaves, swirls of red sparks, tongues of fire that carried upwards in spiralling draughts. Every aperture in the dockyard buildings blazed light and heat, a golden inferno inside.

His heart hammered. His wet clothing chafed against his skin. His coat hung heavy from his shoulders, but he dared not discard the protection it afforded him. The roaring and cracking was awesome, hellish. Then he heard shouts and screams that made him look toward the town. He saw a hundred terrified people – women, children and old folk. They were the poor, those not numbered among the five thousand souls already taken aboard the fleet.

This crowd was stampeding back up towards the Old Town. That could mean only one thing: they were trapped. Earlier they had been fleeing blindly down to the quays and foreshores, just as the rats had fled. Now they were heading back the way they had come. He looked around him, his jaw clenched. The enemy must have got into the district of Ste Anne by now, he thought, remembering what Wilson had told him about hearing Jacobin chanting.

These people are seeking refuge in numbers, he

realized, but in doing so they're gathering into a mob that will only invite violence from invading troops.

According to the usages of war, a town besieged and then overrun would be turned over to the victorious troops for as long as it took to sate their passions. There would be looting and there would be rape. He ran towards them, shouting his warning.

'Stop! Not that way! Disperse, and go back to your homes. Go to your cellars. Hide yourselves.'

Those who saw his gold-laced coat scattered; the rest continued blindly on. He made a lunge for one woman, but she dodged, and when he caught the arm of another she squealed like a pig on a slaughterhouse floor, and he was compelled to let her go.

He came breathlessly to a set of high railings that barred access to a parallel street. The gate had been chained and locked. The bars were topped with fanciful Roman spearheads that rendered them unclimbable. But he jumped up onto the stone coping.

'For God's sake, listen to me! Listen to me, go to your homes, or you're going to die!'

He shouted his rage above the hubbub of the crowd. It was rage born of the impossibility of helping them, but they would not let him save their lives. The insane irony of it struck him suddenly as very funny, but then the humour fast turned sick, and he realized regretfully that the moment had come to think again of his own survival.

It should be possible to reach the shipbuilding slips that flanked the Vieille Darse, and from there to hail one of the gun-boats that would still be plying the inner harbour carrying out his plan of sabotage.

At that moment he leapt down from the stonework and happened to catch sight of two young women. They were in the street on the far side of the railings, hurrying an older woman between them. He looked away, but then instantly back again, because one of them had turned her head momentarily to look behind her.

Smith recognized what was – to him – an unmistakable profile.

That's her! his mind shouted, certain beyond all doubt. The toss of her head, that flash of the eyes as she turns away, the way she wipes the sweat from her face. My God! She's been here all along, he told his guiding spirit. I knew it! I told you, didn't I? I never lost faith that I would see her again.

It was as if the world and everything in it had stilled to silence. The chaos raging around him had become irrelevant. Only one thing mattered now.

He grabbed the bars with both fists.

'Berenice! Berenice!'

His hands reached through the railings.

'Berenice! Berenice, wait for me!'

He shouted so that the cords stood out on his neck, but she did not hear him. He screamed her name again as she passed from view, then he looked up and down the road for a way through. There was none. There was absolutely no way for him to get to her, or even make her hear him. An incredible frustration burned like a fuse inside him. Hundreds of people were hurrying past. Many carried babes in arms, or trailed children after them. Others clutched pathetic bundles of possessions. Smith fought his way back against the tide of bodies.

He saw soldiers – three, no, four of them. He drew his sword. But they were Neapolitans, stragglers whose indiscipline had separated them from their comrades. Perhaps he could send them to search for Berenice! He shouted to them, but they vanished into a side street. He started after them, but then halted. They could not understand him anyway.

He slammed his fists into the iron railings like a madman. Then he looked at his hands as the blood welled from his skinned knuckles. They were bruised and bleeding. For the first time since his boyhood he had broken down into uncontrolled rage. At such a time as this, he thought, a man needs to direct all his energies, not spend them fruitlessly on idle demonstration.

He felt another burst of wild anger but this time he suppressed it severely, and felt triumphant. Now think, damn you! his guiding spirit told him. This is how men die! Use your mind! You've found her at last, and now you've lost her again. But you've proved she's here now, and that's more than you knew before.

'I'll find her,' he said aloud, one frantic thought filling his mind now. 'If I can find her once, I can find her again.'

He struggled to stand against the tide, then, seeing what he must do, turned about, and ascended the slope, making for the market square.

SIX

The market square was packed tight with bodies. Berenice realized too late how acute was the danger. There was not enough time to take stock of the situation before they too were engulfed and were a part of the crush.

They must know that the Republicans will do what they've sworn to do, she thought. They will do here what they've already done at Lyons, where the Rhône rose twenty feet, choked by so many thousands of bodies – and now there is surely no escape for us by sea.

There were thousands of people here now, and more heaving in the bottleneck alleyways that led into the square. Even if Berenice had chosen to go another way, the pressure was now irresistible. People were piling in from behind, closing off all escape. She felt seized by the force of the crowd. Panic was overcoming them all, people following, people ahead, like a flock of stupid sheep, pushing and pushing, until everyone was trapped.

If everyone would just stop pushing no one would be hurt, she thought, angered. All individual sense vanishes when people are thrown together.

'A crowd has a thousand heads but no common sense,' her mother gasped, as if sensing her thoughts. 'People are going to die!'

The darkness was lit by a lurid orange sky glow. As the bodies packed in all around, she held on to her mother's arm, half-supporting her, half-dragging her, leaving Celestine to manage as best she could. Suddenly the mass of people ahead were pressing back, and she saw that a new tide had come swirling into the open space from three roads. Everyone was shoving and fighting, desperate to get away from the soldiers who they supposed to be close behind them.

'Don't get separated!' she shouted. 'And keep your feet, or you'll be trampled!'

'Berenice!'

'Celestine! We're here!'

She tried to turn, but a mass of people pressed in from the road to their right. She braced herself just in time. The pressure became intolerable as they were thrust together. Then she felt her ribs compressed, and the air squeezed from her. The bodies around her were tightly packed.

A man a little way ahead of her lost control and started to thrash, and to try to climb out over the heads of those around him. She felt the struggle communicated through the compacted bodies. She sensed the desperate rage in those close to the panicking man. Then someone gurgled in terror near her, and she saw a woman go down.

It was as if the woman had been dragged down to hell by a demon. A terrible fear came over the woman's face: she knew that she was going to die, and there was nothing anyone could do. Berenice closed her eyes, and when she opened them a moment later the woman was gone.

The towers of flame she had seen rising over the dockyard dappled the buildings with orange light. The mass of people looked like one of the bubbling oceans of hell. Another crush came. This time it was worse than before. Her outstretched arm was trapped and the surge pulled her away from her mother. Berenice felt her own arm bent back. She tried to pull it close to her, but her wrist was held firm, and she knew that if any increase in pressure came now her forearm would be snapped like a stick of firewood.

She wanted to cry out to her mother, but she dared not utter a sound: she knew that if the breath was forced from her she would not be able to draw another. When the crowd heaved again her feet were carried off the ground. She grimaced, holding her breath for dear life.

There were grunts and gasps, and for a few seconds she thought she must suffocate, but then something happened that mercifully changed the direction of the pressure, and she was able to breathe. She stumbled, her feet treading on others' feet, then she was able to use her free elbow to dig the backs of those next to her and make a little space.

Where was her mother? Where was Celestine? The crowd continued to propel her forward. She could not turn her head now, but sensed an old brick wall to her left. She thanked God that at least she was not one of the unfortunates who were being crushed against it. Then the wall gave way, and that sent the surge in another direction. Without warning, she felt her arm come free, and she drew her aching elbow in tight to her chest.

The press had thinned, but all around there was screaming and yelling, incoherent grunts, blasphemies on snatched breath. Bodies lay where they had been trampled. Berenice looked up and saw that she had been pushed almost to the forefront of the crowd.

'Maman!'

Her mother fell into her arms, her face bloody. Then Celestine was disgorged, sobbing. Ahead people were jostling, scattering in terror. There was anguish in their movements and in their voices.

Then she saw the reason. Revolutionary soldiers, no more than fifty paces away!

The street at the head of the square was blocked by a dozen big guns. They were being run forward, the iron-shod wheels of their carriages clattering over the stones as they were manhandled into place. The terrifying muzzles of the weapons were as black as death. Then she saw a mounted officer stand up in his saddle to urge his men. He directed the gun crews to form a precise line.

As soon as she saw him in the rippling, garish light Berenice recognized him, and that recognition sent a thrill of terror through her. He was the rider she had hidden from in the wood, the figure that had invoked in her so powerful a sense of repugnance on the road to St Maximin.

So – it *was* a premonition after all, she thought. Then she felt the dread penetrate to her heart, and she began to tremble. The air around her felt cold, as if the blood was draining from her, and she clasped her mother and sister to her.

'They're sealing off the square!' she heard dimly.

Someone else shouted, 'God save us.'

Berenice stared, fascinated by the pale-faced officer in the uniform of a *chef de bataillon*. He moved like a clockwork automaton, issuing his commands – coolly, crisply, competently, yet he seemed strangely disconnected from the world, and therefore enthralling to those he commanded.

'He's going to fire on us . . .' she said, feeling the certainty of it.

But her rational mind could not fully believe her own whispered words. Is it really possible that anyone would make such an order? she asked herself. To fire grapeshot at point-blank range into a crowd of helpless civilians would be murder in cold blood. It would mean carnage – the bloody slaughter of hundreds of innocents. And there is no reason for it.

She put her hand to her breast, her fingers seeking the looped cross, the *crux ansata*, her lips praying. She saw those well-drilled gunners poised, all eyes on their master like obedient dogs. The officer's arm was raised.

And then, like the blade that had taken her father's head, he let it fall.

As Smith approached the market place he saw the tight-packed crowd that blocked his way. He realized that to go further would be insanely dangerous. He could try to push his way in, but he knew he would not get far. There was the danger of being jammed in as others joined the press from behind. But she's among them, he thought in agony. She must be! I'll have to go in. I'll have to. There's no other way!

He drew his sword once again from its scabbard, and jumped up onto the lip of a stone horse trough to let him see over the heads of the crowd, but what met his eyes filled him with dismay: an ocean of heads stretched for a hundred yards, a mass seething in the half-light, filling most of the square. It would be impossible to find her here.

As he surveyed the scene he saw why the crowd was locked immovably. The people here at the back, unable to see what was happening, were trying to push their way into the square, while those already in it were trying to force their way out again. Then he saw a line of field-pieces drawn up on the far side of the square.

What imbecile has done this? he thought. It's one thing to intimidate a mob by a show of force, but this is idiotic.

'The fool! Can't he see he's killing people? God damn him to hell! He'll kill her!'

He jumped down and fought his way towards the entrance of one of the looted buildings that overlooked the square. The door hung smashed and awry on its hinges. He kicked it down and leapt over it. Hope grew that he might find a back way through to one of the other streets, but then he found there was no way but to mount up a stair.

'I must find her! I must!'

He took the treads three at a time, and found himself in what must once have been the offices of a flourishing mercantile enterprise. Now the room was a shambles. Papers and overturned furniture were scattered over the floor. Everything was lit by the dancing orange light that came through three windows overlooking the square. He ran to the middle window and tried to open it. Maybe from here I'll be able to pick her out, he thought, please let it be so—

His eyes hardly had time to take in the scene before the blast brought in all the windows and threw him across the room, leaving him peppered with spicules of glass. For a moment he could not decide which way was up. He stared at a gaping hole in the wall. The large piece of scrap iron that had taken out the left-hand window and flown past his head had buried itself there. Then he shook his head and jumped up, his heart pumping thunderously, took three drunken strides to the sills and looked down.

The effect of the cannonade was devastation. He stared at it in horror as the acrid smoke thinned over a scene of appalling carnage. The square was littered with bodies.

'Berenice!'

Fear overwhelmed him, then a blinding, blood-red anger rose up inside, as he saw through the clearing smoke the swaggering officer who had made the order. Here was man devoid of all honour and humanity, now calmly ordering his guns to reload to keep the survivors of the massacre cowed.

Smith climbed up over the shattered sill and prepared to leap down.

Berenice threw herself at her mother as the guns whooshed and exploded into deafening thunder. A moment after she slammed down into the cobblestones she felt a crushing weight fall on top of her, then an unbelievable series of shocks. Gun after gun jerked back along the line, as the rolling volley blasted fire and smoke into the terrified crowd. In the confined space the concussion folded back on itself, sound that was louder than anything she had ever experienced, sound that possessed the mind-numbing force of a hammer. It seemed as if a giant's hand had come down from the sky and knocked everyone over as if they were skittles. Shot ripped through human flesh, severed limbs and tore open heads and bodies.

The weight pressed down, preventing Berenice from moving, and when she opened her eyes she saw a trickle of blood moving near her face, dark liquid following precisely a groove between the cobblestones. She watched it stupidly as it turned a right-angle and crawled on, and she thought of the chicken whose neck she had wrung yesterday and the way its body had twitched for a while after death.

She remained held down. Her head was ringing and the air stank: acrid powder smoke, and the shit-stench of torn guts. People were coughing. Here and there among them were pieces of smouldering wadding. Smoke blurred the sky with a pulsing orange haze. Her ears seemed to be plugged up, because beyond the ringing there was a dead silence.

Nothing made sense. What had happened to her? She looked around her, saw a pretty hand lying alone. As she watched it a finger curled, as if beckoning to her. Her mind was too confused to understand it. But as the wisps of smoke coiled in the air above her, she made a tremendous effort and pushed the weight off her back, lifting herself up, sure only that some great crime had been committed.

In the quiet she heard an irresistible voice shout the order 'Reload!', heard the sound of guns being sponged, men busy about the big black barrels. She saw a plume of smoke spurt from a touch-hole and turn into a perfect smoke ring.

The monstrous officer dismounted and climbed onto the plinth of a stone fountain. Black boots, waist sash, gold-laced coat, black in the orange glare, tall collar, shoulder-long hair, dark and lank – and that skull-white face. He surveyed the scene with satisfaction.

He must be Death, she thought, a pang of fear working its way through her confusion. For surely only a thing inhuman could look down with such dispassion upon so grotesque a mass of shattered flesh, knowing that he has caused it to be.

It seemed to her absurd that she should notice, but as he stepped onto the fountain she saw that he moved his leg awkwardly. He was injured. Perhaps that was why the detail was so striking to her – because it showed he was made of human flesh after all. But when he adopted his arrogant pose and braced his shoulders as if to deliver an oration, she heard an unforgettable voice echoing in the silent square.

'*People of Toulon! The vengeance of the Republic is satisfied! Rise up, and go to your homes!*'

Permission had been granted. It was a pardon, a promise, and it broke the spell of disbelief. Groans and screams started to come from the tangle of dead and living flesh that carpeted the square. She saw men and women rising up from among the dead, struggling together, dazed. She recognized her mother's skirts. She was stirring, getting to her feet. They had both been down on the ground when the firing had commenced, shielded by the man whose body had been thrown on top of them.

Berenice stared around, looking for her sister.

'Celestine!'

She screamed the name again, louder this time, then again, her panic mounting, because she felt the certainty again, and knew they were in terrible jeopardy. When she turned there was her sister, twenty paces away, holding out her arms abjectly.

But Berenice's eyes were on her sister's face. It was ghostly pale, her expression that of a wailing child who was unable to draw breath for the next howl. Berenice wanted to comfort her, but there was no dealing with the cause of her horror, for there was now only a bloodied stump where her sister's hand should be.

Berenice saw her mother try to get up, but she dragged her to the ground. 'Get down! Can't you see the evil in him? His mercy is false! He's going to fire again!'

And then, as if in answer, the cannons erupted a second time, obliterating everything.

Smith let himself drop from the ledge, fell a fathom, and landed hard, rolling over on to his side. He heard the sinister voice echo out in the silence, telling the people to rise and go to their homes, that revenge had now sated the bloody appetite of the Republic. And at the command he saw the living begin to rise from the dead. In ones and twos at first, then in swelling numbers, until it seemed to him that everyone who was neither weeping over the dead nor attending the dying had begun to melt away.

He searched like a madman, calling her name, desperate to find her, yet now fearing to find her also. Obscene heaps covered the ground in the centre of the square. He went from one to another, turning bodies, checking faces. Then he heard a shout of defiance, a bellow of rage from a man who stood among the dead.

The Revolutionary officer raised his arm again.

Smith called out, unable to stop himself. 'Berenice!'

But then the cannon vomited flame again, and the lone, defiant figure standing among the corpses of his family was scythed down by a second destroying wave.

Smith felt the blast hit him. He was spun and knocked back by something passing into his shoulder. No pain came as he lay on the ground, stunned. He stared up at the great plume of smoke, its underside lit red from the fire, and to his eye it appeared to stand over the port like a gigantic mocking devil.

He clasped the ragged tear in his coat. Blood welled through his fingers, but the pain in his mind had already overwhelmed everything else.

When he looked up she was staring directly at him.

'Berenice?' he said, the world falling away. He could see nothing but her face, her astonished expression.

She was pale and thin, her cheek bloodied, but there was no doubting those eyes were the same that had looked lovingly upon him so long ago.

They were full of mad torment now. He saw her recoil from him, as if she thought he was a vision sent to deceive her. He grabbed her, but she screamed and tried to fight him off.

'Berenice!'

He seized her and held her. Still she beat at him, screaming unstoppably now, but he knew he must not let her go. Instead he squeezed her tightly and hugged her to him.

'It's all right, Berenice. It's me. It's all right.'

Still she struggled. But the harder she struggled the more he held her to him, until the fight subsided and the sobs came, and he knew that at last she believed.

Smith relied on his instincts to take them toward the waterfront. He carried Celestine in his arms, her gruesome injury bound up tightly with linen torn from his shirt. On the way to the foreshore they were driven to take shelter by a tremendous explosion that lit up the whole sky. It shattered all the remaining windows of Toulon and brought roof tiles raining down all around them. Smith wondered fleetingly at the dreadful force of it.

'What was that?' Berenice asked. When he took off

her filthy bonnet, he saw that her hair was cut short like a boy's. She seemed to be a creature in a trance; her big eyes never moved from him once.

'It came from beyond the dockyard,' he said, unaware of what he was saying or doing. He stared back at her, drinking her in. 'It must have been a part of the arsenal that had escaped the fire until now.'

'Oh.'

He stirred, came somewhat to himself. 'Come. We must —'

'— get on?'

A moment from the past flashed in his mind. 'Yes.'

He negotiated the maze of locked and shuttered dwellings, taking them down deserted, debris-strewn streets. His searches for her had made him familiar with this district, and he brought them down to the shipyard slips, and from there to a spit on the far side of the Vieille Darse.

As he had expected British gun-boats were still plying the Petite Rade. A red glare was reflected in the waters of the harbour, so that they seemed to go upon a sea of blood. When a boat came by close-in Smith ahoyed his identity and waved his intention that it should come for him. It made no acknowledgement, but after being hailed a second time the prow started to come round, and he watched with relief as a figure in the sternsheets raise a cocked hat in salute.

He looked up at the officer. The other's high shirt collar and black neckcloth gave him a magnificently upright aspect. 'Lieutenant Miller, *Windsor Castle*,' the officer drawled. 'We rather thought you must be dead, sir.'

'What did you say?'

'Dead, sir. We supposed you to have perished.'

'Oh, yes . . . perished . . . very good. I would be greatly obliged if you would put myself and these remarkable ladies aboard *Victory* without delay.'

Miller looked at the trio of beggar women and became suddenly solicitous of Smith's sanity. 'I say, Sir Sidney, you don't seem wholly yourself. Are you quite *well*?'

Smith stared back blankly. 'Am I quite well, Mister Miller? I cannot answer you that, for I have never felt like this before.'

SEVEN

To Berenice's eyes the British flagship was a place of bewildering activity. Warnings and orders were being shouted all around.

'Make way there!'

Smith carried Celestine aft to the companionway that led to *Victory*'s middle gun deck. As Berenice followed she felt the foreignness of everything. She saw men in black hats and short blue jackets directing gangs of half-naked sailors to run about the deck, or pull on ropes, or carry buckets, or scramble like monkeys up the rigging. There were soldiers in red coats and boys in white breeches and waistcoats, all busy with some errand or another . . .

Her senses had been overwhelmed, her emotions thrown into chaos. But Smith was taking charge, carrying her sister below to have her wound urgently sutured and dressed. He rattled down the steps, and she followed, passing into an overcrowded, dimly lit world, dominated by the powerful smells of cooking, the sound of young children crying, and the booming noises of heavy work being carried on above their heads. They passed rapidly along a crowded tier of cannon and mess-tables, past hundreds of seamen and marines and soldiers. Wet hempen cables as thick as a man's arm were flaked out on the deck and, nearby, groups of French civilians, equally bedraggled, stared back at them, many with vain hopes in their faces to recognize missing relatives.

Smith refused to let Celestine be taken down to the surgeon's cockpit, and the operation was performed in the purser's cabin. Berenice waited outside until Smith emerged.

'The surgeon has given her laudanum. He says that, God willing, the wound will heal neatly.'

He put his arms around her, hugged her tightly to him, and she clung to him, wanting only to stay in the safety of his embrace, and allow herself to surrender the terrors and responsibilities of the nightmare she had endured. As she felt the warmth of his body huge sobs racked her, and the tears rolled down her cheeks.

He wiped them away, and she saw the tears in his own eyes, and gloried in the joy she knew he was feeling in that intense and private moment.

'This was always meant to be,' he said. 'You know that, don't you?'

'I never doubted. Never.'

But then he looked into her eyes and said with infinite regret, 'Our love has waited so long, Berenice. But I fear it must wait a little longer.'

It was what she had feared. 'No . . . please.'

'I have no choice. I made a bargain with the power that has brought us back together. My promise is to try to my utmost strength to rob the Devil of the means to do evil. That is why I must leave you, Berenice. For I am a sailor and there is one more duty I must perform this night. I must keep my word.'

When Smith turned away from her it was the most difficult thing he had ever done. But he knew that with a captain's rights there came a captain's duties, and so he must learn how his operation had fared. He mastered himself and forced himself to do what was expected. He went on deck to find Hill.

'How has the night gone?'

'Quite well, sir.'

'Only quite well? What was that unusual loud bang I heard?'

Hill inclined his head. 'Ah, most probably the powder ship, *Isis*. She had above a thousand barrels aboard. So it is no surprise that seven hundred and fifty tons of ship were distributed over the entire inner harbour.'

'What happened?'

'One can only suppose she was set afire by the Spaniards, sir.'

Smith felt a jab of annoyance. 'I ordered Lieutenant Riguielme to sink her, not fire her.'

'Well, I'm afraid, sir, Lieutenant Wriggle-Me appears to have disobeyed you.'

Smith turned, concerned, irritated that Hill was not telling him everything. 'Was there loss of life? I should very much like to know what's been happening in my absence, Mister Hill.'

Hill clung to his stiff vapidity in an effort to conceal his emotions. 'The *Union* was the nearest gun-boat to *Isis* when she went up. I regret to say that Mister Young was killed, with three of his men. His vessel was shaken to pieces. Lieutenant Pater of the *Terrible* also lost his boat, however he and his men have all been picked up alive . . .'

Hill's brief report told him that preparations for the burning of the other French ships had gone on apace, courtesy of Lieutenant Priest of the *Wasp*, Lieutenant Morgan of the *Petite Victoire* and Lieutenant Cox of the *Jean Bart*. They had followed his orders to the letter, it seemed, especially the part about using their initiative.

He thought again of the vile enormity he had witnessed in the town square. There had been no need for it, no earthly reason to open fire, yet the commander of those guns had massacred his countrymen – coldly, and with calculation, and not once, but twice. It had not been cowardice, nor even stupidity, it had been deliberate cruelty. There had been no enemy troops there, only men, women and children, the ordinary people of Toulon, unarmed, unthreatening, unimportant.

Mercifully it is not given to many to witness the darkness that is visible, he thought, awed by the mystery. I believe I saw tonight a true irruption of evil into the world. And is it not evil such as this that I am pledged to fight?

He recalled the monster who had ordered the massacre and then the words of the Bailiff of the Temple speaking the Key, '*The people shall have mercy*.' And a silent vow came profoundly to his mind: Before God, I swear that one day I shall know that man's name, and when I do I shall see him brought down. The world may depend upon it!

Now, in the pitch black, he stared down at the *Victory*'s great curving bulwark. The pronounced tumblehome of her flanks gave her the appearance to his eye of a living, breathing organism. He turned, aware of a significant presence. Captain Knight approached him. 'This was addressed to you this afternoon, Sir Sidney.'

He handed Smith an envelope bearing a formal copperplate. From the admiral, he knew at once. He smiled, took the letter, opened and began to read.

My dear Sir Sidney,
I am sorry you are so apprehensive of difficulty in the service you volunteered for. It must be undertaken, and it must succeed to my wishes. The getting off of the governor and the troops in safety is my main object, though the conflagration may be advantageous to us. No enterprise of war is void of danger and difficulty; both must be submitted to.
Ever faithfully yours,
    Hood

Smith felt as if he had been knifed through the heart.

'A true bastard.'

He looked up to see Knight regarding him expressionlessly. 'I beg your pardon, Sir Sidney?'

'Then allow me to grant it, Captain Knight,' he said bitterly. He crumpled the letter. 'I might say that I think this is a kindness quite typical of you.'

As an official communication from His Lordship a copy of the letter would have been made by the admiral's secretary, to be kept aboard the *Victory*. Its insinuations were tantamount to a public reprimand for cowardice. Henceforth his name would be a joke in the fleet, and as dirt at the Admiralty, and there could be no appeal.

Knight looked askance at him. 'What is it?'

'I think you know very well.'

Knight's brow creased at Smith's cold anger. 'Do you mind if I read it?'

He received no answer from Smith, who stared sightlessly out from *Victory*'s rail, but he took the paper from Smith's fingers nevertheless, and straightened it.

After he had finished reading Knight folded the letter and held it out. He said, with difficulty, 'I'm sorry. I want you to know I had absolutely no part in this.'

Smith took the paper back, his composure almost restored. He was certain of Knight's sincerity. 'In that case, captain, I apologize to you. I beg you to disregard what I have just said.'

'I shall. But . . . what did you expect from an admiral like His Lordship?'

Smith sighed, bone weary. 'The semblance of honour, at least.'

Knight crooked his knuckle and knocked twice on Smith's breast, saying, 'That's why you'll never be one, hey, Smith?'

Smith gave him an astonished glance, but then his astonishment turned to ironic laughter. 'Oh, *touché*, Knight. *Touché!*'

Knight's shadowed countenance returned to its customary bleakness. 'His Lordship has expressed himself in writing. Neither he nor I care particularly for your unconventional personality. He takes care always to clip the wings of those he does not care for. However, I may say that after tonight's work upon the quays you'll have the approbation and applause of every other officer and man in His Lordship's fleet. That I can promise you.'

Smith met Knight's eye, appreciating the man's superb honesty. He touched his sleeve briefly. 'Now, that was honourably said. I have misjudged you, sir. Nor shall anyone have just cause to repent a good opinion of me. It may be that I shall not be accounted one of the heroes of Toulon, but that was never my object.'

Smith bowed his head as Knight left. He sighed, contemplating the evening's work. Despite everything, he could not feel total satisfaction. His men had done well, but they had not carried through his plans to uttermost completion. His wounded shoulder burned and ached, but he thought of his newly made vow, and said, shortly. 'Come along with me, Mister Hill.'

Hill's eyebrows lifted in perplexity. 'Sir?'

'The night is yet young. And it's said, is it not, that actions speak louder than words.'

Temporary quarters had been found on the gun deck. The Comtesse du Fay cradled Celestine, and Berenice kept vigil over them both. She was still unable to fully believe what had come to pass. Smith had come back to her, and the ordeal was over. What had happened was real, yet in his absence it seemed otherwise, and she wondered if she would wake up to find herself back in Toulon.

When she went on deck, she was told that Sir Sidney had left the ship. In all her sufferings she had never felt so alone. A terrible panic seized her as she looked out across the separating waters. Her fingers twined anxiously in the hammock netting, and she became blind to the tremendous activity going on all around her as the ship was prepared for imminent sailing, deaf to the interested comments of the officers who spectated the continued destruction. One by one distant fires broke out in the Inner Harbour.

I know what this means, she thought, sunk in black hopelessness. It is the final cruelty. He's not going to come back.

Just then she saw an enormous explosion somewhere in the Petite Rade drive a brilliant plume of fire up into the sky. Seconds later the report of it reached her. She began to shiver, and fingered her cross, offering a prayer to the spirits that guided the fates of men. Only when she began to implore their indulgence did she remember the power that her singular faith had given her.

I did it once, she thought, gathering strength. So I can do it again.

She waited with patience and hope, watching *Victory*'s boats looming up out of the darkness, one by one. Men came on deck, collapsed exhausted onto the gratings, officers shouted, barefoot sailors manhandled boats inboard, helped refugees and wounded shipmates to their ease. She endured the waiting until another boat came in, then another, and another. A dozen had come alongside, but none of them carried Smith. And now only one boat remained.

As she watched it come in she saw a lieutenant stand up near the tiller. The boat was the *Victory*'s overloaded pinnace, loaded with dozens of shivering refugees, their upturned faces reflecting the yellow lantern light as the boat moved queasily. She saw an officer lying prone across the thwarts. When he came up his coat stank of burning; he was badly burned. His face and hands were red and already larded with grease. One eye was sealed.

'Damn me if I didn't leave my eyebrows aboard one of those seventy-fours,' he told one of his fellows.

'A sporting fellow must be prepared to make do without them,' one of the ship's officers called back.

The other guffawed. 'But we *did* it, eh, Hill? We burned them all.'

'Yes, Captain Hare. We certainly did.'

'Where's Smith?' she asked, panic seizing her again.

'I cannot say, mademoiselle.'

A young midshipman came aboard, and was laid close by her. She saw him trembling with shock. His face was blistered and smoke-blackened, which made the white of his eyes stand out in the gloom. His pupils were tiny. He could not take his hands from the poles of his stretcher, nor tear his attention from the coast. The pinnace had been last away; the lad was wrapped in a captain's coat with a rent shoulder. It was Smith's.

'Poor devils,' the lad managed. She could hear the knots tightening in his stomach; his teeth chattered together. 'They were running into the water . . . running in . . . it was *horrible* . . . what could I do? I saw an old woman and her daughter trying to swim after us . . . we were already loaded to the gunwales with soldiers and refugees . . . I ordered an oar to be thrown to them, but I couldn't . . .' The youth broke down and sobbed.

She knelt, feeling unbearable disappointment, but still she squeezed the lad's hand, knowing how his mind was haunted, as was her own, by the pathetic screams they had all heard that night. He had been face to face with the hideous. He was fighting to control himself. He needed a moment, and she gave him that time, shielding his shame from the rest of the ship's company who swarmed on the lantern-lit deck.

'You must not blame yourself,' she said quietly.

'But I watched them drown . . .' The lad grimaced, anger and disgust competing inside him. '*I ordered the men to pull away as I watched them drown!*'

As he gripped her hand tighter she said, 'Even so – you did all you could. You must not blame yourself.'

He began to cry, so she pulled out Smith's hip flask and unscrewed the cap. 'Please, drink this.'

The lad wiped his face, still trembling and burning with shame. He put the flask to his lips again, and took a determined mouthful of good French brandy. She leaned closer to him as he drank again, but this time the brandy draught made him gasp, and he looked past her with wide eyes. 'I'm . . . I'm sorry, sir.'

'So far as I am aware, Mister Eales, it is not actually contrary to the Articles of War for a young gentleman of the king's navy to shed tears – so long as his superior officer considers it appropriate.'

She looked up and saw Smith. He was stripped to the waist, a livid gash in his shoulder, his hair in wild disarray. He was grinning. She threw herself at him, and he held her for a long time before he laid a gentle hand on her face.

'Faith,' he said. 'Didn't I tell you it was always meant to be?'

EIGHT

They stood together wrapped in a single blanket, watching the stars die. Dawn was dimly glimmering beyond the bowsprit. To port the dying fires of Toulon seemed very far away.

Smith noted Admiral Trogoff hoisting his exiled flag in the giant *Commerce de Marseilles*, preparing to weigh. The ships-of-the-line *Puissant* and *Pompée* were being brought away too, as prizes. The frigates *Pearl*, *Arethusa* and *Topaze*, and several large corvettes, had already departed.

He recognized Lieutenant Goddard, who had commanded the seamen upon the Hauteur de Grasse, as he was lifted aboard, wounded. Already *Victory*'s crew were catting her anchors and preparing to set sail for Hyères Bay. Before daylight all His Majesty's ships, with those of Spain and those of the Two Sicilies, must be out of reach of the enemy's shot and shell.

Smith looked at the dark silhouettes, quietly calculating the damage that had been done to France's ability to export her terrible Revolution. He knew it would be a long time before he would be able to erase what had happened in the market place from his mind, or the monster responsible for it, but the final effort he had made tonight had gone some way to squaring accounts.

He closed his eyes now, and breathed deeply, savouring the delicate smells of oak chippings and hempen rope and sea salt. As the sun lifted its golden orb above the eastern horizon he recounted to Berenice how his party had burned to destruction eight fine French ships-of-the-line, then he had gone on to burn two more troublesome 74s lying in the Inner Road. *Hero* and *Themistocle* had lain closest to Toulon dockyard. They had proved to be chock-full of men, so many men that Smith had found his force completely inadequate to effect the disembarkation with any margin of safety for his own men. But then he had thought of Lieutenant Hurd and the American prisoners who had helped save *Unicorn* all those years ago, and the memory had decided him. He had ordered the French crews put ashore.

The landing operation had gone without hitch, and the French sailors' gratitude over his common consideration for their lives had touched him. That they had imagined him capable of having them burned like sheep in a barn had made him shudder.

Then it had been Lieutenant Miller's turn to court personal danger. His zeal for the task in hand had belied his languid style. He had stayed so long aboard *Themistocle* to ensure the fire taking hold that he had been scorched and almost suffocated before being carried to safety by Midshipman Knight.

'Shortly after we came away,' he told her, 'the *Montreal*, the other powder vessel, was hit by shore fire and exploded. I don't expect you could have missed it. The shock was even greater than when the *Isis* went up. Our boat was within the circle of falling timber.'

'I knew you were in danger,' she said, squeezing his hand.

He took out his talisman and put it to his lips and gave thanks to his Tutelary Genius for the apparent miracle – falling debris had made the water foam round them yet not a single piece had touched either the *Swallow* or his three boats.

He smiled a very private smile. 'I must admit, I also

came to a sudden conviction that I had chanced enough, and that to attempt more would be to ask too much of my protector.'

Berenice stared out over the sapphire-blue sea, her eyes fathomless. He wondered if she was thinking of her father, or of the many terrors of her journey, or perhaps the lovely music that had once been played by her sister's skilled hands, music that would never be played again.

She saw Smith recognize her contemplations, and it gave her courage. She would need courage today, because the time had come to fulfil her promise, and tell her mother the truth about her father's death, and so finally to confess the falsehood she had nurtured.

Smith straightened and put a gentle finger to her face. 'This afternoon we shall go aboard a smaller ship, the one taking despatches to England, and once there we shall do as we ought to have done years ago. We shall become man and wife.'

She drew out her looped cross and held it tight. Smith saw it. Immediately he took something from his waist-coat pocket and held it between finger and thumb for her to see.

'I've carried this little figure these six years.'

She looked back in puzzlement to see what it was he was holding. It was a small, silver figure, a man with arms outstretched. She lifted her cross, her ancient Egyptian symbol of life, and brought the two together.

The fit was perfect.